"Gripping, chilling, creepy, and enthralling . . . *Malice House* channels Shirley Jackson, if Shirley Jackson knew how to make me check under the bed every night before going to sleep. *Malice House* is a must for readers who love gothic horror, creaking old houses, attics overflowing with dark secrets, or for anyone who has ever secretly suspected that there is an entire other universe hovering just out of reach."

—Katherine Howe, *New York Times* bestselling author of
Conversion and *The Physick Book of Deliverance Dane*

★ "All is not what it seems at Malice House, and Shepherd uses the conventions of a gothic haunted-house tale to keep readers on the edge of their seats. . . . An intensely spooky and scary tale about the power of stories and the art of creation. Highly recommended."

—*Booklist* (starred review)

"Haunting and atmospheric. Megan Shepherd expertly blends horror and suspense in her captivating book-within-a-book adult debut. Beautifully written and steeped in gothic lore, *Malice House* explores themes of family and legacy, magic and curses, and the mysterious power of stories."

—Megan Miranda, *New York Times* bestselling author
of *All the Missing Girls* and *The Perfect Stranger*

"A twisted tale—made up of even more twisted tales—perfect for adults nostalgic for *Scary Stories to Tell in the Dark*."

—*Library Journal*

"Shepherd crafts a seriously tight mystery with plenty of red herrings, shocking twists, and even a few jump scares, making it a chilling thriller with a totally immersive setting."

—Bookreporter

"This book, like Malice House itself, contains many secrets, and you will read it voraciously to try to find and consume them all. May it compel you as swiftly as it compelled me."

—Chuck Wendig, *New York Times* bestselling author of *Wanderers*

BOOKS IN THE
MALICE COMPENDIUM

Malice House

Midnight Showing

MIDNIGHT SHOWING

MEGAN SHEPHERD

BOOK TWO
of the **MALICE COMPENDIUM**

HYPERION
AVENUE

LOS ANGELES   NEW YORK

All rights reserved. Published by Hyperion Avenue, an imprint of Buena Vista
Books, Inc. No part of this book may be reproduced or transmitted in any
form or by any means, electronic or mechanical, including photocopying,
recording, or by any information storage and retrieval system, without written
permission from the publisher. For information address Hyperion Avenue,
77 West 66th Street, New York, New York 10023.

First Edition, October 2023
10 9 8 7 6 5 4 3 2 1
FAC-004510-23222
Printed in the United States of America

This book is set in Baskerville and News Gothic.
Designed by Amy C. King

Library of Congress Cataloging-in-Publication Data:
Names: Shepherd, Megan, author.
Title: Midnight showing / by Megan Shepherd.
Description: First Edition. • Los Angeles : Hyperion Avenue, 2023. • Series:
The Malice Compendium book 2 • Summary: "Book 2 in The Malice
Compendium series by *New York Times* bestselling author Megan Shepherd,
featuring dark magic and family secrets with a contemporary horror tone"
—Provided by publisher.
Identifiers: LCCN 2023009607 • ISBN 9781368089296 (hardcover) •
ISBN 9781368101547 (trade paperback) • ISBN 9781368091039 (ebk)
Subjects: LCGFT: Gothic fiction. • Horror fiction. • Paranormal fiction. • Novels.
Classification: LCC PS3619.H4565 M53 2023 •
DDC 813/.6—dc23/eng/20230407
LC record available at https://lccn.loc.gov/2023009607

www.HyperionAvenueBooks.com

SUSTAINABLE FORESTRY INITIATIVE

Certified Sourcing

www.forests.org
SFI-01681

Logo Applies to Text Stock Only

FOR MY PARENTS

CHAPTER ONE

—

THE HUNDREDTH STAIR
© 1941 Sigil Pictures

FADE IN:

EXTERIOR — ROCKY SEA CLIFFS — DAY

CAMERA MOVES along rocky sea cliffs battered
with sea spray. At the top of the cliffs looms
an aging Victorian house, connected to the
beach by a staircase so steep it could be
mistaken for a ladder. CAMERA FOLLOWS a GIRL
CHILD climbing the stairs with a wicker basket
of seashells.

CLOSE-UP on child-sized bloody footprints on
the stairs.

—

THE DREAMS ALWAYS began with smoke.

Restless in a cramped hotel bed, in a hiccup of a town halfway down the jagged Portuguese coastline, my sister stole the sheets and muttered sleep-talk beside me while I dreamed again of smoke. There was a shade of paint called Vantablack that was rumored to be the darkest known pigment, but this smoke was darker yet somehow, drinking in all light. The smoke seeped out from under the hotel bed mattress, devouring the color from the room until it had expunged the sunny yellow from the walls, leaving the space grayscale, like an old movie. A dark promise snapped in the air like lightning.

I sat up in bed, sunken-eyed, watching myself from outside my own body. *Another hotel room, another town.* We'd been traveling so long they all blended together. The smoke from under the bed slowly took shape as it pulled itself into a pillar the size of a person, then inclined over me in wormlike form. Immobile, I could only watch as it hovered, hovered, hovered, and then crashed down into a thunderclap of black soot—

I jerked awake. *For real this time.*

Sitting up with a gasp—touching my face, assuring myself I was awake—I checked for Kylie's slumbering body next to mine. She was there. She was safe. Her chest lifting and falling slowly, her lips silent now.

I sagged back against the pillows.

How long had it been now—two weeks? Since we'd boarded the plane in Salt Lake City bound for Portugal, hungry to follow the trail of clues my father had left behind, meager crumbs that might lead us to our family, to answers. We hadn't had much to go off: a thirty-year-old Lisbon return address on an envelope and town names mentioned in his short stories. *Winemakers,* he'd called the Acosta side of the family. *Occultists. Artists.* As though being an artist was the worst thing a person could be.

The thing was, I was starting to believe he was right.

———

"Haven. Um, what the fuck?"

The sound of my sister's voice pulled me out of the bottomless, strange land of sleep. I blinked awake to find not a pillar of smoke inclined over me, but Kylie, frowning.

She held out her hands and turned them front and back to show the dirt that covered them.

I sat up, rubbing tired eyes. It took me a second to place where we were: a hotel room in a town whose name I couldn't recall. Morning sun reached in from the window to paint light-lines on the bed. The walls were yellow again. The curtains once more colorful. The room smelled like shampoo, mothballs.

My mouth felt dry. I swallowed and asked, "Why are your hands dirty?"

"*You* tell *me*." She looked pointedly at the bed.

Only then did I realize the dark substance covered my own hands, too. It wasn't dirt, but something powdery, more like soot. Confused, I threw back the covers to find the substance coating parts of my pajamas and the sheets, like I'd spent the night rolling around in campfire coals.

At a loss, I stared at the mess.

"Haven?" Kylie pressed.

"If I told you I dreamed this to life, would you believe me?"

Her expression flattened. "That isn't funny."

I tried to brush the soot off my hands. I *hadn't* been joking. But that was impossible—the smoke hadn't been real. The Malice House fire was over. It had been almost three months since that terrible night. The smoke, the charred remains of the house; it was half a world away in the Pacific Northwest. *Gone, all of it.* The house, the fire . . . none of it could reach me here.

I glanced at my phone, which showed a notification for an unanswered call from the Lundie Bay Police Department. Just one of a long string of calls that had started a few weeks ago and hadn't let up.

The police couldn't reach me, either—but for how long?

"Aha!" Kylie triumphantly held up a small object she'd found in the sheets.

It was one of my charcoal sticks, the kind I used for sketches before moving on to create a final illustration in watercolor and ink. Those sticks always made a mess, leaving everything they touched filthy.

She pointed to my canvas bag on the bedside table, which was flopped to the side with my keys spilling out. "You must have knocked over your bag in your sleep."

My mind was still trying to catch up with the missed call from the police. I held out a hand. "Sorry. I thought I'd gotten rid of all my charcoal."

I had, in fact, gotten rid of *all* my art supplies, not just the charcoal. Thrown the entire lot in a dumpster behind a gas station in Montana—all my brushes, my pens, my paint tubes, my tools. Everything I had used to illustrate, except for my sketchbook. That had been long gone already.

And yet, bits of my supplies occasionally turned up like old receipts you'd sworn you'd tossed. In pants pockets, in the folds of my bag. They mixed with the pencils and pens I was forever picking up from bill trays and hotel reception desks and slipping into my bag utterly unaware until I discovered them later.

Kylie glanced out the window. "I guess you missed one."

Her eyes were ringed with blue-black shadows—I wasn't the only one still haunted.

A rhythmic churning of waves filtered through the glass. We'd picked this hotel because it was across the street from the ocean. Not that we'd had much choice. It was a two-hotel kind of town, both small family operations with only a few rooms each. Mid-January was the low tourist season in Portugal. According to the hotel clerk, we'd been the only guests for days.

Kylie turned sharply away from the view and plunged into the adjoining bathroom, calling back, "The taxi will be here at ten. Try to dress decently this time, okay? The place looks fancy on their website. And good luck explaining that mess to the maid."

I heard the shower turn on.

I grabbed my phone and deleted the call notification without listening to the message. The calls had started routinely enough. A detective from Lundie Bay PD following up on the house fire to make sure we didn't want an arson investigation. After a few days of no response from me, however, the detective had pointedly broached the subject of Detective Rice's unsolved cases, which he'd acquired after her death. Polite requests had shifted into thinly veiled threats about warrants.

Swallowing, I tried to put the past out of mind—if that was ever possible. I considered my shirt and sweatpants, makeshift pajamas now ruined by charcoal. Then again, there was something perversely pleasing about being dirtied by the medium.

By the time the taxi arrived, I'd managed to wash off most of the charcoal powder and throw on fresh jeans and a shirt that could pass for dressy. Kylie looked better in flowy black pants and a burgundy top, but even her makeup skills couldn't hide her sunken eyes, her nervous lip-chewing.

The taxi driver switched the radio to a *fado* station, and the car drifted along to melancholy warbles over percussive guitar. As we traveled inland, the undulating stretches of farmland lulled my anxious mind into a stupor until my thoughts wandered, my hand trailing down to the scar on my ankle. The skin had grown back, the tendon had healed, but the scar itself would be there forever: seven puncture wounds that matched the seven sharp points of a lobster claw.

When the taxi driver finally stopped the car and indicated with gestures that we'd reached our destination, Kylie slid her hand into mine to give a brief squeeze.

I met her eyes and nodded. Maybe this time would finally be *the* time.

An elegantly rustic sign announced the Vinhos do Vale Winery. Perfectly spaced rows of grapevines rose over the hills, disappearing into the river valley. A tidy gravel path led us from the parking lot, sparsely utilized due to the off-season, to a stately stone barn that served as the welcome center and tasting room.

Kylie paused outside the door, taking in the heavy building materials, the curves of the land, the river meandering down below, and for a second her gaze traveled somewhere else. Someplace far from Portugal.

"Kylie?" I asked.

She blinked, shaking her head. Started chewing on that lip again. "Nothing. It's nothing. Come on, I have to pee."

Most wineries we'd visited since arriving in Portugal had been clustered around the capital, Lisbon, and the touristy towns of Sintra, famous for its fairy-tale castles, and Évora, notorious for its chapel made entirely of human bones. We'd searched everything from commercial-scale vineyards to tiny family farms. None had the sophisticated grandeur of Vinhos do Vale, with its elegant patio overlooking the lazy river.

Inside, a hostess greeted us with a dimpled smile. "Here for the English-language tour?"

I gave her the fake names we'd made the reservation under. As Kylie found the bathroom, I checked out the handful of others milling around the lobby, waiting for the tour to begin: A British couple dutifully reading some informational placards. A pair of elegantly dressed women already holding glasses of vinho verde, though it wasn't yet noon. A few more groups shuffled in: an elderly Japanese couple, a grown family that might have been American.

"Welcome!" A short young man arrived, wearing a white button-down with the vineyard's logo on the pocket. He was cute, with dark curls overgrown like wild vines, though sun damage had given him premature wrinkles. "We are honored to have you visit us here at Vinhos do Vale, the premier winery in central Portugal. I look forward to sharing the passionate story of this farm and its founders, as well as demonstrating to you how we make our award-winning wine. Ah—I see your faces! Don't worry, the tour isn't too long! We all know you're really here for the tasting, eh?" The British couple gave polite chuckles as the tour guide waved us through a set of heavy oak doors. "Started in 2002 by Enzo Clemente . . ."

Kylie rejoined us, and the guide led our group into a bottling room that smelled fruity with a touch of kerosene. Workers attended to machinery designed for bottling and corking and labeling. The tour area was roped off and marked with informational placards detailing the winemaking process in English, Portuguese, and Spanish. Kylie and I drifted to the back of the group. I didn't need to learn the history of the Clemente family. We had already read every word on the business's website, scouring each section for a different name—*Acosta*—like we had with all the others.

And, just like all the others, there had been nothing about our ancestors. One line in the description of Vinhos do Vale's construction had snagged my attention, however—a brief mention that the facility's stone barn had been constructed twenty years ago on top of a natural cavern that now served as a special event space.

A cavern—just like my father wrote about in "Sanctuary."

Our guide led the group out of the bottling room and into a hallway whose posters detailed the grape varieties grown on the grounds. As he continued his well-practiced speech and answered the other tourists' questions, I pulled out the brochure and studied the picture on the front.

"Now," the guide said as he started up a set of stairs, "join me in the tasting room!"

The others followed him up the stairs, but I rested a hand on Kylie's arm. She slowed to a stop.

I jerked my head toward the opposite end of the hallway, which led to a staircase going down to a lower level. I stuffed the brochure into my back pocket.

She nodded.

Once the tasting room door shut, sealing away the sounds of clinking glasses over *fado* music, we went down the staircase and cautiously opened the door. It led to a dark hallway. The fermented-sweet odor was stronger down here and intertwined with a mustier, earthier smell. The door closed behind us, sealing us in darkness broken only by a single small window that cast a square of light.

Kylie started to reach for the light switch, but I stopped her, pointing to the window. If she turned it on, someone might see. I used the light on my new smartphone instead.

Kylie dragged her fingers lightly over the wall as she whispered, "Some of it is bare rock. The rest has been plastered over."

The corridor had a low ceiling, characteristic of an underground cellar. The tour ropes had been pushed to one side along with signs for a wine and cheese pairing event from a few days before. Another sign marked SPECIAL EVENT CELLAR pointed toward a narrow branching tunnel.

Our footsteps echoed on the poured-concrete floor no matter how quietly we tried to move. The passage sloped downward gradually, and the farther we went, the mustier the air became. The walls had less plaster here, exposing more roughly hewn stone. When I turned the corner into the narrow passage, I found myself blocked by a wrought-iron gate. An oversized key rested in the lock, mostly for show, I guessed. They were probably aiming for sophistication with the wrought iron, but in the dark, it read more as "dungeon."

My heartbeat ratcheted up a few gears. *Could this be it? The cave where my father first used the Acosta curse to create life—to create* me?

I slid a sidelong glance to Kylie, glad the darkness masked my face. Of all the things I'd shared with my half sister, the truth about my origin wasn't one of them. Only I had read my father's short story "Sanctuary" in its entirety. And now it was gone, burned in the fire along with so many other secrets.

The hinges groaned as I swung open the gate. I winced. The machinery rumbled overhead, but otherwise all was quiet. I got up the nerve to step inside and shine my phone's flashlight over a grotto-like cavern. It was shallow, the size of a small bedroom, decorated with an ornate table and chairs, shelves of dusty-looking wine bottles, and a trolley cart of cutlery and silver serving dishes. A wooden door was built into the far end of the cavern.

My feet paced, uncertain, not knowing where to take me. Kylie stepped in after me, skirting the table, casting her phone's light up at the low ceiling. My father's story had described a cave filled with decades'—maybe even centuries'—worth of markings on the stone, pencils and pens and paintbrushes and knives jabbing out from the earthen portions of the walls, anything that could be used to create art demanding to be picked up, *used*. The tools of artists; the tools of creators.

I hung back near the entrance and ran my fingers over the stone. Searching for something: a single carved line, or maybe a hole where a pencil might once have rested. My hand began to shake. My eyes briefly closed as I tried to shed the worry over the detective's messages and focus on the feel of the room. *Did my father stand here? Did he hear a baby cry and understand the horror of what he'd done?*

I frowned. This cellar seemed too small to match the cave he'd described. There were no deep underground tunnels, no alcoves, and yet . . . "Sanctuary" had been fictionalized, so there was no way to know what exactly was real and what had been merely creative license.

I glanced at the wooden door at the far end. *Maybe . . .*

The overhead lamps snapped on, baking us like raw sunlight.

I blinked, disoriented. My mind was still back with my father thirty years ago, so my body reacted on its own, pivoting toward the open gate.

The curly-haired tour guide stood there, one hand on the light switch, the other clutching a radio. His face was pinched in confusion.

"What are you doing down here?" he asked in a strange tone. "This area is marked 'For Staff Only.'"

Kylie turned as immobile as the stone walls. There was a lag as my rational brain scrambled to catch up to what was happening. *The door, I still need to look behind the wooden door. . . .*

Our silence was incriminating. The tour guide looked at the phone flashlights in our hands, then the silver serving dishes, the rows of dusty vintage bottles that probably cost hundreds, if not thousands, of dollars, and his expression shifted to one of suspicion.

He thinks we're stealing.

He squeezed the button on his radio, lifting it to his mouth.

I panicked. Only it didn't feel like panic. It felt like, somewhere deep, I knew exactly what I was doing. My hand closed over a stainless-steel cheese cleaver from the cutlery basket. It was like I was back in my dream, watching myself from outside my body. That couldn't be *me* clutching a cleaver. And now *me* talking with such certainty.

"What's behind that door?" I demanded, pointing the edge of the cleaver toward the far end of the cellar. "Unlock it."

The tour guide's face had gone white. He had his hands raised defensively; his already small body shrank even more. Still, there was more confusion behind his eyes than true fear. Kylie and I were well-dressed young women, American tourists . . . hardly the profile of thieves, even less of, what, *murderers?*

"Haven." Kylie hissed my name in a warning whisper. She took a small step forward, clutching the back of one of the wooden chairs. Through her teeth, she muttered, "What the fuck are you doing?"

But it was already happening. Adrenaline shot up from my toes, making my heartbeat wallop, my thoughts erratic.

This is a bad idea.

It's too late.

It's happening.

Might as well find out now . . .

The young man looked uncertainly at the wooden door. "The . . . door?"

I heard my voice pressing, "Does it lead to a tunnel? Are there carvings?"

His face contorted in confusion. "Carvings?"

Suddenly, the cleaver was wrenched out of my hands.

I blinked, my mind too slow—or maybe too fast. Kylie tossed the blade back into the cutlery basket and grabbed my wrist, tugging me out of the cellar faster than my thoughts could follow. I followed her lead numbly, but I kept looking back as an ugly kind of anger rose inside me. *I want to know what's behind that door!* But Kylie moved fast, her confidence overpowering my own. She pulled me into the wider passage and slammed the gate closed, twisting the oversized key to lock it, and then tossed the key on the floor out of the tour guide's reach.

"What are you doing?" he asked from the other side, alarmed.

Instead of answering, Kylie dug her fingers into my upper arm and dragged me away. With every footfall my understanding grew.

I had messed up. I had seriously messed up.

We moved through the hallway with the grape posters, up more stairs, then burst out into the tasting room with its soft chatter and *fado*. A wooden bar was staffed by two bartenders, each with a group of tourists clustered close as they explained notes of honeysuckle and apricot. Kylie cut a direct line toward the patio exit, dragging me along with her, though I wasn't resisting anymore. She only let go once we were outside. We wove through the wine-barrel tables, darted over the gravel path, and hurled ourselves into the vinyl back seat of a taxi.

We rode in heavy silence. I didn't know if the taxi driver spoke English, but neither of us dared speak a word aloud after we named our destination. My mind was muddled pulp as it jerked through the scenarios of what might happen now, if the local police would be called—*shit*, if this would even get back to the Lundie Bay detective—if there was any way the winery could find out our real names. But most of all, how I'd explain to my half sister why I'd threatened a man with a knife—why I'd done so many questionable things.

I fished a hand under my shirt to the plastic travel wallet that hung around my neck, giving it a reassuring squeeze.

We had the taxi drop us off at the other hotel in town in case the police were to question the driver, and then quickly walked the few blocks back to ours.

All the while, I waited. For Kylie's questions. For her curses. For her reprimands.

But she didn't say anything.

Once we were back in our room with the door safely locked, she pushed my suitcase toward me and said simply, "It's time to go home."

CHAPTER TWO

—

THE SANDMAN KILLER
© 1943 Sigil Pictures

INTERIOR — LOBBY — DAY

A beautiful, delicate woman enters through
glass doors beneath a sign that reads LUCERNE
INSTITUTE OF SLEEP. She appears nervous as she
approaches the nurse's check-in desk.

> AGNES
> I'm Agnes Fitzpatrick. My husband
> made me an appointment.

> NURSE
> (checks intake file)
> Insomnia?

> AGNES
> That's right. I've tried everywhere,
> you see. I've nowhere else to turn.
> I fear these sleepless nights will
> make me lose my mind. . . .

—

THE LISBON HUMBERTO DELGADO AIRPORT was crowded for a Monday, but Kylie and I managed to snag an open table at a French-inspired bistro in our terminal, arranging our suitcases as a barrier against the world.

Kylie practically pounced on the server when he came, a wisp of a young man with gentle eyes. "White wine. Bring the whole bottle." Her eyes flickered nervously around the terminal as she mumbled to me, "I swear, when we get home, I'm going to stop drinking. Or at least switch to hard seltzer."

Slumping in my stiff metal chair, a ball cap pulled down low over my forehead, I rubbed the skin around my tired eyes. *Home* was a rather loose term these days. New York City had been home for me until I'd discovered my marriage was a sham and had fled to my late father's place in Lundie Bay. But *that* home was a burned-out cadaver now, the woods around it infested with monsters of my own making—monsters I didn't know how to stop.

"And you're sure this friend of yours can help us? With the . . . *legal stuff?*" Kylie started chewing on her lip again. "Staying under the radar?"

"Yeah. Yeah, he's cool."

The night before had been a sleepless one. Kylie had fretted about the winery incident, constantly glancing out the hotel window. I'd assured her that I could find us a quick way to get back to the United States without alerting any authorities who might have our names flagged. There was only one person I knew who was both paranoid and skilled enough at hacking to turn to: my old friend Rob.

Ten minutes after texting him, he had written me back:

Book this flight.
Tomorrow. Iberia 3107 to LAX
Rental car booth near baggage claim F.
Look for a sign for Nita and Indra Kapur.
No phones, no laptops.

Now Kylie peeked over at my phone screen and said, "Right. So, what exactly do you know about this guy?"

"Rob?" I stuffed the phone back in my pocket. "Not even his last name."

I wasn't even convinced "Rob" was his real first name. I'd known him mostly as SlasherDasher, the administrator of a dark-web site that specialized in underground horror movies and recaps. The movies he'd sent me to summarize had come from different postmarks around the country, and his IP address placed him all over the world. I suspected he was using VPNs to hide his location and was probably holed up in a basement somewhere in the fly-over states, or he was a shut-in inhabiting some cheap apartment, the realm of the Internet Troll.

But Rob had come through for me before. It didn't seem to matter that we'd never met in real life.

Kylie's nails drummed on the tabletop. "What if he's a gamer kid messing with you?"

I paused, then shook my head. "No kid could get his hands on the films I've seen. They're not mainstream. And by that, I mean over the bridge and across multiple dimensions from mainstream. Things you'd probably get arrested for owning. So, whoever Rob is, he either hacked them from somewhere online or has a source who gives him access. An underground movie producer, probably. Or some sicko collector."

"Oh, fantastic. So not out of the question he murders us to wear our skin." Kylie slumped in her seat, her nails continuing to tap the table as she gazed tensely around the airport. "Text him again."

"I've tried. Last night's message was all he sent—just these instructions. That's Rob for you. He likes to play games."

I didn't blame Kylie for her doubts, but Rob had quite literally saved my life when he'd gotten me leverage against my ex-husband. I'd trusted him then; I had no reason not to trust him now.

The waiter returned with our bottle and two glasses. Kylie went stiff as he set the bottle on the table. As soon as he was gone, she picked it up with a frown.

She tilted the label in my direction, dropping her voice. "Look. It's from Vinhos do Vale."

I gave an involuntary shudder as a vent overhead turned on.

She asked, "You think it's a sign?"

In our months together on the road, learning each other's pasts, bonding over shared taste in fast-food specials, fighting over music playlists, I'd discovered that Kylie kept one foot squarely in the world of astrology charts and crystal healing and alien theories. She had a small hamsa tattooed on her left inner wrist and a large reproduction of her star chart on her back, depicted as a constellation of dots—for the longest time, I'd thought they were just freckles.

I didn't want to think about coincidences. "If it's a sign of anything, it's that they're such a big winery they aren't going to bear enough of a grudge to expend resources tracking down a couple of crazy American tourists."

She cocked an eyebrow but didn't challenge the way I'd downplayed what had happened.

I took the bottle and poured us each a glass, holding mine up expectantly until she relented with a sigh and clinked hers against mine.

"It wasn't a real door," she said, throwing back a long sip.

I licked the film of wine off my lips. "What wasn't?"

"In the cellar. That cave. The wooden door was fake—it was only made to look rustic like the iron gate. There was nothing back there. No other tunnels."

My foot started tapping in the air beneath the table. Was that true? If it was, then Vinhos do Vale had been another dead end like all the other wineries. When we'd first made the decision to investigate in Portugal, I'd been fixated on finding distant family who might have answers. But now the prospect of boarding a plane back to the West Coast made me second-guess my motives. Then again, maybe motives didn't matter after the mess I'd made.

"I don't know why I did it," I said quietly, looking off at a terminal sign. "What happened in the wine cellar, I mean. I wish I didn't do a lot of the dumb shit I do."

Kylie studied me with a writer's eye, always observing.

Bristling, I waved over the waiter and handed him my credit card, hoping he didn't notice the man's name on it: Rafe Kahn. When we'd left Lundie Bay, we'd meant to leave everything behind, even Rafe. Maybe *especially* Rafe. But it hadn't been long before we'd run out of cash, and Rafe had offered to keep funds flowing.

Like it or not, we needed him. I'd get insurance money for the house eventually, but it was currently bound and gagged in red tape.

As I signed Rafe's name to the bill, Kylie downed the rest of her wine in one swig. "Did you tell your satanic boyfriend you're coming back?"

I scoffed, ignoring the question. "There's nothing between us."

My foot was still jiggling under the table. Groaning, I realized I'd stolen the waiter's pen and unintentionally slipped it into my bag. *Always hungry to draw.*

I found myself moving to stand up without entirely meaning to. "I'm going to stretch my legs before boarding."

Kylie pinned me with a look that said she knew I was avoiding the topic of Rafe.

The terminal was crowded. I flinched as a businessman brushed by me, knocking his shoulder into mine. I pulled the baseball cap lower over my head, and then spotted a quiet airport bookstore. I plunged inside as if taking refuge in an eddy against the current and found a little alcove to gather myself in. I pulled out my phone, scrolling to Rafe's number and letting my finger hover over the screen, debating.

Should I tell him I was returning to the West Coast? He'd figure it out soon enough from the credit card charges. Kylie was my half sister, but I hadn't known her more than a few months. She didn't know I was pulled off a page just like Rafe was. Only he understood my deepest secrets.

Rafe—the Harbinger. That's what my father had called him in *Bedtime Stories for Monsters*. The herald of dark times.

I was mulling over the reasons I shouldn't text Rafe when a sound on the other side of the shelving unit stole my attention. Though the airport was bustling, the bookstore had the usual one-step-away-from-the-world hush of all bookstores. At first I thought someone was talking on the other side of the shelves, but the voice didn't have the rhythm of someone speaking on their phone. It was low, muted.

Whispering.

My breath stilled. There was something familiar about the voice. Something I'd heard before. A deceptively soft masculine tone with an edge . . .

Fumbling in my pocket, I pulled out an earplug and shoved it into my left ear, then another into my right. My breath came fast, my chest rising and falling hard. The shelving unit was solid wood and six feet tall—whoever was on the opposite side was hidden from me.

Slowly, my feet moved, as though they didn't trust the floor not to give way. I passed stiff rows of tightly packed books until I reached the endcap, where a display of missing-girl thrillers screamed their titles at me as I worked up the courage to take one more step, to look.

Do it.

Around the corner, the aisle was empty. There was no one there.

Disoriented, I whipped my head around, eyes skimming over the usual mass-market romances and sci-fi paperbacks until they snagged upon a familiar name.

Amory Marbury.

I stepped forward slowly, hand reaching out, ghostlike. My fingers hiked the hills and valleys of the row of books until they landed on my father's book.

I slid it out and hefted it in my hand. It was a thick paperback of *Exit, Nebraska* in the original English.

I glanced over my shoulder, checked if I was being watched. Had there *ever* been whispering? Or had a part of me been subconsciously pulled here, to the *M*'s?

I opened the book to its cover flaps, where my father's black-and-white photograph stared back at me. It was his most-used headshot, the one of him standing outside Malice House, arms crossed, looking out in the direction of the ocean, wire-rimmed glasses catching the sunlight and turning his eyes into silver-dollar coins.

I took out my earplugs one at a time and slipped them back into my pocket.

"Hi, Dad," I whispered.

I almost expected his photograph to speak back to me, and it wouldn't have been the most shocking thing to have happened.

I paid for the book, then made my way to the women's restroom next to our gate, where I closed myself in a stall, taking a moment to breathe. Double-checking I'd latched the door, I fished my travel wallet out of my shirt.

When I'd picked up the little wallet in the Seattle airport, Kylie had teased me for looking like a sexagenarian on a cruise. I'd only laughed and gone along with it, letting her think I was worried about passport thieves.

Now I pulled out the yellowed paper inside and unfolded it.

The image was a simple contour line drawing of a baby girl done by a talented but untrained hand, with two words scrawled in the corner: *Amory's Baby.*

Thirty years ago, my father had no way of knowing this combination of art and words would create a mewling little creature deep in those subterranean vineyard tunnels, or that he'd name his creation Haven and take her home, hang a Dora the Explorer poster over her bed, teach her to roller-skate.

My stomach churned when I looked at the picture of this unrecognizable little thing—at *me.*

I shifted on the toilet seat lid and rifled through my bag for a pair of nail scissors. Then I opened the copy of *Exit, Nebraska* to page fifty, a random selection; I needed about half an inch of thickness.

An excerpt caught my eye.

James thought that if hell existed, it would look like Nebraska. He wondered what his old high school art teacher, Miss Saez, would say about the landscape. Miss Saez had always insisted that an artist's job was to see the world honest, but James thought Nebraska needed a few good lies. And maybe, James thought, so did he.

I pressed the scissors into the *a* in *Saez* and started cutting.

In my youth, I'd crafted book safes to hide my valuables in. My dad had done the same, a fact I'd only discovered later while going through his personal collection in Bainbridge University's Clifford Library. Book safes weren't precisely *safe* in the sense that breaking into them was as simple as flipping open the pages, but they had the benefit of being easily overlooked. Now that we were leaving Portugal, it would look strange if I continued to wear the braided-cord necklace of a travel wallet. But Amory Marbury's daughter carrying around a copy of *Exit, Nebraska*? Wouldn't draw a second glance.

It was Rob who'd taught me the value of hiding things in plain sight. Other rare film dealers used password-protected digital downloads to traffic underground movies, but Rob recorded movies onto archaic VHS cassettes with innocuous labels like "2001 Family Trip to Dollywood" or "Gene's Clarinet Recital" and then sent them through the regular mail. He loved to remind me that none of his films had ever been discovered by "the Normies."

Once I'd struggled with the tiny scissors to cut through an inch of paper and make a space about the size of my palm, I refolded my father's drawing and stowed it inside. With the book cover closed, one would never know it was anything other than a simple paperback. I found a rubber band in my bag and stretched it around the book to keep the pages from accidentally opening.

"Haven? You in here?"

It was Kylie's voice. I quickly stuffed the cut pages into the stall's trash can. I arranged a few tissues on top to hide the evidence and stashed the book in my bag.

"Yeah, almost finished," I called.

"Hurry, girl. The plane is boarding."

A half hour later, I was sitting pressed between Kylie and the port-hole window, my bag in my lap, one hand plunged inside. It felt good to palm the hard corner of the book safe; my hands had felt too empty, my bag too light, ever since I'd sacrificed my sketchbook to save Kylie.

It wasn't long before we were nearing the Atlantic, doubling back to the same coast we'd been so anxious to escape, leaving behind an unfinished puzzle in Portugal—if anything could ever truly be left behind.

When I switched off the overhead light and closed my eyes, Kylie reached over to squeeze my hand on the armrest. Only then did I realize that my fingers had been kneading the air, searching for a phantom paintbrush to clutch.

"Haven," she said quietly. "Don't draw."

I forced my hand still as I stared out at the dusting of city lights below, my other hand still clutching the book safe in my bag.

I turned to face her in the red-eye darkness, the call lights throwing cool blues and reds on her face.

"Kylie," I said. "Don't write."

Don't draw, don't write. Our mantra to one another, our sisterly bedtime routine, even forty thousand feet above the ground.

Keep the monsters at bay. Still our hands. Keep away from pencils and keyboards. Away from the darkness.

CHAPTER THREE

———

THE CANDY HOUSE
© 1951 Sigil Pictures

CLOSE ON plain box-style COFFINS rattling
in the back of a horse-drawn wagon. They are
too small for adult bodies. A scrap of paper
pasted on one coffin reads TYPHOID FEVER: WASH
HANDS AFTER HANDLING. The wagon wheels slow to
a stop.

CLOSE ON a shovel digging in wet dirt. PAN
OUT to reveal row after row of holes the right
size for children's coffins.

———

IN FRONT OF the rental-car booth near Baggage Claim F, Kylie sat on her suitcase in travel-rumpled clothes. Messenger bag slung over one shoulder, she swallowed Advil with a chug of bottled water.

She wiped her mouth. "You think your weirdo friend's going to show?"

I chewed on my fingernail. "I told you, he likes to play games."

Our flight had landed two hours ago. We'd followed Rob's strange instructions, but so far there had been no sign of him. Meanwhile, I was discovering that being back on the West Coast aggravated an itchy anxiousness that had taken up residence under my skin. At least abroad, I'd been able to pretend I was someone else. Just a normal person on vacation.

It wasn't as easy to play-act being human here. Though I'd only been in Los Angeles a handful of times, dragged here as a teenager for my father's literary festivals, I couldn't help but feel the uncanny sensation that everyone in the airport could see straight through the skin suit I wore to the *thing* underneath. Maybe I wasn't standing quite naturally enough, or I wasn't doing the right things with my hands. At any moment, I'd be found out for the unnatural creation I was. *The monster.* Pitchforks pulled out of luggage, Kylie and I mobbed and driven out of town . . .

Kylie sat up straight and asked, "What were the names again?"

I glanced down at the message on my phone. "Nita and Indra Kapur."

"There." She jutted her chin in the direction of a twentysomething guy with the bone structure of a cologne model. He wore a casual gray T-shirt, scandalously tight jeans, and reflective sunglasses—hardly the usual car-service driver uniform. He was craning his neck around like he was lost. When he turned our way, I saw the iPad he held had our aliases written out.

"Over here!" I waved to catch his attention. Was this *Rob*? My Internet Troll? Had I been picturing him lurking under a bridge when I should have imagined him on horseback in armor? Of all the various personas I'd imagined, none were a hair-gelled god.

The guy caught my eye and gave me a canned smile that seemed a little nervous around the edges. Doubts rushed in. Maybe I was wrong—Hot Mr. Sunglasses felt more like someone hired from central casting.

He came over and motioned to his iPad. "Nita? Indra?"

Now I felt even more suspicious that he was an actor, not to mention a decent one in that he didn't bat an eye as he read out our clearly false names.

"Yeah, sure." I wasn't sure how long we were going to play out this charade or what Rob was getting at with the secrecy. Mislabel VHS cassettes to throw thieves off the track, but why the cloak-and-dagger with me?

I asked doubtingly, "Rob?"

In lieu of answering, Hot Mr. Sunglasses slid his iPad under his arm. "Come with me." He pulled out his phone, dialed a number, and said to whoever was on the other end, "You can pull around now, we're coming out."

I was feeling less confident by the minute that *this* was SlasherDasher, the man who had once gleefully sent me a horror film called *Anthem*, promising I'd especially like it. A film in which a woman who looked an awful lot like me had gotten decapitated.

Kylie remained rooted to the tile floor, eyeing the spray-tanned guy from a distance. She leaned toward me and muttered, "Yeah, so . . . Black women think twice before getting in a car with a guy who could grace the cover of a frat-house welcome packet." She jerked her chin in the air. "Test him."

"Test him how?"

"Make sure he's thinking for *himself*."

My mouth started to go dry. I instinctively plunged a hand into my pocket, curled my fingers around the earplugs. Kylie was afraid of who might have gotten to our host—who might have whispered in his ear. But there was no way Uncle Arnold could have found us. For all I'd been able to discern, Uncle Arnold was most likely dead and rotting in the Pacific Northwest forests, having bled out from his wound. He had to be.

"You *are* with Rob, right?" I asked.

The man twitched impatiently, one hand going to a rose-crystal bracelet around his wrist. Breezily, he said, "Yeah, yeah, I'm with Rob."

It sounded about as convincing as when I'd claimed my name was Nita Kapur. I stepped close to Kylie and said, "Listen, if you don't feel good about this, we don't have to go with him. We can take a rideshare into town, check into a hotel, try to contact Rob from there."

She shook her head at me like I didn't get it, which I probably didn't. Then she grabbed her suitcase handle with a long-suffering sigh and followed our host, who had already passed through the automatic doors.

Outside, he squinted at the sea of cars, chewing on the inside of his cheek, checking his phone every few seconds.

I extended my hand, forcing him to acknowledge me. "I'm, uh, *Nita*. And you?"

He took my hand distractedly, not looking away from the line of cars and not offering his own name, either. I found myself thinking for the second time that he was nervous, that there was a twitchiness behind his polished exterior.

"Where is Rob having you take us?" I tried again. Then I second-guessed my instincts. "Is Rob even here, in LA?"

Before Hot Mr. Sunglasses could answer, a black town car pulled up. It was the kind that a car service might use, though it didn't have the usual wear and tear, nor a window decal or bumper sticker with a company name. And our host wasn't exactly dressed for business.

The driver let the car idle and came around to get our bags. He was another shockingly well-groomed guy in his mid-twenties—maybe that was just the standard of beauty in Los Angeles—and was styled with more flair than the first. He wrestled our bags into the trunk with enough curses to tell me this wasn't his usual line of work.

"Get in," Hot Mr. Sunglasses said, motioning to the back door as he climbed into the passenger seat.

I started to climb in, but Kylie grabbed my arm. "Wait, *Nita*." Glancing at the two men in the front seats, she whispered, "Now I'm not sure about this. . . . Are *you* sure about this?"

I hesitated, one hand on the open door. Hot Mr. Sunglasses and his friend appeared to be flirting over the single bottle of water in the front console, slapping each other's hands away.

"I don't think this is an elite criminal unit," I muttered to Kylie. "I warned you Rob is strange."

My sister closed her eyes briefly before sliding into the back seat with me, immediately folding her arms and slumping down.

The driver navigated the maze of LAX's exit lanes, which eventually spat us out onto a highway. I felt reassured by the steady thrum of traffic, the nearby drivers engaged in everyday behaviors: talking into their phones, trying to eat a messy burrito. For a moment, I was able to fool myself into thinking the world was just as I had always known it. In a city like Los Angeles it was harder to believe in monsters. There were no endless forests here full of encroaching trees. No pits with claw marks on either side. No whispers on a salt-laden breeze.

And yet, if there were monsters in Lundie Bay, there could be monsters anywhere.

I dug my phone out, checking to see if the detective had left any more messages—if he'd somehow found out I was back on US soil.

Nothing.

I dragged my thumb over the screen. Before I lost my nerve, I dashed out a quick message to Rafe before putting my phone away.

Where are you?

As soon as we'd merged onto the 105, Hot Mr. Sunglasses twisted around from the passenger seat to face us, holding up two rubber masks.

"Put these on."

The masks hung limply in his hand, one a muted green, the other white with streaks of red and black. They were cheap, the kind of thing you'd buy in a costume shop. He tossed them back to us.

Kylie picked up one of the masks between thumb and index finger like it was a dead animal. "No fucking way."

He shrugged. "No masks, no Rob."

She gave me a look that said *This is exactly what I warned you about.* I shifted in the seat, feeling my seat belt seize.

A game, I told myself. *Rob likes to play games.*

But it wasn't just my own safety on the line. I'd dragged Kylie into this. Kylie, who was younger than me, who had warned me about this, who would follow the lead of her big sister.

I held up my mask and recognized the green skin and flat head. It was part of a Frankenstein costume, though someone had covered the eyeholes with duct tape. Now the other mask clicked: a Dracula with painted-on hairline.

"Haven?" Kylie muttered, asking a question for which I had no answer.

Just a game.

I put on the monster mask, and after a beat I heard Kylie do the same, and we rode in darkness in the back of a stranger's car as I worried what the hell I'd gotten us into.

———

After a few minutes, or however long it had been, breathing was hard in the mask. My breath condensed and made everything hotter than it already was. My mascara had to be running, which would no doubt make me look like some tearful victim in a slasher movie when I took it off, the last thing I wanted.

"If this is Rob just being weird," I said tensely to the men in the front seats, the mask distorting my voice, "tell us that. Because this is fucked-up behavior."

There was no answer from the front of the car. It was a small comfort that the men hadn't explicitly threatened us or told us to shut up. In fact, the only time they'd spoken was to debate between themselves if it was okay to listen to a podcast on the drive. The verdict had been no, and we'd kept riding in silence.

At least I had my sister beside me. I found her hand, held it, and was instantly aware of the darting pulse in her wrist. My own head spun with self-recriminations and second-guessing. *Where are they taking us? Is Rob actually behind this? I mentioned Rob's name, not the other guy. Maybe we should we have stayed in Europe, run farther east, away from what we'd left behind in the woods. . . .*

We drove for what felt like over an hour, but judging from the idling engine, half that time was stuck in traffic. The sounds of the city came and went, and I could only imagine what we were passing: shopping centers, restaurants playing ambient music, rows of other cars. Finally, the urban din fell away and the car tipped upward, moving into some hills. We wound around tight hairpin turns, stopping a few times while our hosts complained about having to let a car pass from the other direction. The occasional dog barked in the distance.

Sweat dripped inside the mask. I started to feel the tinges of claustrophobia. The few auditory clues I had could have placed us anywhere from an abandoned factory to an underground parking deck to the suburbs.

Once the car stopped, my heartbeat kicked into overdrive.

"We're going to help you get out of the car now," Hot Mr. Sunglasses said. "Masks stay on until I tell you."

"Or what?" Kylie's voice was muffled.

Our host didn't answer.

The two men guided us out of the car and into what felt like warm sunlight.

So we aren't underground, at least.

I feared being separated from Kylie even for a moment, but then I could hear her footsteps close by again. A sliver of the world was visible at the bottom of my mask, but it only showed my own sweat-stained shirt. A vague smell of motor oil hung in the air, which might have just been the smell of the city.

One of the men gripped my upper arm, guiding me down a set of cement stairs. I felt the edges with my toes, anxious not to trip. A door groaned open, and we were thrust into cool darkness, a space air-conditioned to the point of iciness. I shivered.

The door closed behind us, plunging us into nearly complete black. I breathed unevenly under the rubber mask, which, as much as I hated, I was afraid to take off. Afraid of finding out where we were, what I'd gotten us into. For the first time, I wasn't sure I wanted answers.

CHAPTER FOUR

—

WINTER OF THE WICKED
© 1947 Sigil Pictures

MONTAGE OVER OPENING CREDITS:

As heavy snow falls over an already
snow-covered farm, a malnourished PURITAN
FAMILY goes about their farm drudgery.

FARM HUSBAND carries a bucket of sap from the
maple tap to the outdoor boiling pot.

FARM WIFE breaks the ice that has formed on
the sheep's wooden trough.

YOUNGER DAUGHTER throws grain to the geese in
their muddy pen.

ELDER DAUGHTER, inside, carves wooden puppets
to sell in the market. FIRELIGHT flickers over
the puppets' eerily lifelike faces.

—

"SIT."

I was guided by the shoulders into a hard chair and felt the seat fold down with my weight. The seat next to me rustled as Kylie sat, too. Our hands found each other on the shared armrest, squeezing tightly. Her breath was audibly strained. The room's smell reached me even through the rubber-mask scent. Musty like a basement, cloying like days-old ice cream, and atop that, the reek of something burned.

The space was too silent, too cold, so fears bubbled up in my head to fill the void. What if Rob had lured us to LA as victims? I knew what happened in snuff films. The movies he got his hands on were among the vilest things I'd ever come across. Some were typical monster gore-fests, but some were more disturbing. The psychological ones, the speculative ones about the twisted things regular people did to one another. Had he sold us off to one of his weirdo film producers? Were we being filmed right now?

A sound came from behind us like machinery starting. A series of swift clicks was followed by spinning gears. The room felt cold enough to be a meat locker. Kylie's hand tightened around mine.

Hot Mr. Sunglasses leaned down to speak in my ear, and the unexpected brush of breath against skin made me shudder. "You can take off your masks now. Rob will be here soon."

He dropped something lightweight and warm in my lap. My heart shot up my throat. The urge struck me to toss whatever it was away like a bomb, and I grabbed it—

The scent of popcorn reached my nose.

Fighting with the moist rubber, I ripped off the Frankenstein mask. Beside me, Kylie transformed from a B-movie Dracula into my sister again, as flushed and as sweaty as I was. My other senses were heightened from having been sightless so long, and I felt assaulted by a hundred different sounds and smells as I took in our surroundings.

A movie theater.

I forced myself to take slow, controlled breaths as I scanned the room. It was a small theater with a half-sized projection screen and about twenty old-fashioned wooden seats. The walls were covered with nondescript black curtains. This was no commercial complex—this was a private theater. Which meant no employees, no fire exit. No help.

A vintage projector behind us shone a movie onto the screen. The images were black-and-white, a scene of a farm in winter. A herd of sheep drifted across a barren hill while a solitary woman in a dark dress and white bonnet trudged through the snow.

"Hey!" I pushed myself to my feet, squinting into the shadows at the back of the theater to try to find the men who'd brought us here. "What the *fuck*?"

But the door clicked closed, and we were alone.

"Damn it."

I wound through the maze of seats to the door and shoved my weight against it.

It didn't budge.

Kylie moved into the aisle behind me, clutching her bag of popcorn like she wasn't sure what to do with it. She stopped directly in front of the beam coming from the projector. Strange shapes of light and shadow played out across her body as the film's distorted story unfolded on her torso.

"We're locked in." I paced in tight circles at the rear of the theater.

"Locked in *where*? Where are we?"

I tossed up my hands in ignorance. The movie theater could be anywhere near LA: a basement, a warehouse, part of a strip mall. There had to be thousands of private cinemas in a city that catered to the film industry. I could imagine Rob and his horror aficionados holding screenings down here, reclining in these creaky vintage chairs, chewing stale popcorn. I didn't want to think about the depravity that must have played out on that screen over the years. The air practically vibrated with muscle-memory gore.

Kylie gazed up at the black-curtained ceiling. "This place is seriously creepy, and I was once zip-tied in a garage with a dead body." She looked oddly disembodied with the movie still playing over her, the white-bonneted woman now following the sheep up her shoulder.

I checked for more exits, but there were only the two doors—the one we'd come in through and another on the rear wall—both locked.

Kylie said, "You don't think they're going to *kill* us, right? Like, I am not planning on starring in some podcaster's three-part true crime series."

I ran my hand over my face. "I don't think they'd have made us popcorn if they were planning on murder."

Though on second thought, that sounded exactly like something Rob might do.

"It's just Rob being Rob . . ." I started, though I wondered how much longer I could vouch for a man I'd never met.

Kylie stuck her hand into her pocket and dredged up her phone. A dead goose lying in the snow projected on half of her face, and I found myself unable to look away, both disgusted and fascinated at the distortion. She punched in a few numbers and held it to her ear.

"All due respect to your weirdo friend, but I'm calling 911." After a moment, she tore the phone from her ear. "No signal. You?"

I tried my own phone. After the events in Lundie Bay, I wasn't about to trust any cops, so I dialed the closest thing I had to a friend beside Kylie—Rafe. But I got only a grating beep, not even the option to leave a voicemail.

"We went down a lot of stairs," I said. "So we might be underground. There could be a signal jammer or building materials to block transmission. . . ."

I suddenly felt ill. Like Kylie was right. Like I'd made a huge mistake.

We spent some time looking behind all the black curtains, but found only cinder block. The chairs were bolted to the floor like a traditional theater.

Eventually, we gave up and sat back down, staring blankly at the movie.

All there was to do now was wait. To watch.

The family living on the farm were Puritans on the outskirts of a small village called Fear-Not. The bleakness of the winter setting echoed the bleakness of their lives. The father dissected the dead goose only to find strange glowing insects residing within the organs.

Snow fell steadily on the two-dimensional screen while the air-conditioning kicked on again in three dimensions. The room chilled. The farmer plunged his knife into the goose's eye, and the animal—though dead—cried out in a way that sounded too human.

Kylie cringed deeper into her seat and pressed her hands over her ears.

Curious, I studied her from the corner of my eye. I'd never quite understood why most people found horror movies so affecting. It wasn't as though I never got scared; I did. But from real life, real dangers. Not from actors reading off a script. I'd always found it easy to separate fiction from reality. It puzzled me others couldn't do the same.

With her palms against her ears, Kylie didn't hear the sigh of the door opening behind us. It was painted black like the wall itself, so at first, out of the corner of my eye, it had only looked like shifting shadows. My brain registered it as reality changing. I turned slowly, moving like I was underwater.

A man stepped through the door and let it slowly swing closed behind him.

Rob.

It was him. Somehow, I just knew.

And he wasn't like I'd expected. Neither the stereotypical greasy-haired dweeb nor statuesque like the two men who had abducted us. He was white, on the smaller side, and fell just short of leading-man good looks, with the kind of build that was naturally soft, though he had the misfortune of living in LA, which demanded a keto diet and an hour daily in the gym.

Kylie twisted sharply at the sound of the door, flinching to find the man just steps behind us.

My throat dry, I rasped out, "Rob?"

The man smiled. He had soft cheeks and eyes that twinkled, elf-like, though there were keen points of intelligence fixed in them. His clothes gave off celebrity real-estate agent vibes. There was nothing obvious about him that hinted at a taste for depravity. But then again, was there ever? It was always the quiet neighbor next door, the one everyone said was polite and kept to himself . . .

"It's Donovan, actually. Donovan Robles. You can still call me Rob, just not in public." He tapped the side of his nose three times. "It's good to finally meet you, Haven."

The name *Donovan Robles* struck a familiar chord in my brain, a name I'd seen in closing credits, though not in any of the horror films he'd sent me on VHS cassettes. No, I'd seen his name in Cineplexes in the credits of mainstream movies.

Kylie pushed herself to her feet. "You practically kidnapped us, you psycho!"

Rob ignored her accusation. "You must be the half sister. I'm sorry about . . ." His hand swirled in the air. "All *that*. We had to make sure you were who you said you were. It took a little longer than we wanted. I *did* leave you with entertainment." He tipped his head toward the movie, which seemed to snag his attention. After watching a few frames, he cracked a smile. "I figured you'd like this one, Haven. A virtually unknown masterpiece, *Winter of the Wicked*, 1947. Very hard to get one's hands on." The gleam in his eye turned a little devilish, and—*yes*—*there* was SlasherDasher at last.

"Rob, what the hell is going on?"

He gave the slightest eye roll like I was being dramatic. "Oh, did Tyler scare you? Was it the masks?" With his eyes still glued to the movie, he swatted away a phantom moth and said, "You know the kind of side business I run. A lot of people could get arrested if our identities were leaked. I trust *you*, Haven, but I wasn't sure about your sister."

"Because I'm Black?" Kylie said hotly.

He looked at her in surprise and pressed a hand to his chest. "That hurts my tender liberal heart. In any case, no, not because you're Black. You see, I have leverage on your sister. Incriminating information that would be trouble for her if it got out." He tried to soften his words with polite gestures in my direction. "I don't mean that as a threat; it just makes sense to have an insurance policy when you dabble in the type of business I do." He turned back to my sister. "But *you* were a mystery, Kylie, so we had to find something on you. Before you know my sins, I wanted to know yours."

Kylie's arms entwined defensively over her chest. She muttered begrudgingly, "What, the literary forgeries?"

He scoffed. "No, Kylie. That's slap-on-the-wrist crime. What I found was . . . quite the *enigma*."

He wiggled his fingers conspiratorially in the air.

Kylie's whole attitude shifted. The strength seemed to drain out of her muscles. I waited for her to press Rob, but she didn't. Which, I realized, was an answer in itself.

She knows what he found. There's something big enough to scare her.

I eyed her side-on, but she remained tight-lipped.

Rob pinned her with the knowing look of conjoined liars.

Then his whole energy shifted, and he clapped. "Now that we're all on the same page, would you like to come upstairs? Tyler made sushi!"

The movie continued to run in the background. Facing the projector, I was vaguely aware of the scene, though the imagery played upside down in the machine's small black eye. Glowing maggots wriggled out of the goose's split-open stomach and soared toward the heavens instead of falling to the ground.

I glanced at Kylie, whose eyes held daggers aimed at Rob.

"Upstairs?" she repeated. "Head upstairs for sushi like it's all just that easy? After the masks, locking us in here, showing us some fucked-up movie?"

"Yes, exactly," Rob said, blinking calmly.

Kylie looked at me and muttered, "Your friend is fucking weird."

Rob chuckled gleefully.

I had no idea what *upstairs* held. But we didn't have much choice, so we followed Rob through the door. The stairwell outside the theater was dark, with backlit framed movie posters of classic Romero and Lynch films, and, most troubling of all, a few '80s-era musicals.

Dark, but not *dark*. Not SlasherDasher's taste.

So, who the hell *was* Donovan Robles?

CHAPTER FIVE

THE HUNDREDTH STAIR
© 1941 Sigil Pictures

PROFESSOR BYRD
One hundred stairs up from the
beach? One hundred spindles on
the banister? One hundred colored
shards in the stained-glass window?
You constructed your home based on
superstition, Harrison. Dabbling
in the dark arts is no game. An
architect should know better.

HARRISON SMILEY
I'm a husband and father before
I am an architect, Professor.
And my wife . . . Her illness
isn't natural. All night, I hear
her endless wet rasping like an
incessant clock's ticking . . . so
do not lecture me on the darkness.
(to self) I dwell in it.

WHEN HE OPENED the door at the top of the stairs, I understood immediately who Donovan Robles was.

Donovan Robles was rich.

Mansion in the Hollywood Hills rich. Kelly Wearstler furniture rich. The kind of old-money wealth that liked to congregate on the east or west coast, bumping up against the country's outer edges, wanting nothing to do with real America.

As we exited the stairwell, I felt as though I'd stepped straight into a museum of Old Hollywood. The house had the stucco walls and arched windows of a Spanish Colonial Revival, one of the few remaining original Hollywood homes that hadn't been bulldozed and replaced with a big white box. The first thing to greet us was a life-sized mannequin wearing a sequined gown with a label that read CAROL BUTLER, ACADEMY AWARD GOWN—1931. The plastic woman's painted eyes were chipped. I resisted the urge to tap them with my fingernail.

Rob led us down a few steps into a midcentury sitting room with a Malm freestanding fireplace surrounded by a circular sectional. On the wall was a vintage soda sign, but not for any brand I'd heard of; it was a movie prop, I surmised. A red British phone booth stood in the corner with a charging station inside.

"Like I said," Rob continued over his shoulder, "Tyler's been working his magic in the kitchen while you were downstairs. He sources his fish from the same market in Pasadena as the top seafood restaurants. Very exclusive, very fresh. All the best stuff is gone by five in the morning. The dining room's through here. . . ."

My head was still trying to catch up with the reality that we weren't about to be murdered in a creepy underground theater and were, in fact, in a perfectly normal house—excepting the mannequins. So perhaps not normal at all. From Kylie's wary expression, she was thinking the same.

"So, Tyler's your personal chef?" I asked slowly, taking in two more mannequins flanking a bathroom doorway as I tried to calculate how much money it would take to convince someone's hired staff to pause their nori-wrapping to participate in a creepy, overly elaborate airport pickup.

Rob placed his hand on his chest as though moderately offended. "Tyler is my *fiancé*."

I raised my eyebrows in a silent apology, but my question remained. *How much money would it take to convince your* fiancé *to participate in a creepy, overly elaborate airport pickup?*

Kylie was notably silent behind me, arms still knotted over her torso, eyeing a glass curio cabinet filled with tagged movie props. A chessboard from a famous serial-killer film. A pair of eyeglasses worn in a Hitchcock production. The ivory-handled Damascus knife from *The Gentleman Knife.*

Hot Mr. Sunglasses—Tyler—emerged from a swinging door, looking much more at home in a Williams-Sonoma apron and carrying a wooden tray of canapés than he had playing cloak-and-dagger. His eyes were sharp, warm. A relief. The dining table was set rather formally for ten places, though it seemed to be only the four of us. Someone had set out chopsticks and little terra-cotta bowls of soy sauce.

Tyler presented the sushi tray with the air of someone well aware that what they'd produced was restaurant quality.

"I spent some time in Japan," he explained, though no one had asked.

The dinner began in silence broken only by the gentle slosh of sushi dipped in soy sauce and the glug of the Gewürztraminer wine Rob poured for us.

"So, you're, *what?*" Kylie jabbed the end of her chopstick in the direction of the curio cabinet. "A director?"

"Producer." Rob smiled graciously as he refilled our wineglasses. "I'm working on an adaptation of an Andre West novel right now. We have the actress from *The Callback* attached and—this is not to leave this table—a certain director by the initials of *T.L.* is reading the script this very moment. We got our start together back in '91. We were both baby screenwriters on *Argonauts*." He spoke of his work with the same dismissive sense of modesty that Tyler had with his food, and I found it hard to tell if they were sincere or acting.

"*Argonauts*? The TV show?" The tight set of Kylie's shoulders eased. "I was obsessed with that show in middle school."

"Middle school, huh?" Rob made a face as though he didn't appreciate what that said about their age difference, but he took a sip of wine and reclined in his chair at the head of the table like he was used to holding court. "I'm aware of how campy it's seen as today, all those warrior women in short skirts, low-quality CGI monsters-of-the-week. It was campy back *then*. But there's nothing wrong with genre. Absolutely nothing."

Tyler, keeping his eyes on his wineglass, remained quiet. I imagined that *Argonauts* residuals were paying for the lavish house, his five a.m. mackerel fillets, and his expensive crystal jewelry. If he disagreed, he wasn't about to say so.

Rob sighed. "This town knows me for campy TV series and even campier movies. Few know about my other life as SlasherDasher. But that work is just as important. Do you know why?"

Kylie and I shook our heads.

He wagged a stiff finger over his dinner plate. "The movie complex wants you to see life in terms of happy endings, satisfying character arcs, guessable twists. Predictability is a drug. A literal drug—it rewires your brain to crave it. The audience keeps coming back for more, wanting the same hit again and again. The guy to get the girl. The girl to get the monster. And so forth."

"But not *your* movies," I said.

He nodded slowly with a hint of a smile. "Not my movies. The ones I send you to recap aren't sedatives for anyone's soul. They're the *cure*. They block the urge toward predictability. They're about scares, sure, but so much more. If you really want to affect people—and that's what any good producer ultimately wants—you have to dig around in your audience's brain and destroy their carefully constructed sense of reality."

"If that's the kind of art you like," Kylie challenged, "why don't *you* make it?"

"Fair question. It takes a certain type to make the stuff I collect on my website. My childhood was *disastrously* well adjusted. Raised in Delaware, ski trips over Christmas break. My mother was a pediatrician." He shrugged off the apparent tragedy of a normal childhood. "I don't have the tortured imagination to make those kinds of movies."

Rob's tight smile held a bit of jealousy.

He set down his wineglass with a certain finality. The joviality melted off his face, and his elfin eyes sharpened. He cleared his throat and leaned forward, tenting his hands. "So, that's *me*. But what about you two, hmm? What's the story about fleeing Portugal, needing an untraceable place to stay?"

The table fell silent. I had intimated to Rob that I was tangled up in something strange back in Lundie Bay, something dangerous. He hadn't asked questions then, and I'd been grateful for it. But now, it seemed, his help came with a price.

A wristwatch in the curio cabinet—a costume artifact—ticked steadily.

I sat forward, trying to find the words. "Back in Washington State, Kylie and I ran into a lot of . . ." I swirled my hand in the air. "Strange occurrences."

Rob frowned. "What do you mean, *strange*?"

Kylie set down her chopsticks and tented her own hands. "Unexplainable. Shit that's beyond science. The things you see in your movies but happening in real life. Basically, Haven's house was haunted."

Tyler's hand fluttered to the rose-quartz bracelet around his wrist. He leaned toward Kylie and spoke in a dramatic hush. "Nothing is unexplainable. Ghosts, aliens, Bigfoot—it's just our limited way of perceiving the world. The *hidden* world. We don't have the capacity to fully understand reality, so we label things, turn them into stories. Some more fantastical than others. Just because some things can't be explained with our current vocabulary doesn't mean they don't exist, only that our brains are too undeveloped to comprehend it."

Kylie held my gaze for a second. Then she uncrossed her legs and recrossed them, and asked Tyler, "So you believe in ghosts?"

Rob and Tyler both burst out laughing. I was left feeling lost, like I was missing something.

Tyler motioned to the city outside. "This is LA! You'll find a psychic in every strip mall. People are open-minded here in a way they aren't elsewhere. My grandmother haunted me last year after her death—she kept cranking up the AC because she was always warm."

Right. Or maybe it was just Rob.

What was Kylie making of all this? The novels-in-progress she'd been working on before we'd met had all brushed up against these topics, peeking at dark mysteries in the mirror. And there were her spirituality tattoos, her astrology charts, her alien conspiracies.

I wasn't surprised when she looked at me pointedly. "You hear that? They're open-minded. Tell them."

I bristled, muttering out of the side of my mouth, "We agreed we wouldn't tell *anyone*."

She muttered back, "I know about the detective who keeps leaving you messages. How much longer until they find you? Find *us*? We need help."

The three of them—Kylie, Rob, and Tyler—looked at me expectantly, and I felt targeted, like it was suddenly them against me.

Reluctantly, keeping my eyes on the table, I said to our hosts, "You know the phrase *truth is stranger than fiction*? Well, fiction is fucking strange, too. And it turns out that what Kylie writes, what I draw . . . it doesn't always stay on the page."

I finally looked up from the table.

Kylie added in a hushed tone, "It's a family curse."

Rob and Tyler slowly leaned back in their chairs. I could only imagine what was going through their heads. Tyler toyed faster with his quartz bracelet. A strange light turned on in Rob's eyes.

"Go on," he said.

I described finding *Bedtime Stories for Monsters* in my father's attic and the impulse that had driven me to illustrate its characters. Rob and Tyler listened in silence, glancing at each other with unspoken thoughts; when we finished, Tyler looked frightened, and Rob looked exhilarated.

"They're still out there?" Rob asked in a hushed voice, as though someone might be eavesdropping.

But I assumed we were alone save for the mannequins.

"As far as we know," I admitted. "Yeah, the monsters are out there."

Rob slowly refilled his wineglass and then started to take a sip, pausing. His thoughts seemed to travel elsewhere. When he spoke finally, it was measured. "You know, there's a project that was submitted to us a while back at Insight Entertainment. An urban-legend article pitched as a potential docuseries. It wasn't right for us—the executives passed." He peered at me keenly. "But that thing you suggested about fiction coming to life? This article said the same."

My left eye twitched. *"What?"*

He leaned toward Tyler. "Grab the magazine, will you? It's in my office. The shelves by the window."

Tyler left briefly and returned with a magazine that he set down on the table in front of me. It was the November issue of the *Hollywooder*. I'd occasionally picked up the magazine at airports. A step above *Entertainment Weekly*, a step below the *New Yorker*, mostly middlebrow think pieces about pop culture and the arts, some book and film reviews.

"Page forty," Rob said cryptically.

Picking it up, I flipped to page forty, which was already dog-eared.

THE CURSE OF SIGIL PICTURES

For decades, urban legends have both menaced and entertained a city built on imagination. But what happens when imagination becomes all too real—maybe even deadly?

My toes began to curl in my shoes. "What's this?"

Rob said, "This article has been making a splash throughout town ever since it came out late last year. Even more so because the author died under mysterious circumstances a few weeks after it was published. All the message boards are discussing it, saying the urban legends the author wrote about are real and *killed* her. That's why it came across my desk. You haven't heard of it?"

"We've been traveling. Haven't really been paying attention to the news."

"Well, it's the latest cultural phenomenon to capture the public's attention. For years, everyone's been obsessed with scams, cults. But scams are *so last year*, Haven. Cults are *two* years ago. Urban legends are going to be the next big thing. Trust me." He raised his eyebrows like he was imparting sacred knowledge.

Kylie slid over the magazine to read the headline. "What's Sigil Pictures?"

"A production company that operated back in the 1940s and 1950s. The movie I played for you? *Winter of the Wicked?* That's one of theirs. This article inspired me to hunt down a copy."

"I've never heard of them," I said.

Rob tapped the article with his chopstick. "There's a rundown of their history here. Lots of scandals. The director fell off the Hollywood Hotel; a few years later, the producer overdosed. Kind of eerie, what with the article's author dying too, isn't it? Anyway, I'm not surprised you haven't heard of them. Their films fell into obscurity. They're extremely hard to find copies of, even for me." He gave a self-satisfied smile. "I'm mentioned in the article."

"He means SlasherDasher," Tyler clarified.

I set aside the magazine, swallowing down a lump. "I'll take a look at it later."

After a tight smile, Rob's energy shifted back to one of a gracious host. He gave a dramatic sigh. "Monsters, curses . . . now I understand why you didn't want anyone to trace your location. Well, you're both welcome to stay here as long as you need to. We have plenty of guest rooms. Though I do have a small favor to ask in return, Haven."

My toes curled harder in dark anticipation of what he might ask. "What's that?"

"You start working for me again. My clients are complaining about the quality of my site recaps—the joker I got to fill in for you wouldn't know a false climax if he was standing at the top of one. You can use the theater downstairs."

I was surprised by how my body reacted to the offer, my shoulders falling, head rolling back like I was sinking into a familiar sofa with my imprint in the cushions. I'd actually *missed* horror movies. In the past year they'd become home for me in a world where I had no home, and it would be good to get back to them.

"Sure."

Rob grinned, his elfin sparkle returning as he clapped. "Excellent! Now, how about dessert? Tyler made mochi."

After dinner, Kylie and I discovered that the upstairs hadn't been spared from Rob's eccentric decor. My sister had been set up in a Marilyn Monroe–themed room with a pop art portrait covering one entire wall, a crystal chandelier dangling over the faux-fur bedspread, and a leopard-print settee that held throw pillows shaped like each of the men reputed to have slept with her.

Kylie sauntered into the open doorway between our adjoining rooms, hands on her hips, and said, "I'll trade you." Then she took one look at my room and quickly recanted. "Actually, never mind. Yours is worse."

My room was an ode to Hollywood itself, with a scale version of the famous white letters in place of a headboard and glowing round bulbs around the vanity mirror. But the thing I couldn't take my eyes off—that no one would be able to ignore—was the wax dummies. Life-sized wax statues of waifish beauties looked back at me, Audrey and Elizabeth and Rita, each captured as their most famous characters instead of as themselves; the effect was an erasure of their real identities, trapping them in fiction.

Even worse, the room was drenched in freesia air freshener.

I sank onto the end of the bed, grimacing at the dummies, and ran my nails over my scalp. What time was it? After the red-eye flight, the traffic, our hours in the windowless theater, time might as well have lost all meaning.

"What do you think of them?" I asked, tipping my head toward the hallway.

"Well, Tyler's a woo-woo crystal worshipper, but I've bought a crystal or two in my day, so I get it. I'm not so sure about Rob. *Donovan Robles.*" She dropped her voice. "You know, I googled him in the bathroom. I've seen some of his movies. They're fine, not Oscar contenders or anything. But it's weird that he outwardly makes fluff like *Argonauts* and secretly traffics these underground horror movies. I think that's what he really wants to be making. Your friend has two identities, and the one down in that creepy theater? That's the real one."

"Oh, I know." I dragged my purse across the bed and pulled out the *Hollywooder* magazine, frowning down at it. "I'm relieved he's as normal as he is, considering."

"This doesn't fit *any* definition of normal." Kylie pointed to wax Audrey. "Firmly abnormal."

"We aren't trapped here," I reminded her. "We can leave if you aren't comfortable."

I wasn't actually sure that was true. Not that I worried Rob would lock us in and force us to play dress-up like living mannequins. Rather, we needed him too much to be able to walk away.

"We have a safe place to stay," I assured her. "No one knows we're here. No police. No Uncle Arnold."

Kylie gave a tight nod but remained in the doorway.

"Haven . . ." Her eyes fell to my bag. "I need to tell you something. On the airplane, while you were sleeping . . . I went through your bag.

I was just looking for eye drops, I swear. But I saw your copy of *Exit, Nebraska.*"

I tried to keep my face the very picture of serenity. Had she taken off the rubber band? Seen the drawing inside? Surely not—she would say so if she had.

"Yeah?" I said carefully. "I bought it in the airport bookstore."

Frowning, she looked down at her hamsa tattoo and said, "You don't talk much about him. Our . . . dad."

I let out a tight breath. *She didn't look inside.*

I lifted a blasé shoulder and said, "I guess there's not much to say. Turns out I didn't even know him that well myself."

I hoped that would end the conversation, but she didn't leave. I felt the weight of her unasked questions like a heavy winter blanket. The first few days after leaving Lundie Bay, driving east with little cash and fewer plans, she'd grilled me with questions I didn't want to answer. Had our father been a drinker? What was his favorite movie? What kind of a parent had he been? Liberal or conservative?

"Look, Kylie, I get that you're curious, but there isn't much more I can tell you."

That wasn't true. There were so many memories of him I could share with her. But maybe *I* didn't want to remember. Amory Marbury was dead—gone—and he'd taken a hell of a lot of secrets to the grave with him. Disturb the soil too much, and I was afraid of what would emerge.

I thought she might push the issue, but then she yawned and stood upright, stretching her arms as high as they'd go. "Well, no offense, but I could use a little me time. There's such a thing as *too* much sisterly bonding." She was teasing, but not entirely. For nearly three months, we'd been together almost every minute.

"Yeah, yeah. You know you love my grumpy complaining," I said with a smile.

"Uh, *yeah.* Here's hoping we aren't both taxidermy in the morning." She patted Rita the wax dummy. Then her smirk melted into something more serious as she watched me stretch my fingers, out and in, out and in.

Her voice hollowed. "Don't draw."

I met her eyes, nodding, as my fingers curled into my palms—and stayed there. "Don't write."

CHAPTER SIX

———

PURGATORY'S DOOR
© 1955 Sigil Pictures

DETECTIVE NICK DRAM
All right, kid. You follow up on the
dead girl?

YOUNG COP
Medical examiner's office says she
was mauled by an animal. Maybe a
bull or a ram. Something with horns.

DETECTIVE NICK DRAM
This is New York City, kid. Not
Pamplona. It wasn't bulls she was
running with.

———

THERE *WAS* SUCH a thing as too much sisterly bonding. I let out a long exhale as I closed the door, reveling in being alone. I settled back into the fortress of bed pillows and, under the unflinching gazes of the wax dummies, opened the magazine.

THE CURSE OF SIGIL PICTURES

For decades, urban legends have both menaced and entertained a city built on imagination. But what happens when imagination becomes all too real—and even deadly?

By E. Blackwell

In the summer of 2010, freshly graduated from UCLA and in a new relationship, I watched a movie at my cinephile boyfriend's insistence. . . .

My phone trilled beside me. I glanced down at the screen, then forgot to breathe when I saw the name. Rafe's message was simple.

Why, miss me?

It was in response to my previous message asking where he was. My thumb wavered over the screen, uncertain. By now he must've seen the charge for the plane ticket, would know I was in LA. He knew I was back on the West Coast, yet *I* had to contact him first. Was it another one of his tricks? Trying to get me to miss him?

I rolled onto my side, curling clam-like around the phone as though his response was a pearl. I wrote:

Just making sure your money will last.

Three dots showed he was writing, and then the phone beeped.

There's plenty for you to worry about, but not the money.

And with that one cryptic message I was reminded me of all the ways the Harbinger was bad for me. I tossed the phone aside before I became tempted to keep the conversation going.

I picked up the magazine again.

This wasn't just any movie, my boyfriend claimed—in fact, he only ever referred to it as a film—but rather "an experiment in expanding my perception of reality." (Yes, he was truly that insufferable. I dumped him shortly after, more interested in shrinking him out of my reality.) Ancient and black-and-white, it was called *The Hundredth Stair*, and much like *The Ring*, the blockbuster cult-classic horror movie that still makes me fear static-filled TV screens, it was supposed to transcend two dimensions and bleed into the real world in a metaphysical way that I didn't buy for a second. (He was lucky he was cute—I even sat through *2001: A Space Odyssey* for him.)

Little did I know how deeply *The Hundredth Stair* would worm its way into my psyche. After ditching the lackluster boyfriend, I fell into my own obsession with the movie, as well as the mysterious midcentury studio that brought it into being, Sigil Pictures. I descended, step by step, on my own hundred-stair journey, researching an improbable tale of urban legends, cursed productions, and unexplained deaths a half century old.

The story of the origin of Sigil Pictures reads like a real-life horror movie in its own right. To fully immerse myself in its rich history, I reached out to the famously eccentric Nanette Fields, whose formal title is "Script Consultant," though she's better known by her industry moniker "The Ghostwriter Librarian." At 80, Fields's labyrinthine mind is the repository for all things paranormal in Hollywood. Over black coffees at a hole-in-the-wall diner she's been haunting for 60 years, Fields told me that Sigil Pictures' two creators met in 1938 at a midnight séance at the Bridewater Hotel, where ancestral spirits informed them that they were distantly related. Max Faraday was the creative right brain of the operation, a director who illustrated his own storyboards. The left brain was Richard Alton, heir of a railroad tycoon, who not only bankrolled the studio and ran the business end but wrote the original screenplays. The two-person operation came out with the body-horror thriller *The Hundredth Stair* in 1941, which was immediately embraced by America's growing society of underground horror enthusiasts. According to Fields, they soon after received funding from a mysterious benefactor, which allowed them to produce their roster of cult classics, entering the color-film era in 1951 with the Hansel-and-Gretel riff *The Candy House.*

"But, of course," Fields said as she sipped her fourth coffee on an empty stomach, "you want to know about the murders, don't you?"

I set the magazine down, taking a break from the rest of the article, feeling uncomfortable knowing the author had died not long after writing that. I stood, needing to shake out my legs. Audrey and Elizabeth and Rita crowded the room, so I opened the door and peeked out into the dark hallway.

It had to be past midnight, though the light was still showing under Kylie's door. She was probably reading. She'd begun rereading our father's books, hungry for insight on the man she'd never known. I'd thought it was a bad idea, but it was her life, not mine.

There was no sign of Rob or Tyler, and the light was off beneath the door of their suite.

I made my way downstairs quietly. If Rob's house was eccentric during the day, it was positively ghoulish at night. The movie memorabilia attached to the walls gave the house crooked angles, swollen shapes. Some of the pieces glowed—a horror-movie mask with neon LED threads, a backlit crown from a popular fantasy series. Mannequins stood on the stair landing, in the sitting room, by the hall bathroom.

I hadn't taken a full inventory of them earlier in the day, and every time I turned a corner and found a new pair of eyes looking at me, I had a small heart attack.

I made it to the kitchen and opened the fridge, happy to find a bottle of pinot grigio. I didn't bother with a glass, just tipped it up while standing at the island.

What I'd read in the *Hollywooder* so far left me disturbed. A production company where one member wrote the screenplays and the other—a blood relation, no less—illustrated them was all too familiar. It was Kylie and me all over again. She the writer, I the artist. Before her, my father and me—a collaboration that had even transcended his death.

Not to mention the fact that a curse was involved.

I carried the bottle upstairs and took a long swig before stepping back into the magazine's lurid world, jumping to the last page.

. . . and yet there is ongoing debate about how many Sigil films were made, with some amateur investigators hinting that more have been lost to time. Ask any Sigil film devotee—we call ourselves the Sigilists—and they'll regale you with borderline criminal tales of how they got their hands on these out-of-circulation movies. Ever since the company shuttered, hard-copy reels and videos are nearly nonexistent, and digital downloads are elusive, links popping up for mere minutes on dark-web horror-movie sites like SlasherDasher or VintageScares. (Don't bother googling them. The creators of these sites know how to hide their treasures, and keys to their digital kingdoms require close to a blood sacrifice.)

As something of an internet sleuth myself, I voraciously hunted copies of these films. My ex-boyfriend and his copy of *The Hundredth Stair* had vanished. Google searches returned no solid hits. The most I managed was to view a few grainy clips of *The Candy House* dubbed in Russian—or so I thought, until I later discovered it to be a fan-made reproduction. The dearth of these films, however, doesn't deter online speculation. After a 20-year-old college student was found standing beneath LA's Grand Avenue underpass with a deep cut in one palm, claiming to have sleepwalked under a real-life Sandman Killer's influence, urban rumors hatched and spread. The works of Sigil Pictures had, it seemed, stepped off the screen and into our world.

I was left to ponder:

Had the Sandman Killer actually entered the student's dreams?

Had two gas-masked children left sinister candy trails across Kraków?

Were the recent strange deaths on the LA subway system caused by the fictional tommy gun from *Purgatory's Door*?

Or were these merely baseless urban legends?

Today, a deep dive down an internet rabbit hole or two will lead you to a warren of urban legend message boards, Reddit theories, and paranormal ghost-hunters who claim to have interacted with the real-life terrors spawned by Sigil Pictures' cursed history. Whether the demon living underneath the Hundredth Stair is real, or some trepidatious few actually stumbled upon the ever-shifting location of the predatory Candy House, or the Sandman Killer is still entering viewers' dreams, one thing is certain: The curse of Max Faraday and Richard Alton is far from make-believe to me and countless other Sigilists. As Nanette Fields says, "All stories are based in reality—just maybe not this reality."

As for me, I'll sleep with one eye open. Will you?

I closed the magazine with shaking hands and gulped more wine. Apparently, sleeping with one eye open hadn't spared E. Blackwell. I was tempted to get Kylie and tell her about what I'd read, but her light was off now. Instead, I pulled out my laptop. Sure enough, a few clicks led me to a popular message-board site with a subsite dedicated to the article.

Most of the posts were theories about the production company, dubious facts about the author's death by drowning near the Santa Monica pier, and a few thinly veiled promotions for a Hollywood ghost tour company. Then I found a post from someone with the screen name Decline.A.Copy that had a fair number of responses.

Decline.A.Copy Anyone have the full list of Sigil Pictures films?

HitchMyCock Winter of the Wicked, The Sandman Killer, On the Night Watch, The Candy House, The Hundredth Stair.

TheHorrorGuy On the Night Watch was Gemini, not Sigil. Get your facts straight, HitchMyCock. And you left out Purgatory's Door. There are more out there. No one knows how many.

NEW POST Decline.A.Copy @TheHorrorGuy, what can you tell me about Purgatory's Door? Advice for getting a copy? Is it connected to this site here?

The link led to a cached urban legend blog post about the Killarney Doorman, a demon reputed to guard the entrance to purgatory in the noir *Purgatory's Door*, though the post's author couldn't get his hands on a copy to verify it. According to the author, two boys playing in their Dublin apartment building's basement in 2007 saw a glowing red door with a thuggish, goat-headed man in a suit standing before it. The boys' mother didn't believe them. The next day, the boys returned to the basement and were never seen again.

I made a mental note to do more research on this urban legend, then replied to Decline.A.Copy's post.

OneEyeOpen @Decline.A.Copy, I might be able to get you a copy. Where are you located?

I had no idea if Rob would actually be able to get his hands on a copy of *Purgatory's Door*, but it didn't matter. Decline.A.Copy seemed highly interested in Sigil Pictures and the films that the *Hollywooder* article alluded to; whoever they were, they might have information that could help us find answers, too.

When I finally went to bed, the drained wine bottle beside me, Rita and Audrey and Elizabeth frozen in time, it was no surprise when, once more, nightmares returned.

CHAPTER SEVEN

———

WINTER OF THE WICKED
© 1947 Sigil Pictures

INTERIOR — FARMHOUSE COMMON ROOM — NIGHT —
CONTINUOUS

Farm Husband grabs his Elder Daughter's
half-finished puppet.

> FARM HUSBAND
> What devilry is this? Who taught you
> to make such idolatrous creations?

> ELDER DAUGHTER
> Old Constance Good, Papa. The basket
> maker. While you were away at the
> autumn market in Sturbridge.

> FARM HUSBAND
> A basket maker? Nay, a witch bent on
> bringing evil into this godly home!

He throws the entire basket of puppets and
supplies in the fireplace.

"GREEN JUICE MUFFINS!" Tyler announced over the breakfast table, thrusting a woven basket of fresh-out-of-the-oven baked goods toward us. "Gluten-free, dairy-free, nut-free, but you'd never know. They're delicious!"

He set them between Kylie and me proudly.

Getting coffee that morning, I'd seen the pile of cucumber peels and kale stems in the kitchen, so I had reason to doubt the claim. But I took a muffin, and Kylie did the same.

Rob came trundling down from the upstairs floor, his briefcase messenger bag dangling from one shoulder. He gave Tyler a quick kiss on the lips and then glanced at the muffins with a subtle flash of alarm. *He'd* tried them before.

"Make yourselves at home," he said to Kylie and me. "The door code is six-two-eight-zero. Tyler can show you how to set up movies on the projector downstairs if you'd like to start recapping again. It's an antique—it takes a little skill."

I still didn't touch my muffin. Instead, I picked up the November *Hollywooder* issue, which I'd given to Kylie to read that morning.

"Rob, do you think you could get us a meeting with the script doctor mentioned in this article? Nanette Fields? With the author dead, she's the closest lead we have."

Rob tucked his white button-up shirt into salmon-colored trousers. "Nanette has a reputation in this town. She's been rattling around Hollywood since practically the 1940s herself. I'll see what I can do, but I called around a little back when my studio was considering optioning the article. Nanette doesn't take spec meetings, so it will be a challenge. Still, I *am* resourceful." He winked. "I do have to warn you, she's famously eccentric."

She was eccentric? It took effort not to stare pointedly at the ball gown–dressed mannequins in the corners, the prop guillotine blade adorning the dining room wall.

After Rob left for a Studio City meeting, Tyler showed us how to use the antique film projector in the basement before heading out himself. Quickly, though, Kylie and I split to do our own things, reveling in a little personal space after so many weeks constantly together. I scoured the internet for more information on the history of Sigil Pictures. Everything I found was only rumors, speculation.

That evening, I gave the research a break and switched to the headache of battling my claim for Malice House's insurance payout. Rob and Tyler were still out, so I was alone in the massive kitchen, ninety minutes into a call with the insurance company, when Kylie came down.

"I already submitted that claim . . ." I repeated into the phone.

Kylie grabbed a box of crackers from the pantry. She heard a little of my conversation and gave me a sympathetic look as she slid onto a barstool.

As she rummaged through the cracker box, her hand froze. "Um, Haven, what's that?"

I pulled the phone away from my mouth and whispered, "What?"

She slowly pointed at the counter.

I stepped back, eyes widening.

Someone had poured out a full saltshaker onto the counter. The empty glass jar lay on its side, lid unscrewed.

The customer service rep's tinny voice in my ear fell away.

I had done it, I realized.

Lines ran through the salt. Doodles I hadn't even vaguely been aware of drawing formed the suggestion of a face with three-inch teeth.

Don't draw.

"Shit."

I hung up the phone.

"*Shit.* Sorry," I mumbled to Kylie as I swiped my hand through the salt, banishing the picture.

Kylie closed the box of crackers like she'd lost her appetite. As I cleaned up the mess with a sponge, worries throbbed in the back of my head. This wasn't the first time it had happened, despite our reminders to each other. Not doing something, it turned out, was even more difficult than doing it. And ever since I'd bartered my sketchbook full of my life's work to the Robber Saints, I'd felt its loss keenly; it was like having a cold and not being able to breathe properly.

Kylie climbed off the stool. "That article has you wound up. Not to mention having to deal with the house. You need to relax." She paused. "Come on. I know what will help you."

She led me down to the foyer of Rob's movie theater, where shelves held hundreds of VHS cassettes, DVDs, and even old-fashioned movie reels.

"How about this one?" Kylie ran her finger along the boxes of reels. She slid one out, blowing dust off the label so she could read the writing. "*Stitches 2: Split Seams*. That sounds like your kind of thing."

Leave it to my sister to understand that gore was my preferred form of self-care.

I smiled. "Sure."

I'd seen the entire *Stitches* franchise half a dozen times. It was about a possessed Victorian doll unearthed by a construction crew building a lake house for a family trying to start over after the tragic death of their youngest son. The first installment had been a mainstream sleeper hit in the early nineties that grossed just enough to justify a sequel that tanked. Twenty years later, a couple of low-budget follow-ups came out that practically no one saw . . . except for Rob and me, apparently. He even had the original *reels*.

Kylie managed to get the film going, then dimmed the lights and dropped into the seat next to me. She offered me a packet of candy from her purse.

"Thanks." I pointed to the screen as the credits started. "Keep an eye on the lake. You don't notice unless you've seen the movie a few times, but around the edges, you can see things crawling out of it. In the woods, too. There are faces in some of the trees." I kicked up my sneakers on the back of the chair in front of me.

The projector clicked and spun. The opening credits played out over a backdrop of a Victorian-era sewing shop, with extreme close-ups of needles puncturing leather and measuring tape coiled around a doll's porcelain neck.

Kylie leaned over and whispered, "I forgot to tell you. I got an email today from Patrick Kane."

Though we were alone in the theater, I still whispered from force of habit. "Who's Patrick Kane?"

"The biographer. He did that big compendium of Naja Ann Lundin that came out a few years ago." She swallowed a mouthful of candy. "He's working on a biography of our father."

"What?" My cry cut through the hush of the theater, and I stared at Kylie. "I haven't heard anything about this."

She didn't seem nearly as alarmed as I was. "He said he's been trying to get in touch with you, but you won't pick up his calls."

"I don't answer any unlisted numbers, obviously. It could be the detective."

"Well, he asked if we'd sit for an interview. He said he'd come to us."

My pulse beat a steady alarm. A professional researcher snooping around in our family past was the last thing we wanted. "No chance. How did he even find out about you? *I* didn't even know my father had another daughter until a few months ago."

She flinched like I was reducing her value to that time frame. I gave a quick "Sorry."

"It's . . . okay. It was that genealogy site. He was digging around for Amory's lineage and came across the profiles we uploaded."

The theater chair squeaked beneath me as I settled back, considering this.

Months ago, after leaving Lundie Bay, Kylie and I had each taken a mail-order genetic test and uploaded the results into an ancestry database that was supposed to help connect distant relatives. We'd hoped that it would lead us to Acosta relatives, but we hadn't gotten any results.

I shook my head emphatically. "Block his number."

She sucked on her candy with a small frown.

The hard candy clacking around in my own mouth made me feel like I was sucking on extra teeth. *Of course* Kylie would want to talk to a biographer. Whoever this Patrick Kane was, he probably already had reams of notes on Amory Marbury, the kind of information Kylie had been desperate to have for months despite my one-word answers.

On-screen, the family settled into their house as the construction manager arrived to draw up blueprints. A montage played out of a foreman calling for work to stop because something had been found beneath the old elm tree. My heart spurred into a faster clip, even though I'd watched the scene many times.

"Look, I get that you're curious about our father," I said to Kylie. "It's natural. But it's too dangerous to talk to a biographer."

She grumbled a non-response.

We fell quiet as we watched the movie play out. I felt myself shifting in the wooden chair, struggling to get comfortable. The theater was too cold, making my skin prickle into goose bumps. For some reason, I plunged a hand into my pocket to reassure myself the earplugs were there. *Rob's house is locked. It's safe. No one knows we're here.*

I'd seen *Stitches 2* countless times, and yet something felt different this time. In the movie, the family's nine-year-old daughter took the doll she named Elspeth out onto the dock, combing her hair with a pine cone. From her position she couldn't see into the lake, but the audience could. A dark shape bloomed beneath the dock. At first, it looked like the shadow of a cloud passing overhead. But then it quickly took on a bloodred tinge. The fish began to flop and congregate. Oblivious, the little girl told Elspeth that she was her only friend and sang a song in a strange voice that wasn't her own, an old-fashioned lullaby a modern nine-year-old wouldn't know. The girl got frightened by her own singing and stood up, tried to run to the house, but stepped on a nail.

The nail went straight through her bare foot.

"Shit! Shit!" Kylie threw her hands over her face.

The girl screamed, managed to rip her foot off the nail, and then passed out from the pain. She fell into the lake, dropping Elspeth, who landed perfectly safely on the dock.

"This is why I don't watch horror movies," Kylie muttered while peeking between her fingers. "I can't believe you like this stuff."

I choked out a laugh, but the truth was my heart was suddenly thrashing around like a drowning thing. I gripped the wooden armrests hard enough to turn my knuckles white.

What the fuck, Haven?

Was I *scared?*

I recalled that the last time I saw *Stitches 2*, I was flipping through a catalog, bored, only half paying attention. I'd always been able to separate fiction from reality, so why did I now feel like someone's fist was squeezing the blood from my heart?

I pushed myself to my feet, pivoting away from the screen.

Kylie frowned up at me. "You feeling okay?"

"Yeah." My voice came out hoarse. "Yeah, I . . . I'm tired." I swallowed the rest of the sticky candy. "I think I'll turn in."

She looked a touch concerned but nodded. "Okay. See you in the morning."

I practically scrambled out of the theater, charging up the stairs back to Rob's main floor. Anxious to get out of the low lighting, the relentless reek of burned popcorn. The heel of my palm dug between my breasts, trying to press my heartbeat back into submission. A momentary fright. That was all. I *knew* it wasn't real. A prosthetic foot, a special effect, and not even very well done.

So why had I had such an extreme reaction?

I'd seen hundreds of horror movies, most of them far viler than *Stitches 2: Split Seams*. Things most viewers couldn't stomach, so they had to read my recaps instead. Rob had specifically chosen me because of my ability to digest those films and sleep like a baby afterward.

But this time was different. That scene left me itchy in places I couldn't scratch.

Rob and Tyler were still out. The house was empty, dark except for a few lamps and the backlit memorabilia. The light from a glowing movie poster frame shone on the sitting room mannequin, lighting up her plastic eyes. I stared at her an extra beat just in case she tried to move.

On impulse, I went upstairs and grabbed my bag from my room, threw in my phone and, as an afterthought, my copy of *Exit, Nebraska*.

There was no reason to tell Kylie I was leaving—let her think I'd gone to bed. As far as lies went, this one had no teeth. I just needed air. The cool wash of night to clear my head.

Rob's neighborhood was a labyrinthine knot of narrow winding roads and hairpin curves. There were no sidewalks, and my shoes clattered on the asphalt. It was quiet; this high up in the Hollywood Hills it was only residential homes, most of them mansions rivaling Rob's. For houses in the seven- and eight-figure range, garages were shockingly non-existent. Same for driveways. Teslas and Range Rovers clung to the side of the road like stinkbugs on a windowsill. Gone for the day were the nannies, cleaners, drivers. A few lights shone in the windows of the houses I passed, the blue flicker of television sets throwing mottled lights into the night sky.

I crammed my hands into my hoodie pockets as I wound my way down Egret Drive onto Mockingbird Lane, everything named for the birds whose habitats had been annihilated to build this division. The lights of West Hollywood flooded up from the valley along with the distant thrum of traffic and bar music.

Strange to be back in a city. New York had been home for years, and the twenty-four-hour rumble had become the soundtrack to my life. When I'd moved to Lundie Bay, the silence of the woods had kept me up at night. But now I found the pulsing dance beats grating. I was already anxious, jumpy—I didn't need pounding bass on top of everything.

A dog barked behind me, and I glanced up at a balcony overlooking the street. A Great Dane stood with its nose pressed to iron bars, snarling at me. How did its owners not go crazy with it barking like that at every passing person? But then I realized the dog wasn't barking at *me*—its attention was aimed behind me, farther up the hill, near a cluster of parked Jaguars.

I shaded my eyes against the streetlight, trying to see into the shadows. Was someone there? I didn't see anyone. And yet the dog snarled again, incessantly barking.

I pulled my earplugs out of my pocket and pushed them into my ears. My feet started carrying me toward the main road faster.

I glanced back over my shoulder, checking again to see if I was alone. It was after midnight, but people worked strange shifts. It wouldn't be odd to have someone walking their dog or leaving a party at this hour. Still, I hastened my steps. I didn't like having my sense of hearing cut off with the earplugs—it left me feeling vulnerable, lost.

First I nearly piss myself watching a cheesy doll thriller, and now I'm paranoid.

What was happening to me? I had read enough about trauma to know its effects manifested in myriad ways, and maybe the Malice House fire and everything that had preceded it were fodder for a lifetime of therapy.

A rock tumbled down the road in front of me, and I spun, wide-eyed. Trash cans were out on the curb, parked cars like sleeping beasts. No people—unless they were hiding.

Shit. What if they *are* hiding?

Something had caused that rock to tumble down the road, and it was a still night with no wind. As my eyes dissected the shadows, searching for the outline of a person, my heartbeat started to pick up again.

Maybe I shouldn't be looking for a human shape.

The idea made me pivot sharply, start down the road in double time. My arms crossed tightly across my chest like a shield. The main road that ran through this part of West Hollywood was just a few blocks away, and already the lights were glowing brighter, and a few couples and bar-goers loitered at the bottom of the road.

I reached the safety of Sunset Boulevard and waited for the wave of relief to come, but it never did—the paranoia only changed, replaced by the cacophony of laughing people clustered outside pubs, the herds of girls in crop tops, so loud I could hear them through the earplugs. *I don't belong here.* It was a feeling as certain as hunger.

Sunset Boulevard was one packed bar after another, broken only by cramped parking lots. I glanced back up at Rob's dark street, wishing I'd stayed home. Maybe Rita and Audrey and Elizabeth weren't such bad company after all.

An alleyway caught my eye. A young guy with aquamarine hair strode out, puffing on a vape pen, a motorcycle helmet in hand. Neon lights flashed behind him from a bar set back off the main strip. The sign read PHARMACY BAR. A few stoners loitered by the front door, their chill vibe the opposite of the high-strung bar-goers on Sunset.

I ducked inside.

Pharmacy Bar was a dive bar, but, this being LA, it was still nicer than most dives I'd been to in New York. Inside it was dark to the point of having to squint. Glass cases on the walls held historical pharmacology equipment: a set of brass scales, bottles of various sizes and shapes, medical diagrams. The booths were cracked red vinyl that looked like they'd been picked up by the dumpsters behind a failed burger joint. Each of the tables was covered with hundreds of blue and white pills suspended in solid resin.

I slid onto a stool that was awkwardly high and caught the bartender's attention. Another handsome aspiring model or actor, this one with full sleeves of tattoos and a cultivated mustache. The beauty of everything in this town was starting to get stale.

"Wine, please? I'll have whatever the house red is." With my earplugs in, I wondered if I was shouting.

He came back with a twist-off mini bottle and no glass to pour it into, not that I cared.

I was alone at the bar except for a handsy couple at the far end. I unearthed my copy of *Exit, Nebraska* from my bag and freed it from the rubber band. I peeled back a few pages, peeked into the book's hidden cavern.

My father's drawing was safely inside.

A wave of relief flooded me. I'd already lost my sketchbook, the closest thing I had to a soul. A part of me had been afraid I'd also somehow lost this drawing. That it might somehow have vanished or combusted into ash. That the unfamiliar thrum of fear I'd felt during the movie had been tied to my drawing, my origin—

I felt the presence of a person moving up behind me and slammed the book closed, paperweighting it with my hand. Out of the corner of my eye, I made out a man's shape.

Too tall to be Uncle Arnold. Too young.

But then my back went ramrod straight. My throat constricted. I knew that silhouette. It didn't belong to any wannabe actor or model, though its owner was arguably just as attractive. After all, I'd designed him to be the irresistible man of my dreams—and so he *was*.

I took out my earplugs and swiveled on the vinyl stool to face him.

Rafe Kahn grinned back at me. "Feel like company?"

CHAPTER EIGHT

—

THE SANDMAN KILLER
© 1943 Sigil Pictures

DOCTOR VAUGHN ELLIS
These bruises on your wrist, Mrs.
Fitzpatrick—do they have anything to
do with your insomnia?
    (Pauses meaningfully)
Your husband is a large man, is he
not?

        AGNES
     (quietly)
Yes.

    DOCTOR VAUGHN ELLIS
I see. It's a shame for such a
delicate woman to have nightmares.

He touches her bruises lightly.

—

"YOU WERE FOLLOWING ME," I accused him. "Just now.
In the Bird Streets."

I squeezed the earplugs in my palm and kept one eye on the door.

Rafe draped himself on the stool next to mine like it had been tailor-made for him.

"You were supposed to miss me," he said, leaning on the counter, toying with a sugar packet. His hair had grown out since I'd seen him, and it suited him. "You were supposed to give in to your overwhelming desire to see me again." His look was all smirking dark eyes. "I waited. You never called."

The bartender came over, giving Rafe a wary look. In black jeans and a dark gray top, with his hair a little tousled, Rafe wasn't out of place in the LA crowd, yet a quiet menace radiated off him.

"Get you anything?" the bartender asked Rafe, though his eyes were on me, the thirty-year-old in a hoodie with a novel who probably looked like she didn't want to be hit on. *Want me to kick this guy out?* his eyes asked.

"It's fine," I answered at the same time that Rafe barked, "Have any Caol Ila?"

I bristled. Caol Ila was my father's favorite brand of Scotch, which Rafe well knew. When the bartender returned, Rafe clinked his glass against my mini bottle of merlot.

"*I've* missed *you*, Haven."

His voice slid over my skin, made me cross my legs with a little extra squeeze. He looked good with his longer hair, a five o'clock shadow. His hair was still dark brown, so he must have continued to dye it. Silver hair wouldn't have been out of place in a town where rainbow-colored "mermaid hair" was advertised in the window of every salon, but who knew where the Harbinger had been in the last few months.

"How did you find me?" I asked.

"Darling, I'm paying for your phone plan."

So he *had* tracked me—probably figured out how to remotely install a location app on my phone. My heart began its uncertain knocking. I didn't love the idea of Rafe following me, but given the alternatives, I'd take him as my stalker any day.

"I was going to tell you where we were." I jiggled my foot under the table. "Just not yet. I wasn't sure it was a good idea . . . to see you again."

Far from offended, he offered me a wolfish smile that verified it *definitely* wasn't a good idea. "I get it. Judging by his house, your new boyfriend isn't hurting for cash." He tapped the sugar packet against the bar top. "No wonder you don't need me anymore."

"Rob isn't my boyfriend," I said, fully aware I was playing right into Rafe's hands. "And he isn't giving us money. Just a place to stay and some introductions around town."

"Ah, so you *do* still need me." He drained his drink and signaled to the bartender for another. The bar top was covered in resin-encased tablets just like the tabletops, thousands of tiny pills in a rainbow of powdery colors: Little white Xanaxes. Blue dots of Viagra. Round pink Lexapros.

Were they fake? Expired?

I swirled my fingers over them.

Must drive the stoners nuts.

Rafe dug into his back pocket and came up with a folded piece of paper. He tossed it on the counter in front of me. "As much as I'd like to catch up, there's something you should know about first."

His cryptic text message came back to me. *There's plenty for you to worry about. . . .*

Sitting straighter, I unfolded the paper. It was a color printout. A dark-haired young man's photograph looked back at me. He was grinning from a canoe, the paddle raised in triumph.

I cocked an eyebrow. "Who's this?"

"He was found dead at a campground near Joshua Tree National Park a few days ago. A homicide. Technically, the cause of death was suffocation, but his body was branded with what the police think was an occult symbol." He grabbed a pen left on the bar, flipped over the man's picture, and drew a shape that looked like two crescent moons facing each other, their acute points overlapping like hinges.

He tapped it twice with his middle finger. "Like that. Mean anything to you?"

"No." A shiver ran over my skin. I glanced over my shoulder. Quietly, I asked, "Was the murderer one of yours?"

"I thought it might be at first—that's what got me interested in the case. But no, none of their styles. Then I heard the victim's name and figured you'd want to know."

I looked at him warily, waiting.

Rafe said, "Joao Acosta."

I slid awkwardly off my stool, stepping back from the printout instinctively. Paper and ink, that's what all of us Acostas boiled down to, wasn't it? Gripping the edge of the bar with one hand like a lifeline, I said, "You're sure?"

"Completely. I did my research before coming to you. Stole a few files from the Morongo Police Department—I have them back at my hotel."

"You broke into a police department?"

He grinned. "Of course not. All you have to do is get arrested, and they just escort you right in."

I drummed my nails on my plastic wine bottle, the contents sitting ill at ease in my stomach. My fingers gave an involuntary twitch. Wanting to pick up Rafe's pen. *Wanting to draw.*

For three months Kylie and I had been searching for Acostas, and here one was in a printout from beyond the grave.

Rafe continued. "I saw the crime scene photos on a detective's computer—it wasn't possible to print them out. But if we go there, to the crime scene, I can show you how his body was when he was found."

I didn't answer right away. The bar's low lighting, the murmur of conversation . . . it filled my head so that I couldn't focus.

"Joshua Tree, you said?"

"That's right."

I shifted uneasily on the stool. My father had always told me we had distant family around Joshua Tree, which further supported the possibility that Joao Acosta was a blood relation.

"It's a few hours' drive," Rafe said. "We can go, camp, look around the crime scene, and be back the next day."

"I don't know."

The front door opened. I swiveled toward it, on alert, but it was only a couple of girls in leather jackets.

Rafe rested his hand over mine on the bar top. I could have pulled away, but for some reason, I didn't. His voice dropped as his energy shifted. "You shouldn't be wandering the streets alone at midnight. I might not always be there to protect you."

"Rafe, *you're* the one I should be worried about."

His expression turned dark. "No, Haven. I'm not."

A silence fell between us, and I found myself leaning toward him as though drawn to the warmth of a bonfire. In a barely audible voice, I asked, "Do you know what happened to Uncle Arnold?"

He slowly shook his head. "I've been keeping tabs on all the unidentified bodies found throughout the Pacific Northwest, and none fit his description. There's a chance he survived Pinchy's attack."

I ran a hand over the goose bumps cropping up on my bare upper arm. "In the airport in Lisbon, I thought I heard . . ." I clenched my jaw before shaking my head. "If he's still alive, and out there, what do you think he wants?"

Rafe swirled his glass, ice clinking. "Do you remember his chapter in *Bedtime Stories for Monsters*?"

"I couldn't forget it if I tried."

"Well, Arnold extended beyond the four thousand words your father wrote in those pages. He had an entire life. We all did. When Arnold first got his powers of extreme persuasion after the accident that put him in the hospital, he didn't immediately know how to use it. There was an incident with a wealthy older woman he tried to sell encyclopedias to. He showed up at her door sloppy, and when she insulted his appearance, he attempted to compel her to eat the pages of volume FEN-GIR. He botched it, and she called his boss, who tried to fire him. But by *that* point, Arnold had figured out his powers. He compelled his boss to bludgeon himself to death with the world atlas that came with the set. He then used his voice to have the board vote him in as company president and got them to adopt the slogan *The world in your hands*, to sell the masses on the power of knowledge instead of just catering to the wealthy. Anyway, he grew bored with the role and compelled a warehouse clerk to burn down the entire inventory."

I took a sip of my beer. "Seems tame, for Arnold."

"That was just the beginning, darling."

Rafe placed his sweating glass on the bar, where it magnified the rainbow of pills beneath. "My point is, what Arnold wants is to not be overlooked, ever again."

A votive candle on the bar flickered in the breeze as more patrons came in. I felt a knot in my stomach. "He said he wanted me to help him rewrite the world."

"His gift only lets him control others. He can't actually do much himself—he's still the aging, feeble man he always was. So he needs people who *do* have skills—he needs you."

I crossed and uncrossed my legs as I admitted, "Rafe, I'm scared. I don't know what's happening. I've been afraid before, but not like this."

He listened closely as I told him about watching the movie with Kylie and feeling truly frightened by the nail scene. When I finished, he drew me toward him and wrapped his arms around my back.

I went stiff. It had been a long time since I'd been this close to a man. Once upon a time, I'd thought Rafe and I could have something, but that was before I'd known what he was. Now I felt my muscles softening, melting into his. I pressed my face against his shirt.

He smelled good. No cologne, just an earthiness that took me back to the forest, to the fire.

He pulled back. "What do you say about Joshua Tree? I can take you to the campground where he was killed. I can even get you in to see the body once it's released from the police coroner."

"I don't know. I'll think about it." I glanced at the door. "I should get back."

He gazed at my face, both exploring and suggesting. "Are you sure?"

"What do you mean?"

He dropped his voice to a purr. "I have a hotel room in Santa Monica. Spend the night? We can . . . catch up." His breath brushed over my skin.

My toes curled in my sneakers. This was why I'd been avoiding Rafe Kahn. The way he could make my heart stop with his dark smile, like he was some puppeteer and I was a ball of strings.

I wouldn't go with him, of course. There was no world in which I'd go back to the Harbinger's isolated hotel room with him, but the question stood: Did I want to?

"Why, so you can put a knife in my back?" I asked dryly.

"If you like." He tilted his head with a slow, seductive smile. "I'll do whatever you want me to do to you, Haven." His hand moved down to my wrist, long fingers circling the narrow bone. "Besides, I have something for you. It's in my room. A present. I think you'll like it."

I didn't pull my hand away. I liked being here, being with him. I almost felt like I'd fallen into one of Tyler's alternate dimensions where normal rules didn't apply.

I hesitated before saying, "I can't."

His smile was one of disappointment, though not surprise, as he released my hand.

I sank back on my stool, missing his touch.

He jerked his head toward the alley. "I'll walk you back to your friend's house."

I slid off the stool and Rafe threw too big a bill on the bar.

As we made our way up the winding residential streets, we caught up about my trip to Portugal, the various places he'd wandered. We spoke of monsters like they were old friends.

At Rob's place, his Mercedes was parked just behind his security gate now. Rafe's and my feet drifted to a stop by the gate, and I peered up at the night sky. Los Angeles had even worse light pollution than

New York, but tonight the moon had managed to find its way through the haze.

"I'll go with you to Joshua Tree," I said. "But I should talk to Kylie about it. She'll want to come, too."

"A third wheel. Wonderful."

I fought the urge to smile. Damn it, he was getting to me. I rested a hand on his shoulder, giving it a testing squeeze. *Jesus*. He was in even better shape than before.

"I'll be in touch tomorrow," I promised.

"The body is supposed to be released on Friday or Saturday, which means it'll go in the ground early next week. If we wait too long, we'll have to exhume it. A lot more dirty work. And I'm not partial to digging."

"I get it. Thanks for the escort home."

"Seriously, Haven, you shouldn't go out by yourself until we know where Uncle Arnold is. All it takes is one whisper."

Rafe had moved closer, and my own voice was a whisper now. "Oh, I know."

He looked down at my hand on his bicep, then at my lips. I felt hyperaware of both my body and his.

His shoulders relaxed as he cupped my jaw to tilt my head toward his. I found myself drifting toward him like a moth to a flame. I'd be singed, but so be it.

The kiss came together with a spark and a burn. His hand moved to the back of my skull, fingers curling into my hair. I slid my hands around the back of his neck, then pressed up to tiptoe to get even closer. His other arm curled around my waist.

This is a mistake, Haven, I thought. But my heart didn't agree. There was something in me that only felt whole when I was with Rafe, like he was my long-lost shadow, cut off by a window on the way to Neverland.

He pulled back, his thumb tracing along my bottom jaw. I saw so many questions in his eyes, knew they were reflected in my own.

Slowly, I released his neck and took a step back. Combing my fingers through my hair, I looked up to the swollen moon and repeated, "I'll call you tomorrow."

He bent down to plant a soft kiss on my cheek, then smacked my ass hard as he started back down Egret Drive. "You'd better this time."

I shook my head as I watched him disappear around the corner. My heart was doing that free-wheeling thing again like with the movie, flooding itself with emotion in some crazy Opheliac rush to drown.

What was happening to me? Was this what regular people meant when they talked about romance? I didn't like it at all—except for the parts I did.

It was quiet inside the house. The downstairs was dimly lit, and upstairs all the bedroom lights were off. The mannequins watched me move through the semidarkness until I was in bed, replaying the kiss in my head, wondering what would have happened if I'd taken him up on his hotel room offer.

I pulled out my phone and texted him:

So what was the present?

My phone beeped a few seconds later with his response.

Something you lost a long time ago.

I shook my head, cursing my bad luck that I'd created Rafe Kahn to be my perfect man. But the truth was, I would have given anything not to have been alone in that moment. Already, the memory of Malice House was creeping back under my skin. I thought I smelled smoke. I told myself it was only in my head.

After a little time online, I ended up knocking on the adjoining door, and at Kylie's groggy reply, slipping into the sheets beside my sister.

If I was going to face nightmares tonight, I didn't want to do it alone.

CHAPTER NINE

DIRECTOR'S MEMO ON "THE SANDMAN KILLER"

TO SIGIL PICTURES ART DEPARTMENT:
Please note Richard and I want the
interlocking crescent moons symbol
(referred to in script as "smoke
symbol") to repeatedly appear in the
background. It should be worked into
set design, costuming, and lighting
where indicated in script so as not
to stand out on a first viewing
but be unmistakable upon subsequent
ones. This will be a movie that
demands multiple viewings.

—From the desk of Max Faraday

IN THE MORNING, as Rob filled his travel mug with coffee, he announced, "I have to run to a meeting, but I wanted to let you know I got a lead on Nanette Fields."

Kylie looked up from where she'd been digging around in the refrigerator. "She agreed to meet with us?"

A mischievous smile played on Rob's lips. "Not exactly. She won't take my calls, and neither will her agent. But I worked my connections. Tomorrow, ten o'clock. Be ready to drop in for a visit to the Gemini Entertainment studios."

I didn't love his vague explanation. "We're going to, what, ambush her?"

He shrugged coyly as he screwed on the mug cap, waggling his eyebrows, then said his goodbyes and left.

Tyler poured himself a more leisurely cup of coffee and leaned against the kitchen counter next to me. "So, Haven, who was that gentleman caller I saw you with last night outside the gate?"

Kylie slammed the fridge door, fixing me with a stare. I suddenly found my coffee cup endlessly fascinating.

I cleared my throat. "Just an old friend."

"*Rafe?*" Kylie demanded. "It was Rafe, *wasn't it?*"

I offered an apologetic shrug. "I went out for some fresh air. We kind of ran into each other."

Kylie rolled her eyes and muttered something under her breath. Before she could tell me all the reasons I shouldn't associate with Rafe, I slid a hand out, resting it on the kitchen island in a sign of truce.

"Hey, that biographer? Patrick Kane? I changed my mind. I'll talk to him, but I want something in return."

Kylie perked up at this, temporarily letting go of her disapproval. "Wait, for real?"

"I looked him up last night. He's a genealogy specialist, right? I want him to investigate our family tree. Find every third cousin and second aunt twice removed, or whatever, who lives in the US."

She looked me up and down suspiciously. "Why the sudden change of heart?"

I told them about Joao Acosta, the occult murder ritual, and the trip to Joshua Tree. Kylie listened patiently, nodding at some parts, grimacing at others. Tyler sipped his coffee with wide eyes.

"What did the brand look like?" Kylie asked. "The satanic symbol?"

I grabbed a grocery receipt off the counter and looked for a pen, only to realize I had one in my back pocket—I *had* grabbed Rafe's from the night before.

I paused briefly. I'd fought this for months—a pen in my hand. It felt like slipping into an old glove. *Too comfortable.* I carefully drew the interlocking crescent moons, then immediately set down the pen before the curse compelled me to draw more.

Kylie chewed on her lip as she looked over the emblem. "It looks a little familiar, but I don't think it's from Buddhism or Hinduism. And it isn't any astrological symbol or a rune that I know of. There is something called moon glyphs, but they don't look like this." She handed Tyler the drawing. "What do you think?"

"I don't recognize it," he said. "Did you look it up online?"

I nodded. "Nothing."

Kylie traced a pensive finger over the drawing.

"So, what about Joshua Tree?" I pressed. "Are you in?"

My sister groaned. "God, I hate camping. But yeah. I can stand being in a tent with Rafe overnight if it gets us answers."

Tyler started to clean up from breakfast. "You can borrow my camping gear. I got it for Coachella. I swear, though, I'm getting too old. And Coachella . . . ugh. *Not* what it used to be."

———

After breakfast, I called Rafe to finalize plans for Friday, and then spent the afternoon rereading the *Hollywooder* article in preparation for meeting with Nanette Fields. Unfortunately, there were no new messages on the boards from Decline.A.Copy or anyone else.

At ten the next morning, I found myself in the back seat of Rob's Mercedes with Kylie, listening to Rob yell obscenities into the phone attached to his car speaker. He was cursing at some coproducer on the other line, pausing only to briefly redirect his profanity at other drivers whenever he had to merge.

The rise and fall of *fuck*s drifted into the background as I studied the city through the tinted back windows. When Kylie and I had first arrived in Los Angeles, we'd had cheap rubber masks over our heads. The city had been reduced to muffled traffic sounds. Now I took in strip malls with bargain-price plastic surgery offices, law firms whose signs were adorned with palm trees bearing twinkle lights, trendy restaurants trying too hard to dress themselves down. The city had a worn plastic feel to it as though the entire town had undergone a face-lift years ago and the wrinkles were starting to creep back, but unevenly: patches of sunny perfection, glimpses of ugliness. For every flashy real-estate office touting ten-million-dollar white-box mansions in the Bird Streets, there was a tweaker on the corner. A gaggle of college-aged girls poured out of a brunch place with bright lettering on its sign, walking past a row of posters stapled to telephone poles with missing girls' faces that looked like mirrors of their own.

I couldn't help but scan the crowds. My eyes hunted for the odd fang or black gleam of unnatural eyes. I felt moderately sure that most of the *Bedtime Stories for Monsters* creatures would remain in the vast forests around Lundie Bay, hiding out from the world except for the occasional disappearance of the odd hiker. But not all of them. When I had known Uncle Arnold, he'd worn suspenders and a bowler hat, but if I'd learned anything about the creations, it was that they were quick to adapt. Just look at Rafe.

We pulled up to Gemini Entertainment's main studio entrance, and Rob idled the car. He hung up his phone and rolled down his window, flashing a grin at the oversized security guard hunched inside a too-small booth.

From the outside, the studio looked much as I'd imagined. A tall fence with iron bars surrounded enormous warehouses that presumably stored a city's worth of costumes, props, and sets that could be easily repurposed.

"Hey, Michael," Rob said with great familiarity, though I couldn't be sure if he knew the guard or was just reading off his name tag. "How's it going, man? Donovan Robles. I'm meeting Wayne Morrow on the *Edelweiss Girls* set." He motioned toward us. "Got a few friends in town. Possible investors in a new project. They'll stay out of trouble."

Michael chuckled as he peeked through the window at us. "Sure, sure, Mr. Robles. Don't look like troublemakers to me—not too much. I'll just need some ID, ladies." While we fished out the fake driver's licenses Rob had made for us, the guard rested his hands on his belt and gazed up at the baking sun. "Nice day, huh? Hey, you'll never guess who just came through. Rosemary Bryce Madison. Man, I loved her stuff back in the day."

Rob whistled. "No kidding?"

The more they swapped pleasantries, the more it felt like a rehearsed script that had played out countless times in countless studio security booths, the kind of overly friendly attitude that made me feel like I never quite knew where I stood with someone.

The guard marked our false names in a log and handed the licenses back with a wagging finger and teasing instructions not to bother any celebrities for a picture.

Finding parking was a nightmare, but Rob eventually squeezed between two golf carts parked in an alley.

Getting out of the car, I immediately shielded my hungover eyes with sunglasses. The sun was relentless, bleaching everything in its reach. At least the forests of the Pacific Northwest had offered some form of shelter. Here, in the concrete desert, we were ants under the sun's microscope.

"Let's see," Rob said. "I think it's Stage Twenty-Nine. This way. These places are goddamn mazes." He donned his own sunglasses and led us past warehouses painted in what I'd once heard described as Disney Blue, the shade amusement parks painted their operations buildings so they'd blend in with the sky. Each warehouse had a stage number designation and the usual signage about noise regulations, health and safety disclaimers, as well as a marquee announcing which shows were currently being filmed inside. We turned the corner and suddenly found ourselves standing on what appeared to be a block of Upper East Side town houses.

I went still, instantly transported back to New York. *To another life.*

Rob waved a dismissive hand toward the row houses. "Generic city set. These have been used a hundred times. They change a few details between projects, different doors, coat of paint, that kind of thing."

I'd never given much thought to studio lots or taken the official Universal Studios or Paramount Pictures tours. It felt impossible that such a huge facility existed so close to downtown Los Angeles, but Rob had explained that the studios had all been built back in the 1920s or 1930s when the area was cheap farmland and were now grandfathered in. Still, I wondered why the companies hadn't sold the land for the fortune it must be worth and rebuilt in the cheaper outskirts, where space was unlimited. But there was history here, judging by the DATE CONSTRUCTED sign on each of the buildings, and history stood for something even in a town where change was just one injection away.

We cut through a patch of landscaped bushes, and Rob pointed to a sunken pit occupied by a half dozen parked cars. "That's the dunk tank. A water studio. See those pipes? They fill it for any ocean or water scenes."

"And the cars?" Kylie asked.

He shrugged. "This is LA: You park where you can. If it's drained, it's fair game." He turned his head suddenly. "Oh. Here it is."

Stage 29 was the same Disney Blue, though there was a modern office-building structure attached to it. It wasn't until Rob opened the office door and ushered us in that I realized that the office structure, too, was another facade. Inside, there was no lobby, no elevator bank, no receptionist. Instead, I peered up at a five-story-tall space like an airplane hangar, with scaffolding and a handful of sets built at the far end. The sound of hammering mixed with the shouts of directors and a sudden blast of instrumental music that someone quickly silenced.

"Welcome to Chicago, 1939," Rob said, as a security guard who looked a lot less cheerful than Michael clocked us and made his way toward us with one hand on his radio.

CHAPTER TEN

―

PURGATORY'S DOOR

© 1955 Sigil Pictures

INTERIOR — THE DRUID BAR — DAY

The door swings open, releasing a beam of
daylight like a spotlight on the dark bar.
Patrons grumble. Detective Nick Dram steps
in as the door closes and murky, dim light
returns.

The bartender, BANJAX, a thug whose face and
exposed forearms are covered in pagan tattoos,
is polishing a glass with a dishrag. CAMERA
TIGHT ON his forearm—the tattoos are moving.

They aren't tattoos at all—and he isn't human.

―

THE STUDIO'S SETS might have been 1939 Chicago, but by
way of modular walls, robotic cameras on wheels, and production
assistants trotting around with fanny packs filled with protein bars.

While the security guard grilled Rob about our permission to be on
set, I drifted a few feet away, hugging my arms. It was freezing in the

faux building, which I hadn't expected given the heat outside. They must not want the actors sweating through makeup. The stage's massive overhead lights were off, and instead, giant spotlights were aimed at one set. It was the interior of what looked like an old-fashioned hospital room with a metal bed and scratchy sheets. A wooden rocking chair sat by a fake window closed over with curtains; nearby was a table laden with various-sized steel speculums. Blood was smeared on the wall behind the bed—it looked too real for my liking. Production assistants balancing precariously on a stepladder were busy stringing up a special-effects harness above the bed.

"Art and writing," Kylie mused, coming up to stand beside me.

I hugged myself tighter as I faced her. "What's that you said?"

"Art and writing," she repeated, motioning to the set. "That's all a film is, isn't it? Visuals and text coming together to form something new. Something . . . living."

Her words compounded the chill I already felt. On the road, we'd had many late-night conversations about the nature of art and a creator's relationship to their work. We knew that our family curse required two things: first, that someone with Acosta blood create a written story, and second, that the same person or another family member give the story physical form through artwork. Without both parts—art and writing—it was merely harmless scrawls on paper.

If paper can ever truly be harmless.

I turned back to watch the set workers, even more troubled by the idea she'd raised. A film was the perfect combination of art and writing. Somewhere, a screenwriter pounded out a story on a laptop, transposing the abstract concepts swirling around their brain into *FADE IN on sunrise* and *ENTER a cop*. Then, on a stage just like this one, hundreds of artists—camera operators, set designers, makeup artists, actors—would come together to give those words physical form.

This was what the curse craved even more than the illustrations I'd made of my father's manuscript. Illustrations were two-dimensional, static. Movies *breathed*.

The hair rose on the back of my neck, and I spun around, peering into the shadows of the far end of the stage. It was too dark to see anything but vague, motionless shapes.

"Hey, Wayne!" Rob spotted someone he knew on the set and waved them over. The security guard watched doubtfully as a lanky guy with a mop of dishwater hair sauntered over, the tool belt slung around his waist clattering with makeup brushes and hair-spray bottles.

I heard a few snippets of their exchange in which the makeup artist verified that he knew Rob. The security guard gave Rob a final warning look, then extended a more benevolent nod to Kylie and me before moving back toward the stage, facing us all the while.

"Haven, Kylie. This is Wayne." Rob rested his hand on the makeup artist's shoulder, which was awkward given their height difference. "Wayne's work is incredible. Truly amazing. All the production companies want to work with him."

I was starting to learn that a flood of accolades was expected, or rather *demanded*, when introducing someone in LA.

Wayne gave us a slack stare, not striking me as the prodigy Rob made him out to be. Rob squeezed the man's shoulder, then gave him a coconspirator wink. "Wayne is the little bird who chirped in my ear about Nanette being on the *Edelweiss Girls* set." He put a playful finger to his lips. "Our little secret."

Wayne brushed a portion of the mop off his forehead, looking nervous. I wouldn't have been surprised to learn that money had changed hands between the two of them.

"Yeah, man, Nanette's on break," Wayne said. "Try the kitchen."

"The kitchen?" Rob frowned. "You mean the studio cafeteria?"

"No, man, the kitchen. The main house's kitchen. The *set*." Wayne tipped his head toward a two-story set lurking in the opposite corner of the warehouse. It loomed in the dark portion that wasn't currently being filmed, so only a couple weak spotlights tethered to a power cord were aimed at it.

Our feet echoed as we crossed the vast stage floor and approached the main house set. It was half a house, sliced cleanly down the middle as though prepared for dissection. The angles weren't right; instead of ninety-degree corners, the walls were stretched to accommodate cameras. The effect gave the house a carnival fun-house look, though there was nothing mirthful about the set. It was filled with heavy wooden 1930s furniture and ugly drapes. The shadows from the pair of spotlights' weak beams further exaggerated the unnatural angles.

Rob jogged up a set of industrial stairs to the raised first floor, poking around the empty kitchen set. I hesitated before following. There was something *wrong* about this house that went beyond the missing fourth wall and the swollen angles. I felt almost as though I'd been here before.

Rob poked his head through an open doorway, calling, "Ms. Fields?"

I shambled behind him through the kitchen. Kylie twisted the knob on the oven—nothing happened; it was only a prop. The breakfast table was set with a plate and napkin but no food. The door that should have opened to the living room didn't connect to anything.

Rob jumped down from the set and walked around a wall to the living room area, which was darker than the kitchen. As I followed, something about the arrangement of furniture snagged my eye, again giving me the topsy-turvy feeling of déjà vu.

Rob called, "Ms. Fields? *Oh.*"

A woman was descending the set's staircase in the semidarkness. Though there were doors to what one would assume were upstairs bedrooms, a quick glimpse behind the set confirmed that there was nothing there, which begged the question: What had she been doing up there?

Rob lifted a hand in greeting. "Nanette Fields? Donovan Robles. I'm a producer with Insight Entertainment. I've been trying to reach you. You didn't answer my calls."

Nanette Fields looked like she'd stepped out of an old black-and-white movie herself. She was a fragile woman in her seventies with chopped hair that I suspected she styled to look disheveled, going for a tortured-artist vibe. She wore ill-fitting gray trousers and a flowy black shirt with a single wooden bangle on her wrist. Her black-rimmed glasses were oversized and currently perched atop her head, shackled to her via a beaded chain.

Her body structure suggested she'd been beautiful in her youth and probably would still be if she'd undergone the rounds of facelifts that other aging women found appealing, but I got the sense she relished veering in the opposite direction, neglecting her hygiene, cultivating webs of wrinkles. She took her time descending the stairs, as though she enjoyed the extended period of looking down on us.

I instantly liked her.

"So you staged a surprise attack? You certainly have *balls*," she said at last.

Rob seemed to debate between flashing his impish grin, which I'd seen him turn on now twice for security guards, or his devilish smirk, which was more in keeping with the Rob *I* knew. He settled on devilish, giving Nanette a wolfish smile.

It was the right call. Nanette reached the bottom of the stairs and extended him a long, appraising look.

"I've never heard of you," she announced.

At least she didn't tell him to fuck off.

Rob pressed a hand to his cheek, wincing. "Ah! I hope that slap didn't hurt your hand too much."

A hint of a smile played on her lips as she shifted her posture to take in Kylie and me. "And who are you? Film students?" The words dripped with disdain.

Rob started, "These are friends of mine, Ms. Fields—"

"Nanette is fine, Mr. Producer with Insight Entertainment."

Rob was about to answer with an explanation of who we were when, facing the living-room set, I suddenly jolted with recognition.

I blurted out, "It's Malice House!"

My words shattered whatever delicate rapport had formed in the last few moments as surely as if I'd slashed a knife in the air. I hadn't meant to speak sharply, but the shock of it had burst out of me.

The set, the living room: *It's my father's house.*

Not exactly, of course. The paintings on the wall and furniture placement were different, and there was an old-fashioned radio in place of my father's record player. The dark lighting had thrown me off, but now that I peered closer at the set, it was uncanny. This room was eerily similar to my father's library, down to the fireplace with a wooden mantel made from a ship's hull, to the bar cart full of awards mixed with Scotch bottles—gin, here—to the archway that led into the foyer.

All three of them stared at me like I'd left my mind back at the entrance. Then Kylie spun toward the set to take a closer look and said, "Holy shit, she's right."

Nanette eyed me like I was a strange fish in an aquarium. "I'm afraid I have no idea what you're talking about."

My mouth had gone bone-dry, but I managed to ask, "What's the name of this film? *Edelweiss Girls?*"

"That's the working title," Nanette explained. "Studios give code names to projects that haven't been announced yet to cut down on speculation. The film's real name is *Tulip Carol.*" She gazed at the set as though trying to decipher whatever puzzle had me so disturbed. "It's based on a novel by—"

"Adelaide Martin," I said in a hollow voice. "I know."

I hadn't read the novel, but I knew the author. Now everything made sense. Adelaide Martin was an Australian thriller writer my father had had a long-term on-again, off-again affair with. Perhaps *affair* was the wrong word. There were times when it had tiptoed close to being a proper relationship, and more than once I'd wondered if they would get married. She hadn't come to his funeral because of cancer treatments but had sent an obscenely large floral arrangement. Adelaide had been an occasional presence in the Maine house where I'd grown up, and though my father had never mentioned to me that she'd visited him at Malice House, she must have. She'd turned his final home into fiction. Used my very real house as the inspiration for *Tulip Carol.*

"She must have consulted on the set," I said grimly.

"As a matter of fact, she did," Nanette said, looking more curious about me now than when she'd thought of me as a film student.

Rob cleared his throat. "Haven and Kylie are the daughters of Amory Marbury, the late novelist."

Nanette's sparse eyebrows rose. Her lips pursed a few times, as though a decade ago she would have drawn out a pack of cigarettes and gracefully taken a puff. "Is that so? Can't say I've read much of his work. Not my thing. I don't like realism. I much prefer stories of"—her lips pursed more, searching for either the end of a cigarette or the right words—"the unexpected."

It was the opening I'd been waiting for, and I slipped my hand into my bag and took out the *Hollywooder* magazine.

"You were interviewed in this article about curses—"

Kylie's phone started ringing, and everyone stared at her as she glanced at the screen, distracted. Lifting a finger, she said, "It's Patrick Kane. Go ahead."

I watched as she wandered back into the empty portion of the dark stage, where she began pacing and nodding and occasionally speaking. Something shifted in the shadows behind her, just a small flicker of movement, like a person sighing. I squinted harder, trying to make out a shape.

Is someone back there?

Nanette cleared her throat.

I tore my eyes off the shadows and turned back to her, as I flipped the magazine open to the Sigil story. "We were hoping to ask you about this article. It says you're an expert in cinematic urban legends and Hollywood history."

"Yes, I've been called the Ghostwriter Librarian," she said dryly. "Usually by junior staff who don't realize how many zeros their directors are willing to tack on for my services. You'd be surprised by the number of films that touch on the occult. Even the most contemporary slice-of-life drama craves a few hints here and there of *mystery*. Maybe it's an urban legend, a meaningful dream, a tarot prediction. Directors come to me saying their films fall flat. My diagnosis is always the same: They're trying too hard for verisimilitude when the last thing an audience wants is to see their own dull reality unfold. They don't want a mirror, they want a *story*. They want magic. All any of us want is magic."

With an attitude like that, I was surprised Nanette's and Rob's paths hadn't crossed before.

I continued, "We'd like to know more about Sigil Pictures and this supposed curse. I'm particularly interested in what you had to say in the article: *All fiction is based in reality, just not always* this *reality*."

When she pinned me with an inscrutable look, I shifted from foot to foot, then thought about what she'd said about ample zeros.

I added, "We can pay you a consulting fee, of course."

Nanette smoothed her hand down her elegant throat once more, considering. "Have you even *seen* a Sigil film?"

I motioned to Rob. "Donovan has an original copy of *Winter of the Wicked*."

She turned her attention to Rob, narrowing her eyes. "Where exactly did you find such a thing? They're notoriously hard to obtain."

He shrugged with faux modesty. "I got lucky."

She made a doubting noise in the back of her throat. After glancing at the hospital set where the construction crew was still struggling with the harness, she said finally, "We can talk in the living room. They aren't scheduled to film in the main house until next week, so we won't be disturbed."

She ushered Rob and me toward the cut-open house, and my feet somehow found their way to the steps, though my head was a thousand miles away. Time and space seemed to fracture as she led me through the archway from the foyer to the living room. I was back in Malice House, the real Malice House, and nothing was fire-eaten or smoke-stained, and my father's books lined the walls, carrying the scent of ink and paper pulp; I'd never been sure if he smelled like the books or if the books had come to smell like him.

I stepped on two pieces of blue tape on the floor crossed in an X. I blinked, and the real Malice House was once again far away, on a rocky coast back in Washington State, reduced to ashes. *I* was on a soundstage.

Rob switched on another spotlight. I raised a hand against the light, squinting. Beyond, the rest of the cavernous stage disappeared into darkness. Anything could be out there, anything. Had I really seen someone near Kylie? If so, it was probably a crew member on break, though I hadn't liked how still they'd been as they'd watched my sister. Any person standing there now would have a picture-perfect view of me.

In the distance, the production crew continued to hammer. Closer, a voice came out of the darkness, and I felt my blood pool in my stomach. *A whisper?*

Kylie broke through the blinding spotlight, making me flinch. She shoved her phone back in her pocket.

"Haven? You okay? You've gone pale." Concern was inked across her face. I shook my head against her concern then turned back to the living room set. Nanette sat in a big armchair with a delicate china teacup on a side table next to her, a double-sided axe resting casually on the floor by her feet.

Props. They're only props.

I licked my dry lips. "When you were taking that call, was there anyone else back there? Did you see anyone?"

Kylie gave me an odd look. "It's empty over there."

Rob was hanging back, leaning against the archway, surrendering the living room to us. He knew when to insert himself and when to hold back, though I didn't doubt for a moment he was listening to every word we said.

Shakily, I lowered myself onto the sofa. The angle of the seating was all wrong—I should have been facing Nanette, but that would have put my back to the audience, to the cameras. I had to practically twist myself in knots to face her.

"So, what are you anxious to know about some dusty old company?" Nanette asked breezily, though she had to know it had become a cultural phenomenon.

"You implied in the *Hollywooder* article that the urban legends around Sigil Pictures might have a basis in reality."

"As I told the unfortunate young woman who wrote that article, there have long been Hollywood rumors that the director and producer of Sigil Pictures used occult magic to get their films made. At the time, people argued there was no way such niche films could get distribution otherwise."

Kylie chewed on her lip. "And these supposed occult practices that got their movies made . . . what were they rumored to have involved?"

Nanette only offered a coy shrug as she took a sip from the teacup, which to my surprise, turned out not to be a prop at all. It made me suddenly concerned about the axe.

Kylie tried again. "Do you think it's possible Max Faraday and Richard Alton brought their films to life somehow?"

"Why, that sounds quite ridiculous. What you're talking about are mere urban legends. To believe they're true, well, you'd have to be"—a sly smile stretched her lips—"a bit nutty, wouldn't you?"

She turned to replace the teacup on the side table, then paused to toe the axe's edge with her shoe. I wondered about the plot of *Tulip Carol* and what happened to the fictional resident of this house that was so much like my own. I hoped their fate was better than mine. That they'd escape these walls in a way I never had.

CHAPTER ELEVEN

—

WINTER OF THE WICKED
© 1947 Sigil Pictures

INTERIOR – FARMHOUSE HEARTH – NIGHT –
CONTINUOUS

Elder Daughter fishes burned puppets out of
the dying coals and cradles them like hideous,
mutilated babies. SOUND of PRIMITIVE DRUMS
pounding along with INHUMAN WHISPERING.

CUT TO circle drawn in the farmyard dirt. Farm
animals that should be sleeping gather beneath
the full moon in an unnatural congregation.
A DONKEY brays, earsplitting, in time to the
distant drums.

—

MORE CLATTERING CAME from the hospital set at the
opposite end of the stage, followed by a voice over a megaphone calling
the actors to their places.

"If there's nothing else, I need to be on set for this," Nanette said,
and looked ready to rise. "As to my consulting fee . . ."

"Wait." I unfolded my drawing of the interlocking crescent moons.

"Have you seen this symbol before? Maybe associated with Sigil Pictures? Some of their occult rituals?"

She slid her black-rimmed glasses down from her nest of hair as she took the old receipt. The change in her posture was immediate.

Her eyes snapped to me. "What is this?"

"It was . . ."—I wasn't sure how much to say—"affiliated with a murder victim."

She adjusted her glasses an inch and gave me a quick once-over. "Are you with the police?"

"Jesus, no. Nothing like that."

Still eyeing me suspiciously, she slid her glasses down and handed back the receipt, then said curtly, "I don't recognize it."

"Are you sure?"

"I've seen all the Sigil Pictures films—I'm one of the only people in the world who has. Now, if you'll excuse me, the director isn't known for his patience. . . ."

"If you've seen them all," Kylie said, "can you get us copies?"

Nanette hesitated in the armchair, letting a slender loafer dance in the air before standing. In the distance, a grip yelled camera cues, and there was some clunking as they tested out the harness in the hospital-room set. I became keenly aware of a cool breeze emanating from the darkness and again got the uncanny feeling that someone was out there, watching. Enjoying the show that we were putting on.

I patted my pants pocket to reassure myself the earplugs were there.

Nanette walked to the edge of the living room set. The tips of her loafers hung off the side, and she was so frail that I had to stop myself from jumping up to grab her—a gust of wind might have blown her off.

"I'm afraid I wouldn't even know where to start anymore. I saw them decades ago at a little arthouse cinema in Glendale that's now a strip club. But if your producer friend here got his hands on *Winter of the Wicked*, perhaps he might be able to excavate the others from the Sigil Pictures vaults."

Rob shrugged a little too casually as he leaned in the archway. "I'll ask around. See what I can do."

"Yes, something tells me you have almost as many friends as I do." Her eyes narrowed again. "How good of you to help these women out so *selflessly*."

I glanced at Rob, curious, but his face revealed nothing other than his usual pasted-on smile.

Nanette again smoothed her hand down her long neck. "Now, I'm afraid I truly need to be on the hospital set for this scene. And getting back to my consultation fee . . ."

"You can invoice me." Rob pulled a business card out of his back pocket. "Email address is right there."

She took the card and made her languorous way down the stairs, leaving us in the unfinished shell of Malice House.

Kylie hugged her arms against the air-conditioned chill as she eyed the axe. "And I thought the book industry was fucked-up." She toed the axe with her shoe.

I turned to Rob. "Can you really get copies of the other films?"

His eyes simmered with mischief. In a conspiratorial tone, he said, "That old theater in Glendale? I know which one she's talking about. The original owner is in an assisted-living facility. His daughter goes to my gym. I'll make some calls this afternoon."

He glanced at the time on his phone, then typed in a few notes to himself. The puzzle that was Rob was starting to make more sense now. I'd always wondered what a producer did, but now I got it: Rob got shit done however he had to, whatever—or whoever—he had to produce.

I suddenly wondered: Was he producing *me*? Nanette had certainly seemed to suggest his motives might not be altruistic.

"I have a late lunch in Century City," he said offhand. "Want me to drop you off at the house? Or downtown?"

I waved away the offer. "We'll take a rideshare back."

He wiggled his eyebrows enticingly. "Tyler's making paella tonight."

Once he'd left, dropping by the hospital set to swap a few words with his makeup artist friend, Kylie and I made our way down from the set and gazed up at the house, illuminated by massive spotlights. In my mind's eye, I was climbing the stairs to the second floor with Rafe following, throwing a shy glance at my cute neighbor who'd taken such an interest in my art. I saw us moving through the bedroom to the screened-in porch, letting him peruse my sketchbook, embarrassed and a little turned on that he'd taken an extra-long look at the bras I'd left out on the bed.

My house, but not my house.

"Adelaide Martin?" Kylie asked. "Did you know her well?"

I shrugged, utterly uninterested in my father's affairs. "They dated after I'd already left for college."

"Did they ever talk about getting married?"

My mind was still on Rafe flipping through the sketchbook and telling me I had a unique talent. Ha. I guess that was one way to describe it.

"She was just one in a long line of women. Dad wasn't exactly into monogamy."

Kylie peered up at the house set as though clues were buried in the cue tape, the faux wood paneling. "I thought I might make a trip back to Bainbridge University at some point and read through his journals. I only had a few minutes to look at them when I was there before."

I gave her a quizzical look. "Why? I already told you, I've read them, and they don't say anything about the curse that we don't already know."

Now it was her time to pin me with an odd look. "I'm not talking about the curse, Haven. I'm talking about our *father.*"

Oh. This again.

"Go ahead, if you want," I said. "But they say to never meet your heroes, and I'd say the same goes for fathers like ours. The more you dig, the more you're going to find things you don't like. Addictions. Affairs. Neglectful parenting. Better to keep your mental image of who he was. I promise you it's better than the real one."

Kylie's phone beeped, and she glanced at the screen.

I cocked my head. "Patrick Kane again?"

She slid it back into her pocket. "Yeah . . . I negotiated a deal. He's going to map out our ancestry using the blood sample results and family history we uploaded online, and in exchange, he wants both of us to write personal history statements, including any relevant dates and facts, and, in your case, noteworthy memories of your father. Oh, and he insisted on an in-person interview." She held up a hand. "I talked him down to thirty minutes."

I didn't love it, but it was a deal I could live with. And thirty minutes? I could drag my heels over coffee for thirty minutes.

Kylie, on the other hand, appeared delighted at the idea of speaking to this random writer. Well, of course she did. She wanted to know all she could about her biological father, but I bristled at the idea of someone trying to resurrect the ghost of Amory Marbury.

I bumped her arm with my elbow. "It's a good deal. Well done."

She grinned as she threaded her arm through mine, dragging me toward the soundstage exit, which was open now and blazing sunlight like purgatory's door. "Come on, I want to see where they filmed *Blue Paradise*."

CHAPTER TWELVE

—

THE HUNDREDTH STAIR
© 1941 Sigil Pictures

MEDIUM SHOT - INTERIOR - A VICTORIAN BEDROOM - DAY

A thin, ailing mother reclines in her sickbed
as her daughter shows her seashells collected
from the beach. A BANDAGE on the girl's foot.
SEASHELLS hang from the canopy bed frame like
healing charms.

                    GIRL
                (frightened)
    Momma, did you hear that? It sounded
    like it came from beneath the house.

                    MOTHER
    There's nothing beneath the house
    except the sea caves, silly girl.

—

FRIDAY CAME FAST, and before I knew it, I found myself in the
passenger seat of Rafe's rental Range Rover. The road to Joshua Tree
National Park wound through the Morongo Basin, the kind of place

that touted spiritual vortexes next to gun shops, art installations across from military bases. The high-desert landscape was strangely familiar, a symptom of decades' worth of Hollywood Westerns that had been filmed in these locations and taken up residence in America's psyche.

"I have to pee," Kylie announced from the back seat, where she was piled in with our overnight bags and Tyler's gear.

Rafe, behind the wheel, glanced in the rearview mirror. "Again?"

Kylie jiggled the ice in her empty extra-large soda cup. "Yeah. *Again.*"

He muttered something under his breath but dutifully found a gas station for her. Dream catchers for sale hung in the windows. I climbed out, stretching down toward my toes, eyeing the storm clouds rolling in from the west.

"I don't like the looks of those," I said, nodding toward the sky. "If it rains, it could wash away any remaining evidence at the campsite."

"It's been a week. Any evidence is probably long gone anyway."

Kylie came back out, drying her hands on her pants, and pinned me and Rafe with a suspicious look. I felt suddenly self-conscious, like she thought Rafe and I wouldn't be able to keep our hands off each other while she was gone.

I cleared my throat. "I'm going to pee, too."

The convenience store was full of touristy tchotchkes as well as firewood bundles and last-minute camping supplies. I grabbed a few water bottles and took them to the attendant, a guy with a long black ponytail who looked as dusty as the desert itself.

I glanced around for security cameras. Then, as I slid the bottles across the counter, I casually asked, "Hey, did you happen to hear about a death a week ago in the park?"

"BLM," the guy said.

"BLM?"

"It wasn't in the park. It was in the Bureau of Land Management campground south of the park." He spoke flatly as though rattling off the prices of milk and beer. He turned to blow his nose into a crusty handkerchief. "Every year, we get a few dead tourists. Mostly climbing accidents."

"I heard it was murder, not an accident."

He balled up the dirty handkerchief in his pocket and gave an odd little laugh. "Yeah, we get murders, too, but that's usually locals. Guys getting high and shooting each other over some chick. Or sometimes over a dog. Sometimes chicks *with* dogs."

"Right." I wiped the water bottles on my pants as I stepped back out into the desert air. "Well, thanks."

Outside, Kylie and Rafe were standing by the gas pump, arguing about something. I heard the rise of Kylie's voice as she gestured with her hands. Rafe was frowning, one hand squeezing his chin.

As soon as they saw me, they stopped.

Now it was my turn to eye *them* suspiciously. "Everything okay?"

"Yeah." Kylie's face was flushed. "It's . . . this freaking weather. I was on the fence about camping anyway. I don't see why we can't just stay at a motel and visit the campground in the morning."

I handed her a bottle of water, still side-eyeing them. "It'll be easier to look around without raising suspicion if we're camping near the crime scene."

Kylie tugged open the car door, already climbing inside. "Whatever." She slammed the door.

Alone with Rafe, I muttered, "What was that really about?"

He scoffed. "Nothing. She doesn't like me. Go figure."

We rode the rest of the way to the small town of Twentynine Palms, listening to a moody beat playing on the radio. It was hardly a shock that Kylie and Rafe weren't getting along. He *was* a malignant force pulled out of a cursed manuscript. I'd witnessed him struck by a fire poker, shot by a gun, and fallen through a floor; he'd barely had a scratch on him.

"There," Kylie said, pointing between the seats.

The sign for Twentynine Palms looked like a national park sign with its wooden boards and white paint, but there was nothing of the clean desert scrubland or rock formations I'd associate with a nature park. The town was a simple grid of dated motels and tattoo parlors strung together by telephone wires and towered over by Washingtonia palms. Rafe turned in to a shopping center that had a very out-of-place-looking Victorian home at the far end of the parking lot.

A sign read MORONGO FUNERAL HOME.

How many funeral homes had I seen in Rob's movies? There'd been a zombie film where the freezers started rattling with the undead trying to get out. Another where a serial killer's prey had to strip naked and hide among the dead bodies. But I'd only been in one funeral home in real life, for my dad's service. I stepped inside my second.

Morongo Funeral Home was older than the Lundie Bay mortuary, with cheap folding chairs instead of nice plush armchairs, yet the smell was the same.

Potpourri.

My stomach turned at the sweet floral scent, and I twisted toward a window, closing my eyes briefly.

Approaching footsteps caused me to turn back around. A thirty-something blond woman was clomping toward us in chunky heels and an ill-fitting sleeveless dress that contrasted with her tattooed arms. She had the bad teeth of a former junkie.

Her eyes roved over Rafe. "Mr. Kahn?"

When he nodded, she jutted out a hand palm-up. Rafe smirked and placed an envelope of cash in her hand.

She gave us a tight smile. "I'm Candace Elliot. The guy's downstairs. Ten minutes, that's what we agreed. And that's *it*. I have an appointment at one."

"We won't be long," I said.

Her skeptical look shone on me as she turned the sign in the window to CLOSED FOR LUNCH. "Come on."

She led us past a small chapel room with fake flowers, then past an office where she probably met with family members of the deceased.

She shouldered open a door at the end of the hall and started down a staircase.

"Did the police give you their autopsy report?" I asked.

"Nah, they don't tell me anything," Candace said. "At least not anymore. I used to date a guy on the force. He told me everything."

"Could you still get in touch with him?"

She snorted. "No. And don't offer more cash. It would take a dump truck full of twenties to get me to call that asshole." At the bottom of the stairs, she swung open a door plastered with warning signs about chemical exposures.

She switched on a light. Fluorescent bulbs flickered over a linoleum-floored embalming room with three metal tables. Two were occupied. One by a body draped in a sheet, the other by a tiny old woman pristinely dressed in a peach-colored pantsuit, her gray curls immaculate, lipstick a little too dark.

"Jesus," Kylie muttered, recoiling from the body.

"Mrs. Zalipski," Candace said matter-of-factly. "Her son lives in Las Vegas. He's a dancer. Off the strip, if you get my meaning."

I shifted from one foot to the other as I assessed the dead woman. Behind my eyes, memories of other bodies flashed. *Eddie Chase and Francesca Myers, shot in their car. Detective Rice slumped in a pit. Jonathan Tybee with his head twisted around.*

I turned away sharply. The potpourri smell mixed with formaldehyde was getting to me. I could taste the film of it in my mouth. I worked my tongue around my teeth.

Rafe, leaning against the doorframe with his arms crossed, nodded toward the other table. "That's him?"

"Your friend? Yeah, that's him."

I doubted that Rafe had called Joao a "friend" when he'd arranged this bribe, but Candace was giving us the benefit of the doubt.

"I'll be upstairs in the office." She pointed to the wall clock. "Remember—"

"Ten minutes," I said. "Got it."

She narrowed her eyes a little before leaving, as though suspicious we'd mess up her mortuary. After she'd left, Kylie, Rafe, and I remained silent in the embalming room, and the other two bodies certainly weren't talking. No one moved toward the sheeted figure.

Rafe rolled his eyes. "It's just a *body*."

He started toward it, but I raised a hand.

"No, no, I'll do it." I stalked forward and pulled back the sheet.

Joao Acosta was naked, and unlike Mrs. Zalipski, Candace hadn't yet applied makeup or styled his hair. He was a young guy with a few weeks' beard and shoulder-length dark hair now brushed back from his face. Even pale and stiff, he had a rugged air to him, like he might hop on a mountain bike at any moment.

My attention locked onto the bump in his nose, and I ran a finger over my own.

Kylie wrinkled her nose as she took a baby step closer. "So . . . what exactly are we looking for?"

"The brand," I said, letting my hand fall away from my face.

We all frowned down at his exposed chest. The problem was, as part of the autopsy, the police coroner had sawed through his rib cage in a Y shape and hadn't sewn the skin back up. Though it had been roughly set back in place, it didn't quite match up.

Kylie grimaced as she floated a finger a few inches over of the incisions. "I think you need to . . . rearrange the skin a little. That flap matches up with that flap."

I grabbed a Kleenex and hesitantly used it to clutch the puckered skin. Rafe watched me, not the body, as though I was the one being dissected. He looked amused at my squeamishness.

"Blood and hell. Here, step aside, I'll do it." He batted my hand away and grabbed Joao's skin with his bare fingers, squeezing the flaps together so we could see the brand mark.

"Ew," Kylie muttered.

The brand ran from the left side of Joao's collarbone to the base of his rib cage. Two thin crescents about an inch thick at the widest place.

Rafe released his hold on Joao's skin, and his chest flopped back into pieces again.

Kylie gagged and turned away.

"Check the rest of his body," I told them. "See if there are any other marks."

I'd gotten over my initial reticence, and I was feeling more like myself now, not the kind of person spooked by a little torn flesh. Kylie gingerly lifted the sheet at Joao's feet while Rafe and I lifted his arms, checking his back.

"Tattoos on his legs," Kylie said. "And a mark on his foot like he was burned."

"Take pictures."

She grimaced as she took out her phone and started snapping. I ran my hands over Joao's ribs, feeling for anything broken. He had torn nails and cut marks on his fingers that looked defensive, as though he'd clawed at something. Another wound on his bottom lip. On impulse, I pulled open his mouth. His throat looked red and raw.

I glanced at Rafe. "Can you get a copy of the police report?"

"Probably." He looked down passively at the body as though he'd seen hundreds of cadavers, and considering where he came from, he probably had. "You think he's a, what, cousin?"

I again studied Joao's familiar nose. "Patrick Kane should be able to tell us with certainty. Kylie, do we have a date for the interview?"

"Working on it. He's in Mexico City right now for a writers' conference."

I twitched at the memory of being dragged to generic hotel ballrooms, speakers' cheesy literary puns.

The wall clock read a few minutes until one. I could imagine Candace Elliot upstairs, ready for us to get the hell out of her funeral home.

I took one last look at Joao, my possible distant cousin. If only we'd found him a few weeks ago. What could he have told us about the curse, about whoever—or whatever—was after him?

"Let's get out of here," I said.

Candace was all too happy to walk us out, pulling the funeral home's front door closed behind her. She turned toward the parking lot, glanced briefly up at the clouds congregating overhead as she hunted her jangling ring of keys in her purse. "You know, for a guy with no supposed family, Mr. Acosta must have been either really loved or really hated."

I cocked my head. "Why do you say that?"

She found the door key and slid it into the lock. "You weren't the only ones who tried to pay me off to see the body. You were just the only ones with enough cash."

My head whipped toward Rafe and Kylie, who both looked as surprised as me.

"Who else came by?" I asked, dreading the answer. I was afraid she'd say a middle-aged man with a gut and an uncanny whisper, but as soon as the thought entered my head, I knew that was wrong. If Uncle Arnold wanted to see Joao's body, he didn't need a bribe.

"Some lady." Candace locked up the funeral home. "Called me over the phone this morning. Didn't say her name. She tried to claim she was family, and when it was clear she didn't have the documents to prove it, she offered fifty bucks. *Fifty bucks!*" Candace sneered. I'd glimpsed the bills Rafe had slipped her, and it was ten times that much. "Anyway, you weirdos take care."

Overhead, thunder rumbled. I'd never spent much time in the desert, and I found it unnerving. The sky seemed too vast. I was used to city life, where you were lucky to spot a narrow rectangle of blue between buildings, or Lundie Bay, where trees swallowed most of the horizon. Out here in the open, sky upstaged land, and it left me feeling somehow top-heavy, like I might be crushed under its weight.

We climbed into Rafe's car as a few errant raindrops fell. Kylie fought with the sleeping bags sharing the back seat with her. The plan was to snag a camping spot near the site where Joao's body was found, which shouldn't be hard in the January low season. But I didn't like the idea of spending the night outside in the exposed desert with no locking doors or security gates. Especially now that we knew someone else was poking around.

Rafe looked up at the clouds as he cranked the engine. "You ready to go into the desert?"

I shivered despite the warm day. "No. Never. But let's go."

CHAPTER THIRTEEN

―

THE CANDY HOUSE
© 1951 Sigil Pictures

EXTERIOR — FIELD — NIGHT

MEDIUM CLOSE ON a shallow grave, one of
many. The soil moves. The wooden coffin lid
is thrust upwards. A boy, ANDRZEJ, sits up,
desperate for breath. A Star of David armband
circles his bicep. In the coffin with him is
the cadaver of a young typhoid victim.

Andrzej scrambles out and stumbles to the next
shallow grave. MUFFLED CRIES comes from under
the dirt. He digs to free his sister, HANNA,
from another coffin. They embrace.

Hand in hand, Andrzej and Hanna flee into the
nearby woods. CLOSE ON their two Star of David
armbands left behind in the mud.

―

IF THE RANGE ROVER'S GPS system hadn't directed us
turn by turn to the Bureau of Land Management campground south

of Joshua Tree National Park, we never would have known when we arrived. There were no signs announcing the campground, no booths staffed by a campground attendant, not even a notice board posted with wildlife regulations. Other than the few tents blooming across the scrubby desert like strange, colorful growths, the area was identical to the rest of the empty desert.

"There's nothing here," Kylie grumbled, looking out the backseat window. We'd been warned that the BLM campground didn't have basic amenities like bathrooms or water spigots, so we'd stopped at a convenience store a few miles back to load up on water jugs. But it was one thing to hear about rustic camping and another to be faced with the reality of no toilets.

Kylie looked pale. "What was Joao Acosta even *doing* out here?"

"Not sightseeing," I muttered, mulling over the lack of bathrooms myself.

In the police reports that Rafe had pilfered, he'd learned that Joao had grown up in Twentynine Palms until the age of fifteen, when he'd run away to Albuquerque and proceeded to bum around the Southwest for the next decade, working brief stints in fast-food franchises, never staying one place for more than a few months. According to the police report, his credit card had most recently been used in Pasadena.

"I think it's safe to say he wasn't camping for the fun of it, alone and with no tent." I tucked a loose strand of hair behind my ear as Rafe bumped the vehicle over the gravel road past packed-earth campsites. "Most recently, he was in the LA area. Why? The tax records Rafe dug up suggest he wasn't on any official payroll anywhere in the city. Then he just up and leaves LA to return to his birthplace, but instead of staying with friends or family that might still be in the area, he comes here—the literal middle of nowhere—with no supplies, planning on sleeping in his car?"

"Sounds like some ex-boyfriends I know," Kylie mumbled, then turned more serious. "I mean, it kind of makes sense. A young guy like that, used to moving around a lot, probably low on cash? It's free to camp here and there's no registration. He would have known that fact from growing up nearby."

I twisted in the seat to face her. "You think he didn't want a record of his location?"

Kylie took a swig from a water bottle. "If I was hiding out from the police, this is where I'd come."

"He wasn't hiding from the police," Rafe pointed out. "They weren't after him—I read the police reports. But he very well could have been on the run from something else."

Rafe's words hung in the air as he circled the first campground loop. The BLM property was divided into four loops like a four-leaf clover, with the entrance as the stem, joining the loops. We cruised slowly past a group of college guys grilling on a portable grill; a cooler held a mound of beers nearby. Then an oversized RV with kicked-off shoes in a pile by the front door. The campground wasn't busy, and over half the sites were available, but Rafe drove past them all until he reached orange-and-white traffic barrels blocking the road. He stopped the car.

Gesturing toward the barrels, he said, "The Bureau of Land Management must have put those up to keep anyone from using the loop where Joao was found. This is as close as we can get." He backed up the vehicle and pulled into the closest empty campsite. We climbed out, stretching from the long drive, and surveyed our surroundings.

When we had decided to camp here, I had imagined picturesque rock formations and clusters of the alien-like crooked trees that gave Joshua Tree National Park its name. But this campground technically wasn't *in* the park's boundaries. Instead of tourist-worthy canyons, it was little more than an empty patch of desert that looked exactly like the other miles of desert surrounding it.

The area's flatness was broken by scrubby vegetation I didn't know the names of, though words floated into my mind: *prickly pear, yucca, succulents*. Overhead, turkey vultures circled against clouds that were darkening by the minute. The wind picked up, blowing a ream of sand into my face, and I turned my back to it, wiping my eyes.

"Mahalo, man." A scruffy college-aged guy in the next campsite waved to us as he sauntered over, giving the Range Rover a long look. "First time in the Josh?"

Rafe bared his teeth like an animal. "No."

Undeterred by Rafe's unfriendliness, the dude took a sip of his Natty Lite and motioned toward the sky. "Hope you brought a strong tent, or else you'll be sleeping in your car. They're calling for a serious storm. Winds gnarly enough to blow away anything not staked down reeeally fucking well." He waved his beer can in the direction of a shallow depression behind our tent. "Keep an eye on that wash if there's a flash flood."

The sky emitted a distant roll of thunder, punctuating his warning.

Rafe popped open the back of the Range Rover and started pulling out our supplies. "We'll be fine."

"No doubt, man. If you get bored waiting out the storm, come on over. Cassandra and I are well-stocked. Beer and poker chips." He waved goodbye as he returned to a young woman I assumed was his girlfriend, dressed in a crop top and jean shorts, taking selfies in front of their roaring campfire.

Rafe bristled like he could think of nothing more loathsome than being trapped in a tiny tent with an influencer couple. Kylie came up beside him and unzipped her overnight bag. She sat on the Range Rover's bumper and started swapping her sandals for tennis shoes.

"I'm going to jog around the campground before the rain starts," she said. "See if I can get a sense of the crime scene and if there are other campers nearby. Maybe ask around and see if anyone's heard anything about the murder."

"Be careful," I said.

As she took off, I attempted to help Rafe set up our tent. My only camping experience had been years ago with my ex-husband and his old college friends. Baker had teased me, saying *You can't spend a night without a queen-sized mattress*, and I'd tossed in my sleeping bag on top of hard roots all night, too stubborn to admit he was right.

The disassembled tent was a confusing pile of fiberglass poles, bungee cords, and nylon fabric. I held up two of the poles with a grimace, trying uselessly to fit them together, but the bungee cord kept getting in the way.

Rafe watched me in mild amusement, then chuckled. He stood up and held out his hands. "Give me those before you break something."

I surrendered the poles gratefully and leaned back against the car, munching on a protein bar, while he began erecting the tent. It was a good opportunity to observe the nearby campers. Across from us was a family with three teenagers who all seemed to be sharing the same tent—now *that* was a nightmare. Then there was Cassandra and the Dude, who were currently making s'mores, apparently for the express purpose of photographing them. Next to them, a middle-aged woman was doing yoga in front of a beat-up Winnebago that read DESERT WANDERER in mint-green paint. Her tree pose was impressive. I watched her stand motionless for five minutes until she finally broke and saluted the sky.

I swallowed the last of the protein bar and shoved the wrapper in my pocket.

Turning back toward Rafe, I asked quietly, "Where exactly was Joao found?"

Rafe waved a hand toward the closed-off loop. At the far end, a few wind-worn granite boulders provided the only break from the flat horizon. "By those big rocks. There are a few sites there."

A loud crack of thunder split the sky. In the neighboring site, Cassandra shrieked and dropped a s'more, cursing at the mess. My own heart jumped. I pressed a steadying hand against my chest, breathing hard.

"Afraid of thunder now, Haven?" Rafe asked, eyeing me curiously as he hammered in the first tent stake.

I dragged a shoe through the sand and admitted, "I don't know. . . . I'm kind of falling apart, to be honest. I've been having nightmares."

He walked to the next corner of the tent, sparing me a searching glance. The smoke from the influencer couple's campfire billowed my way, stinging my eyes. I moved to get out of the thick of it, but the winds shifted, and the smoke only seemed more determined to follow me.

Rafe hammered the next stake in. "Tell me about these dreams."

My left hand drifted to the base of my throat and squeezed. "It's like I'm back in Malice House on the night of the fire. There's smoke everywhere."

Rafe pounded in a final stake, then stood and tested out his handiwork by tugging on the cords. Tyler's tent would be a tight fit for the three of us and our supplies, but at least we'd stay dry.

Dusting off his hands, Rafe came over to where I stood. He peeled my hand away from where it was clutched around my neck and took it in his own.

His voice was gravely calm. "You've been through a lot. I'm not surprised you're having nightmares."

"I should probably get therapy," I confessed. "But if I go in talking about monsters, they'll commit me. Pump me full of drugs so I'm a slobbering mess. The curse would *love* that." My father had spent decades fighting the curse; it had only gotten him to create *things* once his mind had been weakened by dementia.

"You don't need therapy." Rafe's big hand swallowed my own. "You need answers."

His thumb absently drew circles on my palm, and I felt a stirring of desire. It had been so long since I'd been close enough to a man to trust him. My disastrous marriage to Baker had shattered any hope of ever having a healthy relationship. I was beyond the point of weekend sci-fi marathons together on the sofa, date nights at breweries. Then again, Rafe had never offered that kind of relationship—I wasn't sure I wanted "date nights" anymore, anyway.

Kylie came jogging back up from her reconnaissance, breathing hard. I quickly let my hand slide out of Rafe's.

"Did you see anything out there?" I asked.

Nodding, she wiped a sheen of sweat off her brow. "A lot of people are packing up and leaving before the storm comes, but even so, there's at least a dozen groups who look like they're staying the night. I went through the closed-off loop, and it isn't exactly private. There's no way we can investigate the crime scene without being spotted by other campers."

"We'll have to wait until dark, then," I said.

Kylie sat on the car bumper and started to untie her shoes. "It'll be hard to see anything at night."

"Yeah, but we can't risk anyone spotting us. You heard what the mortician said: We aren't the only ones looking into Joao's death. Besides, what if they call the police and report someone snooping around the crime scene? I already have the Lundie Bay detective on my ass. I don't need the local cops, too."

Kylie slid on her sandals and walked over to the tent, testing out the nearest stake by tugging on the cord.

"It's secure," Rafe snarled.

She glowered in return as she tested out another cord's strength. "I don't want to be swept off in a flash flood in the middle of the night."

"That's a shame," Rafe answered.

I rolled my eyes. *Bickering like kids.*

I grabbed a roll of toilet paper from our supply bag, then faced the desert, hesitating. In open terrain, how was one supposed to pee without putting on a show?

Someone chuckled behind me. I turned just as thunder cracked across the sky.

The woman who'd been doing yoga beside the Desert Wanderer Winnebago came over with a small orange trowel and a water bottle.

"You don't want to use toilet paper," she said in a lightly accented voice. "It's considered littering unless you pack it out with you. Better to just dig a hole, do your business, wash with some water, and then drip-dry." She offered me the trowel. "Climb down in the wash behind those creosote bushes. No one can see you there."

Grateful, I took the trowel. Tree Pose was in her late forties, though her makeup-free brown face and salt-and-pepper hair gave her the sort of ageless beauty of hard-core wellness gurus.

"You're a lifesaver," I said. "I don't camp much."

"The Range Rover gave it away." She gave me a hearty laugh. "If you can't tell, it's mostly old Subarus and rented RVs around here."

I gave her the warmest smile I could muster. "Hey, can I ask you something? My friends and I heard a rumor that a guy died here recently."

Her brown eyes drifted in the direction we were interested in. "Shocking, isn't it? The police and the Bureau of Land Management closed the campground during the investigation. Everyone had to pack up and move to different campgrounds."

"You were here when he was killed?"

Her mouth firmed into a fine web of wrinkles. "I got here the morning of the day it happened. I moved to the KOA campground until this place reopened."

The wind picked up, but I didn't want to let go of this lead. "Did you see him? Before he died, I mean?"

From the curious look the woman gave me, I realized I was treading on dangerous ground. Most campers probably didn't go around interrogating others about a murder.

She shifted her back to the wind. "Are you working on a podcast or something?"

"No . . ." I forced a laugh. "I just have a morbid sense of curiosity."

She *tsk*ed and muttered under her breath, "Yeah. Apparently so did he."

I cocked my head. "What do you mean?"

She turned again and faced away from me, shrugging at my question. "Oh, I shouldn't have said anything. . . . The police told me it's best to keep it to myself." She bit her lip like she was dying to spill her secret, however. She stepped closer, speaking low. "I found a journal stuck between two of those boulders over there. Before I passed it on to the police, I looked through it to try to find the owner's name. It was filled with stories. I didn't read too much of it—it wasn't my intention to breach anyone's privacy. But the stories I did read were . . . disturbing."

The hair on my arms rose and not just from the falling temperature. If she handed it over to the police, there was a chance Rafe could get it.

"The journal belonged to Joao Acosta?"

She stared at me with growing suspicion. "They already released the victim's name?"

I tried for nonchalance as I shrugged myself. "Yeah. It was online."

"Hm. I didn't know they'd determined his identity. The police said he'd given a fake name when he filled out his campfire permit."

Joao had used a false name? This piqued my interest. The Bureau of Land Management didn't require a permit for camping, but they did for a campfire. The gas station a few miles back kept track of the permits and collected the fees; we hadn't wanted to leave our names, so we'd skipped it, banking on the likelihood that we wouldn't need a fire.

I felt certain now that Joao Acosta had been on the run, probably from something he'd encountered in California. He'd dropped everything and fled here, a place he knew from his childhood as an area of the country that was easy to disappear into.

Tree Pose was eyeing me closely, so I gave an exaggerated shiver and said, "It's scary. Being in a place where someone died."

A hint of sympathy returned to her face. "I'm sure it's safe to camp here now. The police thought it was a domestic dispute, or possibly drug related. The killer was probably someone who knew the victim and didn't stick around until the morning."

Or it was safe to camp here . . . until we arrived, I thought. Rafe, Kylie, and I had a way of leaving disaster in our wake, and I felt a sudden worry for Tree Pose and Cassandra and the Dude and the other campers. Were we putting them in danger just by being close?

I glanced back at Rafe. A literal monster—and I'd brought him here.

A fat raindrop fell on my cheek. I flinched like I'd been slapped. Tree Pose and I both tilted our faces to the sky.

"You'd better hurry and do your business." She gestured toward the wash as she retreated toward her Winnebago. "That storm's about to hit. Just leave the trowel by the van door when you're done."

A few more raindrops hurtled down from the sky, crashing into the sand to form miniature craters at our feet. By the time I scaled down into the wash and squatted to pee, blue-black clouds had lowered over the entire area. The temperature dropped in a matter of minutes. I'd always heard how the desert could go from baking hot to freezing cold quickly, but the sudden shift shocked me, made me feel like I'd left this world and stepped into another one.

When I climbed back up from the wash, raindrops were already falling. Excepting the family with teenagers, who were hurrying to take down the laundry they'd hung up to dry, the campground appeared deserted. Tree Pose had taken shelter in her Winnebago. The influencer couple next to us were blasting music from a speaker inside their tent.

I unzipped our tent door and stepped into the dim interior dome. Kylie and Rafe were both there, hustling to stow our supplies around the edges of the tent to keep everything out of the rain.

"Hey, listen," I said a little breathlessly. They both stopped to look at me. "I think we should go to Joao's site now."

"Now?" Kylie said. "It's pouring."

Heavier rain began pattering on the tent exterior, echoing inside.

"Yeah, exactly," I answered. "All the other campers are taking shelter, settling in for a long evening and night stuck inside. No one's going to venture outside given the weather report. It's like a ghost town out there. No one will be watching to see who might be snooping around the crime scene."

Kylie paused in unpacking her clothes to peer out the partially unzipped doorway behind me. The patter of rain was quickly transforming into a thunderous drumming. Between that and the wind, it was deafening inside our bubble.

She hissed out a sigh. "Ugh. Fine."

"Rafe?" I asked.

"Do I look scared of some rain?"

CHAPTER FOURTEEN

———

WINTER OF THE WICKED
© 1947 Sigil Pictures

EXTERIOR — FARMYARD — DAY

Younger Daughter trudges through snow to the
goose pen with a basket of grain, one of her
morning chores. We hear her gasp.

All the geese are dead except for the big
dark gray one. He is pecking at the corpse of
another. Goose down litters the snow. The dark
gray goose lifts his beak, messily gorging
on his flockmates' flesh, and lets out an
unnatural screech toward the daytime moon.

———

WE PULLED ON rain jackets, grabbed our phones in case we
needed to take pictures, and secured all the zippered windows of the tent.

Then we exited into the storm.

Kylie tried to speak, but the wind stole her words. Sheets of rain
were falling now, blowing horizontally into our faces. The sky had
darkened to a dusk-like shade despite it being only late afternoon. The
clouds were low enough that I felt a fleeting urge to duck.

"It's this way!" Rafe called over the wind as he led us past the orange-and-white barrels to the empty campground loop. I tugged my rain jacket's hood higher over my head as we splashed through rapidly forming puddles. I'd been right about the rain chasing everyone inside: Every tent was tightly zipped. Each camper van as lifeless as a dead beetle husk.

The rain came harder, blowing at an angle, plastering my hair to my face. Within a minute, my shoes felt like I'd been tromping through a knee-high creek. My hood was useless and obstructed my vision, so I pushed it back. Ahead, Rafe pressed on through the wind with an easy grace, unlike Kylie and me, who stumbled behind him. A memory returned to me: the night at Malice House when I'd drawn Rafe for the first time. I'd thought of him as a man made of wind. And it was true—he was as shifting as a storm, reckless and unpredictable.

The gravel road led us toward the boulders. There were fewer campsites here, all empty, squeezed among the rock formations. I could see why Joao had picked this loop—it was much more private than the wide-open area where we'd erected our tent.

Rafe stopped at a large puddle that, I realized, had been a campsite but minutes ago. Only the uppermost portion of the campfire ring rose above the collecting water.

He pushed back his hood and said over the rain, "This is it. Number forty-eight."

My spirits immediately sank. One glance told me there was nothing here that would help us understand why Joao had been running. Any crime-scene evidence—shoe prints in the sand, disturbed vegetation—would have been instantly washed away.

"You saw the crime scene photos," I called to Rafe, sheltering my face with my hands. "What did they look like?"

The storm pelted Rafe as he picked up a stick and considered the campsite. Like me, he'd lowered his hood, but the rain didn't seem to bother him as it did me. The water dripped from his hair and vanished down his neck into his shirt.

He tried to draw the shape of a body in the sand, but the puddles got in the way.

He turned and beckoned toward Kylie. "Kylie, come here for a minute."

She wrinkled her nose. She was the only one of us still pretending her raincoat made a difference. With the hood drawn up tightly over her hair, she splashed her way over to him, scowling.

Thunder broke overhead. At the same time, Rafe grabbed Kylie by the shoulders and started lowering her to the ground.

"Hey! What the hell?" She windmilled her arms against him, but Rafe's strength was superhuman. He didn't let go.

My heartbeat immediately kicked up.

"Rafe, what are you doing? Let her go!" I lunged forward to help Kylie, who let out a scream.

Rafe cupped his palm against Kylie's mouth as he said, "Fuck, if I was trying to hurt you, you'd know it. I'm only trying to show you how Joao's body was positioned on the ground."

He released Kylie, and she stumbled a few feet away, wiping her mouth, throwing him a dagger-filled look. "You could have fucking warned me!"

He scoffed as he crouched near the campfire ring and beckoned her again. At first, she rolled her eyes hotly, pacing tightly in the rain, but then she muttered under her breath and reluctantly clomped forward. "Do *not* touch me like that again. Got it? I'm serious, Harbinger."

Rafe seemed to find her distress amusing. "Do you want to see how his body was found or not? Now, he was found facedown in the dirt." He jerked an expectant finger toward the ground.

"Just do it, please," I said to Kylie "It might be the best clue we have to go on. You have dry clothes back in the tent."

Grumbling, Kylie lay down on her stomach amid the puddles and, at Rafe's instruction, arranged her feet so that one was inside the fire ring, almost like she'd stumbled on one of the stones and fallen. He splayed her hands to her sides. Then he stood up, looked over the position, and nodded.

"This was how the police found him. His hands were out like that, almost a defensive stance. One foot in the fire ring; his right shoe was partly melted, which means he was lying there, presumably dead, long enough for it to burn."

I recalled the burn marks on the cadaver's foot. Either Joao had already been dead when his foot had caught fire in the fire ring, or he'd been too weak to move out of the flames' way.

Rafe frowned, then crouched again next to Kylie, who looked increasingly irritated at being our model. "His mouth was filled with sand, so his head would have been positioned like this." He shoved a hand against Kylie's back, dunking the side of her face into one of the puddles.

Kylie immediately shot up to her hands and knees, coughing out water. She twisted to slap Rafe's hand away. "I said not to handle me like that, you psycho! You did that on purpose! That's it. I'm done being your crash-test dummy. Fuck you, Rafe. I'm going to look around the rocks."

She pushed to her feet, wiping water off her face.

"Kylie—" I started.

"Get your dog under control, Haven." Throwing Rafe one last searing look, she stomped off toward the boulders.

Lightning flashed across the clouds. I flinched, hunching further into my jacket, bracing for the thunder I knew was coming.

"You didn't have to shove her around like that!" I said to Rafe. "What's wrong with you?"

Rafe shrugged as he wiped the mud off his hands onto his jeans. "I was only illustrating a point. And it paid off." He considered the area around the campfire where Kylie had been positioned and then rooted his feet midway through the puddle. "Look. Joao's attacker must have been standing here, given the way his body fell."

A long roll of thunder came, shaking the earth. I glanced after Kylie, worried.

"But there were only Joao's shoe prints," Rafe continued as he pointed through the sheets of rain at the puddle in the sand.

"So what, his attacker flew in?" I said, immediately regretting my choice of words. There were creatures that *could* have flown in and killed Joao. After a pause, I shouted over the wind, "Kestrel?"

Rafe wiped the rain from his face and shook his head. "When he's in bird form, Kestrel kills with his beak and claws. When he's in human form, he twists necks. Besides, he would have left footprints. Joao died from suffocation and the brand."

"What other monsters don't leave prints?" I shouted. By now, the rain had soaked through every layer of my clothing. I could feel my skin erupting into goose bumps. The wind whipped about wildly, making a mess of my hair. A crack sounded behind me, and I turned to see a large branch from a Joshua tree crash down onto the boulders.

Rafe yelled back, "None from Malice."

Movement caught my eye far out in the desert, and I turned, sheltering my face with my hands. For a second, it had looked like something was out there. Something big, something human-sized . . . or bigger. But now there was only the thrashing creosote bushes.

Kylie came jogging back from the rocks. "Did you see that tree? Man, fuck this. Other than Rafe's messed-up display of aggression, there's nothing here to see. I'm going back to the tent."

Hunched against the rain, I nodded. My socks were squelchy in my shoes. Another bolt of lightning appeared far out in the desert, immediately followed by a clap of thunder.

We jogged back to our nylon bubble as the wind wailed around us. The tent was a flimsy barrier against the rage of nature—and whatever else might be lurking in the desert—but I'd learned long ago that the illusion of safety was sometimes the best one could hope for.

I unzipped the tent flap and hurled myself inside, followed by Rafe and Kylie, seconds before the sky opened and let loose even heavier sheets of rain that crashed down, flowing along the sloped sides like miniature waterfalls. The tent's interior was blessedly dry. I let out an exhale, trying to slow down from survival mode.

But then Kylie whirled on Rafe angrily, and I realized the danger wasn't over.

"Not you." She jabbed a finger in the center of his chest. "*You* stay outside."

Her suggestion was hardly unreasonable after the way he'd treated her. Still, Rafe had only acted as he'd been written—the Harbinger wasn't the kind of character to make polite requests.

"Kylie," I said quietly, "where's he supposed to go?"

"The car." Her eyes were sparking. "He's not sleeping *here*, that's for sure. I'm not sharing a tent with a fucking monster."

I shifted from foot to foot, stooped awkwardly beneath the sloping ceiling. I turned to Rafe. "She's right. You should go. . . ."

Rain was dripping off all three of us. Rafe grabbed a towel from his overnight bag and swiped it over his face and limbs. For a moment, I thought he would refuse to leave. There wasn't much we could do to force him out of the tent—his strength was easily greater than both of ours combined.

Finally, he stuffed the towel into his bag, slung it over his shoulder, and snarled in my direction, "Whatever helps you sleep, darling."

I opened my mouth to say something, but what? Rafe had made his own bed. When I remained silent, he unzipped the tent and disappeared back out into the storm. A second later, we heard the car door slam.

I zipped up the flapping door.

Without Rafe, the tension inside the tent eased immediately, and my muscles unwound despite the battering wind outside.

Kylie snatched up her towel, scrunching it over her hair. "I just—I couldn't."

"You don't have to explain. He's *not* a good guy. I get it."

She started peeling off her soaking clothes. I unbuttoned and shimmied out of my wet jeans.

As she balanced on one foot to tug off a damp sock, she blurted out, "*Do* you?"

I didn't know how to answer, so I took a while to dig in my overnight bag for a dry pair of sweatpants.

She threw her socks into our wet clothes pile. "I get he's got the whole sexy bad-boy thing, but you know what he is. What he's *done*. And you let him hang at your heels like a fucking dog—like a *hellhound*—and stick up for him when he's acting psycho—"

"I didn't stick up for him. I *said* he wasn't a good guy." Without meeting her eyes, I struggled through my thoughts. "I do know what he is. But I *made* him, Kylie. At the very least, I gave him form. I feel, I don't know, connected to him. I'd love to tell him to screw off and never see him again, but it just doesn't work like that between us."

What I didn't say was that I was the same as Rafe. Our connection went beyond creator and creation, even beyond our attraction. Rafe and I were children of ink and paper, not flesh and blood. Kylie would never understand that as long as she didn't know about the drawing hidden in my book safe.

She pulled a clean shirt over her head, fighting with the sleeves. "Do you trust him?"

I hesitated. "No, of course not. Not with everything."

She pinned me with a searching look as she brushed out the wrinkles in her shirt. "Have you slept with him since he came back?"

"No! He tried to get me to go back with him to his hotel, but I'm not stupid." I paused, recalling our conversation. "He said he had a 'present' for me there. Wouldn't tell me what it was."

She rested a hand on her hip. "Yeah, no shit, because it was probably a poison apple."

I rolled my eyes as I toweled off my hair. "We didn't come all this way to argue about Rafe. Listen, it's Joao we need to figure out. If what Rafe said about the crime scene having no footprints is true, then a person couldn't have killed him. We also need to face the fact that while it was something inhuman, it likely wasn't one of the Malice creations. That means there are other monsters out there *and* other curseworkers who can do what we can. For all we know, the curse has been going on for centuries."

Kylie moved to sit cross-legged on top of her unrolled sleeping bag, clutching a battery-powered camping lantern in her lap. The wind continued to surge against the tent, making the shadows from the lantern gyrate on the nylon fabric.

"You think Joao was a curseworker?" she asked. "That he created whatever killed him?"

The patter of rain punctuated her words.

I scrubbed the towel against my scalp, thinking through everything we'd learned at the funeral home and the crime scene. "That woman in the Desert Wanderer van found Joao's journal. She described the stories inside as disturbing. I wish we could get our hands on it. I don't know, an Acosta writing down dark stories feels . . ."

"Familiar," Kylie filled in for me.

I nodded.

Shifting on her sleeping bag, Kylie peered down into the battery-powered glow of the lantern and said in a strange voice, "If it's true, I can sympathize with Joao. It *is* an obsessive itch. I know you've felt it, too. All those times your hand gets a mind of its own and reaches for a pen to doodle terrible things on restaurant napkins or wherever. For me—for a writer, I mean—and I suspect for Joao, too, it's a little different."

"You don't feel the urge to write?"

"Not to *write*," she clarified. "Not the act of picking up a pen and writing on paper. For me, the urge is *storytelling*. It happens in my mind, not my hand. I catch my thoughts wandering, and suddenly I've invented some dark new world filled with twisted characters. *I'm* not doing anything; I'm not even an active participant. The stories come to me by force, like an assault." She pressed the pads of her fingers against her temples. "I feel like I'm going crazy at times. It's a struggle to stay present and not get lost in the worlds they want me to make. The only way to exorcise them is to write them down—and of course, I can't. *Don't write, don't draw.*" She swallowed. "So they stay in my mind, whispering to me, trapped in there."

She hunched forward over the lantern like the light was a rescue beacon against whatever cruel forces were clawing inside her skull.

I hesitated. I hadn't realized before how hard on Kylie all this was. Slowly, I sank next to her and placed a hand on her knee. "You should have said something."

She sucked in a deep breath and let it out with a shudder. "You have your own demons."

"It isn't a suffering competition, okay? I didn't know it was this hard for you. That the curse works differently on writers." I squeezed her knee. "It was the same for our father. As soon as the dementia started, his mind didn't stand a chance. The stories beat down the gate. Invaded his innermost kingdoms." I dug my fingers harder into her knee. "I won't let that happen to you."

We listened to the sounds of the wind. I was grateful for the tent's meager shelter, holding off the storm, holding back darker things.

I squeezed her knee again. "Hey, Kylie?"

"Yeah?"

"Don't write."

A lopsided grin broke the tight set of her mouth. "Don't draw."

CHAPTER FIFTEEN

—

```
THE SANDMAN KILLER
© 1943 Sigil Pictures

BEGIN FLASHBACK:


A STRANGE SKY full of lightning but no
rain—heat lightning. YOUNG VAUGHN ELLIS,
age 8, lies unconscious under a charred tree
struck just prior. SMOKE comes off his body.
His LITTLE FINGER twitches. As if responding,
the smoke coils.


END FLASHBACK.
```

—

AS EVENING TURNED into night, the storm showed no sign of lessening. Kylie and I burrowed into our sleeping bags, gnawing on granola bars for dinner. We'd previously brought all our supplies into the tent, so Rafe had nothing to eat in the Range Rover, and no equipment except his flashlight and phone. *Should I take him some food?*

No, I reasoned. Rafe was capable of fending for himself. A man who'd once let the Decaylings drag him to the bottom of Fathom Lake and nibble on his flesh could go a few hours without a snack.

Eventually, Kylie yawned and nodded off to the repetitive drone of the rain. She started snoring. I tried to sleep but just kept staring at the nylon ceiling, thinking of crescent moons. Eventually, I gave up with a groan and sat up. I dragged over my purse.

Might as well do the work for Patrick Kane.

As I dug for my journal, *Exit, Nebraska* fell out, too. For a moment I imagined the rubber band breaking, my secret spilling out.

I glanced at Kylie. The pencil lines of my father's drawing made me *me*. That single sheet of paper forever separated me from my sister.

If I wasn't even human, how could I possibly understand her?

I stuffed the book safe back into my bag, then sat cross-legged with my headlight bowed over the journal, open to a blank page. I'd already written down the dates that Patrick Kane would find relevant—birthdays, graduations, significant trips—but he'd asked for memories, too. I tried to put myself in his shoes, wonder what I, as a biographer, would want to know about the late, great Amory Marbury from his daughter's perspective.

When I was fifteen, my father took me to New York to visit his publishing house's offices in the Flatiron Building. He'd been working on a new manuscript that was a departure from his previous novel, which had been criticized by some for being too pedantic, and he felt this new idea was fresh and experimental. I can't recall the exact premise—something about a young female college student's sexual escapades. The publisher didn't want it. They asked for more of his traditional, award-bait books. It was the first time I'd seen my father get violent. He threw a book at a junior publicist.

I groaned, closing the journal over my pen. Thank god that my father was dead and wouldn't care what I wrote about him. The rain was deafening, distracting. I glanced at Kylie, who muttered something unintelligible in her sleep, thrashing in her sleeping bag first one way, then the other, before gradually settling back into deep slumber.

I opened the journal again, touching the pen to the page, forcing myself to keep writing.

His editor came to our hotel suite that night to discuss the incident. They were both drunk and loud enough that I could hear them arguing in the next room. His editor made the case that they'd built a readership on his previous books and that the public wanted the "Marbury" feel. "The industry will die if it only puts out the same old story," my father argued, "and you'll drag me to the grave with you." My father threatened to get the editor fired, even vowing to start his own publishing company. "Fiction isn't paper and cardboard. It sure as hell isn't awards. Fiction is an entire world in one's hand. Unless you understand that, you'll perish."

The rain was still coming down in sheets when I closed the journal. My throat had gone dry. I stared at the plain black cover as though afraid of the words inside.

I had mostly banished the memory, embarrassed that my father had once thrown a book across a conference room table in front of a dozen senior publishing staff. But now the recollection took on a more sinister edge.

An entire world in one's hands.

Rafe's story about Uncle Arnold buzzed in my head. Uncle Arnold had called encyclopedias "the world in your hands" shortly after he'd ousted his boss and taken over the company, playing out a version of a threat my father had once made in real life.

My father had created Uncle Arnold, and yet it had barely occurred to me to wonder how much of those monsters came from my father himself: His desires. His fears. His failures. There was some of my father in Uncle Arnold. There had been some of the vile creature in him, too.

I buried myself in my sleeping bag and switched off the headlamp.

As I drifted in and out of consciousness, I was back in Malice House, in the attic, kneeling before the broken drawer where I'd found *Bedtime Stories for Monsters*. The scattered pages fanned out across the floor. Whispers emerged from the attic eaves. Somewhere below my feet, a slithering sound rumbled. A stack of books fell off a cardboard box, and I spun, but no one was there.

A smell reached me—*smoke.*

Smoke. Smoke everywhere. Clouding my eyes. Choking me.

I hadn't realized that I'd fallen asleep until I felt a hand on my shoulder, shaking me, and I jerked awake.

———

I gave a startled cry as the remnants of my dream fled from my mind like a colony of rats when the light turns on.

"Haven." Rafe leaned over me in the dark tent, his voice a loud whisper. "You were dreaming. You're safe."

I blinked hard, taking in the unfamiliar sloping nylon walls with blank confusion before it all came back to me.

I'm not in Malice House. Malice House is gone.

I sat up, pressing a hand to the base of my throat. Kylie was still asleep, curled away from us in her sleeping bag like a pill bug. The clock on my phone told me it was nearly one in the morning.

"Sorry," I choked out, massaging my throat. "I was . . . It was another nightmare."

Rafe looked concerned but didn't ask for details. He gestured to the open tent flap behind him, which was whipping in the wind. It was pitch-black out there. The rain still fell in heavy sheets.

"Listen," he said. "There's someone nosing around Joao's campsite."

I went rigid. "You saw someone?"

"The Range Rover is facing that direction. I saw a flashlight beam bouncing that way a few minutes ago. Whoever held it was moving fast, maybe even running. They went straight to the crime scene and shone the light around for a while like they were looking for something."

I reached for my hair tie, pulling the wavy mess off my face. "What did they look like?"

"I couldn't make out much. Only that they were wearing a raincoat."

"They're still there?"

"I don't know. They turned their flashlight off, and I waited a while to see if anyone came back by the Range Rover."

I wriggled out of my sleeping bag as I reached for my own flashlight. "We have to see who it is. It could be the person who wanted to see Joao's body—the other person investigating his murder."

"It could be the *murderer*," Rafe countered.

"I didn't think the killer walked on two feet."

"Darling, with all due respect, you don't know the first thing about monsters. And frankly, neither do I. Not the ones outside of Malice."

He was right, but remaining in the tent wasn't a risk we could take. This could be our only chance. I leaned over to shake Kylie awake. She grumbled something inaudible, then jerked alert, shooting up to a seated position with a wild-eyed look.

"Haven?" Her voice was pitched high. "Fuck. I was dreaming—"

"Listen, Kylie, we have to go back to Joao's campsite. Rafe saw someone there."

Her eyes were still unfocused from sleep. It took her a moment to register what I'd said. She dragged her hand over her hair and said, "Someone's out there?"

I was already tugging on my shoes. "We're going to find out who it is."

"It's pouring!"

"You can stay here if you want." I finished lacing up my sneakers.

"No, no. I'm coming." She wriggled out of her sleeping bag and reached for her overnight bag with a disoriented hand.

We threw on rain gear and plunged back into the storm. What had been a downpour before was now practically a hurricane. Wind assaulted my body hard enough to nearly knock me back into Kylie. In the dark, clouds melded with shadows. Horizontal rain stung my eyes.

"This is crazy!" Kylie yelled.

I could barely hear her. I cupped my hands to shout in her ear. "Don't turn on your flashlight unless it's an emergency!"

Kylie and Rafe were only shadowy outlines before me as we jogged past the orange-and-white barrels. The battering rain drowned out the sounds of our feet, of everything. The rain and stinging sand blinded me. I paused and doubled over against the wind, trying to push grime out of my eyes.

When I looked up again, a beam of light to my left caught my attention. A flashlight beam in the distance. After another second, it shut off.

I sucked in a tight breath.

"Hey!" I shouted to Kylie and Rafe. Except—there was no sign of them. I jogged forward a few steps, but they must have been too far ahead to hear.

I paced tightly, caught in indecision. By the time I ran and found Kylie and Rafe, whoever was out in the desert could have gone anywhere. Unless the mystery person turned their flashlight back on, I'd have no idea which direction they'd gone.

"Damn it!" I said aloud.

Gathering Kylie and Rafe wasn't a risk I could take. Turning away from Joao's campsite, I made my way down into the wash, which had transformed into a stream bed. Six inches of rapidly flowing runoff swept through the shallow ravine. The water soaked my shoes immediately, and I made my way across with squelchy steps. The wet mud formed a powerful suction, trying to pull me down. When I reached the other side of the wash and scrambled out, getting sand all over my hands, I started jogging out into the dark desert, eyes pinned to the area where I'd last seen the beam.

Joshua trees rose like looming specters. Scrubby bushes and prickly pears snagged at my clothes. My pulse thundered in my ears, rivaling the wind's ferocity. My mouth felt dry despite the rain.

Rafe could be right. I could be out here with a murderer.

I stopped and bent over, bracing my hands on my knees, trying to get my bearings. Lightning burst overhead, giving me a brief glimpse of the desert, a split-second snapshot of vegetation blowing violently in the rain.

And something else. A shape moving in the night.

The lightning's illumination had been only a blink—but a glowing afterimage imprinted on my retinas. The shape had been big, maybe six feet tall. It had moved slowly, either floating or slithering. Definitely not moving like a person.

My chest shrank. My whole body wanted to fold itself up, hide. The lightning flash had been so fast that I couldn't be certain of anything. It *could* have been a person. It could have been a monster. It could have simply been one of the fucked-up-looking Joshua trees blowing in the wind.

But the thought persisted: *It wasn't one of mine.*

I knew my monsters. Here, in the desert, I craved *my* monsters. Not something unknown, something I didn't know how to deal with . . .

I spun back toward the campground, only to realize I had no idea which direction the campground was anymore.

"Fuck!" I barked.

What if I couldn't find my way back? The water in the wash was only going to keep rising, and if I waited too long, I could get swept up in a flash flood. . . .

Lightning flashed again, and I briefly glimpsed another shape against the light-colored sand. Smaller this time, not moving. It was too solid to be a bush, too angular to be a boulder. Just the right size for a person hunched over from the storm.

"Hey!" I charged forward as the lightning ended and plunged the world back into blackness. Fumbling for my flashlight, I switched it on, swinging the beam around. As my feet splashed through puddles, the light finally fell on the figure.

I stopped short.

They were lying on the sand, curled in the fetal position.

My feet refused to move. A terrible premonition shrouded me. The person was wearing a rain jacket and dark pants, their back to me. The upper portion of their body was submerged a few inches in a puddle.

Forcing myself forward, I approached the puddle. My heart was thrashing. I could barely catch my breath. Any second, they might jump up. It could be a trick. It could be a *monster*.

I stopped a few feet away, my flashlight still fixed on the figure.

Waiting for movement. Waiting to see the rise and fall of breath. Waiting for a sign of life from the thin, exposed hand.

Moments passed. No movement.

Swallowing my fear, I crouched slowly and reached out a trembling hand. I touched the figure's shoulder through their rain jacket. *Thin. Practically skin and bones.*

I shook them a few times.

"Hey, you okay?"

But I already knew. I'd seen dead bodies before. The person's head, turned away from me, was halfway under water. That wasn't how a living body lay.

Slowly, I rolled the body onto its back. When I shone the flashlight on the person's face, I sucked in a breath.

I know those eyes. I know that mouth.

I turned and dry-heaved into the sand.

CHAPTER SIXTEEN

———

PURGATORY'S DOOR
© 1955 Sigil Pictures

DETECTIVE NICK DRAM
Look, buddy, I don't want trouble.
I'm just looking for information on
the girl.

BANJAX
If you're looking into that dead
girl, trouble is what you'll find.
Now order a pint or get the hell
out.

The intertwining lines of the tattoos on his
forearms twist like coiling snakes.

DETECTIVE NICK DRAM
Hell, huh? Bet you can tell me all
about it, given that's where and
all the other devils around this
city crawled out of.

———

NANETTE FIELDS.

As the stinging rain assaulted me from a nearly horizontal direction, my mind churned with unanswerable questions.

What was Nanette doing *here*? My brain couldn't make sense of it. Nanette belonged in another world, on a soundstage, not drowned in a freak storm a hundred miles from Los Angeles.

Wiping rain out of my face, I fought the urge to panic.

Did she get lost? Hit her head?

With shaking hands, I pushed her rain-jacket hood back from where it obscured the upper portion of her face. Her eyes were open. They already had the glassy sheen of death to them, like two clouded marbles, and were caked with sand in a way that made my own itch.

There was no sign of trauma to her head, and her lips weren't blue. *So she probably didn't drown.* Moving fast, I unzipped her rain jacket down over her black top. There was no blood. Not soaking into the puddle, not staining her shirt. I shone the flashlight over her body in a desperate attempt to figure out what had killed her. Even so, the wind and stinging sand made it impossible to see much. I patted the contours of her chest, looking for bullet holes. There were rips in her shirt I hadn't noticed before. I shifted my position to block the wind as I leaned close to her body.

Up close, it became clear that they weren't bullet holes.

They were burn marks.

A pain hollowed out my stomach. Moving like I was underwater, I slowly peeled her shirt over her chest and shone my flashlight on her bra and pale skin.

Burn marks carved a crescent moon into the left side of her rib cage and another into the right, overlapping near their points.

Feeling sick, I stared at the brand.

The same as Joao . . .

I glanced over my shoulder, searching the dark for movement. Fumbling in my pocket, I pulled out my phone, praying that it hadn't gotten too wet. I had a brief moment of triumph when it turned on. I snapped a photo of Nanette's wounds, then stuffed my phone deep in my bra, where it had the best chance of staying dry. I started digging through her pockets. A gas receipt. A cough-drop wrapper. *Nothing useful.*

Lightning lit up the sky again, and I tossed my head up. There, to the far left—had that been the shape again?

Fear gripped me like a claw around my ankle. A voice inside my head urged me to *run, run.* Instead, I thrust a hand into Nanette's other pocket and came back with a damp card—a business card? Thunder crashed overhead, and I pushed myself to my feet, stuffing the business card into my bra next to the phone.

Get the fuck out of here.

I blinked into the rain. The storm and dark night obscured any indication of which way the campground was. Any footprints I'd made had either been blown or washed away. With the sand in my eyes, I could be ten feet from our car and have no idea. This was how people died on Mount Everest mere steps from their tent.

I spun, then spun again.

A creeping memory climbed into my head of running through the woods outside of Malice House, trying to get to Rafe's house only to find that no matter which direction I went, it was the wrong direction. But this wasn't the Witch of Went bending reality again, only the force of nature.

My flashlight made a brave attempt to light my way, but the beam penetrated just a few feet. Hunching in my rain jacket, I stumbled through the floodwaters in a random direction, hoping for a familiar landmark that could lead me back to the campground. My teeth were chattering in my head like a Halloween skeleton. All I could see in my mind's eye was Nanette's body. The brand.

"Help!" I shouted, but the wind ate my words. Lightning flashed again, and I went still. I tried to take a mental photograph of the landscape it had briefly illuminated: Vegetation bent under the wind. Heavy clouds overhead. A dark patch of sand.

But the sand might not be sand at all—it could be the wash. And our tent was just on the other side.

Pushing through the storm, every step felt like effort. I started to question again if I was lost, but the next step, my foot fell a little too far. I started to stumble forward but managed to catch myself before I tumbled down an incline. My feet splashed into swiftly moving water.

It *was* the wash.

Our tent would be just beyond, but what had been ankle-deep water ten minutes ago was now a fully raging river. Water crested the banks around me. In the churning white rapids, I saw shapes floating: tree branches, uprooted bushes.

What choice did I have? Taking a deep breath, I risked another step into the river. The current was powerful. I had to brace myself so as not to be swept away like the broken logs shooting past me. Holding out my hands for balance, I waded in up to my knees. Then, carefully, to my hips. How much deeper could it get?

A gust of wind tried to knock me down, and I shrieked and windmilled my arms, narrowly maintaining my balance. I fixed my flashlight beam on a spot on the other side of the wash—a scrubby bush that hadn't been uprooted. With shuffling little steps, I inched deeper into the water. Soon, it was up to my waist. I pressed one hand to my bra, reassuring myself of my phone's presence.

Step by step. Step by step.

The ground below me began to shift upward—I'd passed the deepest section. Continuing to push through the water, I started the climb up the other side of the wash. The scrubby bush was only about four feet away, and I reached out a hand toward it.

Something heavy slammed into me from the current. It took me a split second to figure it out—a log. It had happened so fast, coming out of the dark water. There was nothing I could do. I was falling. Pitching backward. That terrible topsy-turvy feeling of lost balance struck me, and I was down, I was in, the water over my head—

Two hands grabbed my shoulders.

Someone dragged me out of the current with effortless strength, helping me partway up onto the higher bank. Floodwater rushed up my throat, erupting in a coughing fit. I clawed my fingers into the dirt, clinging to the safety of the higher bank on the other side.

"Are you hurt?" Rafe asked, pulling me up by my arm to stare at my face.

I shook my head, though my lungs burned and my whole body was shaking. I pushed myself up onto my knees, then grabbed his shoulder, needing the connection, like he was my anchor to reality.

"Nanette . . ." My breath was shaky. "She's . . . there. Dead . . ."

"I'm getting you out of here."

He dragged me to my feet. When I stumbled, he scooped me up in his arms like I weighed no more than a child. I slid my hands around the back of his neck, pressing my face into his shoulder.

I heard a tent flap unzipping, and then Kylie's worried voice. "*Jesus*, Haven! We looked everywhere for you! Rafe, put her on her sleeping bag."

As soon as I was down, Kylie attacked me with towels, cocooning me in them. She pressed a bottle of water into my hands. I took a shaky sip.

"I . . . I saw someone in the desert on the other side of the wash," I stammered when I was finally able to speak. "You two were too far ahead, so I went on my own. I got lost, but . . ." My throat ached, but I forced out the words. "I found Nanette. She's dead. Look at this." I snaked an unsteady hand into my bra and took out the phone, scrolling through the photos and then shoving it at Kylie.

Her eyes went wide when she realized what was in the photo. Rafe, looking over her shoulder, grunted.

"The same brand as Joao?" Kylie asked.

I nodded. "There were no other marks on her that I could see."

"It's the fucking Biblical flood out there," Kylie said, motioning to the storm raging beyond the tent. "How did someone light enough of a fire to heat up a brand? That's impossible."

"Yes, exactly," I said. "No *person* did this."

She went deathly quiet. "Did you see anything else out there?"

I hesitated, remembering the oddly moving shape I'd seen in that flash of lightning. "I'm not sure. Maybe. It was too dark."

The wind blew its steady chorus around us. Shivering, I realized I needed to get out of my wet clothes. My sense of modesty had died in the wash, and I began stripping. When I unhooked my bra, the business card fell out. Kylie picked it up while I tugged on a dry sweatshirt.

"What's this?" she asked.

"It was in Nanette's pocket."

Kylie picked at the damp cardboard with her fingernail, and to my surprise, unfolded what I'd thought was a business card into a bookmark. As soon as she looked at it, her eyes went wide.

"Fuck me," she muttered.

I grabbed the damp bookmark. It read *Books: Your Shield Against Unwanted Conversation*. Beneath the text was the logo for Lundie Bay Books.

Kylie jabbed a finger toward the bookmark and demanded, "Why the hell does Nanette Fields have a bookmark from *that* place?"

No one produced an answer for that.

I pressed my hand against my forehead, kneading the skin. "Okay. Okay. First things first, she's dead, and it wasn't an accident." I gave a full-body shiver at the memory of finding her. "Should we report the body?"

"We're not reporting the body," Rafe said firmly. "What are you going to tell them, that you were going for a night walk in a record flood? You'll be the prime suspect. Especially when they search your name and all the unsolved deaths in Lundie Bay turn up. That detective who keeps calling you? Oh, he'll love to see your name pop up again. And what if Uncle Arnold is tracking police records for you?"

"So, then *what*?" Kylie asked. "We pack up and run?"

I numbly stared down at the bookmark. "There were traffic cameras on the road into the campground. They'll have a video of our rental-car license plate. It'll look suspicious if we leave at three in the morning and a murder victim is found the next day." I drew my knees up to my chest, coming to a decision. "We wait until the morning, pretend that we know nothing when the body is found and the police show up."

I felt confident that my footprints in the desert couldn't be traced back to me. The rain and wind would take care of that. And other than the murderer, we'd been the only ones crazy enough to be out during the storm, so there was slim chance anyone had seen us.

"So we're supposed to stay here like sitting ducks with some kind of demonic killer out there?" Kylie asked.

Rafe pulled out a bottle of whiskey from our grocery bag. He twisted off the cap and offered her the bottle. "Still want me to sleep in the car?"

Kylie gave him a cold glare as she swiped the bottle and took a swig, grimacing at the taste. She wiped her mouth. "You can stay, Harbinger. But try anything and there will be two murder victims in the morning."

We climbed into sleeping bags and tried to sleep, but sleep didn't want to come. I toyed with the bookmark, running through every scenario I could think of as to how Nanette was involved with the Ink Drinkers from that bookstore.

I don't know how long the three of us lay awake listening to the wind, waiting to rise to a world full of new questions.

CHAPTER SEVENTEEN

WINTER OF THE WICKED
© 1947 Sigil Pictures

FARM WIFE
Lord be our shelter. Lord be our
strength. Lord forgive us for the
sins that have so turned us from
thy glory and plunged us into
wickedness.

She clings to her two daughters in shocked
terror as their horse and three sheep eat
flesh from dead Farm Husband's LEG.

CLOSE ON a sheep's bloodshot eye as it turns
to look at the women.

I WOKE TO a ringing phone.

Groggy, I blinked at the sunlight filtering in through the tent dome. I hunted for my phone and checked the caller name, afraid it was the Lundie Bay detective again. To my relief, it wasn't.

I held the phone to my ear. "Rob?"

"I got it."

I glanced at Rafe, who was sound asleep to my right, and Kylie to my left, who was starting to stir awake, grumbling about the early morning as she buried herself further in her sleeping bag.

As I sat up, the ghosts from last night retreated into the shadows. The wind was gone now, no more pelting rain on the tent. "Got what?"

"*The Sandman Killer.* One of the Sigil Pictures film reels." Rob's voice practically danced its way across time and space into my ear. "Nanette thought the films would be hard to find—*ha!* Not for SlasherDasher."

Sitting up fully, I shifted in my sleeping bag, pushing back my messy hair. "You got it through the art-house guy?"

"His daughter called a cousin, who found it in her father's storage unit in Florida. I'll have it in a few days. It's being delivered."

It was a desperately needed win after the night I'd had. Nanette had been the one to tell us about the movie, so it could be the very thing to unlock the mystery of why she'd followed us to the desert and what connected her to Joao Acosta—and to Lundie Bay.

My stomach twisted at the thought of Nanette. "Rob, I need to tell you something—"

A sudden loud blip of a siren made me nearly drop the phone. Kylie murmured something and cracked her eyes open, deep frown lines between her eyebrows.

She grimaced. "The police. Fantastic."

"Rob, I'll call you later," I mumbled.

He tried to say more, but I hung up and tossed the phone on my sleeping bag.

The siren again blipped, and we heard car doors slamming. Rafe still slumbered to my right as though not even police sirens were a reason to get up.

I shoved him hard.

"Rafe. *Up.*" When he groaned and rolled over, I shoved him again. "The police are here."

Kylie looked like the bottle of whiskey had punched her in the face. She pulled her sleeping bag around her shoulders as though the cocoon could protect her from what was coming. "Someone must have found Nanette's body," she said.

Rafe finally got up, running his hands over his scalp. He'd slept in only his boxers, so his extremely attractive torso was on full display. It was entirely unfair—I doubted Rafe had worked out a day in his life, yet he had a body like that.

He should thank me for that, I thought. *I made him.*

Kylie groaned. "Put on a shirt, ew."

Any straight woman would be hard-pressed not to admire Rafe's body, but Kylie was determined to hate him, and for good reason. Rafe cocked a grin and tugged a gray shirt over his head, then started to pull on jeans.

I crawled across the small space and started to unzip the tent flap.

The outside world was a sharp contrast from the one we'd left the night before. The decimating storm had given way to clear skies. Puddles drowned most of the campground, and the water level in the wash had diminished to only ankle-deep. Washed-out vegetation littered the ground. Shifting sands had changed the topography, creating new ditches.

Four police cars sat at the BLM campground entrance. A small crowd of campers gathered around the officers, and I wasn't sure who exactly was questioning who.

As we stood beneath the morning sun, staring at the police circus, Cassandra walked by us in a lacy crop top while filming on her phone.

"This is *beyond*, you guys. I am *freaked*. Tommy and I woke up to the police in our campground because, get this, there's been *a murder*. Okay, let me start at the beginning. There was a storm last night. . . . Now, this is going to be part one of a two-part series, so hit that Subscribe button to make sure you don't miss the ending. You guys are *not* going to want to miss the ending, trust me. . . ."

She stopped in the middle of the gravel road by our site, looked down at her phone, cursed, and then fiddled with it. Making her eyes big for the camera, she started a second take. "This is *beyond*, you guys. . . ."

I pivoted sharply toward Kylie and Rafe. "Listen, Rob called this morning. He has *The Sandman Killer*. We need to get out of here and back to LA."

Kylie's eyes shifted to something behind me. "I'm not sure it's our choice if we can leave."

Two male cops were going around the campground loops, waking up any campers still in their tents and instructing them to join the gathered group. The younger of the two, a baby-faced Black guy who looked about sixteen, signaled to us and walked over with a notepad in hand.

"Hey there. I'm Officer Michaels. We need everyone to move to the campground entrance where the police cars are parked. It's important no one leaves the premises."

"What's happened?" I asked.

"Sergeant Castellucci is going to address all the campers in a few minutes. First, is everyone in your party here? Not missing anyone?"

We shook our heads. The officer checked our false IDs, jotting down our fake names in his notebook, and pointed his pen toward the crowd around the cop cars. "Head that way, please."

Rafe pressed a hand to my back and guided me toward the gathered crowd. "They have no way to identify Nanette's body this fast," he reassured me in a whisper. "And they don't have our real names. There's no way to connect us to her."

We joined the rear of the crowd. Glancing back, I saw Officer Michaels knock on Tree Pose's van. She swung open the door, exchanged a few words with him, and immediately looked troubled. Her head spun toward the crowd—and latched onto me.

I quickly looked away. Was she recalling my questions yesterday about Joao's murder?

The older police officer, a sun-worn Italian man with a graying mustache, climbed onto a wooden bench and raised his hands. "Everyone, please quiet down and listen closely. I'm Sergeant Castellucci. Most of you have already heard, but early this morning, a Bureau of Land Management officer found a body in the desert while evaluating damage from the storm. We're going to need to speak with each of you in small groups. Please think hard about anything unusual you might have seen or heard yesterday. It's very important we know if anyone from your party is missing—"

"Who was it?" a woman from the crowd interrupted. "How did they die?"

"We aren't at liberty to discuss details of the case yet. However—"

The officer who'd taken our names approached the sergeant with his notepad and exchanged a few words. The sergeant nodded and stood back up on the bench. "Officer Michaels just let me know that no groups have thus far reported a missing person. That means it might have been a solo camper or a lost hiker from the national park. Please return to your sites. Remain there until an officer tells you it's okay to leave. Do not leave without our express permission."

The sergeant began answering a few more questions from the crowd. My head felt fuzzy, like a radio station gone to static. The BLM campground had no formal registry, so the traffic cameras would be the only way to verify who'd entered. Would they have captured Nanette's car? A quick look around the campground told me most vehicles had California plates—was one of them Nanette's?

"Terrible, isn't it? And to think, the second death in just over a week." I turned to find Tree Pose sidling up behind me. She wore yoga pants with a light sweater thrown on top, her graying hair swept into a loose ponytail. She folded her arms and clicked her tongue.

Carefully, I said, "Shocking."

She slid her gaze among the crowd and said steadily, "A branch fell on my van around one in the morning. I went outside to check for damage." Her eyes cut sharply to me. "I saw you and your male friend outside."

I told myself to remain calm. Looking flustered would only make me seem guilty. Plunging my hand into my jacket pocket, squeezing a random pen there for reassurance, I said, "I had to pee. Couldn't hold it forever."

"You looked completely soaked."

"Yeah, well . . . it was a crazy storm."

She eyed me for a while, and my heart began to race. The last thing I needed was for the police to know that I'd been outside in the middle of the night and asking around about Joao's murder.

Finally, the woman let out a deep sigh. "Scary to think we both could have been outside with a killer."

I relaxed a little. "What makes you think it was murder? Couldn't the victim just have gotten lost and drowned?"

She tilted her head like I should know better. A mirthless smile played at her lips. "That family with the teenagers? The father saw the body before they loaded it into the ambulance. Seems like it had the same wounds as the one found before."

I pressed a hand to my chest in feigned surprise. "You're serious?"

She watched me closely, then, after a moment, scratched her nose. "The police will want us all out of here as soon as they've taken our statements. You and your friends—where will you go?"

Kylie came out of the tent just then, loaded down with two canvas bags. "Haven, I'm not packing up all your shit."

Relieved, I took the opportunity to move backward toward our tent. I held out my hands helplessly toward Tree Pose. "Good luck. Maybe some other campgrounds have openings."

I could feel her eyes on me as I ducked back into our tent. Once I was away from prying eyes, I was pulled into the whirlwind of rolling up sleeping bags, stuffing wet clothes into plastic ziplock bags, hunting up all our protein bar wrappers to throw away.

As Rafe started dismantling the tent, Officer Michaels and Sergeant Castellucci came to our site. They took a quick inventory of our belongings, and then the sergeant pointed to the Range Rover. "This your vehicle?"

Rafe finished pulling up a tent stake, then sauntered over with the sharp stake still in hand, clutched backward in his fist like a shiv.

"It's a rental," he barked. "My name's on the paperwork."

The police officer gave a pointed look at the stake in his hand.

"Right, so you already gave my partner your names. Want to tell me a bit more about how you all know each other and what brought you to Joshua Tree?"

Rafe started to speak, but I stepped in before he provoked them further.

"We're old friends," I interjected. "From up near Seattle. My father recently passed away and I needed to get away for a while. I'd never been to southern California."

The sergeant wrote this down in his notebook. "To confirm, it's only the three of you?"

"That's correct."

"And did any of you see anything unusual yesterday or last night? Did you leave your tent at all?"

Over his shoulder, I saw Tree Pose shaking wet sand out of her sneakers by her fire ring, watching us.

I said, "I got up around one a.m. to go to the bathroom. It was raining hard, so I just went a few feet from the tent. I know we aren't supposed to do that, but the wash was overflowing. . . . Anyway, that's it. We couldn't exactly go anywhere with the storm, so we just spent time in the tent, finished off a bottle of whiskey." I paused. "Do you think this death was an accident?"

Kylie slid me a questioning look but said nothing.

Sergeant Castellucci didn't immediately acknowledge my question. He finished writing in his notebook and then closed it. "We have photos of your IDs and your contact information. You're free to go, but we'll need you to stay in the area for the next few days in case more questions come up."

I hesitated. "We were going to head to LA. Today, actually."

"That should be fine. Just be sure to remain in the state, Miss—"

A female officer from one of the other cars called him over to speak to the family with teenagers, and the sergeant gave us a nod and left.

Shortly thereafter, we threw our bags into the Range Rover and left Joshua Tree far behind.

CHAPTER EIGHTEEN

———

———

AFTER AN EXHAUSTING return drive to Rob's house, I stood in the shower for an extravagantly long time, trying to scour off the events of the past twenty-four hours. The memory of nearly drowning had a stranglehold on me, and I pressed my forehead against the tiles, feeling the signs of a coming panic attack.

Nanette's body. The flooded wash. Something out there . . .

Returning to the city had done little to ease my nerves. The one benefit of the desert had been that there were few places for danger to hide; returning here, I immediately felt claustrophobic from the tightly packed buildings, the traffic, the throngs of relentlessly moving people that never seemed to sit still. They were always jogging, driving, multitasking. The constant activity made me feel unmoored, like I might as well have been back in the wash, the water level rising, unable to remain rooted. The city was going to sweep me away.

Kylie found me in my bedroom after I'd cleaned up. She settled onto the foot of the bed with two steaming mugs of raspberry tea and passed me one. "How are you holding up?"

Like shit. I stared into my mug. "I'm fine."

She motioned with her own mug toward the wax dummies, which I'd draped three towels over. "What, you don't like creepy life-sized figurines watching your every move?" Then she held up her phone. "I wanted to let you know that Patrick Kane got back to me with a meeting time. He's going to fly in Wednesday and wants to meet with us Monday afternoon. I suggested a café in West Hollywood."

I nodded distractedly, glancing at the notebook on the bedside table.

She noticed the notebook. "How's it been going? Writing down the memories and things he wanted?"

"Not great," I admitted, opening the notebook to the latest entry. "It isn't easy trying to turn a formerly living, breathing person into a series of crossed *t*'s and dotted *i*'s. I'm not a writer like he was. Like you are."

"Rob seems to think you're a good recapper."

"That's different. Recapping is describing a story that someone else—someone much more gifted at storytelling—already created."

She lifted a shoulder as she took a sip of tea. "So, pretend that's what you're doing. You're recapping the life of Amory Marbury. Imagine that it's a movie you saw, only one that stretched out for a lifetime."

I gave her a half-hearted smile until I noticed how she was craning her neck, trying to read the entry.

I sighed but not unkindly, closing the notebook. "Go ahead. Ask."

Her eyebrows rose, confused.

"About our dad. Whatever you want to know, I'll tell you." She clearly wasn't going to give this up, and after everything we'd been through, including Rafe's aggression, she probably deserved answers.

A light sprang into her eyes. She tucked one foot underneath her and leaned forward like we were at a middle school sleepover. "Why didn't he ever remarry? Why all the affairs?"

I bristled, already regretting my offer. Kylie's question was a sticky one, given that I'd never actually had a mother. I'd just been some scribbles in a cave. Everything Kylie had read about Clara Marbury in Amory's journals was a complete fabrication.

I stuck to something simple. "He barely knew my mother. They eloped when he found out he'd gotten her pregnant, and she died soon after I was born. Theirs wasn't some great love story. Basically, he wasn't good with commitment."

My answer hadn't put her off. She pressed, "But he almost married Adelaide Martin?"

"They never actually talked about marriage, at least not that I heard of. Adelaide was a lot like him—brilliant, selfish, not a fan of commitment."

Kylie touched her lips together like she wasn't sure how to frame what she wanted to say next. Finally, she asked, "Did he ever mention my mother? Billie Nance?"

I winced, not wanting to disappoint her. "That would have been when I was just four or five years old. I don't remember anything from back then."

"But he never spoke of her later?"

Softly, I said, "Kylie, he slept with a *lot* of women. From what I gather, it was just a one-night thing with your mom." I shook my head. "He wouldn't have told a kindergartner about that. I'm sorry."

Her face fell, though she tried to hide it with a series of positive nods. She reached over and plucked out the Lundie Bay bookmark, which I'd wedged between the notebook pages. Studying it while she took a long sip of tea, she suddenly asked, "What if Nanette met the Ink Drinkers through Adelaide Martin? Nanette and Adelaide were working together on the *Tulip Carol* production, right? Adelaide based the Chicago house in her novel on Malice House, so what if Nanette went there as part of the script doctoring? Met Catherine and Jonathan Tybee at the bookstore? Maybe Adelaide even introduced them?"

It was an interesting idea. I held out my hand, and she gave me the bookmark back. I examined it again, turning it back and front. Some of the print had rubbed off, but the bookstore logo was mostly intact, as well as the pithy saying.

"If Nanette had been to my father's house," I said, "wouldn't she have said something when she met us?"

Kylie pursed her lips. "Not if she was involved."

I thought through the possibility, but it just didn't make sense. "None of the Ink Drinkers ever mentioned other literary salon members. They never said anything about Los Angeles or the film industry. I just don't see the connection."

Kylie massaged her chin, thinking. "So, what, Nanette just happened to be vacationing in Lundie Bay and dropped by the bookstore? The same store whose owners tried to kill us?"

An idea struck me. "What if Nanette didn't go to Lundie Bay Books? What if someone from Lundie Bay came to *her*?"

Kylie blinked slowly. Then did it again. At last, she said, quietly, "Uncle Arnold?"

It was a possibility I should have considered sooner. Ever since landing back in the United States, I'd had the unsettling sense of being followed. Definitely in Joshua Tree. And someone had been watching us at the Gemini Productions soundstage, I felt sure of it now.

The idea left me clammy, feeling watched even with the towels over the wax dummies' heads.

"How?" she asked. "Uncle Arnold had no way of knowing you were in Los Angeles. We used false names in all our travel documents."

"Maybe something else brought Uncle Arnold to Los Angeles." I paused, rubbing the bookmark between my fingers. "What if he read the *Hollywooder* article, too? You heard what Rob said—it was a small cultural obsession back in November. That's right when Uncle Arnold would have been searching for answers, clues about curses. Nanette was quoted in the article. Uncle Arnold might have seen that and gone to her for answers, just like we did."

"And compelled her?" Kylie asked.

"Why else would a none-too-fit seventy-year-old woman follow us into the desert during a storm?"

When we'd spoken to Nanette at the Gemini Entertainment studios, she hadn't seemed glassy-eyed and hypnotized. So Uncle Arnold might have come to her later—she might have mentioned Amory Marbury's daughters having recently approached her with similar questions. . . .

Uncle Arnold might not have needed to hunt me down at all, I realized. I might have left a perfect bread-crumb trail for him without even knowing it.

And after Rafe's story, I feared more than ever just how intertwined this beast was with my family. With my father. With me.

When I eventually felt human enough to emerge from my bedroom, I found Rob home from work, pouring himself a generous glass of Malbec. As soon as he saw me, he squeaked and dove into his messenger bag, coming out with a large, beat-up reel case.

"What's this?"

"This is it," he said, eyes gleaming. "*The Sandman Killer*. It was delivered today to my office."

Tyler went to the pantry and came out with a plastic jar of popcorn kernels. He gave it a jiggle with a questioning lift of his eyebrow.

"I'll get Kylie," I said.

We reconvened ten minutes later in the basement movie theater, where Tyler had rolled in the popcorn cart, which was popping away beneath its red-and-white awning. As we entered he handed us each a bag.

Kylie looked down skeptically at her popcorn. "Really?"

Rob swooped in, taking a bag for himself. He gave a self-deprecating little laugh. "It's something of a superstition. This theater had a lot of issues when it was being built. And given the movies we play down here, well, you can forgive us for coming up with a fun little tradition to ward off evil energy." He popped a piece into his mouth. "Besides, it's vegan movie theater butter. One of the few things I can eat on this fucking diet."

Being back in the theater made my skin crawl, remembering the first time we'd been here in masks, unsure if we'd been kidnapped or not. And then there was my extreme reaction to the *Stitches* sequel.

"It's one of the original reels from 1943," Rob said as he unlatched the box with a theatrical air, like he was unveiling King Tut's tomb. "The movie was never rerecorded onto VHS, or DVD, or made digital. Tyler, help me get it onto the projector."

As they started to ease the ancient reel out of its box, Rob frowned at the rusted metal edge of the reel. "I don't like the look of that. Water damage, I think. Well, let's see if we can get it playing."

They slid the reel onto the projector and began feeding the eight-millimeter film into the machine. It required a fair amount of cursing, but when Tyler switched on the machine, it churned to life. I pivoted in my seat to face the screen, and watched as blank frames flashed like a strobe light. The reel was dirty, and nothing but fuzz and magnified hairs flashed for a few moments before the credits began. The bottom left corner of the film was stained and blurry, but for something roughly eighty years old that had been sitting in a storage unit, the images were surprisingly intact.

Rob clapped with delight and rushed to take his seat next to me. In the row behind me, Kylie leaned forward and whispered in my ear, "I have the creeps already."

The opening credits played over black-and-white images of a snowstorm in what looked like the high Swiss Alps. The orchestral music was gratingly dramatic as it led us through the names of the director, Max Faraday, who fell off a hotel, and the producer, Richard Alton, who'd overdosed. With each name, my stomach dropped further.

The camera zoomed in on a mountain pass, and small cottages appeared, then a little town. Towering over the village was a monumental building made of stone. It cut to a sign that read LUCERNE INSTITUTE OF SLEEP.

Rob leaned over, his breath carrying notes of vegan popcorn butter. "The opening shots were done in the Alps, but the movie was actually filmed in a hotel in Colorado." He pointed his popcorn bag toward the screen.

The film cut to the title card. THE SANDMAN KILLER wavered in white letters before fading away into the snowstorm. Then we were in the interior of the asylum-like institute where a new patient, Agnes, was being admitted by a nurse.

I shifted in my seat, glancing over my shoulder at Kylie. She was slumped down, staring apprehensively at the screen. I couldn't imagine such an old movie would frighten her. It had been made in the 1940s, when the bar for horror was so much lower. They were more slow burn, more psychological. Hitchcock films might as well have been Disney cartoons.

And yet, I felt a strange increase in my heartbeat. I told myself it was a consequence of so recently discovering a dead body—that would shake anybody up.

But still, something felt wrong. I was starting to feel like the protagonist of a movie that opens in black and white and switches to color halfway through. Was this how most people felt? So emotional all the time, unable to separate fiction from reality? People came to Los Angeles to reinvent themselves, but not me. I had no desire to transform if it meant opening myself up to these terrifying rushes of seesaw emotions.

I sank deeper into my seat, shoving popcorn down my throat.

In the movie, the nurse led Agnes, played by a beautiful young carbon copy of Ingrid Bergman, up a concrete staircase to a dormitory floor, where she was checked into a small bedroom. Through the window, the snow blew fiercely, and the pair discussed the possibility of getting cut off during an avalanche. The nurse reassured her they were well stocked, and noted that the doctor would meet with her later that afternoon. Left alone, Agnes explored the institute, where the few other patients appeared warm and friendly, inviting her for a game of gin rummy in the recreation room, but she declined and wandered into an office. There, she was caught by Doctor Vaughn Ellis, the leading sleep researcher.

Far from chastising her for snooping, Doctor Ellis invited Agnes to begin their initial session, where she confessed to having terrible nightmares that bled into her waking life as hallucinations. Doctor Ellis assured her this was a result of insufficient sleep and explained how he'd hook her up to a machine for observation overnight. He was a handsome man—though leaning a little Dr. Strangelove, with intense eyes barely visible behind shaded glasses—and the two seemed to have an instant attraction. When Agnes admitted she had an estranged husband, Doctor Ellis suggested her tense marriage could be part of her sleep psychosis. That night, he stood behind a two-way mirror, watching Agnes as she slept. A melodramatic voice-over told us that the equipment was only for show; Doctor Ellis could, in fact, enter his patients' dreams, and, in walking through their dreamworld thoughts and memories, solve the source of their insomnia.

The movie's pace was painfully slow. Long shots of the snowstorm outside were interspersed with Agnes's nonsensical dreamscape, most of which focused on her abusive husband. Halfway through the movie, an avalanche cut off the institute just as word came through to Doctor Ellis that Agnes's husband was found dead back in England. While the cause of death was suffocation, the police report noted strange burn marks on the body, and Doctor Ellis sketched them on his notepad as the officer described them over the phone.

When it cut to the drawing, Kylie dropped her popcorn and jumped to her feet. "That's it! *Holy shit—that's it!*"

She was right. It was the same symbol that had been branded into both Joao and Nanette—the interlocking crescent moons.

Kylie threw a finger toward the screen, which had cut to another long snowstorm shot. "That sleep doctor killed her husband! He went into his dreams and killed him just like Joao and Nanette were killed!"

"Wait, what are you saying?" Rob asked, twisting around in his seat. "A fictional character is alive and has been for eighty years, killing off your acquaintances?"

Kylie rested her hands on her hips. "I don't know *how*, but *yes*! That's sort of exactly what I'm saying! We know the killer has some kind of paranormal abilities."

"Hang on," I said, feeling shaken by the symbol's appearance. "Nanette had seen this movie and swore she'd never seen the symbol before."

"She was *lying*," Kylie emphasized, now pacing the aisle. "That's why she didn't want to answer any of our questions. She was trying to throw us off track."

"But why?"

"Maybe because she was in on it somehow, probably with her old chums the Ink Drinkers? And it got her killed?"

Kylie had a point; the crescent moons appearing in the film was too uncanny to be a coincidence, and Nanette *had* reacted strangely when I'd shown her my drawing of it.

Was it possible *Uncle Arnold* had shown it to her before?

"Kylie," I said firmly. "Sit. Let's just finish the movie." My voice came out moderately confident, though that was the last thing I felt.

Kylie folded her arms and sat back down, chewing hard on her lip.

On the screen, Doctor Ellis hung up the phone, then slowly tore the drawing of moons into pieces and threw it in the wastepaper bin. When Agnes arrived for their next session, he said nothing about the police call or her dead husband. They continued their sessions in the isolated, cut-off institute. A prying nurse was soon found dead, with the same crescent-moon-shaped wounds, but the snow precluded the police coming to investigate the body. Agnes and Doctor Ellis were trapped with a murderer.

"It's *him*, you idiot," Kylie muttered at the screen. "*He's* the murderer. That guy you're clinging to and falling in love with."

As a third body was found, this time the institute's founder, I was riveted. The image of interlocking crescent moons began to appear everywhere throughout the hotel, in the sun's reflection on the windows, in a puddle of spilled champagne. Reality started to bend in strange ways, almost as if the institute didn't exist at all, and the events of the movie were happening inside Agnes's head while she was dreaming in bed. Just as she began to realize Doctor Ellis was behind it all—

The screen went fuzzy.

A few moments passed, and I hoped it would clear, but it only got worse. The fuzziness turned into blank patches, and the actors' voices grew distorted, the background music warbling off-key. The reel suddenly snapped, and the screen went bright white.

I whirled toward Rob. "The reel . . ."

He was already making his way to the projector. He poked around the machinery and then called Tyler over. The two of them argued quietly over how to fix it.

"Must be the water damage," Rob muttered as he pulled out the metal wheel, holding it up to the light. "Yes, I think it's rust from the reel case that ate through the film. Well, fuck."

I stood up in alarm. "We can't watch the ending?"

Kylie cried, "Agnes was just about to learn he was the killer! Can't you get another copy?"

Rob made a face. "Do you have *any* appreciation for the lengths I went to for *this* one?"

Tyler offered him more popcorn, but he waved it away with a grimace.

Kylie let out a long breath. "Well, we saw enough to know the movie is definitely connected to the recent murders."

"Yes, but we don't know *how* Doctor Ellis killed his victims," I pointed out. "Or is maybe still killing them. It has something to do with their dreams—but *how* does he suffocate them without touching them? He was half a continent away from Agnes's husband when the man died. And we have no idea how or why he brands them, or what the symbol means."

"Yes, and let's not forget that he's *fictional*," Tyler pointed out.

"Couldn't it be a copycat?" Rob suggested. "Someone who read the *Hollywooder* article, saw the movie, and is killing in a similar way?"

I paced up and down the row of theater chairs. "You saw how hard it was for us to get our hands on the movie. Who else could possibly get a copy?"

My feet slowed as an idea struck me. Someone else *was* out there searching for Sigil Pictures films. The anonymous Decline.A.Copy on the message boards.

I started for the stairs, but Kylie called for me. "Girl, where are you going?"

"I need to talk to another Internet Troll," I called back.

When I logged on to the *Hollywooder* article message board on my laptop, there was a response waiting from Decline.A.Copy.

OneEyeOpen @Decline.A.Copy, I might be able to get you a copy. Where are you located?

NEW MESSAGE **Decline.A.Copy** I can come to you. Message me. Text Crypt Decline.A.Copy

It didn't take me long to find that Text Crypt was an anonymous messaging service that masked IP addresses. Whoever Decline.A.Copy was, wherever he was, he knew how to hide his tracks. I downloaded the app to my phone, then messaged Decline.A.Copy that I was in LA and could meet him at Pharmacy Bar to hand over the film.

Tossing my phone aside, I glanced at the vintage wall clock. It was just a few minutes until midnight, the small and large hands almost meeting.

I went to the window, looking down on the city at night. The legendary Sunset Strip was artificially bright, snaking through the valley below the hills. There was something about those distant lights that made the observer an empty promise—an escape, but fleeting. Not really an escape at all.

Gazing out over the city, I pulled out my phone and leaned against the windowsill, feeling emotionally charged for no reason.

He picked up on the first ring. "Rafe. I could use that company around now."

CHAPTER NINETEEN

THE CANDY HOUSE
© 1951 Sigil Pictures

                    HANNA
          Look—a light ahead beyond those
          trees. It's a house!

                    ANDRZEJ
          We are blessed!

With renewed energy, the siblings hurry
through the forest toward the lamplight. Hanna
trips on a root, falling to her hands and
knees. In front of her, a PIECE OF SALTWATER
TAFFY in the mud.

                    HANNA
                 (to herself)
          Candy?

THIRTY MINUTES LATER, we were cruising in Rafe's Range
Rover down Sunset Boulevard. The streets were quieter than I'd ever
seen them. Other than a few girls shivering outside chintzy restaurants

in short skirts, the city felt oddly empty, and I had the sensation that reality had inverted again. That we weren't in Los Angeles at all, but some alternative universe where something terrible had happened, along the lines of a virus or war, leaving the streets sparse. Rafe didn't play music on the radio. The gentle, steady *thunk* of the wheels over breaks in the pavement lulled me into a calm.

"It was the present, wasn't it?" he said at last, glancing my way with a grin. "I knew I could lure you with presents."

"Sure," I said, rolling my eyes. "It was the present."

Our eyes met.

Fuck, why did I make him so handsome?

After another few blocks, he rubbed a hand over his chin and, with a hitch in his voice, asked, "You aren't afraid to be alone with me?"

I glanced out the window, slipping my hand into my bag to curl my fingers around the *Exit, Nebraska* book safe. "I never said that."

He took a hand off the wheel to tuck a piece of loose hair behind my ear, then focused again on the road. "Good."

It wasn't long before glimpses of ocean winked between the dark shapes of palm trees, and he turned onto a wide avenue flanking the water.

I realized that I was no longer clutching the book safe in my bag. My hand had gotten a mind of its own again and found a pen to squeeze, something I appeared to have swiped from Haywood Family Pharmacy in Billings, Montana.

I moved my bag between my feet and tucked my hands under my legs.

Rafe glanced over. "Something on your mind?"

He already knows about the drawing in the book safe. I'd kept so many secrets that I had to forcibly remind myself that I could talk freely to Rafe.

"I haven't drawn anything since leaving Lundie Bay. It hasn't been easy, but I've resisted. That means something, doesn't it? Like I'm getting stronger?"

He didn't answer immediately, and I felt the weight of unspoken thoughts. He navigated the car down the ocean drive and finally said, "I guess that depends."

"On what?"

"You and I have always felt differently about the Acosta talents. To you, it's a curse. To me, it's the best thing that ever happened."

I eyed him with a whiff of fresh suspicion. In the hotel room, was he going to try to make a case for me to draw again? *You and me, doll, we're going to rewrite this world*, Uncle Arnold had said. Rafe had never asked anything of me—yet.

He pulled the car into the circular drive of the Beverly Rockwell, ending our conversation. I stared up at the monumental Art Deco structure. The hotel's bones looked like they'd been forged during the Gilded Age and undergone a massive remodeling in recent years. Sleek elevators ran up the outside of the building.

"For some reason," I said as the valet headed our way, "I'd thought you'd have stayed in a cheap roadside motel."

He put the car in park. "How was I supposed to entice you to spend the night with me in a dive?"

My face warmed all over again. We surrendered the car to the valet and stepped into the glittering lobby, with its massive crystal chandelier overhead, its modernist fountains babbling water, the soft piano music coming from unseen speakers. We were soon whooshing up the side of the hotel in one of the elevators. I rested my hands lightly on the glass, looking out on the city as we rose. Below, cars glided down Ocean Avenue, the dark palms swaying in the night. I felt removed from it all in the glass bubble—though I wasn't sure if my feelings leaned more toward *protected* or *trapped*.

Rafe's room was on a high floor, a suite that must have cost a small fortune. Not that he cared about draining the real Rafe Kahn's bank account. Floor-to-ceiling windows revealed an unimpeded view of the ocean, the shifting waves making small, almost imperceptible movements in the dark.

Rafe slipped a hand around my waist and my heart leaped. A rush of desire mingled with the spark of danger.

He brushed my hair to one side, exposing my neck, and then pressed his lips against my skin. My head tilted as my eyes sank closed.

"Rafe . . ."

He spun me around, pressing my back against the cool glass. Without warning, he crushed his lips to mine. A bolt of pleasure shot through my skin. God, I'd missed this. I'd missed *him*. I chased away the voices that told me this was a bad idea and surrendered to the kiss, matching his impatience. His hand slipped up to graze the bottom of my breast and I broke away, breathing hard.

"*Rafe.*"

He pulled back with a faintly satisfied smirk. He rested his hands on either side of me, caging me between his body and the sky. His eyes simmered. "You knew what would happen when you came back to my hotel room."

I pressed a hand to his chest to hold him back—to give me some space. *Of course I knew.* But now my pulse was too fast, my resolve was faltering, and I blurted out, "You said you had a gift for me."

I wasn't sure he would take no for an answer, but after a second, his lips curled into a smile. His hands fell, freeing me, and he retreated a step.

He wiped a hand over the bottom half of his face. "Wait here."

He sauntered into the connected bedroom. My head fell back against the glass as my eyes sank closed. My skin was buzzing. My stomach felt hollow, hungry.

What are you doing, Haven?

Rafe reappeared in the bedroom doorway and beckoned me with a finger.

Swallowing, I pushed up from the window and made my way into the bedroom. It was as sleek and modern as the rest of the hotel, with Rothko-esque squares on the wall and a king-sized bed that my eyes were drawn to instantly, imagining what might happen later.

Rafe had retreated to the corner and now leaned casually against the dresser with his arms folded. He nodded toward the far side of the bed, which was hidden from my view.

"It wasn't easy to get my hands on," he said. "Let's just say it involved a meeting with your ex-husband, who wasn't exactly pleased when I told him who I was."

Alarm shot through me. "You found *Baker*?"

Rafe gave me his wolfish grin.

My heart started pounding with true fear again. Now I had a new reason to be afraid. I was suddenly apprehensive to see whatever twisted thing Rafe had brought me from my abusive ex. Rafe wasn't the type of man to give chocolates or flowers. He was the kind to murder my former husband and bring me his severed head in a box.

I stepped slowly around the bed. My eyes fell to the floor.

I stared in utter shock at the last thing—*things*—I thought I would ever see again.

I pivoted sharply toward Rafe.

"My paintings?" I said in surprise.

He smiled that secretive smile of his. Eyes wide, I turned back to the framed artwork that leaned against the nightstand. These were my paintings that had decorated my New York apartment walls, which I had framed and hung as soon as I'd moved in with Baker. When I'd run away to Lundie Bay, I'd asked Baker to send them along, but the request had gone unanswered.

I dropped to my knees, and with shaking hands, rifled through the pieces. There was the self-portrait with a dark crosshatch aura I'd done for my RISD graduate program. A lonely Medusa ankle-deep in Fingal's Cave. A Mother Nature being either devoured by or born from mushrooms, depending on how you looked at it.

Cool relief washed away my fear. My heart latched onto the paintings like a missing part of my soul, finally found.

"You went to New York to get my paintings?"

"Boston, actually. He moved there a few months ago and had

everything of yours from the old apartment in a storage unit."

"You saw him? You saw Baker?"

The corner of his mouth lifted slowly. "We had quite the little *chat*."

My stomach plummeted. "You didn't . . . hurt him? Right?"

He took his time admiring his fingernails, running a finger over their short, sharp edges. "I didn't *kill* him."

I pushed myself to my feet. "Rafe, what did you do?"

He swatted away the question. "Humans don't *need* spleens. They aren't biologically necessary."

When I stared at him in utter horror, he scoffed, "Oh, he'll be fine. He seemed to make it to a taxi without any issues, so I presume he made it to the hospital. I boxed up the spleen on ice and sent it to Dahlia."

"You're still in touch with her?"

Once upon a time, that name had belonged to my father's housekeeper, who'd poisoned him before her own death. After the Malice House fire, the Witch of Went had taken the name.

"But of course. She's in Portland. She owns a witchy little shop—crystals and tarot in the front, *real* magic in the back. Why? You don't care about that guy, do you?"

I blinked, then blinked again. Arguments were forming in my head, but then I let out a long exhale and let them dissipate. I turned back to the paintings.

"Why did you get these for me?"

Rafe settled back against the dresser. "You gave your sketchbook to the Robber Saints in exchange for Kylie's life. I know what that sketchbook contained—the best pieces you'd made since you first learned to draw. People like us—people born of ink—we aren't like humans. We don't find meaning in some inner soul, but rather in something we carry outside our body. Something external." His eyes darkened. "I know what that sketchbook meant to you."

Everything, I thought. *It meant everything to me.*

I'd always wondered why I had trouble making friends and maintaining relationships. Like Rafe had said, that sketchbook had been the closest I'd come to finding meaning, truth. I'd felt its absence keenly since surrendering it to the Robber Saints, my hands seeking out the familiar weight in other books or notebooks but never finding the right fit.

Rafe had surprised me—a trickster, a monster. The last thing I had expected of him was *to see me for exactly who I was.*

I scraped my teeth over my bottom lip, aware I was staring at him. He didn't seem to mind. My fingers trailed over the base of my neck.

"Fuck," I said softly, and closed the distance between us.

I wasn't sure who started the kiss. Only that his hands encircled my waist and that mine slid against the plane of his chest, curving against his shoulders, twisting in his shirt's stiff fabric. He pushed his lips against mine, craving, devouring. My body softened. Our bodies flush, I could feel his heartbeat vibrating in his chest and my own answering it a beat off-sync. His hand wrapped around my throat, his thumb caressing the pulse he found there.

I undid his shirt's top buttons, then broke the kiss to lean into the crook where his neck met his shoulder, touching my face to his bare skin there. His fingers curled in the fabric around my waist, pulling my shirt free from my jeans. He muttered my name as he lifted me off the floor and carried me to the bed, where he tossed me down like I weighed nothing.

A groan slipped from my mouth.

Before I could even lift myself to my elbows, he'd crawled on top of me, stealing another kiss I was all too ready to give. I tilted my head back to deepen the play of our mouths, all the while thinking with a flare of angry desire, *This monster knows me better than anyone.*

Our arms were a tangled knot as buttons came undone; clothing was shed like two snakes twisted together. His hot touch was all over my body. Exploring me. Claiming me. I met his intensity with my own possessive need, dragging my nails through the hair at his nape and pulling his mouth down to join mine.

The sex was like the kiss itself, immaterial who took charge, who wanted it more. We were two lonely, soulless beasts who'd found in each other a matching half; we were the concave and convex of a curve, different yet the same.

When we finally broke apart, spent and shivering from pleasure, I rolled over and stared out at the dark ocean through the full-length windows. The moon had been out before but was now hidden by hazy clouds. A few lights bobbed in the darkness, lonely boats stranded in the endless expanse of water.

Rafe sank onto the side of the bed, gently stroking the curve of my waist. I didn't realize he'd even left. On impulse, he bent down to fasten a kiss to my hipbone.

I leaned on one elbow and studied him in the dusky hotel light. "So, what do *you* carry outside your body?"

His smile didn't falter as he cocked his head curiously. "Darling, I thought you knew."

At my blank look, he leaned in and whispered in my ear, "It's *you*."

CHAPTER TWENTY

—

THE HUNDREDTH STAIR

© 1941 Sigil Pictures

MEDIUM SHOT - A VICTORIAN HALLWAY - INTERIOR - NIGHT

TIGHT ON a GIRL'S tearful face as she
eavesdrops by her mother's cracked bedroom
door.

> HARRISON SMILEY [V.O. FROM INSIDE BEDROOM]
>   (sobbing)
>   Shall I go ahead and say it? You're
>   dying. There. Let us no longer
>   pretend. It is only by confronting
>   the truth that we may yet find a
>   cure.

> MOTHER [V.O. FROM INSIDE BEDROOM]
>   Confront the truth? The truth is
>   there is something evil beneath this
>   house, Harrison. And who would dare
>   venture within those caves to stop
>   it?

—

WE KISSED AGAIN, softer this time. Rafe's cool fingers mapped every curve and freckle on my skin like he was lost, searching for an end to some long journey that he'd never reached in his own story.

And what about my destination? Since I'd left Lundie Bay, the future hadn't been something I'd much considered. I had a whole new reality to try and learn to live with. And besides, my ambitions for a career in illustration were dead if I couldn't draw.

Your father found a way, a voice whispered in my head.

And it was true. Amory tried something he called *averted writing*: Giving in to the curse's urge but only partway. Writing, but not exactly what the curse wanted to bring to life.

If I could learn to do averted drawing—

My phone beeped, and I broke the kiss, rolling over to retrieve it from the nightstand. There was a missed call from the Lundie Bay detective, but I ignored that. I focused instead on a notification from the Text Crypt message service; Decline.A.Copy had replied to my request to meet.

I immediately sat up, swinging my legs off the bed. "Sorry, Rafe. Just a minute."

My thumbs began to tingle as I opened the program.

Decline.A.Copy: Pharmacy Bar. Saturday, 10 p.m. Bring the film. Big things coming. Get ready to rewrite the fucking world.

The phone slipped out of my hand. It clattered to the hotel carpet as adrenaline shot through my system.

My fingers went numb.

Then, suddenly, I was on my feet and halfway across the room, rooting a hand to the wall to keep from swaying.

Rafe glided off the bed, grabbing his flannel shirt from a chair and wrapping it around my naked body. "What is it, Haven? What *happened?*"

My fingers tugged the flannel tighter around my shoulders, trying to form a shield. Once I could drag oxygen into my lungs, I found my voice.

"It's him. It's Uncle Arnold."

Rafe peered at the phone on the floor.

My legs were draining of strength. Rafe helped me back to the bed, where the moment my weight settled on the tousled sheets, I immediately jumped right back up. I felt trapped, under attack.

Fuck, I missed it.

The username "Decline.A.Copy" was an anagram of "encyclopedia." An encyclopedia salesman. All this time, I'd been writing back to the man who was trying to find me. The *Hollywooder* article, the Sigil Pictures curse, the message boards—they had pulled our divergent paths together. There was only one trail now, and both of us were on it.

Rafe picked up the phone and read the message. A shadow crossed his face. I thought he might curse, but he turned instead toward the windows, looking out at the dark ocean. "Does he know it's you?"

"I used a different screen name, OneEyeOpen. I don't think he knows. But . . ."

"But?"

"I'm not sure."

Rafe muttered something under his breath that sounded like an incantation. Then he dug through the rumpled clothes strewn about the room until he located his pants.

I found myself pacing aimlessly, but he caught me in the circle of his arms, drew me close.

"He's ours," he murmured in my ear. "Do you hear me, Haven? He's one of ours."

My shoulders eased. I understood what Rafe meant. I had created Uncle Arnold, and in *Bedtime Stories for Monsters*, Rafe had served the role of the minder of monsters. We knew the vile salesman better than anyone, and as Uncle Arnold would say himself, the greatest weapon of all was knowledge.

"Well, it's obvious what we do about it," Kylie said, hands on her hips.

We were gathered in Rob's living room—Kylie, Rafe, Rob, Tyler, and me. I'd called an emergency meeting when Rafe and I left his hotel in the morning, though Rob had been so tied up in meetings we couldn't all convene until late afternoon.

"Nothing." Kylie punctuated the word with a clap of her hands. "You do nothing. If Uncle Arnold doesn't know it's you that he's been talking to, then you're fine. This is LA, not some small town with two coffee shops. So what if you mentioned a bar near here? There must be ten thousand people within half a mile of Sunset Boulevard. As long as you didn't tell him exactly where you were, he has no way of finding you. Just keep hiding. And obviously, *don't* go to that meeting." She turned toward Rafe, who hung back in the doorway, one shoulder lodged against the threshold. "I mean, right? Back me up here."

Rafe only shifted to lean against the other side of the doorway.

In *Bedtime Stories for Monsters*, Uncle Arnold had been long overlooked in his low-level job as a door-to-door encyclopedia salesman. But that hot point of rage also gave him a valuable camouflage. In a city like Los Angeles, anyone who didn't have the right dress size, the right skin color, the right address, was virtually invisible. Slovenly Uncle Arnold could pass through the city undetected, using his vocal ability to juice information out of whoever he pleased, leaving their minds a pithy rind.

Tyler switched on the midcentury gas fireplace—the weather had turned in Los Angeles, becoming cooler than usual for January. My back was to a mannequin displaying a French satin gown that Grace Kelly had worn to the Oscars, and every time I caught the human shape out of the corner of my eye, I ran my hand over the back of my neck, feeling exposed.

"We can't keep hiding forever," I said quietly. "Uncle Arnold is on the same trail we are. The Sigil curse is just the Acosta curse by a different name. Now it's a race to see who gets answers first, him or us. And we have an advantage. We know his online identity, but he might not know that I'm OneEyeOpen. We could set a trap."

Kylie looked at me like I'd lost my mind. "You want to talk *advantages*? Uncle Arnold is the one with all the advantages, not us. He doesn't have to slip bribes to morticians or question script doctors. He can simply whisper in *anyone's* ear and get all the answers he wants. If it's a race, then he's already miles ahead of us."

I pulled my legs under me on the sofa as I considered this. "What do you think, Rob? Can Uncle Arnold trace my username back to me?"

Rob, the producer-turned-hacker, leaned back on the sofa, Italian leather shoe bobbing in space. "Doubtful, given what you've told me about him." He switched positions and leaned forward, tenting his hands. "I'm much more interested in his motives than in his hacking abilities. The first thing I ask any screenwriter when they pitch me an idea is: *Why? Why now? What does your character hope to gain?*"

The words of "Everyone's Favorite Uncle" played back in my mind. Uncle Arnold's story had been one of the shortest in *Bedtime Stories for Monsters*, and yet I'd found it among the most disturbing. Pinchy snipped off feet and the Hellhound gnawed on human bones, yet their motives made perfect sense. They were predictable in their monstrosity. Uncle Arnold, however, was a different kind of devil.

I turned toward Rafe. "You're the only one who knew him outside his story. What does Arnold want, truly?"

Rafe hadn't talked much about his history in Malice, his erstwhile role as the Harbinger. I didn't know if this was because Rafe wasn't the kind to live in the past or simply liked this life better, reveling in his new freedom.

"First off, Uncle Arnold wasn't anyone's uncle," Rafe started. "*He* was the one who started calling himself that. He lived alone, whiskey his only companion. All those quiet nights in his own head—I think he got angry. Knocking on doors all day, peddling encyclopedias to housewives who sneered at him. Having to answer to bosses who were younger, born into wealth and handed a place at the head of the company. One day, he was walking home across a bridge. A group of teenagers taunted him, threw his briefcase in the river. Beat him, strangled him, left him for dead. But he survived, and when he woke up in the hospital, he found that the pretty nurse would bring him extra Jell-O whenever he whispered a particular way. Then he got her to give him extra morphine. Then she was sucking his cock." Rafe shrugged. "That's when he decided to reinvent himself. He started calling himself everyone's favorite uncle. He's always been a son of a bitch—but after that, he was a powerful one."

Kylie hugged her arms, looking queasy.

Rob gazed into the gas flames, lost in thought. "If he's after reinvention, he's come to the right town. Don't like your past? Reinvent yourself. Every day, that's the conversation around the studio tables. Rebooting *Argonauts*, doing a spin-off. Making the old relevant." He scoffed. "No one wants anything original. Anything daring. That's why I . . ." He cut himself off, shaking his head. "It doesn't matter."

Tyler reached over, squeezed his fiancé's arm.

Kylie toyed with her earring as she paced in front of a backlit movie poster. "Reaching out to Decline.A.Copy again will only give our enemy more clues to figure out you're the person he's been messaging. He thrives off information, like Rafe said. You might think what you tell him is safe, but he's clever. Better to shut off communication entirely."

When I hesitated, Kylie gave me a pointed look. "Haven?"

"All right," I said, relenting. "I won't contact him again, but it doesn't change the fact that he's out there, beating us to answers. He can get anyone to talk. Look at what happened to Nanette. And what do we have to *our* advantage?" I looked at the ceiling and let out a frustrated sigh. "A Sigil film reel he can't get his hands on . . . but we can't even watch the ending. Without knowing how the Sandman Killer murders his victims . . ."

Something unlocked in my head, opening a door I hadn't known was there. I snaked a hand down to my ankle, covering the scar there. Despite the fire, I felt a strange kind of chill, the kind that carried a tinge of excitement, like the first frost in fall.

"Rafe," I said. "Can you get in touch with Dahlia?"

In "Kaleidoscope," the Witch of Went had the unique ability to alter the fabric of perception. Without warning, the jangling bells of merchant stalls would mix with birdsong, and what was once a woodland clearing became an ever-moving market of clandestine wares.

Now I explained to the others, "We need to know the ending of *The Sandman Killer* if we're ever going to figure out how Doctor Ellis killed Joao and Nanette. Dahlia has the ability to bend reality. If we can't *watch* the end of the movie, maybe we can . . ." I felt a flicker of fear, suddenly doubting myself, but I pressed on. "*Enter* it."

Rafe's hand drifted to his abdomen, where a scar remained from his own dark deal with her. "She'll want something in return. And it might not be something you want to give, Haven."

It was true that Dahlia wasn't just mistress of the Night Market—she was also a vendor. She found the worst kind of men and turned their organs into potions to sell at her stall; what had started as justifiable retribution against men who wronged women had turned evil, unhinged—culminating in Kylie almost ending up on her dissection table.

Reaching out to Dahlia, I knew, could go either very well for us or very badly—and unlike Rafe, I wasn't inclined to pull out my own spleen as payment.

"Call her," I said before I lost my nerve.

He nodded slowly, but watched me.

The meeting ended with no definitive answers, but at least we had a plan. Rafe returned to his hotel, Rob and Tyler went out for a late dinner, and Kylie settled in to read for the evening. I found myself drifting from room to room, unable to concentrate, examining Rob's memorabilia. The longer I was in his house, the more claustrophobic the space felt. It had always been more of a gallery than a house, and being here late, alone in these rooms, made me feel like I'd lost track of time, gotten myself locked in a museum overnight. The memorabilia spanned not just decades but worlds. There were rubber alien masks, maps of kingdoms that had never existed. At times, Rob's house felt like the epicenter of all realities. In a way, maybe it was. What were movies if not two-hour interdimensional voyages?

"Haven."

I jumped, pivoting away from a framed autographed screenplay. My hands balled into fists on instinct.

Kylie loomed in the darkness, the same size and shape as the mannequin behind her. "I'm turning in. Tomorrow morning—you'll be ready?"

It took me a moment to remember the meeting with Patrick Kane. I thought briefly of my notebook upstairs, the half-finished entries.

"Right," I promised. "I'll be ready."

She shifted, and her outline separated from the mannequin behind her, breaking one silhouette into two. The light from inside the phone booth charging station reflected on her teeth.

"Don't draw," she said from the darkness.

I loosened my fists. "Don't write."

She disappeared back upstairs, and only the mannequin remained. If I was being honest, sometimes it felt like that between me and Kylie. Like we were pulling apart, one forging ahead, the other staying in place. Nothing as dramatic as a crack in our sisterly bond, no fissure caused by a specific fight or disagreement. It was a softer premonition—a slow yawn, two lips stretching apart. The things that sparked her interest were the things that repulsed me like a magnet's opposing pole. The last thing I wanted to think about was our father, a dead man who'd kept so many secrets. Conversely, the things that drew me in—Rafe, becoming acquainted with one's own darkness—were repellent to her.

CHAPTER TWENTY-ONE

———

PURGATORY'S DOOR
© 1955 Sigil Pictures

THE DRUID BAR - INTERIOR - NIGHT

BAR SOUNDS fade as Banjax leads the way to the
back office. CLOSE ON Detective Nick Dram's
shoes sticking to the dirty floor. As they
enter the office, his feet COME TO A STOP.

MEDIUM SHOT on THE KILLARNEY DOORMAN, a
goat-headed thug dressed in a worn three-piece
suit standing guard before a mysterious
interior door. CLOSE ON submachine gun in his
giant hands. CLOSE ON his sharp horns.

> MICKEY KELLY (V.O. WHILE SEATED AT DESK)
> Detective Dram, ain't it? I
> hear you've been asking a lot of
> questions. Well, I got answers.

———

THE NEXT DAY, traveling across town in the back of a rideshare,
Kylie and I both deep in our thoughts, I mulled over my feelings toward

Los Angeles. It wasn't the veneer of sunny perfection that irritated me; that could be forgiven. Of course the swaying palms, the pastel-colored boutiques, the glimpses of glittering blue-green ocean were picturesque. I didn't fault the city; in fact, I admired its near-violent determination to be cheery.

I just hated that I didn't belong here. Everything about the city reflected that fact back at me like each passing mirrored shopwindow. I stood out in my dark New York clothes with my awkward slouch. And inside, the differences were tenfold. This sunny sanctuary wasn't for the likes of me. I belonged in the dark and damp. A cave, forest, swamp. Places with space to hide. Places to lie in wait.

Kylie, with her chic athleisure wear and tattoos and piercings, went a lot further toward belonging here. There was an independence about her that made me think she'd never fully belong anywhere—she was a drifter, apart from any one place—but unlike me, she could almost be at home here.

Almost.

When we reached a cute little café called the Chocolate Lounge, squeezed between a bookstore and a vintage clothing boutique, Kylie slid off her sunglasses.

A bell sounded as we entered. Inside was all dark wood and exposed industrial pipes, though with an air of inauthenticity; this wasn't a hundred-year-old converted factory, it was a strip mall designed to capture a certain aesthetic. My eyes went to the glass cases of confectionary offerings. Chocolate brownies, chocolate cookies, tiny ceramic ramekins of *pots de crème*, rows of bonbons in dozens of flavors. Behind the counter, vats of hot chocolate bubbled. My stomach rumbled.

Kylie gripped my arm. "That's him."

I searched the tables until I saw a Black man in his fifties, stiff in his sport coat with the graying temples and haircut of a newscaster from the eighties. He was bent over a notebook, one hand pressed against his ear. He glanced up and caught our eyes, recognizing us. He gave us a brief nod. A footnote of a smile followed.

We placed an order, and once we were laden down with pastries and cold sipping chocolate, we made our way to the biographer's table, where he moved aside his notebooks to make room.

"Patrick Kane?" Excitement was sprinkled in Kylie's voice.

The man stood, reaching out a hand. "Yes, yes, it's a pleasure to meet you. Ms. Nance, right? And Ms. Marbury?"

"Haven." I flinched as his big hand swallowed my own. He motioned to two empty seats. We scooted closer to the table to make room for a family with young children trying to squeeze by.

He smoothed a hand over his tie—I realized I'd barely seen a *tie* in months—as he tapped the blunt end of his pen against his notebook, a monstrous thing stuffed with newspaper clippings and printouts.

"Is all that about our dad?" I asked, motioning to the mass. "Looks like you've done your research."

"I have four more like this back home." He peered at me over his glasses. "For the Naja Ann Lundin biography, I filled twelve notebooks. They're all boxed up in my attic."

I flinched at the image of boxes pushed under attic eaves.

I glanced at the clock on my phone. "We promised thirty minutes."

He nodded crisply, aware of our agreement, and opened his notebook. "Yes, so let's get started. First of all, allow me to give you a brief summary of the project's scope. Every biography has a focus: for some it's the subject's formative years, others the career accomplishments, others the scandals." He slid me a searching look to gauge my reaction. When I kept a poker face, he smiled almost approvingly. "In your father's case, I want to focus on a sort of overlay of his writing on top of his life. How his real life shaped his fiction and vice versa."

An irritating buzz was coming from somewhere in the café. I rested my hands on my knees under the table, squeezing them tightly.

"I don't know how much I'll be able to tell you," I said. At least I was being honest. I *couldn't* tell him anything about the curse or *Bedtime Stories for Monsters* without painting a dotted line straight from me to a bunch of murders.

His response was a patience-tested nod. He turned to Kylie. "Ms. Nance—"

"Kylie." Kylie was on the edge of her seat, hands tented under her chin.

He gave her a grandfatherly smile. "Kylie, we've already spoken on the phone, but is there anything else that occurred to you? Things your mother might have told you about your father?"

Kylie's brow turned serious. "Well, she never said he died in an accident or anything like that. I figured he was, I don't know, a bad guy and she didn't want me dragged into that life. When I finished college, she was already sick. I never got up the courage to ask for the truth—she'd made it clear she didn't consider him a part of our lives. I only found out his identity later from my aunt."

Mr. Kane wrote down everything she said. "Did your mother read his works? I mean, were there Marbury books in your childhood home?"

Kylie's eyes drifted to the left in recollection. "Yes, *Feast of Flowers* and *The Desecration of Johnny Jim*, I think. But she was a cultural arts reporter, so our house was filled with books. It never occurred to me that *those* books could have special relevance."

He jotted this down and then turned to me. "Now, Haven, I've located all your biographical details from public records, so there is no need to waste precious time on confirming those. What I'm interested in hearing from you here are stories you can tell me. Memories that would give context to your father's writings."

The pastries on my plate looked unappealing beneath the too-bright overhead lighting. I pushed them around with a fork, focusing on anything but the man across from me.

Patrick Kane watched me carefully, then took out a manila envelope from beneath his notebook. He rested a hand on it. "I should note that I was able to find your extended family's history, including living relatives." He tapped his index finger heavily on the envelope.

Kylie went quiet, but her body said everything in the way she leaned forward like a hungry cat before a bird's nest.

I told myself that whatever names were on that paper were strangers'; they weren't *family*. They were only a means to an end. The only family I had was sitting next to me, twisting her hoop earring.

I cleared my throat as I pulled out my own notebook and pushed it across the table. "I wrote down a few memories, like you asked."

He picked up the notebook but didn't break eye contact. "Yes, thank you, but I want to hear it *from* you." He patted my notebook. "There are stories, and then there are the ways people *tell* stories. They aren't the same."

I wasn't fond of the way Patrick Kane was steering a meeting that *I* had planned to control.

I said carefully, "I haven't read all my father's books, so I can't speak to specific inspirations for scenes or characters, whatever you writers conjure in your heads." I waved my hand toward both Kylie and Patrick, who were the type to think in scenes, not pictures. "But I do remember one story that might be interesting for your biography. About a novelist he dated for a few years, on and off. Adelaide Martin. They're adapting her novel *Tulip Carol* over at Gemini Entertainment."

He nodded for me to continue as though he already knew this information.

I fixed my gaze on the industrial pipes overhead. "She was a grouch. Brilliant but caustic. I always thought of her as a rosebush in winter—no buds, only the spiny core. Not that I minded; she was very similar to my father, and she and I got along decently. She stayed with us for a few weeks in Maine one summer when I was in college. My father was a pack rat—she hated that about him. One night, she talked him into burning down a shed on the property that he'd filled with old junk. Broken appliances, moldering books, exercise equipment he'd barely touched. I thought he'd refuse, but he stood up from the dinner table and got a matchbook. The shed burned all night. All of that old junk, gone. He never spoke about it again. He simply moved on. That's how my father was. He wasn't sentimental about the things he kept—it was just his nature not to let things go until poked. It was the same with his writing. He wasn't attached to his work. As soon as he finished a book and it was published, the book tour finished, he forgot about it. You'd ask him a year later about a character and he'd have no idea what you were talking about."

Patrick Kane wrote fervently as I spoke, and Kylie was hanging on my every word, too, her cookie untouched.

Finally, Patrick looked up and adjusted his glasses. "What about people? Was he as unsentimental about his relationships, such as with Ms. Martin?"

I let my gaze trail off from the ceiling as I crossed and uncrossed my legs. It wasn't as simple as a yes or a no. Even my story about Dad burning down the shed wasn't the complete truth. It turned out that he *had* been attached to some things. In Malice House, I'd found boxes of my childhood schoolwork, photographs, and art projects in the attic.

It turned out he'd been sentimental about *me*.

But I didn't want to say that in front of Kylie, the daughter he'd never acknowledged.

"No," I said gingerly. "He was just as unsentimental with people. He'd meet some woman and within a few months, it was like she'd never existed. He'd moved onto the next. He was always moving on to the next. The next affair. The next book. The next house."

Patrick Kane's pen paused. Without looking up, he said, "Speaking of, I was sorry to hear about the Lundie Bay house. A fire, wasn't it?"

I forced myself to remain perfectly still. Beside me, Kylie became very interested in her cookie. "That's right. An accident."

"So all of his personal records . . ."

"Gone," I said quickly. Kylie whipped her head around, mid-bite. It *wasn't* all gone—we'd saved one of his journals, along with several pieces of his artwork, and boxes of books and other valuables.

It wasn't much longer before Patrick's phone timer, set to half an hour, trilled, making me flinch. He tapped it to turn it off, then slowly removed his glasses and rubbed the bridge of his nose.

"How quickly time passes. I do hope you'll consider speaking to me again if more stories return to your recollection, but a deal is a deal." He unfastened the manila envelope and took out a stack of papers, turning the pile around to face Kylie and me.

A rush of air raced up my throat; I swallowed it back. We would look through them at length at home, but my curiosity got the better of me. My eyes were too excited, hunting over the top paper, a branching family tree, for familiar names. *Acosta? Joao?*

Patrick Kane used his pen to circle two names at the bottom of the tree: mine and Kylie's. "Here you two are. The only known direct offspring of Amory Marbury. Tracing it back to your father, here is your mother, Haven, of which very little is known. I found the marriage certificate and her death certificate, but it's been a challenge to locate any of the officers who worked on her case, or any of her family."

There was a question in his voice, and I lifted a stiff shoulder and said tersely, "I don't know much either, sorry."

He held my gaze as though he wasn't sure he believed me, but then traced a line in the opposite direction. "And here is your mother, Kylie. Much easier to identify her side of the family. Several generations in the Charleston area dating back to the mid-1800s. The records get fuzzy before that. As I'm sure you are well aware, many slave owners didn't prioritize record-keeping. Your DNA sample identified your ethnic group on your mother's side as—"

"Ghanaian," Kylie said. "Yeah, my mom knew that much."

He nodded. "Right, so let's focus on the Marbury side, the side the two of you share." Patrick traced the line up from Amory's name. "Amory's father, Thomas Marbury, was a history professor born in Philadelphia. Amory's great-grandparents immigrated to the United States from Wales in 1889. His mother, Isabel Acosta, was a first-born immigrant from Portugal. Now this side of the family is quite interesting." He continued to use the pen to connect our family members with lines. "Isabel's parents, your great-grandparents, immigrated to America and tried to start a vineyard here in California, but it went bankrupt, and your great-grandfather went to jail, where he passed away."

I slid the stack of papers closer, flipping through the other pages.

"You'll find copies of any official documents I could locate," Patrick explained. "As well as biographical summaries, though I'm afraid most are sparse. There are a few pictures, too—"

I stopped on Isabel's family tree. Branching off from her sister's side of the family were four offspring. I sucked in a breath, then tapped on a name, looking at Kylie.

Joao Acosta.

There it was. Proof of our blood relation with the body in the morgue.

"What can you tell us about this man?" I pointed to Joao's name.

Patrick took the stack of papers back briefly to look over them. "Well, I believe that would be your third cousin. . . . I'll have to check the exact relation. I found his driver's license photo. I have a photocopy somewhere. . . ." He located the page he was looking for and held it up. There was Joao—the body on the table, only this time full of life in a DMV photo.

Patrick cleared his throat. "I'm afraid he recently passed away. I've included the death certificate."

I made a small noncommittal noise in the back of my throat that I hoped he would dismiss as mild sympathy.

As Kylie took the photo of Joao to study it closer, I dragged my thumb over a few more pages. I stopped on a color photocopy of a mug shot and froze.

The paper began to shake in my hand.

Noticing my reaction but misreading the cause, Patrick glanced at the mug shot and said, "Ah, yes. Miracle Acosta. A cousin of your father's, which would make her your first cousin once removed. She was arrested in 2019 for trying to bribe a police officer. I told you the Acosta side of the family was interesting."

I slid my elbow to bump against Kylie's arm and snag her attention, not trusting my voice not to shake.

The face looking back at me was agelessly serene even in a mug shot, her salt-and-pepper hair loose around her shoulders, brown eyes filled with winking mischief.

In the campground outside Joshua Tree National Park, I'd nicknamed her Tree Pose. I'd been worried that she might report my suspicious activity to the police.

But perhaps I should have been afraid of her for darker reasons.

CHAPTER TWENTY-TWO

WINTER OF THE WICKED
© 1947 Sigil Pictures

INTERIOR — BARN — NIGHT

A single dying CANDLE shows Farm Wife cowering
in an empty stall with her two daughters.
ANIMAL SHRIEKS AND MOANS come from outside.
Hooves slam against the barn door. The
barricade splinters but holds.

A POSSESSED MOUSE with bloodshot eyes slips
through a crack and bites Younger Daughter.

"SHE'S OUR DAD'S COUSIN, Kylie. His *cousin*."

Outside the Chocolate Lounge after our meeting with Patrick Kane, I paced tightly along the stretch of sidewalk that spanned from the clothing boutique to the bookstore, feeling like my legs had gone boneless. Kylie leaned against the bookstore window, toying anxiously with her earring.

Now that I thought back to Tree Pose—Miracle Acosta—I saw everything with fresh eyes.

"Do you think she knew who we were?" Kylie asked.

"She *had* to," I said emphatically. "She approached me, not the other way around. I think she completely made up that story about finding Joao's 'journal' to test me. And I'll bet you anything it wasn't a coincidence she just happened to also be awake and outside at one a.m. on the night of the storm. She was watching us."

"Why not tell us who she was?"

I didn't have an answer for that. I slowed to a stop as I dug out my phone and punched in a number.

"Who are you call—" Kylie started, but I held up a finger as someone picked up on the other side.

"Hello?" I said into the phone. "Candace Elliot? It's Haven Marbury. You might remember— Yes. Listen, you mentioned someone else had been trying to get into your funeral home to examine Joao's body. A woman. Did she have a slight accent, by chance?"

At Candace's response, I hung up and pressed my fingers against my eyes.

"Candace verified it," I muttered. "The other woman investigating Joao's murder *wasn't* Nanette. She had an accent, so it must have been Miracle. It was *her* that Rafe saw searching the crime scene during the storm."

Kylie slumped further against the bookstore's window. Its display of literary thrillers soured my stomach. I was afraid to look too closely at the titles. Afraid I'd see an Amory Marbury or an Adelaide Martin or a Patrick Kane—as though forces beyond our control were reaching out, forming connections that should never be made.

Kylie's eyes darted toward a nearby couple looking at the menu posted outside the Chocolate Lounge. She lowered her voice to a whisper. "Do you think Miracle killed Nanette?"

Honestly, I didn't know *what* to think. That night had been so dark, turbulent. My glimpse of the mysterious shapes I'd seen had spanned a single lightning flash—person or monster or tree, I hadn't been sure.

I slumped onto the bookstore windowsill next to her. "If she did kill Nanette, why? What does Nanette have to do with her nephew's murder?"

Kylie gave an involuntary shiver. "Unless Miracle killed Joao, too."

When I let out a small exhalation of surprise, Kylie jabbed a matter-of-fact finger against her palm. "Think about it. Maybe Miracle was at the campground to return to the scene of the crime. Make sure no one was tracing Joao's murder back to her. Nanette was out there spying on us, Miracle ran into her, was afraid she'd seen too much. . . ."

The couple walked past us, and we fell quiet. Even once it was safe to speak again, we let the silence stretch. I found my eyes latching onto every passing face, looking for Uncle Arnold's. What if Nanette hadn't been the only one that he'd compelled? What if he'd whispered to Miracle, too?

"The killer wasn't human, though: no footprints," Kylie said.

"I don't know, maybe we're wrong about that."

We returned to Rob's, finding the house empty, and dug through the pantry for something resembling dinner. The packet of family history Patrick Kane had given us was overwhelming, and we spent much of the night and following day going through it in an attempt to piece together the Acosta lineage into a complete picture. But it didn't want to snap together.

When we'd finally gone through everything, I fell into bed, exhausted.

My phone lit up with a notification. I reached for it, dreading what I'd find as soon as I saw it was from the Text Crypt app.

Decline.A.Copy: OneEyeOpen, you there? Meeting time/location a go? Need a confirmation.

My hands were shaking. I worried irrationally that Uncle Arnold could somehow see me through the internet connection. *It's just a text*, I reminded myself. *Texts can't hurt me.*

My fingers hovered over my phone's keyboard. I had promised Kylie that I wouldn't go to the meeting with Decline.A.Copy now that we knew it was Uncle Arnold, but there was something deep inside me that wanted to push those buttons. This was the only time we'd ever had the upper hand on Uncle Arnold.

I know exactly where he'll be on Saturday at ten p.m.

No more hiding, no more stalking. We could flush him out into the open.

But I had promised I wouldn't, and for good reason. I tossed the phone onto the bedside table, watching it from a distance until it went black again, once more letting Uncle Arnold escape into the dark.

———

"What's the name again?" Rob asked the following day, seated at an ancient desktop computer that called to mind the clunky, pixelated PC games of my youth. It was the first time I'd seen a floppy-disk drive since elementary school.

"Miracle Acosta," I said, leaning over his shoulder. "And it's the Morongo Police Department. You might try the Bureau of Land Management office, too. Their rangers were also interviewing campers."

Rob navigated away from the Central Casting website he'd had open to the police department's database. As his fingers flew over the clanking keyboard, pulling up code that looked like gibberish to me, I let my eyes drift around his home office, though *home office* conjured a different image. On the house's main level, in a stylish room down a hallway from the living room, Rob had the executive desk and trappings one would expect of a successful producer. *This* office was in the basement, in a closet off the movie theater's foyer. No windows. No memorabilia, though with the ancient desktop and equally ancient VHS players, it retained a museum-like feel. A TV screen was paused on an image of a tentacled alien slipping its appendage down a sobbing man's throat. There was another copy of the November *Hollywooder* issue on top of a cabinet, open to the Sigil Pictures article, a few passages underlined.

Rob patted the old computer affectionately. "They don't make them like this anymore. No—and I mean absolutely no—software is compatible because I wrote this operating system myself. There's more chance of Vincent Price rising from the grave than someone hacking into this beast."

He soon pulled up the Morongo Police Department's internal network and gave a dark snicker of delight as he sorted through digital folders.

"That one," I said, pointing to the screen. "It has the date they found Nanette's body."

The folder contained typed-up entries of Sergeant Castellucci's and Officer Michaels's interviews with each of the campers at the BLM campground. Rob skimmed over the entries labeled with our fake names, and stopped on one near the end.

He opened the notes on Miracle. Leaning in, I scanned the statement she'd made to the police. To my surprise, she hadn't mentioned anything about Rafe or me. I wasn't sure why not—was she protecting me? Or rather, somehow protecting herself?

"Hang on," I said. "Let me write this down."

I jotted down the phone number they'd taken from Miracle. From somewhere upstairs, the doorbell chimed. Footsteps crossed above our heads—Tyler, I supposed, headed to the door.

Glancing back down at my phone, I mused aloud, "How does one go about asking one's distant cousin if she murdered a few people?"

Rob held out his hand, palm up. "Give the phone to me."

I handed the phone over hesitantly, and he typed quickly before I could stop him.

"Hey—!"

He handed the phone back with that impish gleam in his eyes. I glanced down at the message he'd sent to her number.

It's Haven. I know everything.

"There," he said simply. "When in doubt, the less you say, the better. You have to give people enough rope to hang themselves. Now *she* knows that *you* know her identity, and it's up to her to reveal her hand."

"And if she doesn't respond?"

"That's an answer in itself."

Something caught my eye behind him. A red light was blinking on an old VHS camcorder. Wait—was he *recording* this? But as soon as I stepped closer for a look, Kylie stuck her head in the open doorway.

"Haven—" Her words stalled when she saw the image of the man with a tentacle down his throat. Exhaling in a way that emphasized how fucked-up she thought everything in Rob's house was, she started again: "Better come upstairs. We have a visitor."

There was an ominous ring to her words. I glanced once more at the video recorder.

Rob had security cameras all around the house, standard for any Los Angeles mansion—I'd accepted them as the price of crashing free at his place. But a twenty-year-old camera in his secret basement office? Was it always recording, or had he only just switched it on to record me?

Rob tapped his ancient keyboard and put his computer to sleep.

I watched him closely as he led Kylie and me up the stairs. But as soon as we made our way into the living room, all worries about Rob and cameras fell away. My feet felt stuck to the ground, too heavy, while my head was much too light.

The Witch of Went sat on the sectional sofa, sipping from a promotional *Argonauts* mug.

Tyler sat across from her, talking excitedly with his hands about some new Michelin-starred restaurant he wanted to visit in Portland. His voice was a little too forceful, too friendly. He knew what she was.

I felt as though a bird had struck me straight in the chest.

Rafe hung back near the windows, arms folded, watching in dark delight as Tyler squirmed in his attempt to make chitchat with a bona fide witch.

As soon as I entered, Dahlia locked eyes with me. "Haven." No hellos, no polite exchanges. Her eyes scraped over me like she could read all she needed to in the shadows under my eyes. "I thought you'd be dead by now."

She took another slow sip from her mug.

"Hi, Dahlia."

The last I'd seen the Witch of Went, she'd warned me about all the ways the world could be unkind to women like us—and part of me felt like we'd forged some connection when she saved my sketchbook from the Malice House fire, even if I lost it shortly thereafter. Still, I knew better than to expect any more kindness from her.

She wore dangling silver earrings and a V-neck teal dress that hugged her thick frame. Gone was the oversized men's shirt tucked into a gauzy black skirt from *Bedtime Stories for Monsters*. Her black hair was glossy, pulled to one side, hanging nearly to her waist. And yet the more I took in her new appearance, the more I felt she hadn't changed in the slightest. The Witch of Went had never cared about her looks, and she still didn't—but she was, above all else, a survivor. The makeup, the dress—it was a means to an end.

Tyler stood up, tugging nervously at his shirt. "I'll let you all catch up—"

"No." Her hand shot out, grabbing his wrist. "You stay. You all stay."

A moment of panic crossed his face before he dutifully sat back down, throwing me a desperate plea for help over his shoulder. I stepped into the sunken area, waving him away. He gratefully scooted a few seats down, and I took his place across from Dahlia.

"I take it Rafe explained the situation."

I glanced behind her at Rafe. Of all of us, he was the only one not visibly shaken by her presence. In *Bedtime Stories for Monsters*, the Harbinger and the Witch of Went had been something close to friends, even one-time lovers. I told myself it wasn't jealousy I felt—only apprehension.

"So, can you do it?" I asked.

She set her mug down on the coffee table and blinked languorously at me. "Enter a movie? I can't quite say. I haven't ever tried before. Though I suppose it isn't that different from what I do for the Night Market. I patch together the perception of realities. Poking a hole in one, pulling through another."

Kylie got up the nerve to speak. "The movie is fictional, though—it *isn't* reality."

Dahlia pinned her with a stare. "Who is to say that imagined realities are not true realities? Are you so certain that this"—she motioned to the room with its backlit posters and view of the Hollywood hills—"wasn't dreamed up by some bored god wanting to play dollhouse? Unless I'm mistaken, that's *exactly* what you teach your children to believe."

Everyone was quiet enough to hear the clock ticking in the curio cabinet. There was something deeply unnerving about a witch explaining reality with a mannequin dressed in a frilly Grace Kelly gown behind her.

Finally, I scooted forward, clasped my hands, and looked her in the eye. "So you'll give it a try?" I paused. "What about payment?"

I couldn't stop myself from glancing at Rafe, thinking about the scar that cut across his abdomen. What could I spare—tonsils? Teeth? A few pints of blood?

Dahlia matched my look at Rafe with a secretive little smile. "The Harbinger and I have already come to an agreement regarding payment."

My face fell. *This* disturbed me more than if she'd asked for one of my kidneys. When I raised my eyebrows at Rafe in a silent question, he shrugged a tight shoulder as though telling me to drop it.

But I certainly *wouldn't* be dropping it.

Rob broke the tension by clapping. "So it's on, then?" He flashed one of his rehearsed grins. "In that case, ladies and gentlemen, may I invite you all down to the theater for a showing? Tyler, heat up the popcorn machine."

It was easy to see beyond Rob's impishness now—he couldn't hide how delighted he was to have us all here in his curio-filled house, a living exhibit, like one of his coveted horror movies come to life. *Always the producer.*

I thought of the VHS camcorder downstairs and again had the uncanny sense that Rob's latest project was somehow producing *me.*

We filed down the basement stairs in a single line. Tyler turned on the popcorn machine. Rob uncased the *Sandman Killer* reel and hooked it up to the antique projector. Kylie pulled a sweater tightly around her shoulders as she took a seat in one of the wooden theater chairs. Dahlia went straight to the front row and sat in the middle seat, five feet from the screen.

I stopped Rafe at the door, holding him back. "What did you trade her for her help?" I asked quietly.

There were no smirks or smiles this time. "The only thing I have that she wants," he said. "Time."

My face must have filled with alarm, because Rafe cupped my jaw and brushed a kiss against my forehead as though to dispel my fears. "Don't worry about it, darling. Not long. She needs me for something in Portland, that's all."

But gentle words, soft kisses—they could never banish fear. Fear would always prevail.

CHAPTER TWENTY-THREE

———

THE SANDMAN KILLER
© 1943 Sigil Pictures

FADE IN:

INTERIOR — MEDICATION CLOSET - DAY

CAMERA PANS past clean, orderly shelves of
glass pill bottles. As we move to the lower
shelves, the bottles are in disarray. When
we reach the FLOOR, the bottles are broken.
Pills scattered. CONTINUE PAN along floor, as
we discover a puddle of blood. Then a woman's
hand. Then the dead body of INTAKE NURSE.

CLOSE ON the nurse's white uniform, where
SMOKE SYMBOL appears in blood.

———

THE THEATER LIGHTS DIMMED, popcorn bags were
passed around the room, and *The Sandman Killer* returned to the screen
in flashing frames until the reel caught.

Dahlia wanted to watch the film from the beginning. She sat alone
in the front row, her long black hair trailing over the back of the

wooden seat. Tyler hung back behind us all with Rob, crunching popcorn nervously.

With Kylie to one side and Rafe a few seats over to my other side, I watched the events of the first half of the movie unfold again. Agnes's arrival at the institute, that fearful first dream, the call to Doctor Ellis's office that Agnes's husband had perished, his decision not to tell her. That unreachable itchiness began to tingle again under my skin. I felt the need to get up, to do something.

When a jump scare flashed showing the nurse's mangled body, I gripped the armrests on either side of my chair, hard.

Kylie glanced at me and leaned over to whisper, "What's wrong with you?"

"Nothing."

She held my gaze, her eyes searching mine. "I didn't think you got scared at movies."

"I don't. I'm not scared," I lied.

Doubtful, she stuffed some popcorn into her mouth and went back to watching the movie.

It was almost like I had two selves, I felt. One was Haven, the creation. The other was . . . what? *Human?* I didn't yet know which one was which, or, perhaps more tellingly, which one I wanted to be. A part of me craved the monster. I'd seen the pendulum swings of human life, and I shied away from it, more at home in the dark.

The truth was, I *wasn't* human, so if I was undergoing a transformation, the question was: Into *what?*

The film played until we reached the point where water damage began to blur the reel, and then it clicked a few times, and the broken reel flapped to an abrupt ending.

Rob called from the back of the theater, "Should I wind it back?"

For a moment, the witch said nothing. Her head was immobile, tilted up at the blank white screen as though the film was still playing, her face hidden from us.

Then she called without turning, "I'll do it."

As she twirled a slow finger in the air, the film began to run backward. On-screen, Agnes climbed backward out of bed and paced backward through her room. I glanced over my shoulder. Neither Rob nor Tyler was at the projector. They had stepped back a few feet, staring as the crank moved on its own.

Dahlia stopped her finger, and the film paused at the image of a champagne puddle containing two overlapping crescent moons.

She stood, turning to us. The projector's beam shone near her head like a lighthouse signal calling out danger.

"I'll need all of you down here with me," she said.

Rafe sauntered down toward the screen. Kylie and I exchanged a glance, then shuffled out of the row of chairs.

Tyler made a small, hesitant sound from the back of the room, but Rob cajoled him with a mix of what sounded like encouragement and threats until they walked together down the outer aisle.

Once we were gathered in a loose circle at the front of the theater, Dahlia said, "You. The pretty one." She meant Tyler. "Stand here."

Tyler slid Rob a look that warned their engagement might soon be over as he took his place where Dahlia pointed. Then she motioned to Rob. "And you, here."

Next, she directed Kylie to stand a few feet from the screen, and then gave Rafe a place closer to the seats. The four of them stood in a shallow rectangle beneath the screen. Dahlia studied the still image of the spilled champagne on the floor, saying nothing.

I asked, "Where do you want me to stand?"

"I don't." She spoke over her shoulder. Her hand rose slowly in the air as though reaching for something near the screen—or holding something off. "They are making a doorway." She pointed her other hand toward the outer edges of their rectangle. "*You* are going through the doorway."

A spark of fear spread up from my toes. I forced myself to keep looking at the screen.

With her left hand still raised, braced against an unseen force,

Dahlia lifted the first two fingers of her right hand. Her fingers began to move in a pantomime of scissors. Cutting, cutting. I recalled the night of the Malice House fire when she'd stood outside the sealed front door, tapping a book with two fingers, drawing out one nail at a time in mimicry of a hammer.

Dahlia's hand began to shake as though the effort was taxing her. Her face was focused, her attention riveted to the screen.

"There." A vein of triumph ran through her voice. "Do you see it?"

I shook my head. "See what?"

"The fissure. The door." She tore her gaze from the screen long enough to look annoyed. "Well, *go* before it closes. We can't hold it forever."

I could only stare, confused. The screen was four feet off the ground. There was no type of tear or rip I could see, certainly no open doorway. But strain showed on her face as she scowled. *"Climb.* Why do you think I stopped on a frame of the floor? Did you want to drop from the top of a mountain, girl?"

I took a hesitant step forward. Kylie looked like she was afraid she'd never see me again. Rafe appeared a little angry, like he'd been duped.

"I need to go in with Haven," he growled.

Dahlia scoffed at his concern. "If you do, the door will collapse."

"It's okay," I said to Rafe. "It's just a movie. It isn't real."

From his corner of the rectangle, Tyler let out a squeak of uncertainty. When I reached the front wall, I extended my hands slowly. Chair rail molding ran along the wall at about waist height, and the bottom of the screen began not far above that. I took another step forward, expecting to touch the screen. But my hands didn't stop on the vinyl panel as they should have. A coolness settled over them like I was reaching deep into a freezer. Something wet brushed my palm, and I jerked my hand back.

I sniffed it—champagne.

"Go on," Rob urged from the rear corner of the rectangle. The screen reflected in his impish eyes, made them gleam devilishly.

I gripped the bottom of the screen, which had transformed into some kind of ledge—or had the ledge always been there? I was able to get one foot on the chair rail and push off to lift myself onto my forearms, then kick against the molding, hoisting myself *into* the screen.

That freezer chill spread over my torso and arms as I scrambled farther onto the ledge, finally feeling stable. I paused to catch my breath and realized that the surface beneath me wasn't a ledge at all. What I'd thought was a ledge was the sleep institute's *floor*. White linoleum squares with flecks of gray spanned beneath me. I twisted around to see if the others saw what I was seeing, and froze.

The others were gone.

All that stretched behind me was a long hallway with many closed doors. White linoleum floor, white cement-block walls. I whirled around to face the other way—an identical hallway except for a single door at the far end.

I pushed myself to my feet, finding it hard to breathe.

There was something wrong with this place, with the colors. It wasn't white flooring and white paint, I realized. It was monochrome. I was in the black-and-white movie, so the world was black and white now. Everything except for myself. My skin was still warm pale with toffee freckles, my jeans faded blue, my blouse a soft tan. I'd always dressed in plain, basic hues—but now I felt like a Harlequin performer clad in garish rainbow colors.

The overhead lights flickered. I recalled that at this point in the film, there was a snowstorm blustering outside. The power hadn't cut out yet, though it threatened to.

"Hello?" I called tentatively, turning in another circle.

Were Kylie and Rafe and the others watching me on the theater screen? Or had only I entered the second half of the movie, and to them it was still the frozen scene of spilled champagne?

I crouched down to pick up the broken champagne glass and, testing, felt its jagged edge. On impulse I dragged my finger through the spilled alcohol and then touched it to my tongue, testing this new reality to see how real it was.

Authentic champagne.

I took a cautious step down the monochrome hallway, wincing at the echo of my footsteps. All the doors were closed except for one, and I wandered into a space I recognized as Agnes's hospital room. There was the book she'd been reading, dog-eared on the nightstand. Various medication bottles lined up on a table. The framed photograph of her husband, the one personal item she'd brought with her.

I shook the medicine bottles—pills inside rattled. They weren't just props. Dahlia hadn't opened a doorway to the old production set; she'd placed me straight inside the actual *movie world.*

Footsteps sounded in the hallway, and I flinched, dropping the bottle. Tiny gray pills spilled out all over the floor.

"Damn it," I hissed, starting to pick them up. But the footsteps were rapidly approaching. I searched the room for a place to hide. There was nowhere. Maybe behind the door . . .

I was only halfway across the room when Agnes entered. She was as monochrome as everything else: grayscale skin, grayscale hair. I froze, clearly exposed in plain sight, but she didn't seem to see me. She was wringing her hands, pacing back and forth theatrically. She glanced over her shoulder toward the open door, took a hesitant step toward the hall, and then seemed to change her mind.

She closed the door and crossed the room to sit on the bed. Her shoes crunched over the spilled pills, but she didn't appear to notice them, though in the original movie they'd never spilled.

I dared to take a small step toward the bed. Then I waved my hand in front of her face.

Nothing.

It was like I was a ghost.

She picked up the framed photograph of her husband, and after staring at it for a moment, turned it facedown and changed into her silk nightgown. She climbed under the sheets, dimmed the bedside lamp, and rolled over to sleep.

This was as far as the movie had played the first time that I'd watched it. The reel broke here, with Agnes falling asleep after a troubled argument with Doctor Ellis. But the hospital room didn't flicker or shatter or turn rust-colored as I would expect if the damaged reel had reached its end. The world continued, and I continued to exist within it, ghostlike.

Was this what Rafe had felt like for years, rattling around Malice House with an identity but no form? I felt vaguely perplexed now that *I* was the one doing the haunting of poor sweet Agnes.

I was about to leave to explore the rest of the sleep institute when the door opened again, and I froze for a second time.

Very quietly, Doctor Vaughn Ellis slipped in, and I felt my breath still. My heartbeat stomped so loudly I felt certain he must hear it—*must see me*—but he didn't look my way.

The grayscale tones made his skin look sickly, almost rotting, in a way that Agnes's hadn't looked. His round dark spectacles hid his eyes. Otherwise, he was textbook handsome and taller than he'd seemed in the movie. Still, the more I looked, the more I felt certain there was something wrong with his skin. Its texture was strange. Then I realized the actor must have worn makeup, only there wasn't makeup in this reality the same way there weren't props—the medicine was real, the doctor himself was real, and the caked-on makeup had become his *actual* skin.

Doctor Ellis gazed down at the sleeping Agnes for some time. I didn't like that I didn't know what would happen next.

He can't see me, I reminded myself. *He can't hurt me.*

I took a small step toward the door, but he didn't flinch or look my way. He lowered a hand to Agnes's cheek and gently stroked her soft skin. A shudder ran up my spine. Dreading a man doing that to me, seeing it happen to someone else. I wanted to tell myself it was just a movie and Agnes was just a character, but I couldn't be sure of that anymore. Dahlia had suggested that all realities existed once created, which meant this was all *really* happening to poor Agnes. Which, I realized, meant every horror movie I'd ever seen had been real in *some* alternate reality.

I felt a little faint.

"My darling Agnes," Doctor Ellis muttered in a quiet voice. "Soon it will be you and me, as it was always meant to be. Until then, sleep soundly. Sleep sweetly."

Something crashed out in the hallway. Doctor Ellis spun toward the door, and I mirrored his movement. He grabbed a scalpel from the hospital tray that contained Agnes's medication. Clutching the blade, he threw open the door and disappeared into the hallway. I followed, unbothered by the noise I was making. As far as I'd seen, in the first half of the movie it was only the two of them left in the institute, Agnes and the doctor. Everyone else had been evacuated before the avalanche except for a nurse and the institute's founder—and Doctor Ellis had subsequently killed them both.

As soon as I was in the hallway, I saw him disappear through the door at the far end. I sprinted after him, finding myself in a stairwell. He was one flight below me and moving fast. He exited onto the floor below, and when I got there I burst out through the door, breathing hard.

Ahead of me, he was striding into the institute's lobby with its monochrome midcentury benches and now-empty nurse's station. He stopped suddenly, the scalpel clutched in his hand, facing something I couldn't yet see.

I rushed up behind him, slowing to a stop—only to realize we weren't the only ones in the institute, after all.

CHAPTER TWENTY-FOUR

—

THE SANDMAN KILLER
© 1943 Sigil Pictures

INTERIOR - INSTITUTE OFFICE - LABORATORY - NIGHT

CLOSE ON hands cleaning stainless steel
surgical tools with a rag, including a
SCALPEL. PAN OUT to Doctor Vaughn Ellis,
seemingly alone at work.

> DOCTOR VAUGHN ELLIS
> (to himself)
> These days the medical profession
> is all about the march forward into
> so-called progress, but their eyes
> are facing the wrong direction.
> They should be looking toward the
> past. Only by preserving tradition,
> understanding the lessons history
> has delivered through hard-won
> battles, will true power be
> unlocked. For it is not science that
> gave me my ability—it is something
> else entirely. Something ancient.

```
PAN FARTHER OUT to reveal the Lucerne
Institute of Sleep founder's deceased body
slumped in an office chair, his neck recently
slashed by the very scalpel in Doctor Ellis's
hand.
```

━━

A SWISS POLICE OFFICER stood in the foyer. His black-and-white uniform was caked in snow, and he was tearing off the straps of old-fashioned wooden snowshoes. The officer tossed the snowshoes to the side and then dramatically threw back his hood to reveal good looks rivaling those of the doctor himself.

"Doctor Vaughn Ellis, I presume?" The officer was breathing hard after his journey up the mountain. "We've had rescue teams trying to reach you ever since the avalanche."

Doctor Ellis moved the hand with the scalpel behind his back. "And here you are. The cavalry arrives." He cocked his head. "Is it only you?"

"I grew up snowshoeing in these mountains," the officer explained. "Hunting rabbits in winter at my grandfather's farm. I told the others not to attempt the crossing—it was too dangerous."

"Well, what a relief."

The officer gave a weary nod. "Yes, you're safe now."

"That isn't what I meant," the somnologist continued smoothly. "I never wanted the cavalry to arrive, you see. My relief comes from the fact that it's only one of you. Easier to dispatch that way."

He revealed his scalpel with vaudevillian theatricality.

The police officer, exhausted from the hike, took a moment too long to understand the danger he was in. He drew a pistol, aiming it at Doctor Ellis. The doctor didn't seem troubled, but *I* took a few steps back. Dahlia hadn't told me what would happen if I was killed in a fictional reality.

"Drop your weapon!" the officer commanded.

Doctor Ellis smiled thinly as he paced in a wide circle around the officer. He raised a slow hand to his left temple like a carnival mind-reader. "We're after solitude, you see. Agnes and I have fallen in love. And we can be together here, as long as we're alone."

A chill spread up my ankles. I looked down to find black smoke seeping across the foyer's floor. It crawled in an almost sentient fashion until it began pulling itself together into a pillar.

Eyeing the smoke, the police officer took a step back toward the front door.

As the doctor moved closer, the smoke followed in his wake. He pressed his scalpel hand against his opposite temple, the instrument jutting out between his fingers like a lone, slender horn.

"Do you know what kind of research I do at this institute, Officer? I'm aware the sign above the door indicates it's for sleep disorders, but this isn't a place for patients to come to be healed. It's a place for me to perform my experimentation. Ever since I was struck by heat lightning as a boy, I've had the unique ability to control dreams. For a while, I thought it was limited to my own. I spent decades perfecting what I call the Ellis Method, a partial trance that allows me to be both awake and dreaming at the same time. I even devised a way to bring this dream smoke—a physical manifestation of my power—into the waking world. It wasn't until I was well into my research that I discovered I also had the power to cast my dream smoke into the dreams of others. I could use it to experience their minds and learn everything about them."

He pressed his fingers harder against his temples, and the smoke swirled in a whirlpool around the officer. Bits of debris and broken glass were sucked up into its vortex.

The officer kicked at the smoke, tried to wave it away. He pointed his gun at it uselessly—before turning it on Doctor Ellis again. "You're a demon!"

As the officer moved to pull the trigger, the doctor dug his fingers even deeper into the sides of his head and grimaced. The scalpel horn twitched. The smoke rushed to form the rough shape of a person, which reached out and grabbed the officer's gun from his hand. The frightened officer staggered back as the smoke-person stalked forward, towering over him.

Then it shifted once more into a pillar.

And the thin, snakelike pillar shot down the throat of the startled officer.

I watched in horror, unable to look away.

For a second, the officer made strange expressions as the smoke moved around inside his body. Then he cried out as it burst out of his chest with a violent tear. The sharp bits of debris the smoke had gathered had coalesced into makeshift teeth. The smoke shot to the ceiling, higher and higher.

Doctor Ellis dropped his hands, and the dream smoke dissipated. Bits of broken glass and dust rained down.

The officer fell to his knees, then crashed to the floor, dead.

Doctor Ellis approached the body slowly. Using his foot, he turned over the officer's corpse so the man's dead eyes looked up at the ceiling.

"Agnes and I need our privacy, you see," he hissed to the body.

My attention, too, was on the body. But for different reasons. For the place where the dream smoke had burst out of the officer's chest bore *tooth marks* in the shape of interlocking crescent moons.

It was never a brand, I realized.

There had never been any satanic ritual involved in Joao's and Nanette's deaths. There hadn't even been any symbol. It wasn't two crescent moons—that was simply the shape that the dream smoke's "jaw" left behind when it ate its way out of its victim's body.

My hand slid to the base of my throat as I thought about all the nightmares I'd had of late. Smoke, always smoke. All this time, I'd believed it was trauma from the Malice House fire. But now it seemed that that belief was wrong, too.

A woman's scream made me spin, and a few steps away, Doctor Ellis did the same.

Agnes stood at the top of the staircase, a hand pressed to her lips as she peered down at the dead officer.

On impulse, I shouted, "Agnes, no!"

Doctor Ellis turned to look at me.

His eyes behind his dark spectacles were fixed directly on me. I was in the middle of an open lobby—there could be no mistaking what had his attention. I blinked, stunned. This whole time, I'd been shadowing his moves and he hadn't flinched, hadn't looked at me once.

I'm a ghost here.

Or was I?

I felt a chill around my ankles again, and not coming from the direction of the cracked front door. For a beat, Doctor Ellis and I stared at each other.

He adjusted his grip on the scalpel. He started to smile slowly.

I took a step back—then I felt myself slipping. The floor was no longer flat. My heel tottered on some indiscernible precipice, and I threw my arms out for balance. But it all happened too fast to think.

Without warning, I was falling.

My hand shot out, trying to find anything to hold on to. My fingers landed on the doctor's spectacles as he lunged toward me. I ripped them off his face as I fell backward.

For a second, I saw his eyes: The irises were dulled, overtaken with a cloudy sheen.

And then I was falling not onto the floor but through it, passing through a wall of frigid air, falling, falling—

I collapsed onto the movie theater floor, surrounded by Kylie and Rafe and Rob and Tyler and Dahlia.

For a moment, my head rang. I dug the heel of my hand against my forehead. The colors in the theater were jarring, too intense. Realities warred in my head, making me doubt which one was real.

Rafe dropped to one knee. "Haven, you're out. It's okay, you're out."

Dahlia stood ramrod straight with her hand outstretched toward the screen.

Breathing hard, I rolled myself into Rafe's chest, pressing my face against his shoulder. "He looked at me," I said between breaths. "He *saw* me."

I heard Kylie gasp behind me. I slowly looked back up at the screen. Dahlia had paused the film on a frame of Doctor Ellis standing over the officer's body as Agnes started down the stairs, but something strange was happening. The doctor was moving despite the still frame.

"He's coming," Kylie yelled. "He's trying to get out!"

Doctor Ellis was moving in slow motion as though underwater, his hand outstretched toward the place where I'd fallen through the floor, one hand pressed to his temple. Those glassy grayscale eyes fixed on us as though he could see straight through the movie screen and into the theater.

Can he see us?

Dahlia's face remained stiff, but her eyes widened as though not even she had anticipated this possibility. "Cut it off," she commanded quickly, turning to Rob. "Stop the reel."

Rob kicked into an erratic run up the outer aisle to the back of the theater, but I wasn't sure he would make it in time. On the screen, Doctor Ellis stretched a hand toward us. There was a surge of light, and then his fingertips appeared.

Pushing *through* the screen, gray fingertips touched a world of color.

Doctor Ellis's entire arm thrust through the screen, fingers straining and clawlike, as Kylie screamed.

Then the movie went black.

The screen was blank now. The fingers and the arm were gone.

I whipped around toward the back of the theater, where Rob stood with the projector's plug in one hand, his chest heaving.

I let out a shaky exhalation and then slumped against the theater wall, not sure anymore who was the ghost and who was real.

Once we'd taken time to recover from the incident in the movie theater, we gathered in the living room, where Tyler threw his nervous energy around by serving cups of herbal tea and Rob's phone pinged constantly with reminders for whatever studio meeting he was supposed to be at.

"Sorry," he said, silencing his phone.

Rafe asked Dahlia, "Did you know that the Sandman Killer could get out of the movie?"

She sipped Tyler's tea probingly and seemed to approve. "I didn't. Though if Haven got in, it stands to reason he could get out."

"He already *did* get out," Kylie interjected. "He got out back in 1943 when the movie was made. That's what the *Hollywooder* article was getting at, wasn't it? That characters from the Sigil Pictures films are more than just urban legends? Now we know how he uses his dreams to kill his victims—through that black smoke. He killed Joao and Nanette, here in our world, with it, too."

"So if that creepy doctor is actually *here* in our world . . ." Tyler tapped the throw pillow to his left. "How was he also *there* in the movie?" He tapped the pillow to his right.

"Echoes of himself," the witch explained. "It happened to us when we were trapped in Malice House before Haven gave us form. We existed as disembodied spirits while echoes of ourselves still lived within the world of Malice. The Sandman Killer did step out of his movie in 1943, but he left one foot back in the film, so to speak."

Kylie dropped onto the sofa, frustrated. "So ever since 1943, a black-and-white serial killer has been living in the real world? What's he been doing that entire time?"

"Well, he killed Joao and Nanette," Rafe offered.

Kylie scraped her nails through her hair. "Yes, but that's about eighty years that he *didn't* kill anyone—or at least anyone that made it into the news. What changed? In Rob's words: *Why now?*"

I dragged over my bag and took out the November *Hollywooder* issue.

I tossed it onto the coffee table with a thud. "That. That changed. The article about Sigil Pictures came out, the whole world learned about the cinematic urban legends, and someone went looking for him."

Kylie grimaced. "Uncle Arnold."

I squeezed my hands together to keep them steady. "Yes. We know for a fact that Arnold found him: Doctor Ellis was hypnotized. I know that look in people's eyes. Kylie had it. *I* had it. The Sandman Killer might have murdered Joao and Nanette, but I bet you anything Uncle Arnold was giving the orders."

A car honked outside somewhere down the road. Someone honked in response. It struck me that I had no idea what time it was. Night had come while we'd been in the theater, and the glow from Sunset Boulevard filtered skyward, making the city look radioactive.

"There's something else," I said quietly. "You watched the movie unfold while I was in it, right? You heard Doctor Ellis describe how his ability works. He can get his dream smoke inside dreamers' heads and learn about them." I looked squarely at each of them, one at a time. "*I've* been having dreams about smoke. I thought it was just recollections of the Malice House fire, but seeing that dream smoke and the way it moved made me think Doctor Ellis might have been in my head."

Tyler made a strangled noise. He switched on an extra lamp as though to chase away the darkness.

Rafe leaned forward, resting his elbows on his knees. "Are you certain?"

"Almost positive. I've dreamed that smoke."

Rafe considered this with a grave expression. We all knew what it meant: If Doctor Ellis had been inside my head, then he knew everything about me, my location, my secrets.

Kylie cleared her throat and announced, "I've had them, too."

My spine shot straight. "*What?*"

Her face looked pale as she nodded. "This whole time, I thought it was the memory of the fire, too. Lately, the dreams have been more vivid. I wake up thinking I taste smoke. So, what does this mean? He's been in my head, too? He knows where we are?"

I didn't answer because I doubted my response would comfort her. She grabbed the magazine and started flipping through it to the article as though it would suddenly reveal answers it hadn't before. I stood up, needing to move.

I paced closer to the kitchen while the others continued to speculate about what the dreams could mean. Rafe joined me, laying a hand on my upper arm.

"You look exhausted," he said quietly. "You need to sleep."

I gave a dark laugh. "And dream? Lead him right to us?"

"I'll stay here the next few days to keep watch. You'll be safe."

I clenched my jaw, looking back at the others in the living room. "The Sandman Killer has been inside my head, watching my dreams. For all I know, I dreamed about the fucking house numbers on Rob's front door. Uncle Arnold might know exactly where we are."

"If he knew, he'd have come for you already."

"Not if he's studying us like ants under glass, watching to see what other monsters we might lead him to. But we still may have one advantage," I whispered. "We know that Uncle Arnold is going to be at Pharmacy Bar on Saturday night at ten o'clock to meet OneEyeOpen. It doesn't matter if he knows that's me or not—he's still planning on being there. This could be our chance to corner him. Go after him before he comes after us. I can't afford to wait around for a better opportunity. I have the Lundie Bay police calling me, asking questions. It might not be long before the Joshua Tree police start in on me, too."

"Kylie was adamant about you not contacting Decline.A.Copy."

"That was before we knew that Uncle Arnold knows our location." I stepped closer, wetting my lips. "Listen, I don't want Kylie or any of them involved. Kylie was already hypnotized by Uncle Arnold once—I can't put her at risk of that happening again. And it isn't fair to drag Rob and Tyler into more danger."

"Then what are you saying?"

I squeezed his arm. "You and me. Like you said, Uncle Arnold is one of our monsters. If anyone knows how to deal with him, it's us."

Rafe smoothed an errant strand of hair back from my face. His jaw relaxed. "Okay."

I raised my eyebrows, surprised at his ready acceptance. "Okay?"

"You let me deal with him directly, got it?" There was an edge in his voice. "Uncle Arnold's ability doesn't work on me. He's a weak man physically. I can overpower him."

I nodded shakily. "Yes, all right."

"Do you have a plan?"

"I'm working on one." I let my hand fall away from his arm and leaned back against the wall, tapping my heel against the floor. "You'll really stay here for a while?"

"I told you—I'll do anything you ask, darling."

Our eyes met.

Before I could answer, Kylie called my name.

Dahlia came near, slinging a leather purse onto one shoulder. She ran her eyes up and down Rafe and me standing close together and then said, "I need to get back to Portland. And, Rafe?" A sly smile cracked her face. "Be seeing you soon."

It gave me goose bumps to hear her cryptic allusion to their deal. Rob walked her out of the house, speaking quietly to her in his producer way, and even after she was gone, I didn't feel as though she'd entirely left.

Rafe busied himself by cleaning up the mugs from the living room and said nothing else.

CHAPTER TWENTY-FIVE

———

THE HUNDREDTH STAIR
© 1941 Sigil Pictures

EXTERIOR — SEA CLIFFS - DAY

CAMERA PANS WITH Jane, nervous yet brave,
entering one of the sea caves beneath their
Victorian house. She wears her seashell charms
as though for protection. A wet, slithering
sound comes from deep within the cave.

Jane pauses, then takes another step inside.

———

WITH THE MEETING at Pharmacy Bar looming, I didn't have
much time to put gears into motion. I told Kylie a small lie that I'd
found a lead on an urban legends blog, and I closed myself up in my
bedroom under the guise of doing research.

Fortunately, I'd remembered the name of the casting website I'd
briefly glimpsed on Rob's computer screen. It was the kind of site that
hired actors for one-off roles for music videos or background work.
I navigated to the site and selected Los Angeles as the location, then
searched for female actors between twenty-five and thirty-five years of
age. Hundreds of faces stared back at me in polished headshots, each

taken from the same angle, designed to make their eyes look big, their necks matchstick-like. I settled on a serious-looking woman named Carla with shoulder-length brown hair that was similar to mine. I offered her two hundred dollars for a few hours' work, claiming it was a stand-in gig as part of a location scouting project and wouldn't yet be filmed.

As soon as it was done, I tossed my laptop aside, feeling antsy.

She won't be at risk. I would be there. Rafe would be there. The plan was that Uncle Arnold wouldn't even make it to Carla—or anyone else—before Rafe got to him first.

When Saturday arrived, I made the excuse that I was going to Rafe's hotel to pick up my artwork. Rob had gone to a dinner meeting with his team, and Kylie had barely stepped out of her room all day; Patrick Kane had sent her the first draft chapters of his Amory Marbury biography, so she was clearly absorbed in that.

I checked the time—nine o'clock. The actress, Carla, was scheduled to arrive at Pharmacy Bar in thirty minutes.

I knocked lightly on Kylie's door. When she called that it was open, I cracked it enough to press my face through. "Rafe will be here soon to pick me up. I just wanted to say—" I swallowed. "Bye."

She was sprawled on the bed in loose pajama bottoms and a T-shirt that advertised a singer who'd been dead since before she was born. She looked so young. My chest seized up.

She peered over her laptop. "You sure you don't need help carrying the artwork?"

"Rafe and I can handle it. It isn't that much."

"Okay, then."

Her eyes had already darted back to the computer screen, hungry to devour paragraph after paragraph of our father's life. Briefly, I wondered what was in those pages. How had Patrick Kane classified my relationship with him? Strained? Distant? Or was Mr. Kane perceptive enough to read between the lines and see the small glow of warmth there?

Tyler was walking down the hall as I was headed back to my room. He gave me a sly wink. "He's cute, you know. Your boyfriend or whatever you want to call him. *I* get it."

"Thanks, Tyler."

In my room, I stripped out of my jeans. I didn't dare go to the Pharmacy Bar rendezvous looking anything like myself, so I'd borrowed one of the least extravagant dresses from Rob's mannequins, a waist-hugging black minidress that had been worn in *Sweet Morning Light*. I dressed quickly, then tucked my hair into a twist so it looked like a bob.

When I went downstairs, Rafe's Range Rover wasn't in the driveway yet, so I waited out on the deck that overlooked the city.

The world beyond Rob's house was a mystery. The mannequins might startle me, but at least they stayed in one place. Out there, the city was too loud, too frenetic, three million lives lived in neon. New York had a weight to it that made me feel pleasantly smothered. Manhattan changed, but glacially. Skyscrapers didn't come down and go up overnight. Here, though, everything felt afloat—the roads, the houses, the shops. Tomorrow everything could look different.

It was the people, too—people like Carla, whose profile said she was from Milwaukee—who had washed up on this shore from elsewhere, either running toward a dream or from a nightmare. In my case, it was both, though running just left me feeling like all I was doing was turning in circles.

My phone's ringtone trilled, and I dragged it out of my pocket. It was an unlisted number.

Thumb hesitating over the button, I sucked in a breath. The Lundie Bay detective's caller ID had always come up when he'd called before.

"Hello?" I asked tentatively.

No one immediately spoke. Then a woman's lightly accented voice said, "How did you figure it out? I thought I scrubbed all the genealogy websites."

Miracle Acosta.

I clutched the phone hard, glancing inside through the windows. Kylie was reading upstairs in her room, and Rafe hadn't arrived yet.

I swallowed a lump that had formed in my throat. "It was a genealogy specialist." I spoke slowly, knowing I needed to be careful with my words.

Miracle clicked her tongue. "Well, I guess murder doesn't scare *you* off after what happened in Washington."

So she knew about the Malice House fire, probably even about the murders that came before it. She must have gotten her hands on the police reports.

I asked cautiously, "You knew who Kylie and I were in Joshua Tree, didn't you?"

"You? Yes. Your sister? No. Amory never said anything about another daughter. It took some work to figure out her role here. Joao was always better than me at hacking into police reports."

A hitch of regret hung in her voice, giving me an opening.

Walking to the edge of the deck, I looked down over the city. "I don't think you killed Nanette Fields—the woman out in Joshua Tree. Or Joao."

Miracle snorted. "You don't think I killed my own beloved nephew and a random stranger? How *gracious* of you. For the record, I don't think you killed them, either. Or any of those people up in Washington." She paused. "But I suspect you know *what* did."

Her voice held dark meaning. No who, but *what.* Gone was the dippy yoga practitioner driving around in a Desert Wanderer van. This Miracle Acosta was thornier, and I liked it.

"Why was Joao in LA before he was killed?"

"We were researching an article that had recently come out. Maybe you've seen it—maybe it brought you to LA, too. Those film people mentioned in the article, Max Faraday and Richard Alton, had Acosta blood."

So the *Hollywooder* article had drawn all of us to the city: Uncle Arnold, Kylie and me through Rob, and Joao and Miracle. Almost as though the curse itself was at work in the printed words.

"Was Joao a . . . curseworker?" According to what Miracle had told me, he had written disturbing, macabre stories in his journal—but she could have been lying to me about that.

She didn't answer right away. "You know, that's the same word Amory used for it. Joao and I, we preferred plainer terms."

"Like?"

"Monster."

I flinched. "Monsters are what we create, not what we are."

She laughed out loud at this. "Cousin, come on. The curse doesn't care which end you are on. The creation and the creator are just different sides of the same evil."

My chest felt tight at her words, and I wondered if my father, whom she must have had some contact with to know the things she did, had told her about my origin.

"So, then, you and Joao—that's what you are? Monsters?"

Her laughter was gone now. Breathing hard into the phone, she said, "No, cousin. Every curseworker, as you call us, has a choice. A choice that hundreds of us have faced—those with the Acosta blood, working in film, in fiction, in fine art, all over the world. You can either be what you create—or you can hunt it."

My hand holding the phone trembled.

Her voice turned softer, more like the woman I'd first met at the campground. "Joao and I went to LA to track down the monsters listed in that article, but one of them got to him first. Be careful, cousin. It isn't only the creations out there you should fear. Not all of us Acosta curseworkers have made the *right* choice." She paused. "I hope you and your sister do."

She hung up before I could ask more questions. I stared at the blank phone screen, trying to process the information Miracle had given me.

"Haven? Ready?"

Rafe slid open the deck's gliding door, his head sticking out, and I jumped. I shoved my phone in my purse and nodded. He took a minute to look me over in the dress, letting out a low whistle.

"Don't get used to it," I said.

Rafe grinned. "I prefer the baggy sweatpants anyway. Easier to take off."

I rolled my eyes, worries still creeping into my mind. I checked the time. "We should go."

As we climbed into his Range Rover, he counted off on his fingers. "Duct tape. Rope. Ketamine." He reached into the back seat and dropped something heavy into my lap. "And this."

I picked up the stun gun, hefting its weight, as he steered down Egret Drive. "How'd you get a stun gun?"

"How? Crime. Usually, crime is the answer." Reading the worry on my face, he reached out to squeeze my hand in my lap. "It's going to work out, Haven."

I watched the houses roll by, wishing I had his confidence. It had been almost three months since I'd faced Uncle Arnold. My body tensed as muscle memory kicked in, recalling the feeling of being under his spell. My consciousness had divided, with one part of me shoved back into the cobwebs and the other part—the one Arnold controlled—hurling myself at Pinchy to kill him at his command.

I slid the stun gun into my purse.

⎯⎯

Sunset Boulevard was busy.

"Good. It's still here." Rafe pulled the Range Rover into a street parking spot beside a palm tree that had been marked with a city notice closing off the spot for a special event. When we climbed out of the car, Rafe ripped the notice down and shoved it into a trash can.

"Are *you* the city government in this case?"

He chuckled wickedly.

I pulled my jacket collar up around my neck. This time of year, it was too hot for a jacket, but I'd found this one in Rob's coat closet and wanted something to hide behind. One more layer between Uncle Arnold and me.

"The actor has what she needs?" Rafe asked, his eyes canvassing the street.

I gave a slight nod. "A courier delivered everything to her apartment yesterday." I'd sent a film reel box that I'd borrowed from Rob's collection without his knowledge, as well as the green canvas jacket that I'd worn the night of the Malice House fire—a jacket Uncle Arnold had seen me in.

Music thumped down the alley from Pharmacy Bar's open door.

Rafe pressed a hand to the small of my back. "Get a seat in the booth in the back by the bathrooms. I already paid the bartender to hold it for you. It's dark back there—Arnold won't see you. He'll go straight for the woman at the bar he's supposed to meet."

I pulled out my phone and scrolled back through my Text Crypt messages with Arnold to double-check.

Decline.A.Copy: Pharmacy Bar. Saturday, 10 p.m. Bring the film. Big things coming. Get ready to rewrite the fucking world.

Decline.A.Copy: OneEyeOpen, you there? Meeting time/location a go? Need a confirmation.

OneEyeOpen: Meeting a go. I have the reel. Pharmacy Bar. Saturday. 10 p.m. I'll be in a green jacket at the bar—I'm female if it matters lol.

We couldn't be certain that Uncle Arnold didn't know he was talking to me on the Text Crypt app, so I had selected an actor from the casting website who looked like me from the back. We needed to lure Arnold into the bar—a busy public place with too many people to compel at once, complete with loud music to drown out his whispers.

Rafe cupped my jaw. "I'll be in the Range Rover, watching. I'll follow him into the bar—you just stay in the back."

I nodded and slipped in my earplugs. Rafe hadn't wanted me to go into Pharmacy Bar at all, but I had insisted. The actor I'd hired, Carla, would be alone with Uncle Arnold otherwise, and my conscience couldn't allow me to leave her with him.

I wasn't *that* much of a monster.

As Rafe headed back to the car, I pulled my collar up higher and made my way down the alley. Stoners and Gen X hipsters littered the area, sharing joints or waiting for rideshares. The earplugs dulled my awareness in a way I didn't like, but I didn't have a choice.

As soon as I pushed open the bar door, the chill of air-conditioning blew over me. It was busy, just as we wanted. Nearly every seat and table was filled. Nineties throwbacks blasted on the speakers, the beat pulsing up from the floor.

I went to the bar and got the bartender's attention. It was the same handlebar-mustache guy as before, and he must have recognized me because he pointed toward the back and yelled over the crowd, "The one in the corner. Saved for you."

I could barely hear him over the earplugs. I got a beer and shuffled through the crowd to the rear portion, where a couple was sitting in the booth near the restrooms despite the RESERVED sign. They were making out like one of them had been away at war.

When I set my beer down hard on the table, they broke apart. I pointed emphatically toward the sign, and they grumbled as they slid out of the booth.

I took their place, settling into the shadows. From here, I had a clear view of the bar and a nearly clear view of the front door. I squeezed my legs together under the table, taking an anxious swig of beer.

It wasn't long before a woman came in, dressed in my green cargo jacket. Carla. She stopped a few feet into the bar and looked around like she thought there might be cameras after all, but I'd been clear in my instructions that our "producers" would be planted in the crowd and she was to simply go to the bar, order a glass of wine, and wait for an hour. After that, she could leave. I'd already paid her half the fee up front.

Squaring her shoulders, she pushed through the crowd. She *did* look a lot like me from the back. From the front, her face was prettier, more delicate than mine. But I didn't intend for Uncle Arnold to get close enough to her to see her features.

I glanced down at my phone on the table. The screen was black, no updates from Rafe.

My foot jiggled under the table.

The song switched to "Zombie" by the Cranberries. A few drunk guys near my booth started jumping around like they were in a mosh pit. I hunched down farther in Rob's coat, picking at the beer bottle's label.

Then, from the corner of my eye, I saw the door swing open. My view was somewhat hidden by a corner, so there was a lag before I saw whoever had come in. I leaned forward, trying to get a better look.

My phone suddenly lit up on the table. I glanced down and saw a text from Rafe:

He's here. It's him. He's going in now.

"Shit." I grabbed the phone and slid it into my lap, clutching it tightly. A thick figure appeared at the edge of my vision, still hanging just inside the front door. It was a man, on the short side. All I could glimpse through the crowd was a section of his shoulder and a slice of the side of his head. He was balding, but what white hair remained was cut short on the sides. He was wearing a windbreaker.

He turned to look toward the bar, and my breath stopped. Now I had a clear view of his face. It was Arnold, but he had changed. Gone were the glasses. His 1950s-style clean shave had been replaced with a sparse goatee.

A chill ran up the length of my arms.

He strained to look over the crowd, looking irritated. I found myself sinking deeper into the booth, wishing I could disappear into it. My phone vibrated in my lap.

I'm just outside. Ready.

Once Arnold approached Carla—whether he thought it was me or not—and realized there was a mistake, he'd leave. Rafe was waiting in the alley to incapacitate him and drag him into the back of the Range Rover.

Arnold moved around a cluster of college-aged guys at a high top, then stopped. He was staring fixedly at Carla at the bar. My throat tightened in fear. Had he come here expecting to find me? I felt sure of it.

He watched Carla take a sip of wine. Once she set down her drink, his lips pursed slightly in a grim smile, and he took a step toward the bar.

The front door swung open suddenly behind him, and a tall, attractive man came striding in. It took me a minute to recognize who I was looking at.

Tyler?

I drew in a sharp breath as my mind twisted in circles. What was Tyler doing here? Had he followed me and Rafe? I gripped the edge of the table. This was wrong. Tyler wasn't supposed to be here. . . .

I grabbed my phone to text Rafe but froze as Tyler spotted Carla sitting at the bar. He immediately pushed his way to her—right past Uncle Arnold, who hung back uncertainly—and placed his hand on the woman's shoulder.

She turned, a confused look on her face. Whatever Tyler had been saying to her, he stopped when he realized it wasn't me.

Now it was Tyler's turn to look confused. He stepped back, turning in a slow circle around the bar, searching the crowd. He called out loudly. I couldn't hear him with my earplugs in, but I could guess the syllables from the movement of his lips. He was calling my name.

No, I thought. *No!*

He locked eyes with me in the back booth and let out a visible sigh of relief. He crossed toward my booth just as I was raising my hand, waving frantically for him to stop.

Uncle Arnold had retreated from the bar the second he'd seen that Carla wasn't me. Now he was following Tyler's movements with his gaze.

No, no . . .

Everything was happening too fast. My head couldn't catch up with reality.

Tyler stopped at my booth, raking his hands over his face. He started saying something urgent, but I shook my head, already sliding out of the booth. I grabbed him and pulled him close.

"What the hell are you doing here?"

I couldn't hear his response with the earplugs. I pulled one out just far enough to hear him saying, ". . . told him it was wrong to do it behind your back. They've already optioned the article. It's done. He's trying to find old Sigil Pictures props now. . . ."

My heart was racing faster than my head. I practically slurred, "Tyler, what are you talking about?"

"Donovan! He was finally able to convince Insight Entertainment to option the *Hollywooder* article because of *you*. He'd always been missing an entry point into the story—personal stakes the audience could connect with. When you showed up that first night talking about real-life curses, he realized he could use you as that entry point. He's been recording everything. The interview with Nanette, filming you around the house . . . Honestly, Haven, I *told* him it was fucked-up—"

I shoved the earplug back into my ear and grabbed my phone, trying to text with thumbs that had gone numb.

This had all gone wrong so fast.

Before I could send the text to Rafe, I felt a shadow blocking the light from the bar and looked up in slow dread to find Uncle Arnold standing over my table, grinning widely, his yellow teeth still behind lips that were moving ever so slightly.

CHAPTER TWENTY-SIX

PURGATORY'S DOOR
© 1955 Sigil Pictures

INTERIOR — THE DRUID BAR — NIGHT

              MICKEY KELLY
     The girl ain't gone.

              DETECTIVE NICK DRAM
     I have a body in the city morgue
     that says otherwise.

              MICKEY KELLY
                (smirking)
     I didn't say she ain't dead. I said
     she ain't gone. You ever heard of
     nuance, Dram? Horns, open the door
     for our detective friend. Give him a
     good look at . . . Purgatory.

CLOSE ON the goat-headed doorman taking a
MAGIC BRASS DOORKNOB out of his pocket.

FOR A SECOND, I could only stare. It was as though I'd forgotten Uncle Arnold was real. In my mind, he was still just a character in an old, forgotten manuscript. His existence limited to twelve-point Times New Roman.

Then reason slammed back into me, and I hit Send on as much of the message as I'd been able to write.

Need Yo.

Fuck. Hopefully Rafe would understand. I pressed my hands over my ears. My palms, the earplugs—I wasn't taking any chances. Arnold's hot gaze scoured over me, then flickered to the speakers still blasting Dolores O'Riordan's ethereal voice.

His eyes narrowed.

Arnold suddenly grabbed Tyler's arm and pulled him close. Tyler flinched, but Arnold had already started whispering before he pulled away.

"Shut up!" I shouted, shaking my head, not daring to take my hands off my ears.

But it was too late.

The change in Tyler was immediate. His body softened. His eyes took on the glassy sheen that I'd seen so many times before. I scooted to the farthest corner of the booth, afraid of what he might have commanded Tyler to do.

I had a stun gun, but could I really hurt Tyler if he attacked me?

But Tyler didn't lunge for me. He calmly picked up the votive candle from the table, then filched the half-full vodka bottle from the neighboring table. The bar goers shouted obscenities, but Tyler ignored them as he overturned the bottle on the floor. A hipster guy jumped up, yelling at him, and Tyler answered by splashing him and his friends with vodka, too.

I understood then.

The front door slammed open, and Rafe came hurtling in. He took in the situation with a quick sweep of his head, his focus settling on me amid the chaos.

He stalked toward my booth, his eyes throwing daggers at Uncle Arnold. He dropped a heavy hand on the old man's shoulder, spinning him around so they were face-to-face.

If Uncle Arnold was shocked to see Rafe, he didn't show it. He grinned ghoulishly and said something I couldn't hear with my earplugs in. Rafe answered, his hand like a vise on his shoulder, ready to drag him out.

Behind them, Tyler raised the candle over the area he'd soaked with vodka. A few people who'd been seated at the table were on their feet now, mopping up the alcohol on their clothes and faces with paper napkins.

"Rafe!" I yelled. "Tyler—stop Tyler!"

Rafe moved toward Tyler, dragging Uncle Arnold with him. A second before Rafe swiped his free hand at him, Tyler dropped the candle.

It struck the vodka puddle. Flames erupted across the bar floor in quick succession. A film of fire bloomed on the alcohol-soaked couples, who jumped up, shrieking. The room filled with screams.

Tyler gave no reaction other than jumping on the bar, grabbing another bottle, and pouring it onto the bar top, glassy-eyed and eerily calm the entire time.

"Rafe!" I yelled.

He was busy trying to wrestle a broken bottle away from Arnold.

"Shit. Shit. Shit." I shoved up from the booth, pushed my way to the bar, and threw myself on Tyler's pant leg, trying to pull him down from the bar. But Tyler was well over six feet tall and spent hours every day lifting weights. He gave me a single sharp kick that sent me staggering back.

I scrambled back to the booth to get my purse and pulled out the stun gun. I struggled my way through the panicked crowd until I could return to the bar, and then jabbed the stun gun against Tyler's calf.

It pulsed and snapped, causing Tyler's body to gyrate, but he still didn't stop. He was compelled by Uncle Arnold to light the bar on fire, and nothing could break that, not even fifty thousand volts. I'd once been there, too—I'd fought Pinchy with every ounce of my strength, unable to break the spell.

Rafe reached toward Tyler with one hand while clinging to Uncle Arnold's collar with the other. He managed to wrestle the bottle out of Tyler's hand, but Uncle Arnold did a little twist and slipped right out of his windbreaker. It hung limp in Rafe's hand.

Uncle Arnold bolted for the door.

Rafe threw me a sharp look full of questions.

I had to yell over the noise. "You've got to get Tyler out of here! I'll get Arnold!"

Rafe started to object, but I wasn't enough of a physical match to stop Tyler from setting fire to everyone in the bar.

But the stun gun will work on Arnold.

Rafe tossed me a roll of duct tape. "Don't try to take him on your own. Just distract him, make sure he doesn't get out of your sight—I'll be there as soon as I can."

I shoved out the door as patrons pushed their way out after me, frantic to escape the flames. In the distance, sirens wailed to life. The alley was packed with people running toward Sunset Boulevard, where a crowd of onlookers had gathered, filming the bar fire with their phones. There was no sign of Uncle Arnold.

He wouldn't flee toward the cameras, I reasoned.

I spun around—the other end of the alley was deserted. Everyone who'd been loitering there must have hurried to Sunset when the fire began. But after a moment, a shadow on the brick wall showed a portly figure shuffling away.

I ran into the alley, stun gun in hand, and turned the corner. The passage extended past the rear entrances of Pharmacy Bar and several other bars. A few people were scurrying out the bar's open back door and racing off. Uncle Arnold was about twenty feet ahead of me, limping and winded.

He was an out-of-shape elderly man riddled with a lifetime of disease and alcoholism—and slowed down by Pinchy's old wound.

I can do this.

My lungs burned as I sprinted after him. He flashed a wide-eyed look over his shoulder, shambling toward the alley's corner with all his strength. Sirens blared in the distance, drawing closer. The smell of smoke permeated everything.

"Stop, Arnold!" I yelled.

But he didn't. He limped toward a dead-end portion of the alley where the streetlight had gone out. My pulse kicked up, warning me. Something wasn't right. Did he think he could hide? *Here?*

I ran up behind him, throwing myself on his back and tackling him to the ground. He came down readily, tripping over his own feet. His front collided hard with the ground. His body cushioned my own fall, though my right knee smacked into the concrete, shooting pain up my body.

He tried to scramble onto his hands and knees to crawl away, but I dug my fingers into his shoulder, using my weight to pin him down while I fumbled with the stun gun.

He shouted something that my earplugs muffled. It sounded like *"Get off."*

"Rewrite the world, huh?" I hit the stun gun's ON button, then let it crackle a moment. "That'll be hard to do when Rafe cuts out your tongue."

I jammed the stun gun into his side. His body started flopping like a landed fish. He screamed something, and this time the words were audible.

"Get her off!"

Get *her* off—it took a second to process what that meant, but I tossed my head around at the shadows, fearful that I'd misjudged the situation.

A man lunged out of the shadows. No—not a man. A *thing.* It towered seven feet tall over me, hulking arms outstretched. The dark suit it wore hid rippling muscles. Resting on its human shoulders was a massive goat's head. Two brown horns curved out from either side of the creature's skull, glistening in the low light.

I'd seen this thing before. . . . No, I'd heard about it.

The Killarney Doorman.

The beast snatched me by the shoulders with preternatural strength and hoisted me off Uncle Arnold. The old man's body sagged on the dirty ground, stunned from the voltage.

I kicked and screamed, but the Doorman's strength was too great. He carried me deeper into the unlit portion of the alley, amid overflowing trash cans that reeked of rotting bar food. Rats scurried away from us.

Without saying a word, he pinned my hands behind my back so I couldn't gain leverage. He was holding me from behind, so all I could see from the corner of my eye was a sliver of his terrible face. His odor was worse than that of the trash.

Uncle Arnold moved. Gingerly, in clear pain, he pushed himself to his hands and knees. His head swiveled toward where the Killarney Doorman had me trapped in the darkness. Exhaustion and anger twisted his features, but there was a small lick of triumph there, too.

He managed to get to his feet, shakily brushing the dirt and trash off his shirt, and then limped over to join us.

I couldn't catch my breath. My sweaty hair had come out of the faux bob and now streaked my face. The black dress was ripped, hitched up on one side to my hip.

All I could see of Arnold's face as he entered the shadows was a gleam catching on his eyes and teeth. He reached up to remove the earplug from my left ear.

"No!" I twisted my head away, but Arnold grabbed a fistful of my hair and wrenched my head to the side. He pulled out first the left earplug, then the right. He tossed them into one of the overflowing trash heaps.

"Hello, OneEyeOpen." His voice was strained, struggling to catch his breath. He leaned to the side and coughed hard. "I suspected it was you."

"Because you've been in my head," I hissed. "Or your *friend* has, since apparently you can't do shit for yourself. Doctor Ellis, right?" I threw the accusation at him, hoping to make him worry he'd misjudged how much I knew.

But Arnold only gave a tight shrug, unconcerned. "Every living creature seeks out its own kind. Yes, I found Doctor Ellis. And this fellow."

I flinched as the Killarney Doorman shifted behind me, his massive chest like a redwood tree trunk against my back.

"What, you were lonely?" I quipped.

"No, not really." He had caught his breath now. He snapped sharply, "Give me your phone."

He hadn't compelled me to do it—that took a particular kind of whisper.

"Fuck you," I spat.

He sidled up, pressing his pudgy face close to my left ear. "We both know how easy I could make you do it, Haven. One whisper and you'd be on your knees, sucking my cock. Don't make me compel you. It makes people dolts, and I don't like working with dolts. Wouldn't you rather have your rational mind working? Hmm?" He practically bared his teeth as he hissed, "So I'll ask one more time. Give me your phone."

Chin raised against his hot breath, I begrudgingly felt through the objects in my purse and came out with my phone.

He snatched it out of my hand. "The passcode?"

I reluctantly told him. He turned away as he entered in my code and typed into my phone. Then he slid my phone into his pocket.

"What did you do?" I asked through a clenched jaw.

Instead of answering, he signaled to the Killarney Doorman. "My suite. We'll wait there." He pulled out a handkerchief to pat the sweat beading his balding head.

A wave of panic rose in my chest. I struggled to try to get away from the Doorman, though it was useless. He was too strong. My eyes went to the end of the alley, urging Rafe to appear. What had happened back at the bar?

The Killarney Doorman let me go and shoved me against the brick wall. My back smacked it hard, air rushing out of my lungs. He had positioned himself between me and freedom, holding out a meaty hand to warn me against an escape attempt. His goat eyes blinked mechanically, his snout softly sampling the air.

His eyes didn't have the cloudy sheen of Uncle Arnold's hypnotism victims. Maybe I could reason with him? *Or maybe he's perfectly willing to be Arnold's thug.*

With his other hand, he removed a doorknob from his suit pocket. It was old-fashioned and ornate, an etched brass bulb. He lumbered over to a gatelike door that capped off one building's exterior fire escape. He thrust the knob into the wrong side of the door—the hinge side—and the whole metal rectangle began to glow crimson around the edges.

Back against the bricks, breathing hard, I slid a step away from the glowing door.

The Doorman turned the knob, pulling it open to reveal such a strongly burning light that I had to shield my eyes.

"Come on," Arnold snapped. "Don't be shy now."

He signaled to the Doorman, who pulled me by the wrist toward the opening. Beyond were hazy shapes I couldn't quite make out with the red light stinging my eyes.

I dug in my heels, but the monster's grip was unyielding.

"Haven!"

I turned to see Rafe at the far end of the alley, chest rising and falling hard. Soot streaked one side of his face. His clothes were disheveled, torn. As soon as our eyes locked, he burst into a sprint.

Uncle Arnold's body tensed behind me. "Time to go."

The Killarney Doorman loomed behind me, blocking any return to the alley. As I was opening my mouth to scream for Rafe, the old man gave me a hard shove. I stumbled toward the crimson light, wincing as its dry energy hit me like a chemical burn.

I fell forward.

The last thing I saw before the light blinded me was Uncle Arnold giving a mean little wave to Rafe before he, too, stepped through the doorway.

CHAPTER TWENTY-SEVEN

—

THE CANDY HOUSE
© 1951 Sigil Pictures

EXTERIOR — FRONT DOOR — NIGHT

A FACE looms in the window. A moment later, a
BEAUTIFUL WOMAN opens the door.

> NURSE
> Children? Out on your own? Where
> have you come from? Hurry inside
> before you freeze to death, you poor
> teddy bears!

> ANDRZEJ
> This is your house?

> NURSE
> A rural hospital, in fact. I care
> for those who have suffered in the
> war. It's only me now. Come, come. I
> haven't much, but I do have beds and
> broth. Even a little candy.

She SMILES WARMLY. From somewhere inside, a
patient SCREAMS.

———

TIME MOVED TOO FAST, too slow. The air, the light—both
burned. It was like a dream that stretched for what felt like years only
to pop like a soap bubble. Once my head stopped spinning, it took
three hard blinks to chase away the lingering imprint of the crimson
light to see where I was.

The dark shapes I'd glimpsed through the glowing doorway were
furniture. I was on my hands and knees in the foyer of a presidential
hotel suite. It was opulent, but utterly filthy. Food delivery cartons
littered the tables. Clothes were balled up on the floor. The bedsheets
looked stained by some kind of sauce—maybe ketchup.

Not purgatory, at least. Just a trashed hotel room.

The Killarney Doorman grabbed my collar, hoisting me to my feet.
A second later, Uncle Arnold stepped through the hotel door, pressing
the pads of his fingers against his eyes, blinking as hard as I had. The
Doorman closed the door behind him, removed the brass doorknob,
and placed it in his suit pocket. The portal's glowing edges dissipated
until it was once more a simple hotel door, and the monster stood
before it at calm attention, guarding against my escape.

Uncle Arnold mopped his face with his handkerchief. He cut a line
for the room's kitchenette, where he poured himself a shaky glass of
whiskey, downing it in a few gulps.

I did a quick survey for anything I could use as a weapon—there
was a butter knife on a room-service tray, a heavy alarm clock on the
side table, plenty of sharp corners on the furniture. It was the kind
of place that cost thousands of dollars a night, but what was money
to a man who could whisper his way through the front desk staff? It

looked like Uncle Arnold had been holed up here for weeks, eating room service and delivery meals. I quickly scanned the papers stacked in messy piles on the table. Underlined photocopies of the *Hollywooder* article, notebooks filled with lists of names.

Nanette's name was there, circled twice.

"Don't touch anything." My captor jabbed a finger toward the upholstered sofa. "Sit and shut up."

He poured himself another drink and, once his hands had stopped shaking, he tugged fresh clothes out of the dresser before disappearing into the bathroom.

I took the opportunity to look closer at the Killarney Doorman. The alley's shadows had blurred his edges, muddied his details. Here in the hotel suite, a weak entryway light shone over his massive head, highlighting his curving horns. I knew that lore from several different cultures included a creature with a man's body and a goat's head, but the quasi-religious image that rose in my memory was godlike, reverential: a prophet seated on a golden throne. However, the last thing I'd call the Killarney Doorman was regal. Beneath his worn three-piece suit, he had the body of a warrior if none of the bearing. His fur was matted and dirty around his mouth. A secretion oozed from his eyes, making him look sickly. His horns, while massive, were chipped from years of battle.

He was no deity—he was a thug.

Uncle Arnold came out of the bathroom wearing rumpled but clean clothes. The sticky remnants of alley trash were gone from his face. He returned to the whiskey bottle as though he hadn't taken two shots a moment before.

He held up the bottle toward me in a silent question.

I crossed my legs on the sofa and sneered. "No thanks."

Once he'd poured his drink, he collapsed into a lounge chair opposite the sofa, releasing a long, thin sigh. He raised his glass to his lips.

"You were at the Gemini Entertainment soundstage when we spoke to Nanette Fields, weren't you?" I demanded. "You've known where I've been ever since you had Doctor Ellis watching me through my dreams."

He gave a mirthless smile. "The thing about dreams is they're inexact. Doctor Ellis can only pick up clues. He thought you were in LA but wasn't certain, so I staked out Nanette Fields for a few days, figuring you'd show up to ask her about the article sooner or later."

Something turned rotten in my stomach. *He was watching me for a while.* I squeezed my legs tighter together. "How many Sigil monsters have you rounded up? Just the Killarney Doorman and Doctor Ellis? Where *is* Doctor Ellis?"

Arnold leveled a calculated smile at me that said his secrets would die with him.

I let out a frustrated breath, then leaned forward to switch tactics. "But why kill them?"

He paused, head cocking. In a drawn-out way that made my skin tingle, he said, "You'll have to be more specific."

"Joao Acosta and Nanette Fields."

"Oh. Them."

Chilled, I asked, "Why, have there been more?"

He leaned back in the lounge chair, the whiskey glass dangling from his hand, a strange light in his eyes. "Joao was hunting monsters—monsters that I needed. He got in the way." The drink had loosened his limbs and made his tongue sluggish.

"So you had Doctor Ellis kill him with his dream smoke."

"Joao wasn't only hunting monsters, doll. He was also hunting the people who brought them to life. It wouldn't have been long before he heard about the unexplained deaths up in the Pacific Northwest and came looking for you." He pointed the bottle my way. "Frankly, I did you a favor."

My jaw clenched. "And Nanette?"

He stood up, taking his time, drifting to the table to rifle through several bags of junk food. He finally returned with a half-eaten bag of pretzels. He popped one into his mouth, chewing infuriatingly slowly.

"Nanette," he echoed at last. "Her mind was sharper than I anticipated for a woman of her age. She figured out how to break the compulsion. She was going to warn you. Obviously, I couldn't have that."

I swallowed. "And the others? There have been others, haven't there?"

Arnold crumpled the pretzel bag, giving a shrug. "Of course. But I suspect you're interested in Emily Blackwell, the journalist who wrote the Hollywooder article. Her I told to jump off the Santa Monica pier . . . and to forget how to swim."

"*Why?*" I whispered.

"To blow up the story, of course. Make sure you heard about it and came to LA."

I covered my face with one hand, fingers digging hard into my skull as I tried to wrap my mind around yet another death.

Uncle Arnold tossed the pretzel bag on the floor. "You have such a unique ability, Haven. I don't know why you think we have to be enemies. There's so much we could do together. You think I'm some storybook villain, but you must give your father more credit than that. His writing was nuanced, not some dime-store thriller. Is it so hard to believe I'm just a person walking life's bumpy path, guessing at switchbacks, uncertain what may lie at the end? I want the same thing everyone wants. Safety, comfort. To leave a mark."

It was like he'd forgotten I'd already read "Everyone's Favorite Uncle," and the part where he forced women to obey him. The man before me was no plucky protagonist.

I straightened my back with what strength I could scrape together. "Bullshit. You don't want safety. You want control."

Annoyance flitted over his features, twisting his lips and nose, but there were burning coals of satisfaction in his eyes, too. I'd called him on his lies, and he *liked* it.

Someone knocked on the door.

My pulse quickened. I sucked in a breath; anything could walk through that door. *Or slither.*

Uncle Arnold bobbed a nod toward the Doorman, who turned with his slow, laborious gait to open the door.

Kylie stepped in.

She was looking down at her phone with twitchy, distracted energy. Her purse dangled carelessly from one shoulder. She wore the same band T-shirt as before but had swapped the pajama bottoms for blue leggings.

"Hey—" She froze when she saw the goat-headed man looming over her. Her eyes widened. "Oh, *fuck.*"

I shoved myself up to my feet. *"Kylie?"*

The Doorman caged her thin arm with his massive hand, dragging her into the room as he kicked the door shut behind her. She shrieked and tried to tug out of his grasp, but he only let her go once he'd brought her over by the bed.

She stumbled away from him, breathing hard. Once my sister's eyes fell on me, she practically pounced. "Haven!"

I wrapped my arms around her, trying to shelter her face against my shoulder like she was a child afraid of the dark. But she was too jittery, and she pulled back, though she kept one hand clamped on my wrist like a lifeline.

"What the fuck is going on?"

Uncle Arnold texted Kylie to come here, pretending to be me, I realized. That's what he had done with my phone.

The lounge chair's soft leather sighed as Uncle Arnold stood and wiped crumbs from his shirt. Kylie's eyes locked on the butter knife on the room-service tray. I pressed my free hand over hers, shaking my head. "Don't try anything. He'll compel you if you do."

"He'll compel me anyway!"

Arnold *tsk*ed. "Not if you behave."

The fight slowly bled out of my sister. Her eyes remained round and frightened, but her arms fell by her sides. She gave me an utterly lost look.

I explained in a rush, "Rafe and I thought we could trap him. But Tyler showed up, it all went wrong—"

I ran out of breath.

She let out a long exhalation. "Fuck."

Uncle Arnold indulged himself with a quiet chortle. Then he held out his hand. "I'll take your phone now, Kylie."

Begrudgingly, she handed it over. He tossed it into a leather suitcase, then started adding clothes and toiletries. *Packing, but for where?* Kylie and I kept the hotel bed between ourselves and Uncle Arnold, as though that could keep us safe.

When Arnold went into the bathroom to finish packing, Kylie whispered, "He's going to kill us."

I flicked a glance at the Doorman, wondering how much he was observing and reporting back, though I wasn't sure he could even talk. "He needs us. You to write, me to draw."

"To write *what?* To draw *what?*"

I shook my head; I didn't have an answer for that.

Arnold came out of the bathroom. He slung the suitcase strap over his shoulder and, as an afterthought, grabbed the half-full whiskey bottle.

"Come on, ladies. We're taking a trip."

He motioned to the Doorman, who reached into his suit pocket for the antique doorknob. Its intricate carvings caught the overhead light, making it gleam.

"A trip to where?" I asked cautiously.

Arnold came around the bed and shoved my shoulder, pushing me roughly toward the door. "*Move it*, doll."

The Doorman thrust the doorknob's stalk into the hinged side of the door. A crimson glow began to flicker around the door's edges, tongues of burning light licking out toward us.

Kylie dug her heels into the carpet, but Arnold snarled and gave her a shove.

The old man extended his hand in a mockery of manners. "You first, ladies."

The Killarney Doorman turned the knob, and we were bathed in shades of scarlet and amber that washed over our bodies like hellfire.

CHAPTER TWENTY-EIGHT

WINTER OF THE WICKED
© 1947 Sigil Pictures

INTERIOR — BARN — NIGHT

Farm Wife soothes and rocks Younger Daughter.
Younger Daughter looks up. Her eyes are
bloodshot. Snarling, she bites her mother's
cheek.

Elder Daughter screams.

Farm Wife backs away. She touches her bloody
face. Turns around to face her two daughters.

> FARM WIFE
> I'll not harm you, my children. God
> keep you.

Farm Wife takes the puppet-carving knife and
slits her own throat.

BRIGHT LIGHT.

The heady rush of falling.

Then solid floor beneath my shoes.

We stepped out of the Doorman's portal into an expansive, natural-light-filled lobby supported by timber columns. The oak-beamed ceiling towered two stories overhead, with twin staircases leading to an upper balcony and a frosted-glass elevator between them. It had clearly once been a grand entryway, though currently a film of dust coated everything. The wire in the folding doors of the elevator was badly damaged. Nature had encroached by way of birds' nests in the rafters, moss sprouting between broken tiles. The only light came from large, grimy windows.

When I turned, I was surprised to see we'd entered through a glass set of double doors that looked jarringly familiar.

Kylie muttered in a daze, "It's the institute."

She was right. We were standing in the lobby of the Lucerne Institute of Sleep, though it was hardly recognizable in its current state. When I had entered the *Sandman Killer* movie world, I had been transported back to a version of 1943, when the building had been in its heyday: glistening linoleum floors, sleek midcentury furniture, the orderly check-in desk. Now mouse-nibbled sheets covered most of the furniture, with some ratty Adirondack-style sofas left bare to bleach unevenly. A mangy, taxidermic grizzly bear loomed near one of the columns. A rack of faded brochures advertised local hikes.

"Wrong," Uncle Arnold said neatly in response, flicking a dead beetle off a sofa back. "The Lucerne Institute of Sleep doesn't exist in this world. You're standing in what was formerly the Jackrabbit Hotel. A premier mountain resort decades ago. It closed down midway through the last century after the management discovered structural damage that was too costly to repair."

A topographical map hung on the wall near the grizzly bear. I made my way over, spooking a crow that had been perched on the bear's shoulder. It cawed and flapped off into the rafters.

On the map, a red dot placed the Jackrabbit Hotel deep in the Rocky Mountains, a bit outside of Durango, Colorado.

"This is *The Sandman Killer*'s filming location," I said.

Uncle Arnold's gaze followed a black crow feather that fell lazily from the rafters. When it landed, he explained, "The filmmakers converted the Jackrabbit Hotel into the movie set for a few weeks one winter when the hotel was closed for the season."

Kylie joined me at the map.

Uncle Arnold waved his hand in contempt. "Don't bother looking for a means to escape. The main road has long since washed out. We're ten miles from the nearest town, and good luck getting there with no roads or trails." He jerked his thumb toward the Killarney Doorman. "You need his little gizmo to get here."

With the Doorman standing sentry at the entrance, our chances of even exiting the building's grounds were slim.

"Come here." Uncle Arnold pointed toward an archway next to the left-hand staircase. He scratched his nose. "There's someone you should meet."

He limped off with the confidence of a man who expected his dogs to follow at his heels. Anger gripped my throat like a hand. This was wrong, all of it. I wanted to scream loud enough to wake myself up, but this time, I wasn't in one of my dreams. Kylie snarled a toothy curse under her breath.

Still, we followed.

As we trudged behind him, Uncle Arnold spoke over his shoulder with calm authority. "Back in 1943, the Sigil Pictures production team used a real-life Swiss hospital for the exterior shots of the institute, but it was costly to film the entire production abroad, so they rented the Jackrabbit for the interiors. They brought in props, costumes. The actors and crew slept in the guest rooms for a month. The hotel reopened the following summer, but that was its last. Old buildings like this cost a fortune to maintain, and newer hotels were cropping up—too much competition. The Jackrabbit couldn't get new investors, so they had no choice but to shut down. And then it sat vacant for a long, long time." He gave a mean-spirited laugh. "Its new owner got quite the deal."

Kylie said, "New owner? Let me guess. You."

Arnold stopped at the bottom of the left-hand staircase, resting his hand affectionately on the wooden railing as he turned to us. "The bank representative was exceedingly generous. She handed over the deed for one dollar. *Just one dollar!* Can you believe it?"

"You compelled her," Kylie answered bluntly.

Uncle Arnold gave his odd little chortle.

I pointed to a placard above the archway that read PATIENT WAITING ROOM. I blurted out, "But *that's* from the movie."

Uncle Arnold seemed pleased that I'd noticed. He was too short to reach the placard to tap it, so he patted the wall instead. "The manager at the time bought a lot of movie props off Sigil Pictures. He was hoping the film would be a hit and renew interest in the old place. I found notes in his office that he was planning to install display cases here in the lobby and decorate the guest hallways with memorabilia. But he didn't make much progress before the hotel choked. That placard was about all he managed to put up. There's a storage unit in the basement full of *Sandman Killer* keepsakes and filming equipment. *He's* been through most of it."

"Who has?" I asked.

Uncle Arnold raised his eyebrows as he tipped his head toward the archway. "See for yourself. The Durango Ballroom. Go on ahead. Say hello."

The archway opened to a ballroom whose vaulted ceiling was embellished with plaster medallions, some of which had fallen and now rested in dusty chunks on the floor. A tiered crystal chandelier hung at an odd angle, one of its support chains dangling. Rectangular buffet tables had been pushed to one side of the room and covered with sheets—all save one.

Directly under the broken chandelier, a table was set up with a full service. China plates and glassware waited at all ten places. A floral arrangement, long dried and desiccated and crawling with spider mites, occupied a waterless crystal vase.

My feet drifted to a halt. This was a scene almost identical to one in *The Sandman Killer.* After the institute's evacuation, when it was only Agnes and Doctor Vaughn Ellis left in the building, he set up this disconcerting banquet for the two of them.

Movie world, real world—I felt like realms were colliding.

A man sat at the head of the table, silver knife and fork in hand, slowly cutting a piece of unidentifiable meat that oozed red juices.

"Jesus Christ," Kylie muttered.

Doctor Vaughn Ellis was black-and-white; *actually* black-and-white, exactly as his movie had been. When I'd stepped into his world through Rob's movie screen, I'd retained my color in a monochrome world, and now the doctor had kept his grayscale appearance in ours.

The doctor wore his trademark round spectacles and white lab coat, but otherwise he appeared a specter of the robust character that I'd watched on-screen and interacted with. His body was shrunken, hunched over with sarcopenia, his skin sagging around his jowls. He looked as threadbare as the hotel itself. As though he, too, had been languishing for decades.

But he hasn't actually aged, I realized. His dark hair and youthful hands still marked him as a man in his prime, midforties. His worn appearance couldn't have been caused by age, but some other trauma.

Doctor Vaughn Ellis continued eating, almost moving in slow motion. Finally, he gathered up a napkin and dabbed his gray lips, then returned it to his lap. He peered up at us slowly as though only then noticing our presence. I couldn't see his eyes behind his dark lenses, but I knew they'd be dazed.

Arnold circled the table, hand tapping lightly on each chair back as though playing a game of duck-duck-goose, until he came to Doctor Ellis. He rested a heavy hand on the frail doctor's shoulder.

The somnologist paused briefly, as though touched by a ghost, then continued his slow-motion eating.

"What happened to him?" I asked.

"His unique coloration? Sigil Pictures was making films at the time when color-motion was the newest technology. Some of their later projects, like *The Candy House* and *Purgatory's Door*, were actually filmed in color"—he gestured at his servant—"which gave the Killarney Doorman his lovely caramel horns. But our friend here came from an earlier project." He looked down at the older man's scalp. "Sadly for him."

Something creaked in the rafters overhead. Kylie eyed the chandelier doubtingly.

"But why is he so slowed down?" she asked.

Uncle Arnold patted the Sandman Killer with the same tender condescension that Rob gave to his mannequins. "*Obsolescence*, that's why. After Doctor Ellis stepped out of the film in 1943, he racked up a few real-life murders. Rumors spread and he fled here, to the location where his story was filmed. He's been here ever since, rattling around the abandoned hotel alone. Persisting but not thriving. This is what happens when ideas stagnate." Arnold's lip curled in mild derision. "He's a relic from another time, like this building itself. Things left untended will naturally crumble. Relevancy requires renovation." He paused as though another thought hung on his tongue, but then his face settled into a strange smile.

A swinging door at the far end of the ballroom eased open with a groan of hinges. A haggard woman came out carrying a tray with more of the meat dish.

She moved strangely, an unsteady lurch-slide toward us.

She, too, was black-and-white, though her unusual coloration wasn't as immediately obvious as it had been with Doctor Ellis; dressed in a heavy black dress and white apron, with fair skin and dirty dark hair, she could have simply been a very pale person. It was the old-fashioned clothes that gave her away. She was the farmer's wife from *Winter of the Wicked*, who had gone in search of the lost sheep on the outskirts of the Puritanical village of Fear-Not. And it was immediately evident that she was dead.

Her throat had been cut open. Jagged lines ran across her face like something had clawed her, but they were too precise for an animal attack. *Maybe a pitchfork*, I thought. Through slashes in her sleeves, raw wounds showed, including a few gashes down to the winking white bone. A chunk of her bottom lip was missing, revealing uneven teeth.

I'd only seen the first few minutes of *Winter of the Wicked*, when her character had been alive and well—it was anyone's guess what horrors had befallen her by the end.

The woman moved awkwardly on her undead limbs. She set the tray on the table roughly. The plates rattled; the meat looked raw. Her jaws snapped a few times, teeth clattering.

Kylie breathed a curse and drew backward.

Uncle Arnold gripped the backs of two banquet chairs. "Sit, ladies. I've had the Fear-Not Wife prepare a meal for you, though I must warn you, her tastes veer toward the extreme. You've found her in a good mood; when she's grumpy, she gets the overwhelming urge to consume raw human flesh."

He dismissed the shambling figure with a flick of his fingers. The woman's unsteady body turned, and she shuffled over to the wall, taking her place next to the Killarney Doorman.

Neither Kylie nor I moved.

The smile fell off Uncle Arnold's face. He took a seat opposite the doctor and used his foot under the table to push out the two chairs, their legs squealing across the floor.

"I said *sit*."

CHAPTER TWENTY-NINE

—

THE CANDY HOUSE
© 1951 Sigil Pictures

INTERIOR — DARK HOSPITAL HALL — NIGHT

PAINED MOANS come from the other side of the
door. Andrzej holds the STOLEN KEY. His hand
shakes. He GLANCES down the hall to verify his
sister is keeping watch.

He UNLOCKS the door. Inside, weak lantern
light reveals a grisly scene. The nurse's
wartime PATIENTS lie on floor pallets, wrapped
in bandages. They've been disfigured and
drugged. SCIENTIFIC EQUIPMENT and a NAZI
JACKET cover a table on the other side of the
room.

Andrzej sniffs, then covers his nose.

                    ANDRZEJ
                  (to himself)
          Wintergreen. . . . It's the candy!

—

HIS WHISPER WASN'T *that* whisper, but it held the threat of terrible compulsions.

Kylie and I grudgingly took our places at the table. At the far end, Doctor Ellis continued to eat slowly, as though unaware of our presence. His movements were so repetitive that they almost felt caught in a loop, and I wondered what he'd been doing in the foreclosed hotel for nearly eighty years other than dragging up old props from the basement.

Uncle Arnold dove into the meat dish with gusto, a sharp contrast to the withered man at the opposite end of the table. Between bits, he jabbed a fork in the Sandman Killer's direction.

"Once I found the doctor and revived him—yes, this pathetic display before you *is* a vast improvement from the state he was in a few months ago—I compelled him to use his dream smoke to see into their minds and search for other Sigil creations." His fork gestured backward and something fell from it. "That's how I located our friends here. And of course . . ." Mashed bits of meat caught in his small teeth as he turned the fork on us. "The two of you."

He cut again into his slab of meat. The knife squealed on the plate, making me cringe.

There has to be a way out, I thought. The Killarney Doorman could only guard one door at a time, and a hotel this size must have dozens of exits, or at least first-floor windows we could climb out of. But the hotel was isolated—if we got out, what would Arnold send to hunt us down in the wilderness?

Our host pushed away his empty plate and waved over the Fear-Not Wife. A hiss escaped her slashed throat like an angry wild animal. He snapped his fingers sharply at her, and she finally lurched forward to clear the plates.

As she gathered them with her erratic movements, I thought it would be impossible that she wouldn't send everything crashing to the floor. But she managed to make it to the kitchen with the dishes intact. The swinging door swayed behind her, revealing rhythmic glimpses of stainless-steel counters, an old enamel fridge.

A familiar beep came from Uncle Arnold's pocket.

He wiped his mouth with a napkin, took out my phone, and casually started scrolling through it.

"Hey!" I cried, gripping the edge of the table.

He reclined in his chair, taking his time reading whatever text had come through. "The Harbinger has been relentless in his attempts to reach you, dollface. So many calls and messages. All unanswered." He *tsk*ed and continued scrolling through my phone as he picked his teeth with his fingernail. "Someone named Rob has been trying to contact you, too." His eyes widened as he read through Rob's messages. When he set the phone down, he looked at me in delighted curiosity. "A *movie?* He's trying to make a *movie* about the Sigil curse?"

I kept my jaw clenched, looking down at my untouched meal.

Uncle Arnold chuckled as he tucked my phone in his pocket. "Maybe I should respond to this Rob fellow on your behalf. He seems very apologetic about something. I'm sure he'd appreciate a message saying where you are. I wonder, if you said you needed help, would he come?"

An angry fist tightened in my stomach. Uncle Arnold was making it clear that he could hurt those I cared about. Rob might have betrayed my trust, but he was still Rob. The number of people I considered friends was painfully slim, and Rob was among them.

"Rob doesn't matter." I leaned back in my chair, trying to trump Uncle Arnold's nonchalance. "He'll never even get the movie made. If he tries to, there are ways to stop him—ways that hurt only his pride."

Uncle Arnold ran a hand down the loose skin around his neck. "Oh, I believe you misunderstand. I have no reason for a movie about the Sigil curse not to get made."

Kylie twisted around sharply in her chair. "You *want* people to know about the curse? About you?"

Arnold tossed his napkin on the table and stood up. "Let's go for a walk."

The Killarney Doorman moved aside to let us pass. A wave of animal musk rolled off him as he brought up the rear. We followed Arnold into the lobby and then up a set of stairs to the second-floor guest rooms.

The hallway there was narrow, the wood floor sun-bleached around the edges and darker in the middle where a runner had once rested. The air had a lazy, stagnant quality, full of dust motes suspended in the late-afternoon sunlight. None of the lamps were on, though a few glowing red EXIT signs told me the electricity was working. The hallway was frigid. Either the boiler was broken, or the cold didn't bother the hotel's current residents. I hugged myself, shivering.

On the hallway's side tables, guidebooks to the Rockies and other tourist tchotchkes had been shoved to the floor to make room for old surgical instruments, medical encyclopedias on sleep disorders, and framed photos of the Swiss Alps. As we passed closed guest-room doors, I felt a sense of déjà vu. I had been in this hallway. This was the filming location of Agnes Fitzpatrick's hospital room.

The old floors squeaked underfoot, mixing with the persistent buzz of wires in the walls and a crunch like insects chewing on the insulation. Beneath the smell of mildew, there lingered a note of something damp and long dead, like the carcass of a sheep left to rot in a marsh.

We reached the end of the hall and climbed a stairwell to the third floor. The walls became closer together, more constricted. Unlike the second floor, where the Sandman Killer had tried to re-create his own movie set, this floor looked untouched from when the Jackrabbit Hotel had been operational. A dirty runner muffled our footsteps. Broken picture frames of faded mountainous vignettes dotted the walls. One guest-room door was cracked open; I peeked inside to find a stiff iron-frame bed with linens stained by years of roof leaks.

A little way ahead, hinges creaked. A door slammed.

Kylie scrambled back a step and grabbed my arm, pointing to a guest room. "There was something there. Wearing a mask like a . . . like an old army mask."

ROOM 323, the door was marked. On the rug outside was a trail of old-fashioned candy like the kind found in touristy general stores:

Saltwater taffy in wax paper. Green-spiraled wintergreen mints. Foil-wrapped caramels.

A metallic squeal came from inside Room 323 like someone bouncing on a rusty-springed mattress.

More of Uncle Arnold's foundlings.

The disembodied giggle of children arose from the closed room.

Uncle Arnold motioned briefly to Room 323. "Andrzej and Hanna. I found them in Poland—you aren't the only ones whose search took you abroad. I started in Ireland, where I was looking for the Doorman. After that, travel was much easier with his doorknob. No more airports." He made a face. "I hate fucking airports."

"They're from *The Candy House*," I concluded.

"They can't hurt us, can they?" Kylie whispered.

"I haven't seen their movie," I answered. "I'm not assuming anything."

According to message boards, *The Candy House* was about two children who escaped the Warsaw ghettos and fled into the Polish countryside only to stumble upon an evil spirit disguised as an old nurse in a rural hospital. It was Hansel and Gretel by way of Nazi supernatural experimentation.

"Have you seen it?" Uncle Arnold peered at me with what looked like sincere curiosity. When I shook my head, his expression fell. "Yes, no one can seem to get me a copy. My latest source turned out to be a bust."

He gave that odd giggle that made my skin want to turn itself inside out.

As we passed another open door, a sigh of movement caught my eye. The Fear-Not Wife was inside Room 340, lying supine on the bed covers, her chest rising and falling in gurgling breaths as she slept. A crude wooden-handled pitchfork rested against her dresser.

Uncle Arnold stopped across the hall, at Room 341. "You'd be surprised by how many of us are out there," he said, then gave me a searching look. "Monsters dream too, you know. The Sandman Killer has seen into many of their dreams and reported to me what he's discovered. Most creations tend to hide. The ones who don't hide don't tend to last long. There are the hunters like Joao Acosta, among many other threats."

"And you?" I challenged. "Do you want to hide? Is that why you're here?"

Arnold made his *tsk* sound. "I suppose the answer to that depends on semantics."

I didn't like the cryptic remark but didn't ask for details.

To my surprise, Room 341 had been repurposed as a makeshift office, with modern computer monitors and TVs plugged into wall outlets. Empty food wrappers littered the tabletops just like in Arnold's trashed hotel suite back in LA.

One television was tuned to international news. The other was set to a channel that leaned toward ancient aliens and Bigfoot chase shows. Currently, it played a ghost-hunting program.

Uncle Arnold nudged a laptop on a desk awake. It was paused on a YouTube video of an attractive blond man with a Jesus complex. He stood on a rocky outcropping by a lake in a white robe, arms raised high while an audience of mostly young women gazed on adoringly.

"Do you know who this is?" Uncle Arnold asked.

I had no idea, but Kylie answered, "Yeah. I've heard of him. Some lifestyle guru-slash-cult leader. There's a documentary coming out about him. He's called something ridiculous . . . . LoneWolf—that's it."

Uncle Arnold opened another laptop tab, which showed a still image of a bearded man speaking directly into the camera from an ultramodern beach house.

"And this?" At our silence, he continued, "Balan Erner. The founder of AvalonTech and now a metaphysics coach and author. He has nearly three million followers on social media."

I was finding it hard to concentrate. My head was still in the hallway, glimpsing monsters through cracked doorways. I couldn't figure out why Uncle Arnold was showing us a series of Gen Z influencers.

He picked up a remote to turn off the television sets. The sudden silence roared up to fill the void.

"You saw the somnologist," he said in a measured voice. "Such a sad, pathetic case. Back in his era, he was what every man aspired to be: virile, well employed, highly respected. Now look at him—*utterly irrelevant*. When I first found him, I tried to spur him to change. If he'd only embraced the modern world and found a new place in it, he could have been great again. But he refused—he's trapped in the past."

A tingle of premonition spread up from my toes. Doctor Vaughn Ellis and Uncle Arnold came from different realms but similar eras. The sleep doctor had been in his prime in the 1940s when all power and influence was held by white men, and Uncle Arnold had aged in a similar 1950s-inspired world.

"The only way to thrive is to adapt," Uncle Arnold said matter-of-factly. "Look at the film industry your friend is so enamored with. Movies that were once beloved stale in time. The solution that Hollywood found? Revivals. Sequels. Retellings, whatever you want to call them. Taking an outdated story and making it fresh again. Younger actors, a modern setting, all the current technical marvels. And *bam*." He snapped his chubby fingers. "You have a new hit. In twenty years, do it all over again."

The room felt even colder than the rest of the hotel. Kylie shivered as she moved her foot away from snaking wires that covered the floor like tentacles. My breath felt heavy when I looked at her. *My sister.* I had to get her out of there.

"You're going to need to start making some sense before we freeze to death," Kylie said. She was trying to sound tough—it almost worked.

She might not understand the point Arnold was getting at, but I did. That hot tingle had spread up from my toes to my fingertips. I felt the need to sit down, but I didn't want to be lower than Arnold, give him even that small measure of power.

He gazed with longing at the images on the computer screens. "I've been gathering monsters and cataloging their abilities. Each one is so fascinatingly unique. So much potential, if one can bend them to one's will. Fortunately, I can—with most. The doctor downstairs has already proven so useful. But the most useful thing he ever did was lead me to you two. You see, you're monsters, too. And now I need *your* talents."

I stole a glance at Kylie to gauge how she was taking this. It was true that I was as much a creation as the preternatural creatures stalking the Jackrabbit Hotel hallways, but *she* wasn't, though she did have the Acosta curse.

Uncle Arnold spiraled a fat finger toward the two of us. "It's my turn for a revival, and the two of you are going to make it possible."

CHAPTER THIRTY

PURGATORY'S DOOR
© 1955 Sigil Pictures

INTERIOR — THE DRUID BAR BACK OFFICE - NIGHT

The goat-headed Doorman opens a closet door
with his magic doorknob. Instead of brooms,
a crimson glow emanates. Beyond it, murky
outlines of people.

                MICKEY KELLY
     Voilà, pal. You want the girl?
     Welcome to Purgatory. Population:
     the Damned.
         (He nods to the Doorman.)
     And about to increase by one.

            DETECTIVE NICK DRAM
     Hey! Wait!

A skirmish as the thuggish Doorman tries to
push Detective Nick Dram through the doorway.
Nick lands a punch. Then a GIRL'S CRY FOR HELP
from within the doorway. Nick turns.

The Doorman lowers his horns, stamps his foot
twice, and gores Nick in the side.

UNCLE ARNOLD'S WORDS sat heavy in the air, a weight to
them like humidity.

Before I'd met Kylie, I hadn't known what it was like to have a
sister. My only family had been my dad, and it was generous to call
our relationship *distant*. I'd never known how to talk to him, and he
hadn't figured out how to connect with me, so we had existed near
each other for years like furniture occupying the same room, shoved
to either end, never quite falling under the same light.

When I'd learned about my origin, I'd assumed that was the answer.
How could I have connected to my dad—to anyone at all—if I wasn't
human?

Yet over the past few months, I'd come to doubt that assumption.
Kylie and I had been together nearly every day on airplanes, in hotels,
in countless rental cars as we traversed the country and even crossed
oceans. We'd gotten annoyed with each other, recounted tales of old
boyfriends, snickered over inside jokes that would have annoyed the
rest of the world. We'd connected.

What Uncle Arnold suggested about change and relevancy lodged
deeply in me. Ever since I'd had an unexpected emotional reaction
to *Stitches 2*, I had felt changed myself. Like I'd been living my life in
black and white, bumping through a marriage, surface-level friends
and jobs, emotionally unreachable. But now, like Dorothy Gale, I was
floating into color. It was both wonderful and terrible; above all, it
was bewildering.

"A revival?" Kylie scrunched her nose, though her eyes flashed with
fear. "As in . . . ?"

Uncle Arnold wasn't deterred by her sneer. His face remained
studious, his eyes sharply focused, like two knife points.

"You write me a new story, of course." He aimed his finger at her, then twirled it through the air toward me. "And you draw me a new form. Something fresh, not this diseased geezer's body that your father thrust upon me."

My eyes shifted to the computer screens behind him, paused on LoneWolf and Balan Erner. Young men with actor-like good looks and modern sensibilities. No saggy suspenders there. It reminded me of what my father had said to his editor after the incident when he'd thrown a book.

The industry will die if it only puts out the same old story. Unless you understand that, you'll perish.

At once, I comprehended how dangerous Arnold's plan was. His ability to compel paired with a persuasive appearance would leave him extremely influential.

"It won't work." My hands balled into fists at my sides. "I burned your illustration and the *Bedtime Stories for Monsters* manuscript. Even if we could rewrite someone's story—and there's no guarantee that would work—we'd need the original pages."

Kylie looked down and to the left, running a hand along the back of her neck.

Did she think I was bluffing? I wasn't.

Uncle Arnold had clearly already thought of this, judging by the way he went to the closet and produced our two purses. He removed Kylie's battered laptop from hers. Then, from the desk drawer, he took out a pack of Copic markers, still new-smelling, and a blank spiral-bound sketchbook.

He tapped a finger against his left temple.

"I'm not talking about editing an existing draft. Does Hollywood dredge up the original script when it makes a reboot? Of course not. It starts with a blank page and makes a new version."

"Something new?" I blurted out. "That's impossible. We'd have to kill you and start over fresh."

I'd spat the words at him, hoping to scare him into realizing the absurdity of his plan. But he only gazed at me with condescending patience, and my small spark of hope was doused. He blinked a few times as though waiting to see if I'd make another outburst, then held out the laptop and art supplies.

"Starting over won't be a problem," he prompted, trying to press the pack of markers on me.

I shook my head, confused. "You'll *die*."

"I'll come back."

I still couldn't bring myself to accept the markers. My body felt tight, numb, except for that itch I couldn't ever get at. Vague questions tangled in my head, never quite coming together to form words, just pounding into the inside of my skull like fists.

Uncle Arnold took my hand forcefully, shoving the markers into it. He set his hands on my shoulders and turned me around to face the desk. He had to stand on tiptoe to whisper in my ear.

I dropped the markers so I could close my hands over my ears, but he was faster.

"Stop what you're doing."

My hands froze half an inch from either ear.

Kylie also tried to cover her ears, but his attention snapped to her. "You, too. *Stop what you're doing."*

Pain writhed over her face as she tried to fight his control.

"Hands down, Kylie."

Slowly, her hands lowered.

Uncle Arnold dug his fingers deeper into my shoulders. His hot breath stirred the loose hairs around my nape. *"Be a good girl like your sister. Hands down."*

In an instant, I was pulled apart, like bread dough, into two separate selves. There was a piece of me that took a step forward, responding with perfect willingness to Uncle Arnold's order. Another part—my true self—remained one step behind, watching it all happen.

My hands lowered.

Uncle Arnold took his time scrutinizing us as though worried we might have figured out how to avoid his compulsion. He poked my shoulder, testing.

When I didn't fight back, he waggled a finger between the two of us. "Compelling two people at once can prove challenging. I've realized that my ability works through sound waves. You've heard of the Doppler effect? Sound produces a higher pitch when moving toward you and a lower pitch when moving away from you. I have to direct my whisper squarely at my target for it to be effective. Someone who merely overhears it from an angle won't be affected. So you'll forgive me if sometimes I have to repeat myself to each of you." He smiled tightly. "As to your concerns for my life, Haven, I'll admit I have concerns, too. No one knowingly faces their own death without fear. I've decided to use narcotics—the Killarney Doorman was kind enough to let me into a hospital's storage room, and Doctor Ellis advised me on what to get. Call me fussy, but I don't like the idea of blown-out brains or slit wrists. The poor Fear-Not Wife would find me like that and have to lick up all the blood."

I forced my throat to work. "When are you going to do it?"

"Once I'm certain my new self exists and is satisfactory." He consulted his wristwatch. "At the risk of rushing creative brilliance, you have an hour. When I come back, I want to see a draft."

He dragged a second chair over to the desk.

"Sit," he commanded Kylie. *"Start working. Don't try to break the compulsion. Don't leave your chair."*

He turned to me and repeated the commands in my direction.

Kylie and I moved like puppets, taking our seats beside each other. She faced her laptop. Me, the markers and a blank sketchpad.

When Arnold left, I got a glimpse of the Killarney Doorman standing guard outside before the door shut and locked.

"He posted the Doorman outside," I whispered.

"Of course he did," Kylie muttered.

I dragged over my purse and dug through it. Uncle Arnold had kept both our phones with him, so there was no chance of calling Rafe or anyone else for help. I dragged out fistfuls of pens I'd haphazardly collected from our travels and paused at the rubber-banded copy of *Exit, Nebraska*.

I set it on the desk, resting my hand briefly on the cover before selecting a pencil with *Hotel Ibérico* printed on it in gold letters.

"One hour." Her eyes had a glassy sheen. I knew mine must look the same. Already, the hypnotized part of me was gripping the pencil, pressing the familiar shape between the calluses on my thumb and first finger.

"How do we break his hold?" Kylie whispered.

There were ways to end Uncle Arnold's hypnotism: The compulsion faded in time, though never in under an hour from what I could tell. The only other means we'd discovered was by experiencing pain sharp enough to cut through the spell—but it didn't always work, and he'd forbidden us from taking that course, anyway.

She gritted her teeth as she placed the laptop in front of her and opened it with a shaking hand. "I have to, Haven. It's like a knee jerk. I can't *not* do it."

I knew what she meant. I fought to keep the pencil from the blank page, but my hand moved involuntarily, pressing the pencil tip to the paper, tracing upward in the curvature of a skull.

She started typing. Moving slowly at first, key by key, but the more her mind worked, the faster her hands worked. The bright screen reflected in the mirrors of her eyes as her hands flew over the keyboard.

I gave myself over to the urge, too. Let the pencil do as it wished. When I stopped trying to fight Uncle Arnold's compulsion, my whole body relaxed into the flow state, and it felt wondrously, addictively good. Uncle Arnold wanted a physical form that was attractive yet approachable. Charismatic but intense.

A figure began to take shape in graphite. A man around thirty years old—not so young as to be easily discredited—with chin-length hair in a cut that was somewhere between professional and casual, with a well-trimmed beard to give him some edge. Tortoiseshell glasses for the intellectual look. A simple V-neck shirt and vest combo suggested hip modesty but was paired with an expensive watch. I added a tattoo of crescent moons on his forearm.

When I finally pulled out of the flow state, the first attempt at his sketch all but finished, I found Kylie looking ill. She angled her laptop toward me. The blank document was now filled with lines of black text.

"Arne Koning." She gestured toward the document. "That's his new identity. I titled the story 'The Encyclopedic Life of Arne Koning.'"

A shiver ran through me. I blinked at my drawing, arguably complete except for some areas around his jaw that weren't fully rendered. "What time is it?"

She peered at the clock on her computer. "Seven minutes until the hour is up." She rubbed her chest like she had heartburn. "What happens now? It's done, right?"

I shook my head. "Not until I add my signature. Arnold's new form won't come to life until then. And I sure as hell won't sign anything other than the final draft. Otherwise, we might end up with multiple Arnolds creeping around."

She pressed her fingers into her temples. "I keep thinking that there must be some way to fight his compulsion. If only you could slap me hard enough to wake me up. That worked last time."

"He ordered us not to try to break it." I raised my hand uselessly.

Her eyes suddenly lit up as she studied my drawing. Hesitantly, she picked up a black Copic marker. "What if instead of trying to break the compulsion, we work around it?"

"How do we accomplish that?"

She licked her lips, getting excited. "Arnold ordered us to create his new identity, right? He didn't say we couldn't create something else, too."

My eyes narrowed. "You mean make something else with the curse? We always say *Don't write*—"

"*Don't draw*. I know." Her fingertips tapped open a new blank document. She looked at me with an eager gaze. Seeking permission.

I took a deep breath as I glanced out the window at the dying light. For months, we'd resisted the urge to create. I'd been proud of myself for fighting its pull, knowing the curse only ever created monsters. I thought back to Kylie's confession in Joshua Tree about how hard it was for her to resist the curse.

"It's too much of a risk," I said. "Nothing good comes from the curse."

"Rafe came from it. He's good to you. And you yourself are—" She stopped herself. "You aren't thinking big picture, Haven. Arnold controls the other monsters, so we can control what we create, too, if we make it that way."

I checked the clock on her computer. "We only have five minutes—"

She spoke in a rush. "Come on, we can do this. Everyone's always overlooked both of us, Haven. This is our chance to prove we're more than just our father's progeny."

Goose bumps prickled over my skin. "It's the curse, Kylie. It's pushing you toward this plan."

She shook her head. "It isn't. Besides, can you think of another way to get out of here?"

I dragged my head back and forth slowly. Finally, I let my head sag. I closed my eyes, thinking, then lifted my chin.

"Birds," I said.

"Birds?"

"Arnold won't notice a bird as unusual. There are crows roosting in the lobby rafters."

Kylie chewed on her fingernail as anxious energy coursed through her.

I pointed out, "Besides, crows like to steal."

"Steal what?"

I selected a Copic marker from the set. E-110, Special Black. "Shiny objects."

As I explained my plan to her, we began swapping ideas, brainstorming possibilities. Kylie's fingers flew over the keys in fits and starts. As she worked, I tore out a fresh piece of paper and laid it on top of Arne Koning's drawing. I sketched as fast as I could. Outstretched wings, a sharp beak, keen eyes. The crow would need a place to store its shiny stolen objects, so I gave it a marsupial-like pouch miraculously able to hold as much loot as it could pickpocket, like a magician's endlessly vast top hat. I sketched a few different versions of the bird to capture the exact effect I wanted.

"One more minute," Kylie muttered tightly, her fingers flying over the keys. "Shit—I shouldn't have made it obedient to my voice in case Arnold forbids me from speaking again. Hang on, let me change this. . . ."

I rushed through a final version of the illustration, then snatched up a ballpoint pen to sign my name to the bottom, but paused.

Once I did this, there was no going back.

Don't write, don't draw.

Kylie sagged back in her seat, taking her hands off the keyboard. "Time's up." She glanced at my pen hovering over the paper and said, "Haven?"

"Right." I signed my name quickly while I still had the nerve. My heart was thundering. I folded the bird illustration and tucked it into my bra.

"So that's it," I said, feeling like I might have made an awful mistake.

Kylie's eyes shot to the window as though she was listening for the sound of wings. "How long before . . . ?"

"I don't know. It'll come from the hotel basement. That's where creations always come out: someplace dark, deep."

Her face paled.

I knew the unwritten rules of horror movies: *Beware the basement* was high on the list. That logic especially held true in an abandoned hotel full of actual monsters. But that was also an old rule. In newer movies, edicts like that got turned on their head. I'd recapped one for Rob called *On the Night Watch* where the heroine used the basement's hidden tunnels to her advantage.

The hallway outside creaked.

I turned my attention to the door. Arnold would be back at any minute. "What did you title the story?"

"'The Thieving Crow.'"

"Let me read it. Quick."

She slid the laptop over to me. "It's in Track Changes mode, so it reads a little janky."

The word-processing document took up about half her screen, the rest filled with other open tabs and desktop icons.

It wanted the gleam of stars—pinpricks of fire set in night's dark ~~fabric~~ skin. Flying high, always flying high. Never far enough. And so instead it settled on ~~the shiniest of objects~~ those things that lustered within reach. . . .

My attention was jumpy, worried about Arnold. Only a few lines into "The Thieving Crow," I glanced at the desktop icons visible to the side. They were blue folder symbols labeled with the titles of her novels-in-progress.

My eye caught a folder icon labeled *Enigma.*

Enigma. Where had I heard that before?

I let my eyes drift through space. They settled on Kylie, who was playing with her earring, like she did when she got nervous.

A memory unearthed itself: the first time we had met Rob in person. *Quite the enigma,* he had said, and the pointed way he'd emphasized the final word when talking about the collateral he'd found on Kylie—not to mention her reaction to it—had snagged in my mind like a thorn.

"Kylie," I whispered, all too aware that at any moment Uncle Arnold would open the door, "what's that?"

I pointed at the file on her screen. Her fingers curled into her palms. She sucked a tight breath through her nose, eyes flashing.

Quite the enigma.

I realized in that moment that we had both been keeping secrets. All those months on the road, just an arm's length across the gearbox from one another. All the inside jokes, shared take-out pizzas, confessions over third and fourth glasses of wine. I'd always assumed my secrets had been worse than hers, but now I had the sudden fear that I'd been wrong about that, too.

CHAPTER THIRTY-ONE

———

```
THE  HUNDREDTH  STAIR
© 1941 Sigil Pictures

INTERIOR — ARCHITECT'S OFFICE - NIGHT

Harrison Smiley stands before an ancient book
of demonology. CAMERA CLOSE ON a block print
illustration of a demon composed of human body
parts fused together in the shape of a giant
tentacled sea monster. CLOSE-UP ON Harrison.


                  HARRISON
     Dear god. What have I done?
```

———

"OPEN THE ENIGMA FOLDER," I ordered in a voice I barely recognized.

For a few tense seconds, Kylie didn't make a move. Then she lurched for the laptop, sliding it close to her and clutching its base with blood-less fingers.

"It's just some book ideas," she said weakly and with so little conviction that it was clear she didn't intend for me to believe her.

"Have you been writing stories?" My voice grew into a high pitch. "After all the times we said *Don't draw, don't write?*"

Her voice rasped like fall leaves. "It isn't like that."

I pressed a steadying palm against the table. "Then *what* is it *like*?"

Her shoulders sagged as she seemed to give in. Her eyes closed as though pained. She whispered, "It started with Rafe."

"What the hell does Rafe have to do with anything?"

She remained still as I wondered what secrets she could possibly be withholding. When she finally opened her eyes, she picked up the rubber-banded copy of *Exit, Nebraska.*

My heart gave a peculiar thump.

She handed the book to me with a familiarity that made my stomach squeeze.

In a barely audible voice, she said, "I know you cut out the pages. I know what's inside."

I hadn't opened the book safe since the night we'd watched *Stitches 2,* after that strange overblown rush of fear had made me want to confirm the drawing was still inside. Now, feeling unsteady, I slid off the rubber band and cracked open the pages with quaking fingers.

There was the drawing, still folded in a tidy square.

Relief flooded me. I couldn't open it fast enough, verify that it was real and unchanged. The chubby baby legs, the tender fold of the little ear. My father's pencil lines that held so much confidence for his amateur talent.

I stole a look at the door, listening for Arnold, but it was quiet. Then I pinned her with a brutal look. "I don't understand. What did you do?"

She wouldn't meet my eyes. Her fingers curled around her laptop. "I was worried about you, Haven. After the fire, when you and I left Lundie Bay, and we spent those weeks driving out through Montana? You wouldn't talk to me. You were shut as tight as a jail cell. The things that happened in that house, the violence, the things *you* did . . . you ignored it all."

My skin began to itch.

Her voice grew muted. "I reached out to Rafe—it was all I could think of to do. He was the only person who might have insight into what was going on with you." She paused as the direction of her eyes shifted to the paper in my hand. "He told me about the drawing."

I sucked in a breath, but she was quick to hold out a staying hand.

"He thought I already knew about it!" she continued in a rush. "He assumed you'd told me. He explained how you were different, like him. When he realized his mistake, he threatened to hurt me if I ever let you know that I knew. He said if you wanted to pretend to be human, it was your business."

I could only stare.

She's known the whole time. Kylie had known that I was just as much a creation as the monsters slithering throughout the Jackrabbit Hotel. All that time on the road, when I'd kept my secret self hidden away in a novel, she had known.

"I don't *care*, Haven." Her eyes finally rose to meet mine. "It isn't my business how you started in life. . . ." Her voice hitched, suddenly uncertain, before she continued. "But I saw how you were struggling. You couldn't emotionally connect, not just to me . . . to *anything*. I mean, you watch these gruesome movies like they're cartoons." She paused, choked up. "I thought I could help you."

Something had gone very still, very cold inside me.

Kylie slowly eased her grip off her laptop, then clicked to pull up a document titled "Work in Progress."

She slid the laptop around to face me.

"And I *did* help you. It worked." Her voice rang with reverence for her own power.

I could only bear peeking at the open document from the corner of my eye, afraid that, like a star, it would disappear if looked at straight on.

Haven Marbury was born with a scream on her lips and a sob in her heart. . . .

I slammed the laptop closed. I didn't need to read any more. The idea felt dangerous, like if I read one line more, the screen might spark and catch fire.

"That's . . . impossible," I managed.

"Rewriting someone's story? Yeah, I know what you said to Uncle Arnold. You don't believe it's possible to rewrite his story even if you hadn't burned the pages. But the difference is, Uncle Arnold *had* a story. Our father wrote him as a fully developed character. You never had that. You only ever had two words: *Amory's Baby*. It was enough to bring you into existence, but not to give you a real, true self. You've always been a half-finished character. A first draft. Not even that—a brainstorm."

I flinched. When I replayed what she had said in my head, it felt no less cold the second time.

"A *first draft*?" I echoed.

She backpedaled quickly. "I didn't mean it to sound like that. Of course you've always been a person, but you said yourself you aren't like everyone else. Rafe told me that you feel like you're missing some key ingredient. That's the way you described it, isn't it?" She held out her hands as though extending a gift. "I wanted to give you that ingredient."

My fingers curled into my palm. "I'm not a fucking cake."

Kylie's hands dropped, and her frustration was clear. "You're misunderstanding. There's never been anything wrong with you—I shouldn't have said it like that. You're my sister, and I love you. You did so much for me the night of the fire. If you hadn't worked out a deal with the Robber Saints, they would have lobotomized me. Ever since we met, you've always been this larger-than-life character. You got your ankle sliced open by a lobster monster. You convinced a hacker to frame your ex-husband. You're *scary*—and I mean that as a compliment." She paused, rewetting her lips. "Then Portugal happened. You attacked that tour guide—"

"I didn't *attack* him. . . ."

But that wasn't true, was it?

I took a breath and started again. "I wasn't going to actually hurt him."

"It didn't look like that to me." Kylie's voice dropped back to a whisper. "You looked like a wolf with a fluffy little rabbit under its paws. You said in the airport that you didn't know why you did it. You said you wish you didn't do things like that. So I . . . *tweaked* your story to give you what you wanted."

Finally, it all made sense. Ever since leaving Portugal, I'd felt a shift in myself that I hadn't been able to fix a name to. It had started with those feelings of intense fear.

"*Tweaked?*" I repeated breathlessly. For a few moments, all I could do was stare at her. "Kylie, you changed me. You made me *soft*."

Her "Work in Progress" had awakened a latent fright response that made me flinch at Hollywood jump scares, blurred the lines between how I reacted to fiction and reality. I'd been changing in a town that was all about reinvention.

We were locked in a silent impasse when Uncle Arnold knocked sharply on the door. His voice was muffled as he called out, "Your time is up, ladies." His soft chortle followed.

I breathed in a jagged, gulping breath.

The door creaked open.

I wondered if Uncle Arnold would sense the shift in the room when he entered. If he'd feel the buzzing tautness between Kylie and me, the heaviness of the secrets that still rested at our feet, broken and bleeding.

But he was too concerned with himself.

"Your sketchbook," he snapped at me. "Let's see what that clever noggin of yours came up with."

I passed it to him like a manned marionette. Next to me, Kylie quietly pressed a key on her laptop to change the open document from "Work in Progress" to "The Encyclopedic Life of Arne Koning."

Uncle Arnold seemed pleased by my sketch. He held the notebook at a distance, cocking his head. He rubbed a hand self-consciously over his thinning white hair, admiring the mane of dark locks I'd given him.

"A few notes," he said with a chuckle. "But all of them minor."

He snapped his fingers at Kylie, who slid her laptop around so he could read the document. He drank in her story greedily, nodding, covering his smile with a hand at one point. She'd been shrewd to structure the narrative in encyclopedic entries for "Childhood Life," "Early Accomplishments," "Business Influence."

She was a good writer—she'd known what her audience wanted.

Had she known what *I* wanted? Had she put that knowledge into "Work in Progress"? I slid her a sidelong look, feeling a rumble of anger in my chest.

"Good," Uncle Arnold pronounced. "Kylie, tighten up that part about the high school years, and add a few more mentions of romantic entanglements with celebrities. Haven, for the final illustration, let's cut the glasses. Too pretentious, not to mention I want excellent vision. And make the nose a little straighter."

He flipped the sketchbook to a fresh page and handed it to me. Then he went to the edge of the bed and settled in, rooting around in his jacket pocket.

"Go ahead," he prompted us. "I'll wait. I have everything ready for the transition to my new self." He produced a baggie with a filled syringe and set it on the foot of the bed, then patted the mattress. "As good a final resting place as any, once the new Arne Koning graces us with his presence."

It didn't take Kylie long to make her edits. I fiddled longer with my revisions, taking my time with the blank page as I thought through the final drawing.

Just as I started to touch my pencil to the page, Kylie said suddenly, "The basement."

Uncle Arnold looked at her in surprise, as did I. When I'd brought up the basement, she'd looked disturbed by the mere thought of it.

"What about the basement?" he prompted.

She flicked a glance in my direction, catching my eye with meaning, though there was also uncertainty there and even a little fear.

That goddamn "Work in Progress."

"Well, creations always come out of someplace dark and deep," she said. "Arne Koning will emerge from the hotel's basement. Who is to say what he might do between his arrival and the time it takes for him to find you up here? Do you really trust your other self? He'll have a whole hotel to explore, and a lot of time to think. To scheme."

Arnold held up the syringe. "I intend for him to kill me. What exactly could he scheme that's worse than that?"

"I don't know what he's capable of. You wanted him clever, so that's how I made him. Cleverer than *you*."

Arnold slowly tucked the syringe baggie back into his jacket pocket. His brow was furrowed—Kylie's seeds of doubt had found ground to settle in. She glanced at me again, and I gave a small nod. Now I understood what she was doing: Our Thieving Crow would be born in the basement just like Arne Koning. If Arnold killed himself here in the third-floor bedroom, the crow might not be of use to us so far away. Besides, I wanted to be there when Arne Koning awoke, to make sure he never made it out of that basement.

"It's true," I added. "You crawled out of the dirt around Malice House, didn't you?"

Uncle Arnold cocked his head as he considered this. There was distaste in his voice when he said, "The hotel basement is . . . Well, you'll see for yourself. But you make a good point. It's a risk, but perhaps worth it. Fine. Gather your supplies for the final story and illustration, Haven. You can draw it in the basement so we'll be ready for Arne Koning the moment he makes his appearance."

Kylie looked nervous as she closed her laptop and unplugged it from the charger. I scooped up the sketchbook and a handful of markers.

The weight of Kylie's revelation unbalanced me like dialed-up gravity. It was hard to focus on Arnold, on what we had to do. I could barely look her in the eye, knowing she'd manipulated my story as much as his. I squeezed the markers, trying to contain my anger.

We followed Arnold into the hall, which had grown darker. The Killarney Doorman took up the rear of our group, a doorknob-shaped lump in his pocket. I still felt pulled between two selves. Since I'd satisfied Arnold's direct command by drawing a draft of his new identity, the compulsion had lessened, but the lingering film of his hypnotism left me disoriented.

Ahead of me, Kylie's feet slowed. Several sticky-looking mints littered the floor. We stepped around them and soon were at the stairway that returned us to the Durango Ballroom. Light from the tall windows stung my eyes even though it was thin and gray outside; it darkened early in Colorado in January. Doctor Ellis still sat at the head of the banquet table, though dinner had long ago been cleared. A stack of timeworn magazines rested by his side.

Uncle Arnold patted the doctor's shoulder condescendingly as he passed. Doctor Ellis continued flipping through a magazine in his eerie, slow-motion way, yet when I passed, his hand suddenly darted out, fast.

Black-and-white fingers curled around my sleeve.

Behind his dark spectacles, I could barely make out the doctor's cloudy, hypnotized eyes. Still, he looked at me like he remembered reaching through a movie screen, fingers pushing from one reality into another. . . .

I jerked away, and his clawlike hand hovered a moment in space. Then, as though nothing had happened, he picked up his cup of tea and took another sip, turning a page of *Life* magazine.

The Killarney Doorman gave me a shove to catch up with the others.

In the hotel lobby, my attention latched onto the trail maps on the walls—anything that tethered this place to *my* reality instead of theirs. It was getting harder and harder to know what was real and what wasn't; my mind kept wanting to pull me back into the movie world of *The Sandman Killer*, convince me it was the Swiss Alps outside, a *gendarme* hiking nearby, perhaps to save us.

"Haven," Kylie whispered over her shoulder. "Look."

Black dream smoke was seeping in from the lobby's edges. It hugged the floor like early-morning fog, but as Uncle Arnold tromped through it, he merely gave it a kick to send it swirling.

"The doctor likes to watch," he said.

When Kylie slowed down to pass through the smoke, Uncle Arnold gave an impatient *tsk*. He chided, "The smoke won't hurt you like this. It only becomes sentient if the Sandman Killer wants it to be—and you saw him; he's a joke unless I'm pulling his strings."

Arnold led us into a large area that a sign declared the hotel management's offices. The rooms inside were musty and dark. Furniture had been haphazardly moved around like someone had started a renovation but abandoned the project halfway through. Mouse droppings covered the carpet.

Uncle Arnold kicked aside more pieces of saltwater taffy; a giggle came from not far off, and I spun toward the sound. A closet door was cracked open, but nothing came out of it.

At the end of the hall, a door marked STAFF ONLY was barred by a heavy oak desk and a cluster of rolling cleaning carts. This went beyond moving furniture around for a possible renovation. It looked more like a battle had occurred here, though there was no blood spatter on the walls to indicate a struggle. I thought of *Zombie Train*, a movie I'd recapped for Rob, where passengers had barricaded themselves in a train station to keep out the undead. Had Uncle Arnold set up this barricade against something in the basement? He'd said that it was a risk to go down there.

"What happened here?" I asked.

Uncle Arnold wheeled the cleaning carts out of the way, then signaled to the Killarney Doorman. "Move the desk."

The lumbering monster picked up the heavy oak piece like it was made of straw, tossing it into the nearest office, where it landed with a floor-shaking thud.

Kylie shrieked and covered her ears.

When the noise settled, I thought I heard light footsteps behind me, and I turned to the empty offices. Again, there was no one there. As I started to turn back, a round gumball rolled down the floor along the baseboard.

My adrenaline spiked. I felt damp sweat at my armpits.

Once the Doorman had cleared the blockade, Uncle Arnold wove between the maze of cleaning carts and opened the basement door. A narrow wooden staircase descended into darkness. I braced myself, leg muscles tightening, but no monsters came hurtling out. All that emerged was the odor of stagnant water.

Beads of sweat had broken out on Uncle Arnold's upper lip. Grabbing the doorframe tightly, he warned, "Stick to the center of the stairs. Don't use the handrails."

"Why?" Kylie asked. "What's down there?"

As he stepped down the stairs, disappearing into darkness, he simply said, "I'm serious about the handrails."

As I entered the dark space, Uncle Arnold's warnings buzzed around me like biting insects. Wooden handrails ran along either side of the stairs, but I kept my hands folded together, squeezing the markers. My feet felt oddly hollow as I stepped in the center of each stair. It was a fossil of a staircase, doubtlessly original to the building, and probably never repaired. Each board groaned under my weight. My eyes darted to the stairs' edges, where the drop-off revealed utter blackness. Other than our footsteps and the usual clicks of a settling building, it was silent as we descended.

Until I heard a dragging sound like someone pulling on a wet sleeping bag.

I stopped, whisper-shouting, "Arnold, seriously. What's down in the basement?"

A board moaned beneath the Doorman's heavy weight right behind me. I heard more of the dragging sound, and I felt that our footsteps had awoken something sleeping in the dark.

"Not all the creations in the hotel are ones I found," Arnold answered. "One of them found *me*."

A thought itched at my mind: *The Hundredth Stair.*

It was the first Sigil Pictures film. I knew little about it other than from brief mentions in the *Hollywooder* article, but now my ankles felt chilled, exposed to the gaps between the stairs. I wished I knew what the movie was about, regardless of how terrible it might be. Nothing was worse than the blank sensation of not knowing.

Uncle Arnold's shoes finally clattered on the basement's cement floor. His shoulders slackened in relief now that he was away from the stairs. In the minimal light provided from the doorway above us, I saw him shuffle through the shadows until he found a control panel and threw on the ceiling lights. Most of the bulbs were burned out, but some weak ones flickered to life.

I blinked, still on edge. The hotel's basement was sprawling and low-ceilinged, packed with furniture in need of repair, expired cleaning supplies, stacks of bygone luggage. The wooden staircase cast a heavy shadow, hiding whatever might be lurking there beneath it.

Kylie's attention skittered around the room's corners. She tugged on my sleeve lightly, then intertwined her thumbs and made a faint flapping gesture.

I looked around, too, but there was no sign yet of our Thieving Crow.

"Over here, ladies." Uncle Arnold shoved aside desiccated cardboard boxes near a gigantic black boiler that was long cold and silent. "Yes—here."

A wire storage cage the size of a large closet partitioned a section of the basement near the old boiler. It contained a steamer trunk, a few green banker's boxes, and some ghostlike objects draped in white sheeting. Uncle Arnold took out a key and let himself in. He waded through the boxes until he could tug a sheet off a tall contraption that turned out to be a lighting rig. He removed another sheet from a 1940s-era motion-picture camera.

He picked his way over to the steamer trunk and threw it open. Gesturing toward the boxes' contents, he said, "Memorabilia the hotel management bought off Max Faraday and Richard Alton. Doctor Ellis raided much of it over the decades for his own purposes, but there are still some treasures."

Cautiously, I entered the cage and set down my notebook and markers on a trunk. I poked through the closest banker's box, finding a glass pill bottle and shaking it gently. The label said *Agnes Fitzpatrick*, but the pills inside were balled-up slips of paper, not actual pills.

"Ah. Here. This is what I wanted." Arnold plugged in the lighting rig and switched it on.

Kylie and I raised our hands against the sudden wash of light. It lit up the Killarney Doorman, who'd been standing just outside the storage cage and now turned away with a pained bleat like the brightness hurt his eyes.

"That should give you enough light," Uncle Arnold said, clapping his hands clean and then dragging over a footstool for me. He looked at me expectantly. "Well, go on. Do I have to compel you? Let's get this done."

He settled onto the steamer trunk to wait.

From the opposite end of the basement, one of the wooden stairs creaked.

Kylie spun toward the noise. A marker slipped from my hand. Uncle Arnold jumped up from the steamer trunk, his pinprick eyes focused on the stairs. He made his way out of the storage cage to cower behind the safety of the Killarney Doorman.

My mind raced as my fight-or-flight mechanism engaged. My instinct was to protect Kylie, my sister—but did she deserve it after what she'd done?

Another board creaked. The footsteps were light. Someone was coming down the stairs, rather than anything crawling out from under it. Our company reached the bottom and stopped where I couldn't see, somewhere behind a stack of draped furniture.

Uncle Arnold's shoulders relaxed—he wasn't afraid of whoever had joined us. He strode over impatiently to meet this new arrival.

"Well?" he snapped. "What is it?"

From my position, I could only make out a portion of the newcomer's shadow where it hit the floor, distorted from the light's angle. Whoever it was seemed very small.

The shadow beckoned Uncle Arnold forward, and he moved closer and bent low.

It's a child, I realized, the height difference apparent when the old man's shadow moved next to the smaller one.

A strangely muffled voice came. I caught a whiff of wintergreen.

I glanced at Kylie, who was hugging herself. The child said something else I couldn't make out, and Uncle Arnold snapped, "Speak up, Andrzej, I can't hear you with that damn mask on."

The boy lifted his voice. "Someone is outside the hotel. They're circling the perimeter trying to find a way in."

Uncle Arnold grunted, *"Here?* Someone is *here?* How the fuck did they get here? There's no road."

"I don't know."

"Is it a lost hiker? What did they look like?"

"I don't know."

"Yeah, you and your sister not knowing much? That's a common theme I'm noticing. Clearly, I took the wrong characters out of your movie." He sighed, his patience tested. "Show me. I'll be up in a minute."

The child turned and scampered back up the stairs. The wet dragging awoke again at the sound of the boy's footsteps.

Uncle Arnold didn't look pleased when he returned to the storage cage. He closed the wire door, locking Kylie and me inside with a twist of the key.

"I have to take care of some business upstairs. Don't do anything until I get back. *You*—" He handed the jangling key ring to the hulking Doorman. "Stay here. Guard them. I only need their hands—you can break their legs if you need to."

I looked at Kylie and knew immediately she was thinking the same thing I was. There might be secrets between us, broken trust, anger that snapped like a live wire.

But the only way we were going to get out of this was together.

This is our chance.

CHAPTER THIRTY-TWO

———

THE HUNDREDTH STAIR
© 1941 Sigil Pictures

INTERIOR — VICTORIAN BEACH HOUSE — ENTRYWAY

Jane is entirely on her own. She is covered
in algae and blood as she locks the front door
behind her. She's terrified. But—she escaped!

A tentacle made of humanlike arms and fingers
bursts through the floor—she hasn't escaped at
all.

Jane runs upstairs to her mother's sickroom.
CAMERA PANS WITH the snakelike, seemingly
never-ending tentacle as it pursues her.

———

THOUGH IT WAS a relief to hear Uncle Arnold's footsteps going
up the basement stairs, the rustling beneath the treads had me holding
back a cry. Whatever monster from *The Hundredth Stair* was down there,
it was definitely awake now.

The Killarney Doorman stood guard outside the cage, his back to
the old-fashioned spotlight. Kylie lightly jabbed me in the side to get

my attention. She tilted her head toward the shadows near the boiler.

She made the flapping gesture again.

"Did you see it?" I mouthed.

She nodded, but there was something uncertain about the movement. She glanced at the Doorman, close enough to overhear anything we said.

Quietly, she poked through the contents of a banker's box full of memorabilia and counted out a handful of silver-dollar coins that the sleep institute's rec room jukebox had used in *The Sandman Killer*. She jangled them in her hand.

The Doorman glanced over his shoulder at their jangle.

"We're just looking for things to pass the time," I said in his direction. "Unless you want to let us out of this cage?"

Uninterested, he grunted and turned away from us again.

In the second that his back was turned, he missed what I saw—the shadow near the boiler had moved. Two bright dots had glinted in the darkness under the pipes. Then . . . they'd blinked.

"Haven, let's play a game to see who can roll a coin farther," Kylie said loudly, crouching down. Her acting ability was shameful, but the Doorman was too dumb to pick up on it and seemed to take her words at face value. She rolled a coin through the cage's wires toward the boiler. It drifted to a stop a few feet outside of the cage. She rolled another one that stopped farther away, near a draped wardrobe.

Fluttering came from the boiler's direction.

Picking up my own coin, I glanced at the Killarney Doorman, but he didn't seem to care about our supposed game, and the fluttering sound could easily have been air from the vents.

"I wrote the Thieving Crow to like shiny things like coins," Kylie whispered low enough for only me to hear. "I didn't see it at first because it blends in with the shadows. Look closely—you can see it when it moves."

In an angry flash, I wondered what she'd rewritten *me* to like.

Crouching, I rolled a dollar, and indeed, the shadows seemed to shift. Something vaguely the shape of a crow hopped toward the coin. "Make a trail," Kylie whispered. "Lure it closer."

There was an urgent edge to her actions that wasn't just about our imprisonment. After my discovery of "Work in Progress," she was acting like she had something to prove: her worth, her loyalty.

Maybe she does.

We took turns rolling silver dollars into a line for the bird to follow. We waited, watching the shadows, all too aware that the Doorman could crush our windpipes with a single gesture.

Near the boiler, another flutter sounded so faint and quick that I almost missed it. When I checked, the coin closest to that area had disappeared.

I whispered, "How did the bird move so fast?"

Kylie frowned. "I didn't see it, but the air around it reacted . . . strangely."

Suddenly, rustling from the opposite corner of the basement caught my attention. My fingers closed over the loose coins as my adrenaline surged. "I thought the crow was under the boiler."

"So did I."

"So what's over there?" I asked.

"There's . . . more than one Thieving Crow," she whispered, looking startled by her own revelation.

"How?" I mouthed back, holding up a finger. "I only drew one."

She dragged a shaky hand down the length of her neck. "No, you drew several different versions."

"To get the picture right—there was only one *final* version."

She lifted a shoulder. "You drew them all on the same paper, and you drew each version with rough, overlapping lines. When you signed the paper, all those iterations of *all* those versions might have come to life."

My heart squeezed a staccato rhythm. I didn't like her accusing me of being as careless with the curse as she had been.

"Maybe it's okay." Kylie licked her lips. "In fact, maybe it's a good thing." Without offering any more explanation, she quickly sorted through the prop box and came out with a handful of stainless-steel surgical equipment props. She set down a small pair of scissors, a pair of tweezers, and a mercury thermometer along the cage's outer edge, leading a trail to where the Killarney Doorman stood guard. Then she stepped back.

Another flutter sounded near the boiler, so faint and quick that I almost missed it.

"Look, the tweezers are gone!" I whispered. "I didn't see anything! How are the birds moving so fast?"

A flash of movement from the rear of the basement caught my eye as something broke apart from the shadows like a pool of oil separating. As soon as the shape came out onto the concrete floor, it transformed from the color I'd given it, E-110 Special Black, to a shade closer to W-3 Warm Gray. I suddenly understood. The Thieving Crows weren't fast—they were camouflaged.

"They can change color," Kylie hissed breathlessly, seeing it too. "They're like chameleons."

"It's the curse." My voice was tight. "I knew something like this would happen. We rushed the drawing, and the curse took advantage."

I had drawn so many versions of the crow using different shades and roughly sketched lines meant to give the birds a sense of movement, but the curse had misinterpreted my intention.

Squeezing the cage wires, I searched for the birds. Now that I knew what to look for, I could spot the nebulous shape of the closest cement-colored bird. It was larger than a normal crow. Against the floor, its feathers appeared a stony gray mottled with dirty patches of tawny brown, even a few dark lines to perfectly match the floor's cracks.

The bird hopped forward, peered at the scissors.

One of the other Thieving Crows squawked near the stairs, and the Killarney Doorman looked that way. His goat nose sniffed the air. While his attention was elsewhere, the closer bird flapped its camouflaged wings, nearly undetectable as it rustled around the brute's pockets. I heard a soft, swift clink of metal along with fabric swishing.

The Killarney Doorman patted his clothes like he'd felt the brush of an insect.

"Crows," Kylie said aloud. "I heard them, too. I saw some roosting upstairs in the lobby. A few must have gotten down here. I think one just flew by."

The Killarney Doorman scratched the side of his neck but seemed to accept her explanation. He faced away from us once more.

The bird that had pickpocketed the Doorman now eyed the shiny pair of nail scissors. It lurched forward to snatch them, but Kylie was ready. She thrust her hands through the wire cage, grabbed the bird, and pulled it through the bars. She squeezed her knees together, pinning the bird's wings, and wrapped her hands around its beak to keep it silent.

In a fraction of a second, its feathers transformed from gray to B-39 Prussian Blue, the color of her leggings. It spasmed once in an attempt to get free before calming under her hold.

Metallic objects clattered together softly as Kylie felt through the bird's ever-expanding marsupial pouch. Though the bird's chest appeared unswollen, Kylie was able to fit her whole hand to the wrist in. She grimaced at the squelch of wet mucous noises as she dug around. When her hand emerged, the Killarney Doorman's brass doorknob gleamed in her palm amid silver-dollar coins. All in all, the loot took up about as much space as the bird itself.

She released the bird, who transformed back to concrete gray and hopped through the bars toward the boiler. More squawking came, this time from near the pile of old rugs.

The Doorman took a step to his right, trying to see into the shadows.

"On second thought," Kylie said loudly. "That sounds like more than just a few stray birds. I wonder if your boss has been at work collecting more monsters—maybe some that could replace *you*. If I were you, I'd investigate."

The Doorman took a few lumbering steps toward the boiler, crouched down, trying to see what was squawking.

"Okay," I whispered. "Now."

I held my hand out for the knob. The second Kylie passed it to me, I thrust it into the wire door. A crimson glow began to emanate from the edges. Kylie scrambled back, momentarily wary of the light, but I grabbed her shoulder and kept her close as I twisted the knob.

Red light blinded us. Beyond, through the portal's bleeding haze, I could just make out the rigid outlines of people on the other side.

The Doorman pivoted sharply back toward our cage. Hand clasped on his pocket, feeling the emptiness there, he let out an earsplitting bleat.

I threw my weight against the glowing door, dragging Kylie with me, and then we were both falling into a crimson wash like hellfire's glow.

A second too late, I realized I'd left behind the notebook.

A savage weightlessness overtook me. My body sizzled. My thoughts clawed and scrambled. Then—a half second after we'd entered the portal—we landed on a rug with a thud.

The Jackrabbit basement was gone. The air was crisp, air-conditioned. I smelled freesia.

A deep voice from somewhere close by barked, "*Blood and hell.* Haven? Is that you?"

———

We were in my bedroom at Rob's house.

My eyes were still tender from the portal light as I blinked at the miniature Hollywood sign behind the bed, the chandelier, the looming wax Rita and Audrey and Elizabeth, whose shapes I'd glimpsed through the portal.

I pushed to hands and knees, wincing at my cramped muscles. "Oh, god . . . the notebook . . . I left it behind."

Rafe dropped into a crouch. "What notebook? How the hell did you two get here?"

I sat back on my heels, dragging a hand through my hair. "It's a long story . . . Uncle Arnold compelled us to create him a new identity.

Kylie wrote him a story. I drew him a body. And I left the illustration back in the hotel. . . ."

"It's okay," Kylie reassured me. "You didn't sign your name to it. It can't manifest his new self."

I tried to convince myself she was right. I tested out my body gingerly as I stood up with Rafe's help. I flexed my fingers. The tendons ached from straining against the pencil for so long while I'd been illustrating. But at least my mind was my own again.

"Is Tyler okay?" I asked. "And Rob?"

"They're at the hospital. Tyler had severe burns. Rob's staying with him." Rafe motioned around the guest bedroom. "I've been searching for clues as to where you might have gone. You didn't answer your phone."

I noticed then that the dresser drawers had been thrown open, my clothes rifled through. My books were strewn around the floor, my laptop open on the bed.

"Arnold took both our phones," I said. "He still has them."

"Where were you?"

"Yeah, that's part of the long story. An abandoned hotel in Colorado. Arnold's been gathering Sigil Pictures monsters there. That portal doorknob—we stole it off one of them."

Rafe's hand tightened reassuringly on my arm. "Good. Then he doesn't have a way to get you back, at least not quickly. By the time he gets here, we'll be long gone."

My legs felt weak—I wasn't sure I could keep standing for long. Kylie looked exhausted, too. She leaned back against the windowsill, letting her head slump forward.

Maybe I should rewrite her *to have a little more fucking stamina*, I thought bitterly.

I sank onto the foot of the bed. The faux fur comforter cradled my aching muscles. I felt tempted to relax back into the pillows and sleep for ages.

Taking a tired breath, I said, "No, we can't run. Uncle Arnold has my illustration of him, and he has Kylie's laptop with his story on it, too. I know I didn't sign it, but I don't trust he can't figure out how to bring it to life regardless. Look what happened with the Thieving Crow. The curse is clever. It found a way to twist our intentions. We have to go back."

Kylie let out a burst of air. "There's no way he can finish the drawing on his own. He isn't our real uncle. He doesn't have Acosta blood."

I chewed on my lip. "Sure, but for all we know he could have some other curseworker in his back pocket who could finish the job."

I rubbed my exhausted face as I turned to Rafe. "Speaking of, have you heard anything else from Miracle Acosta, Rafe? If we're headed back there, we could really use the help of a monster hunter."

He shook his head. "When I couldn't find you, I tried calling her on the line she used before. It was disconnected."

"We can't trust her, anyway," Kylie said, incredulous I would even suggest it.

"Arnold was the murderer, not her. He admitted it. Besides, she's family, isn't she? I'll take my chances with family over 'Uncle' Arnold. Then again, I guess you can't even trust family these days." I shot Kylie a glare as I hefted myself to my feet, wincing at my collection of aches and bruises. "I lost the stun gun in the alley—"

"I brought it back here," Rafe said. "It's downstairs."

"Well, that's something," I said as I began pacing. "Not all of Rob's props are purely decorative. I know for a fact that the Damascus knife from *The Gentleman Knife* in the curio cabinet is real."

"Hell, let's just go to a gun store," Kylie said. "I wouldn't have the first clue what to buy, but I'm guessing *he's* a fucking expert." She jerked her thumb at Rafe.

"There isn't time," I said. "We have to get back to the Jackrabbit before Arnold manipulates that drawing."

Rafe folded his arms, looking grave. "I agree that someone must go back to stop Arnold, but not the two of you. You're exhausted. And you know fuckall about how to fight. Give me that magic doorknob. I'll go after Arnold on my own. I've faced him before. This is what I do—manage other monsters."

"No." Kylie's voice was sharp as she snatched the doorknob from my hand before Rafe could reach it. "I don't trust that you won't work some deal with Arnold on your own, Harbinger. You want to tag along, fine. I'll admit that we could use the help. But Haven and I are in charge." She glanced at me, suddenly hesitant. "Haven is, I mean."

Kylie was trying to make up for her sins, but it wasn't her deference I wanted.

I sighed. As tempting as Rafe's offer was, hiding under the covers and pretending like none of this nightmare had happened was impossible. The nightmare would find me.

It would find Kylie.

And I didn't want that—*right?* For her to suffer? I reminded myself that she was still my sister despite the sting of her betrayal.

I tipped my chin at Rafe. "Kylie's right."

He scrubbed a hand over his jaw. "Now you don't trust me either, Haven?"

"I didn't say that." Weariness weighed me down as I turned toward the bathroom. "We'll take a half hour to prepare. I, for one, want out of this fucking dress. Then we head back to the Jackrabbit. All three of us."

I was eager to calm my racing heart. Desperate for a shower. But no matter how the water scoured the smell of the musty old hotel off me, I could feel the Jackrabbit's dark hallways waiting for us to return.

It was hungry to have us back.

CHAPTER THIRTY-THREE

—

INTERIOR — THE DRUID BAR BACK OFFICE - NIGHT

Detective Nick Dram lies on the sticky floor.
Blood pools beneath his body. A CRIMSON GLOW
spills out of the open closet door, bathing
everything in harsh red light. CLOSE ON Nick's
fatal chest wounds. CLOSE ON the Killarney
Doorman's horns, now bloody.

—

"THE JACKRABBIT HOTEL. BASEMENT."

Standing in front of Rob's kitchen pantry with Rafe and Kylie on either side of me, I jabbed the brass doorknob into the door's opposite side. The portal's red glow burned hotter this time. Angrier.

The portal took us to the Jackrabbit's boiler door and into a space so narrow we had to crawl out of it onto the floor. The minute I dusted soot off my clothes and looked around the basement, I knew something had gone wrong.

We're too late, I thought sharply.

In the storage cage, the banker's boxes of props had been overturned and were dented like someone had kicked them in. The old light rig was still on, though knocked over so that its glow was skewed. The cage door hung open, unlocked. Thieving Crows were everywhere. Deafening caws echoed against the low ceiling. There were too many to count now—their chameleonic feathers took on the hues of Agnes's hospital gown, the cobalt gleam of the moving-picture camera, the dull green of the banker's boxes.

Rafe held out a hand to shield his face from the birds. "Arnold's new friends?"

Kylie grimaced. "Ours, actually."

She pushed her way through the birds, nudging them aside with her toe. Their camouflaged shapes flitted with reptile grace, slipping between the gaps in the cage's wire walls.

I crouched, searching the floor for the sketchbook. I spotted a couple markers first, then finally found the notebook, overturned behind the steamer trunk. I grabbed it and flipped through the pages.

My breath hitched. "The illustration is gone. Ripped out."

Kylie came over to see for herself, running her fingers over the blank page that had been beneath Arne Koning's sketch. It still bore the imprint of some of my pen strokes. We could afford to lose Kylie's laptop, since, ultimately, it was the artwork that triggered a manifestation, but we couldn't lose my drawing.

She groaned. "Arnold must have come back and realized what happened."

"So, we find him before he knows we're back," Rafe said, peering up at the basement rafters as though calculating. "How big's this hotel?"

"Big," Kylie answered. "Three stories. The upper two are guest rooms. Arnold set up an office for himself in the last guest room on the third floor. Room 341."

Rafe kicked his way through the birds toward the wooden stairs leading up to the first floor, but I caught up to him, resting a hand on his arm. The carcasses of several dead crows lined the perimeter of the stairs, and a viscous goo streaked the concrete.

"Wait, Rafe. Don't touch the railing. Stay in the middle of the stairs."

He took in the dead birds. "Why?"

"There's something living under the stairs. I don't think it can leave the shadows, but given what happened to those birds, it must have some reach. Don't get close enough for it to catch you."

Rafe took the stun gun out of the rear waistband of his jeans and pressed it into my hand. "Listen. You should keep this."

I didn't argue. The device felt like what my palm had been craving ever since I'd lost my original sketchbook. I tucked it into my jeans' back pocket.

"Sorry," he barked roughly to Kylie. "I'm short on stun guns."

"I bet you are," she muttered wryly, and then pulled out the nine-inch blade of the Damascus knife. "Good thing I didn't rely on you."

We ascended the stairs single file, keeping close together and away from the edges. The door at the top was open a crack, and a light beyond flashed. Once inside the hotel manager's office, we found a silent alarm was going off, causing the strobes, but there was no sign of what had triggered it.

"A Thieving Crow?" Kylie asked.

I gave an uncertain shrug. Night darkened the windows, the moon's light too weak to illuminate more than outlines of overturned furniture.

Kylie suddenly clutched my shoulder, her fingers digging into my skin. "Look."

She pointed toward the hallway, where black dream smoke billowed across the floor. Pieces of broken glass, nails, and other debris glittered within it. Something rippled across the smoke like a water beast under a lake's surface.

Alarmed, I rested a hand on my stun gun.

Rafe muttered darkly, "I thought Doctor Ellis had to be asleep to summon dream smoke."

I shook my head, not taking my eyes off the anomaly. "He can put himself in a trance on command. Arnold is behind this. Telling the doctor what to do. Spying on us."

Remarkably, the dream smoke seemed to hear me and respond,

rippling snakelike in my direction. Some of the debris it carried coalesced into a sharp, toothy shape.

"*Shit.*" I took a quick sidestep away.

I thought of Joao's corpse in the morgue, the wound that we'd mistaken for a ritualistic brand but that had in reality been made from the inside out. A *bite mark.* The dream smoke began to consolidate into a pillar the thickness of my wrist, rising toward the ceiling.

I shifted my weight backward. "That's how Doctor Ellis kills. . . . He sends the smoke down their throat and has it eat its way out of their chest."

"If Arnold is behind it, then he must be in close proximity to the somnologist," Rafe pointed out.

"The Durango Ballroom," Kylie said in a rush. "I don't think Doctor Ellis ever leaves it. It's on the far side of the hotel lobby."

Rafe kicked the broken furniture around until he found a metal desk chair. Straining, he wrenched off one of the legs as easily as if he were snapping a tree branch.

He rested the metal over one shoulder like a baseball bat.

"You insisted on being the leader," he said to Kylie. "So *lead.*"

Before we could make our way to the lobby, however, a dozen birds gathered to block the hallway in front of us, screeching. One bird hopped forward. Its wavering outline was nearly twice as large as any of the others. It was the one from the basement that had stolen the scissors.

"It's okay, I've got this. I wrote them to obey me." Kylie waved the Damascus knife toward the birds to shoo them away. A few of the birds fluttered back, but the big one let out a sharp caw, wings batting aggressively in the air.

Kylie looked suddenly doubtful. The bird darted forward, pecking at her shoe.

"Hey!" she cried.

"Real obedient," Rafe observed.

The big crow cawed at the others. One of them alighted and flew close enough to Kylie to claw her shoulder before she could swing the knife at it. She gave a frustrated cry. "They're supposed to listen to me!"

I assessed the big bird warily, not liking the gleam in its eye. "We were rushed when we made them. We made mistakes with both the art and the writing. And now we have to deal with the consequences."

Behind us, more Thieving Crows had flown up from the basement to join the flock gathered at the top of the stairs. Now we were surrounded by birds on both sides of the hall. They were growing more aggressive, daring pecks at Kylie's shoes. Above the birds, the pillar of dream smoke snaked through the air in zigzags, watching us.

Rafe pointed the chair leg toward the lobby. "We need to get to that ballroom. Now."

"The birds are blocking us in," I said. "And that smoke has a way of sucking up debris to give itself fucking *teeth*."

"I'll handle the birds," Rafe said. "When I say so, run."

"And the smoke?"

"Run faster than it can make teeth."

Kylie grimaced, shielding her body from a bird who tried to peck her knee. Rafe put himself between us and the birds. He waited until most of them had settled back onto the floor, and then rolled the chair leg down the hall. The birds took flight all at once to avoid it, lighting upon the high roosts of doorways and light fixtures with angry squawks.

"Run!" Rafe said.

Dodging the few remaining birds, we made a break for it through the dream smoke. It was knee-deep now, and cold, swirling like river eddies around us. A second pillar sprouted from the smoky mass to coil behind us.

It swooped in my direction; a maw the size of my fist yawned a few inches wide.

"Haven!" Kylie jerked me by the elbow just before the pillar smashed into the wall where my head would have been.

We ran until we reached the lobby, where the open space meant the dream smoke was more dispersed. It was only ankle-deep here, billowing away from our footsteps like ripples in a puddle. The snakelike smoke pillars were gone for the time being, but I had a feeling they could return at any moment.

We jogged over to the reception desk, where we stopped to catch our breath. In a flash, a memory came to me of the opening scene from *The Sandman Killer*, when Agnes Fitzgerald signed in with one hand pressed to her aching head.

Kylie pointed the Damascus knife's tip at the archway on the far side of the lobby. "The Durango Ballroom is through that arch."

But before we could head for it, the elevator gears groaned to life with a jangle of chains. Inch by inch, it slowly descended from the third floor. A familiar shape paced beyond the frosted glass. There was no mistaking those massive horns.

"The Killarney Doorman is coming down in the elevator," I breathed. "I don't even think he's compelled. He either likes working for Arnold, or Arnold has something on him."

Kylie scanned the lobby for a place to retreat. "The staircase. He won't see us if we're going up at the same time he's coming down."

"*Go,*" I ordered.

We hurried across the length of the lobby, weaving between massive oak columns. From the corner of my eye, I watched the Doorman move behind the frosted glass.

Small pebble-like objects crunched under my feet, but the smoke was so dark and dense that I couldn't see the floor. Kylie slipped on one of the objects, losing her balance and crashing down on her hip.

Rafe and I both skidded to a stop and backtracked to help her.

Wincing, Kylie rocked back and forth as she clutched her ankle. "I think I twisted it. I need a second."

"We don't have a second." I knelt by her, feeling my way through the smoke to see what she'd tripped on. My hand closed over a crinkling plastic wrapper. I held up a handful of wintergreen mints.

They smelled strange, and I leaned in on instinct to sniff them.

"Don't!" Rafe called. "Not the wintergreen ones, they're—"

It was too late. The plastic wrapper had come partly undone, and a burst of saccharine powder puffed out into my face. Gagging, I tossed aside the candy.

My body reacted almost immediately.

Burning eyes. Swirling vision. A lack of smell.

Rafe dropped down beside me. "Haven? Blood and hell. Those wintergreen candies are poisonous."

"What?" My voice sounded dazed.

"When you disappeared, Rob leaned on his film connections to give us information that might help us find you. One of them had seen *The Candy House* as a young boy. He told us what he could remember about it."

As the colors in the lobby sharpened almost painfully, Rafe's words felt distant. Whites brightened. Blues cranked up their hues. Browns practically glowed. As an artist, I knew such psychedelic colors didn't exist in the real world. No paint pigment could capture the fantastical lengths the mind could go to. Objects around me started to move and twist; the nearest oak column swelled like a blood-fat tick. The stuffed grizzly bear clawed at the air, angry that its feet were still bolted to the floor.

"The bear—it's alive!"

As I started to panic, Rafe grabbed my shoulders. "You're hallucinating, Haven! Kylie, can you stand?"

She struggled to her feet, grimacing with the effort. Rafe helped me up, not letting go of my hand, as if he was afraid that I'd run away in the throes of delirium.

His breath warmed my ear. "The stairs aren't far, Haven. We can make it."

I clutched his arm like a lifeline, trusting that the floor I was about to put my foot on wasn't undulating as much as it looked like it was.

The elevator dinged, making me stumble.

He's here.

"Shit," Kylie hissed.

My heart palpitated. I let go of Rafe, shoving him toward my limping sister. "*Go.* Help her get to the stairs. I'll be okay."

Rafe was poised to argue, but when the elevator doors rumbled open, he changed his mind and backtracked to Kylie, wrapping her arm over his shoulders so he could help her move more swiftly. I stumbled after them through the smoke.

As we skirted the reception desk, a pillar of smoke rose from behind it like a seated receptionist taking to her feet. It towered eight feet tall, as thick around as a person, huge in comparison to the smaller pillars we'd seen previously.

My chest squeezed inward like a squashed balloon. Was the giant smoke pillar in my head? Another hallucination?

I heard the Killarney Doorman's heavy footsteps go from elevator to tile floor.

A dizzy sort of terror overcame me. I pulled the stun gun out of my jeans pocket, squeezing it tightly. My vision slid and jumped as a result of the psychedelic gas. *There.* Coming from the direction of the elevator, the monstrous Killarney Doorman was crossing toward us in great strides, ankle-deep smoke parting to clear his path. His leather shoes crunched over colorful twists of candy, but the poison gas clouds didn't reach above his knees.

And *there*. Behind us, a murder of Thieving Crows poured out of the manager's office wing. In my disoriented state, their iridescent feathers rippled with wild, improbable colors. Their caws burned holes in my skull.

And *here*. The pillar of dream smoke rose from the center of the reception desk, looming over me just like in my nightmares, the maw already parting like a set of broken-glass jaws yawning open.

"Haven!" Kylie screamed.

I snapped out of my delirium. The smoke wasn't just in my imagination. *None of it is.*

The Killarney Doorman, the birds, the smoke: Everything descended on me at once.

CHAPTER THIRTY-FOUR

THE CANDY HOUSE
© 1951 Sigil Pictures

EXTERIOR — ROOFTOP — NIGHT

SMOKE rises from the hospital cremation kiln's
chimney.

INTERIOR — NURSE'S BEDROOM — NIGHT

TIGHT ON Andrzej's and Hanna's faces as they
hide under the nurse's bed. They're terrified.
Trying to keep quiet. TIGHT ON the bowl of
wintergreen mints on the nightstand. TIGHT ON
Andrzej's eyes, spotting it. He's devising a
plan. FOOTSTEPS enter the room.

RAFE GRABBED ME by the bicep, jerking me backward a second
before the smoke pillar hurled itself down to where I'd been standing,
yawning jaws crashing into the floor as the smoke burst apart against it.

Kylie fell back against the support of one of the oak columns, clutching the Damascus knife in front of her chest. "Haven! Behind you!"

A swarm of Thieving Crows dive-bombed my head. I jabbed the

stun-gun button, which sent the device crackling to life. I thrust it into the air, where it connected with one of the birds, causing it to explode into a shower of multihued feathers. Its carcass collapsed to the ground, turning E-110 Special Black again. Silver-dollar coins rolled out from its pouch.

I barely had time to charge the stun gun again before the Killarney Doorman was barreling down on us, nostrils flaring.

"Stay back," Rafe ordered, putting himself between us and the monster. He held out a steady hand and called to the beast, "*Wait.* You're going to want to listen to me. Whatever you want, I can get it for you."

I hobbled over to Kylie. The room was still swirling, its angles swelling and shrinking. I collapsed next to her against the oak column, breathing as hard as she was.

The Killarney Doorman ignored Rafe as he continued forward, steam rising from his nostrils.

"You want to work for yourself?" Rafe tried again in a rush. "Not have to answer to that old man? I can arrange that."

The Doorman remained undeterred.

"He doesn't speak!" I shouted to Rafe over the smoke.

Rafe slicked his hair back, keeping distance between him and the advancing monster. "He can fucking nod. What is it you want? Money?"

The beast snorted.

"To kill? Is that what you want, victims? I know a witch who'd pay you well for your services disposing of her enemies. Or if you don't care for money, she can get you willing females. Human or . . . goat. Whichever you prefer."

The Killarney Doorman, only a few feet away now, raised his massive fist.

Rafe kept one eye on the fist, ready to dodge it. "Or maybe you want back into your world? Lonely here, is that it? I get it. This can be a harsh reality."

The Doorman pulled back his fist.

Rafe muttered, "Fine. Fuck a deal, then. I tried."

He raised the chair leg behind his shoulder and stepped forward with a snarl on his lips, his hair mussed, swinging the rod at the Doorman's head with explosive strength. The Doorman opened his hand to catch it but wasn't fast enough; it glanced off his arm to slam into his shoulder, sending him staggering to the side.

Rafe doubled over, resting one hand on his knee to catch his breath.

The Doorman pulled up fast, rounding on Rafe with a flying fist. Rafe sidestepped the blow, but the Doorman caught hold of the end of the chair leg. He gave it a powerful tug, and it was all Rafe could do to hold on to the other end.

Closer, a Thieving Crow suddenly plunged toward Kylie.

She shielded her face with one arm while slashing blindly with the knife. The bird sank its beak into her forearm, ripping through her jacket. A second one latched onto her hair, pecking at her scalp.

She cried out in panic.

"Get away from her!" I waved my hand in an attempt to shove them away. Dizzily, I realized a book was burning in my hand. *No, not a book.* It was the stun gun, sparking.

I jabbed the stun gun into the Thieving Crow. The device crackled, and the bird jerked, its wings spasming.

Another bird dove for Kylie, but she moved aside in time, and it collided with the column. With a yell, she stabbed the Damascus knife into its spine. Its feathers rippled in a prismatic burst of color, then turned dull and black.

I had no chance to catch my breath before more birds swooped at us. My spinning vision made it hard to follow exactly what was happening in the fight between Rafe and the Killarney Doorman over by the elevator. They seemed to be wrestling over the chair leg, though in my poison-induced daze, both their heads appeared cartoonishly swollen. A crimson streak covered half of Rafe's face. More blood stained the Doorman's white shirtsleeves.

At the reception desk, billows of black smoke pulled themselves together again into a pillar.

Arnold is behind all this.

Whatever form Uncle Arnold was in now, we had to kill him. It was the only way the monsters at his command would fall back. I tossed a glance toward the ballroom, but another bird launched itself at my face. I jabbed the air with the stun gun, but the combination of my impaired vision and the bird's camouflage made it impossible to get a solid hit.

Kylie grasped the bird by its wing, dragging it off my face. "I *seriously* regret making you!" In response it flapped harder, battering me. Kylie pinned it against the oak column and stabbed the Damascus knife blade into its chest.

"The smoke . . ." My chest heaved as I pointed to the fog gathering in the center of the reception desk. Kylie held up the knife uselessly. Neither it nor my stun gun could do anything against smoke. I shouted across the lobby, "Rafe, the dream smoke!"

"Just give me a damn second!" He had gotten the upper hand with the Doorman, thrusting his weight behind the metal chair leg that they wrestled over. The Doorman's right side was streaked with blood from a puncture wound on his chest. Rafe wrenched the weapon away from him, raised it high, and then stabbed it into the already-oozing wound.

The Doorman let out a half-human, half-animal cry.

Breathing hard, Rafe slammed the chair leg down on the Doorman's head. It glanced off one horn but struck him in the temple. The creature sank to his hands and knees.

I grasped Kylie's sleeve, not trusting my own eyes. "Is Rafe—"

"Rafe is okay. I think your boyfriend *likes* this."

Rafe swiped his sleeve over his blood-soaked brow. The weapon dangled from his exhausted arm. He turned in our direction, breathing hard, and then cast a slow look of apprehension up the length of the smoke pillar.

The pillar had begun to spin like a tornado vortex, pulling in more of the smoke and debris that covered the lobby floor. The maw was already starting to writhe like a cobra before striking.

The pillar whipped around to face Kylie and me.

I shoved Kylie away from the oak column. "Run!"

She moved as fast as her twisted ankle would let her. I barreled in the other direction back toward the manager's office wing, hoping to draw it away from her. The smoke's head whipped back and forth as though undecided about which one of us to pursue.

I ducked behind the taxidermic bear, breathing hard, and then peeked out to see if the smoke was following me.

Shit. It had gone after Kylie.

The mangy fur pressing against my cheek suddenly felt warm, alive. The bear growled low in its chest. *It isn't real,* I told myself, but it didn't *feel* unreal.

Rafe snatched up the chair leg again, his chest rising and falling in unsteady bursts as he started after the smoke pillar. Did he think he was going to stop it with a piece of metal and his two fists?

Out of the corner of my eye, I saw movement coming from where the Killarney Doorman's body rested on the floor. Slowly, the beast pushed himself to his hands and knees. I rubbed my eyes, not sure I was seeing correctly. The Doorman slowly staggered to his feet behind Rafe. His head was bowed—at first, it seemed, as a consequence of his wounds—but then he stamped his foot twice, and I understood.

It was the same move a bull made before striking.

My mind's eye saw everything a second before it happened. The Killarney Doorman was going to pierce Rafe's kidney area with those sharp horns, gore him to death.

My fingers clutched the bear's matted fur hard enough to rip it out. I screamed, "Rafe—!"

My cry was drowned out by the thunder of gunshots.

The Killarney Doorman, poised to charge, jolted backward as though a ten-foot tidal wave had crashed into him.

Whipping my head around to follow the gunshots' trajectory, I couldn't believe what I saw. Reality shifted like a sliding door, and suddenly I was back inside the black-and-white movie world of *The Sandman Killer*, standing exactly here in the lobby while a Swiss gendarme in snowshoes thrust open the glass entryway. Only it wasn't fictional police this time.

It was Miracle Acosta.

She clutched a rusty-barreled tommy gun, stepping over the cadavers of crows as she aimed again at the Killarney Doorman. She wore a canvas military-style backpack over black leggings and a long-sleeve white tee that read LIVE, LAUGH, FUCK OFF.

I collapsed my shoulder against the bear, trying to calm my breath.

Despite the bullet wounds, again the Doorman managed to push himself to his hands and knees. Blood gushed out of his chest. Rafe backtracked a few feet, his body primed for another attack.

Without taking her sights off the Doorman, Miracle gave Rafe a sharp command. "Get back."

Rafe didn't argue. He retreated to the oak column where Kylie was holding off the birds, turning his back on them to shelter her.

When Miracle was ten feet from the Doorman, she muttered, "Bye."

She let loose a few rounds from the antique submachine gun. The Doorman's body jolted. A squeal ripped up his throat. There was a second when I thought he might have the strength to stand again, but his body hovered for a moment, blood dripping from the matted fur around his mouth, and then he slumped to the floor.

In the silence that followed, no one moved. Rafe's eyes gleamed with adrenaline. Miracle kept the weapon aimed at the monster's body as though she didn't trust that he was truly dead. Her stance was nothing like the gentle-spirited yogi I'd met in Joshua Tree.

She's done this before, I realized. *Many times.*

When the Doorman still didn't move as blood pooled beneath his head, Miracle took a few steps forward, prodding his shoulder with the tip of the gun barrel. Then she lowered her weapon and canvassed the lobby, focusing on the Thieving Crows flocking Kylie and Rafe.

She turned to me. "Is there a secure room? An office or a coat check?"

I tried hard to snap to attention, running a shaky hand over my pulled-back hair. "To the right of the staircases."

"Those birds?"

"We created them—" I swallowed. "It got out of hand."

"No shit. Do you know how to kill them?"

Even my blinks felt out of sync, still sluggish from the poison gas, though the worst of the effects were fading. "A stun gun will do it. A knife, too. They like shiny objects."

Letting her gun dangle from a shoulder strap, she pulled out a handful of bullets from the backpack's side pocket and tossed them across the floor in the direction of the hotel manager's wing. The crows circling Kylie and Rafe peeled off when they heard the plinking tin sounds, diving toward the shiny bullets.

"Get to the coatroom!" Miracle ordered.

We wasted no time, Rafe helping Kylie hobble. I reached the coatroom first. It was musty inside, as though no one had entered in half a century. Wooden hangers spanned one wall, holding a few dusty wool garments and a mangy fur coat that seemed to *breathe*, though I still didn't trust my perception. Hard-sided suitcases were stacked in the back corner. A canvas duffel bag was open, mouse-nibbled wrinkled clothes pulled out onto the floor.

Rafe and Kylie barreled in behind me, with Miracle bringing up the rear. She scanned the lobby, then closed the door firmly.

"Put Kylie there," I said, pointing to the suitcases.

Rafe helped Kylie slump onto the stack of old luggage. I was less concerned about her ankle than about the beak puncture wounds freckling her arms and face, weeping blood.

"Are you okay?" I asked.

She nodded shakily as she grabbed the edge of a coat and used it to mop her face. "Are *you*?"

I rested a hand on the wall, still struggling to steady my vision. The fur coat had stopped moving, at least. The walls weren't undulating quite as fervently.

I gave a nod. "Miracle. How did you—"

"I tracked your phone." Miracle stashed the remaining bullets in her backpack's side pocket. "It's easy—you got a text offering a weather app, right? You declined? Doesn't matter—I can still get into your location services. When I saw that you traveled from downtown Los Angeles to Colorado in a three-second span, I knew the curse was involved."

"You can't have gotten a flight so fast," Kylie said.

Miracle patted her backpack. "You two have a lot to learn. Teleportation is rampant in fiction. Find the right world, get your hands on a tool, you can go anywhere."

"Like the Killarney Doorman's doorknob," Kylie said.

"It was a map, in my case. But, yes, I know about that goat-demon's brass device. We saw *Purgatory's Door.* Joao and I tried to get the doorknob for weeks."

Rafe rustled past the hanging coats and touched the small of my back. "The smoke?"

"It didn't get me." I swallowed, relaxing at his touch. "But I'm guessing it can pass under that door."

Miracle started gathering the loose garments, which she passed to Rafe and me. "Stuff these under the door. Block the crack the best you can."

"That will work?" I asked.

"I have no idea, but it's worth a shot."

As we made our barricade, I took a few breaths to clear the haze from my mind. I told Miracle what we knew about the characters from *The Candy House, Winter of the Wicked,* and *The Hundredth Stair,* then finally about the smoke that killed the others and Arnold's control over its creator.

Miracle listened closely as I explained how Uncle Arnold's voice worked and the rebooted version of himself that he had ordered Kylie and me to create.

"Arnold's voice doesn't work on me," Rafe said matter-of-factly. "You three handle Doctor Ellis, and I'll head to the third floor. I can kill the old man."

Miracle made a doubting *tsk*.

Rafe cocked his head at her with something like a snarl. "I *can* kill him."

"I don't doubt you're capable of a lot of things," Miracle said evenly. "But if you accomplish this plan, you will only put an end to the monster's physical form. You know it takes art and story together to summon one, right? You need to end both."

"End both the physical and the spiritual side?" It was an idea that hadn't occurred to me despite knowing that the characters from *Bedtime Stories for Monsters* had existed for years in a poltergeist-like state, rattling around Malice House. "What happens if we don't?"

"If you only kill their bodies, they persist spiritually. Ghostlike. Whatever you want to call it."

A tense silence filled the coatroom before Kylie pointed out, "Killing their physical forms sounds pretty fucking sufficient to me. I can *handle* ghosts; heck, we can just leave them here."

Miracle shook her head. "You don't want formless stories wandering around. They have ways of finding bodies for themselves again. Ways of tormenting you. Believe me, I know."

She crouched down and unzipped her backpack.

"So how do we kill both their physical and story forms?" I asked.

She laid open her backpack to show an impressive array of supplies. A ziplock bag held a variety of passports and ID cards. There was a small pistol and several hunting knives, and stranger objects, too. Plastic water bottles filled with oily liquids. A length of roughly spun wool yarn. A hammer with chipped green paint on the handle.

She pored over the implements like a surgeon selecting a scalpel.

"You weren't far off when you created those crows," she said to me and Kylie. "Only you shouldn't have introduced new stories—like you quickly discovered, it never ends well. The only thing that can kill their spirit is their story itself: You fight them from within their own world."

It took a moment to wrap my thoughts around that.

"So that submachine gun isn't from our world?" Kylie sat with her hands braced on her knees, nodding toward the gun.

Miracle adjusted the gun strap around her shoulder. "It's called the Chicago Typewriter, and no, it isn't from this world. It's from *his*." She angled the barrel toward the lobby where the monster's body lay. "The Killarney Doorman was the first Sigil monster that Joao and I targeted after the *Hollywooder* article surfaced. We took the gun off another creature who'd stepped out of *Purgatory's Door*, Banjax, who was prowling around the LA subway system, picking off riders. That's why I was able to effectively kill the Killarney Doorman. A gun from *this* reality wouldn't have ended his story. I needed something with the van Doornik touch."

"What's van Doornik?" I asked.

Miracle unzipped another internal backpack pocket, sorting through a variety of skeleton keys. "Not a *what*, a *who*. It's a family name. Van Doornik, Acosta . . . it's all the same. The curse has gone by many different names over the centuries. Joao and I called it the Creator's Curse. Van Doornik was the first curseworker anyone has identified. Hugo van Doornik, a Dutch painter in the early sixteenth century. He did mostly oil on oakwood, a lot of scenes of hell. But he wasn't the actual artist. It was his wife, Gaudicine. She painted nightmares that arose in her dreams. Her husband took credit for the works against her will, and her rage took revenge."

A prickly apprehension traveled through my limbs. "That was how the curse started?"

"I have no idea. That's only as far back as we've traced it. It was a different time. The occult, witchcraft . . . it was accepted then as reality. It's mostly *always* been accepted throughout history. Now we call curses folklore, unscientific, but really we've just forgotten them. We've turned curses into fiction when they never were—and still aren't now."

Out of the corner of my eye, I thought I glimpsed movement near the door. When I looked closer, the vintage clothes Rafe had stuffed under the crack appeared to have been pushed out. A small wisp of smoke sidewinded its way into the coatroom.

I straightened. "Everyone else is seeing that, right?"

"Yeah," Kylie breathed.

Rafe hurriedly kicked the shirts back under the door.

"The curse isn't fiction," I agreed in a rush. "And we don't have much time before the things it brought forth come for us. You said monsters could only fully be destroyed when we turn their own stories on them, Miracle?"

"That's right."

"So, we need to find new ways to end this—to end them." My eyes fell on the suitcases Kylie was sitting on, and I thought of the Sigil Pictures equipment in the basement. "I might have an idea."

Miracle crossed her arms, drumming her fingers as she lifted an eyebrow. "Go on."

I turned reluctantly to Kylie. "I don't think you're going to like it."

Kylie stiffened. The taut string of tension still hummed between us. We hadn't spoken of the revisions she had made to my story, or the fact that she even thought my life *needed* rewriting, as though I was half a person, or worse, a minor character in the background of someone else's tale.

But I didn't care if she thought I was a hero, a villain, a martyr, a victim.

It didn't matter. Whatever I was, she was going to hate me for what I was about to suggest.

CHAPTER THIRTY-FIVE

—

```
       WINTER OF THE WICKED
        © 1947 Sigil Pictures

INTERIOR — BARN — NIGHT

Possessed Farm Wife sways as straw falls like
snow from the hayloft. Her face is deeply
scratched. Blood soaks her dress from her
fatally cut neck. At her feet, her daughters'
battered bodies lie. Elder Daughter's hand
still clutches a pitchfork.

A puppet is covered by falling straw as the
Possessed Farm Wife lets the POSSESSED ANIMALS
into the barn to feast.

Farm Wife snaps her teeth.
```

—

"FIRST OFF," I said, "we need to clear the birds from the lobby. Their calls give our location away. Your bullets distracted them before, Miracle. We can use the same trick again."

"The bullets are from the same world as the Chicago Typewriter," she said. "Once they're used up, that's it. I don't have enough to shoot every bird."

"I'm not suggesting you use the bullets."

"So, what's the lure if not bullets?"

I held up a foil-wrapped caramel from my pocket. "Only the wintergreen mints give off poison gas. That means Miracle can use the caramels to draw the birds outside. Rafe, you take care of the dream smoke. You'll have to find Doctor Ellis in the ballroom and snap him out of his trance."

"With pleasure." He toed Miracle's open backpack with a gleam in his eye. "I could use that butcher knife there—the one with the ivory handle. In case negotiations with Doctor Ellis go as poorly as they did with the Doorman."

Miracle's answering stare was cold. "I'm not voluntarily lending a weapon to a monster. You aren't the first product of the Creator's Curse who has offered their *help*." She zipped up the backpack, swinging it onto her shoulders, then tipped her head in my direction. "Haven might trust you—for now—but she hasn't seen the things I have. It won't take me long to draw off the birds. Then I'll come keep an eye on *you*." She raised her gun at Rafe. "To make sure you don't decide to flip on us."

Rafe mirrored her cold smile, unflustered.

"That leaves you and me to deal with Arnold," Kylie said uncertainly. "What part of this aren't I going to like?"

Quietly, I said, "We're headed to the third floor. You're going to let Arnold whisper in your ear."

Her eyes widened with shock. *"Voluntarily?"*

"Yes, voluntarily."

It was hard to muster sympathy for Kylie. She was my sister, yes, but she'd also taken away *my* will by rewriting my story in a way that wasn't all that different from Uncle Arnold's compulsion. Was it wrong of me now to ask her to make the same sacrifice?

Kylie's foot bounced repeatedly. I could only imagine what was going through her head. She'd broken my trust with "Work in Progress," and she had to be wondering if this was a form of retaliation.

Maybe it is. Maybe you need to remember how it feels to have someone else pulling the strings.

"Okay," Kylie said quietly.

I nodded sharply. "We'll need some equipment from downstairs. Uncle Arnold has been using his voice for years, and he's developed go-to phrases to control people. The first thing that he whispers is *Stop what you're doing.* That makes his victim stop whatever specific action they were intending to carry out. He used that phrase on both of us in his office when we tried to cover our ears. If we can record his voice saying it, I can play it back for him. As soon as he tries to compel me, his own voice will order him to stop trying to compel me."

Kylie rubbed her thumb over the grooves on the Damascus knife's hilt. "Then you'll kill him?"

"According to Miracle, that would only put an end to his body. It will take something from within his own story to kill his spirit."

"How are we supposed to get that?" Kylie's grip tightened on the knife hilt. "The manuscript is gone."

I pressed my fingertips together. "The night of the Malice House fire, two police officers got in Arnold's way. He addressed the incident by ordering them to kill themselves. It didn't feel like the first time he'd used that tactic, either. I think it's another go-to command he uses. If we could get him to state that command and record it, I can play it back so that he'll be compelled to kill himself."

The knife nearly slipped out of Kylie's hand before she caught it. "Uh, he'll be giving *me* that command. You want me to kill myself, too?"

I quickly reassured her, "That won't happen. Arnold's room is 341. The Fear-Not Wife was asleep in 340 last we saw, and there's been no sign of her since then, so there's a good chance she's still sleeping. When the time is right, I'll wake her up. While she causes a distraction, I'll snap you out of the compulsion before you even come close to hurting yourself."

"How?" she challenged.

I held up the stun gun from my back pocket. It hadn't done much to slow Tyler at Pharmacy Bar, but he was insanely fit at over two hundred pounds. Kylie didn't weigh much more than half that.

The others were quiet. Rafe was the first to break the silence, holding up a finger to make a point. "Tactfully, might I suggest a zombie might not be the best way to solve our problems?"

I pushed myself up from where I'd been sitting on the trunk. "Honestly? I think the only way we're going to get out of here is to use the monsters against each other."

Miracle thrust a water bottle at me. "Maybe you aren't hopeless after all."

I took a swig and then passed it to Kylie, who hesitated before accepting it, fixing her gaze to mine. "I trust you, Haven. I'll do whatever I have to."

I held her gaze, nodding.

Rafe pressed a hand on the small of my back. His eyes combed down the length of my body, coming back to rest on my face. "As soon as I take care of the doctor, I'll come up to the third floor. Try not to get yourself killed before then?"

My mouth twitched in a reluctant smirk. My chest tightened with memories of his woodsmoke scent. Miracle didn't trust him—but did I?

I want to.

"You too, Rafe."

He scoffed as though he was indestructible, but we both knew he wasn't.

Kylie handed him the water bottle, and he tipped it back.

I peeked through the coatroom's keyhole to assess the situation in the lobby. The smoke was still ankle-deep on the floor. My fingers plucked at my shirt collar anxiously. A gentle hand rested on my shoulder. I flinched, but it was only Miracle.

"Haven. Take a breath. You can't fight anything if you pass out."

Her voice had settled into the gentle rhythm of the free spirit I'd first met in Joshua Tree, and I wondered if maybe Tree Pose hadn't been a complete fabrication.

I clasped my hands to steady them. Quietly, I asked, "Is it always like this?"

"Hunting monsters, you mean?" She adjusted the strap of her tommy gun. "Joao and I, we usually tracked one at a time. We had time to research, to create a plan, even backup plans in the event that something went wrong."

"But you've faced this kind of thing before." I needed to press, to convince myself we could rely on her.

She didn't answer right away. Then she clutched my wrist stiffly, a gesture I wasn't sure was meant to be comforting. "Yes. From what I hear, so have you."

My lungs pulled in a sharp breath. Memories rushed back, sending my limbs twitching. My throat felt choked by phantom smoke, reliving what had happened within the walls of Malice House.

"That night, it wasn't the monsters trying to kill us," I intimated. "It was regular people."

Her hand tightened on my wrist in a single strong squeeze. "Is there a difference?"

Silence.

I didn't have an answer.

Rafe finished draining the water bottle and tossed it into the corner. He wiped his mouth with his shirtsleeve. The four of us faced the coat-check door.

"You first, darling. May I suggest you use your shortcut?"

Heart racing, I took out the brass doorknob.

The red glow, the weightless tug, and then Kylie and I were stepping out of the coatroom into the basement storage cage.

I took a moment to get my bearings.

A handful of crows perched on boxes and the draped furniture, matching the color of their chosen roost. It wasn't so many birds as to be an immediate threat—most of the swarm was still upstairs in the lobby—but we kept our distance regardless.

The piles of bird carcasses lining the stairs had swelled to small mountains.

I tugged on Kylie's sleeve. "Keep an eye under the stairs."

"Whatever lives there has been busy," she muttered darkly. "At least we know its reach. It looks like about six inches from the perimeter."

A caw that cut off mid-squawk told us another bird had met its end.

I picked my way toward the Sigil Pictures trunk and lifted the lid. "We need to find recording equipment. I don't think motion-picture cameras in the 1940s captured sound, but there had to be something they used."

Kylie sorted through clunky pieces of hundred-year-old audiovisual equipment tangled in their own cords. She moved aside several bulbous microphones. I set the microphones out of the way, my heart knocking hard in my rib cage. We examined cords and boxes, lighting equipment and handheld cameras.

"I think I found something," she said.

She held up a metal case about the size of a dictionary with a leather carrying strap. A small handheld microphone was attached to it by a wire. She read the case's label. "It says it's a Bell Portable Dictaphone. That's a recorder, right?"

I took the contraption to assess how it worked. A portion of the metal lid folded open, revealing a plastic disk inside with a record-player-like arm.

I handed Kylie the machine's fraying cord. "Plug it in. Let's see if it still works."

She found an outlet on the wall behind the trunk. The Dictaphone's controls were simple, with only a single button and a dial, so I pressed the button. The machine whirred to life in my hands. The disk spun with a faint rusty groan.

I handed her the microphone. "Let's try it. Say something."

"Live, laugh, fuck off," Kylie pronounced.

I fiddled with the dial until I figured out how to run a playback. Out of a speaker in the rear of the Dictaphone, Kylie's disembodied voice fed out of the speaker, distorted by audio static and carrying a mild echo.

"Live, laugh, fuck off."

"I'd say that will do it." I switched off the machine, then slid the strap over my shoulder. I stole a final, wary gaze at the basement stairs.

Kylie turned to me with worried brows, holding out a hand for me to wait. "Haven, about 'Work in Progress,' I—"

"Don't. Not now." I reached out to squeeze her wrist, not unlike Miracle's dubious brand of comfort. "We're in this together, and we'll get out of it that way. And then we'll sort through our own shit. Right?"

She nodded, though her jaw firmed with guilt.

For a second, a ripple caught my attention in the gap between two of the stairs' wooden slats. I frowned, unsure what I was looking at. A crow landed on the edge of one stair, its body immediately shifting into a woody brown color, but before it could fold in its wings, a pale appendage shot out from the shadows and snatched it.

I covered my gasp. In the brief glimpse I'd gotten, it had looked like human fingers grabbing the bird.

A sound like clattering human teeth came from the shadows. Then the crow's decapitated body was thrown out from the shadows to join one of the piles.

Kylie's eyes had gone huge. "Did you—"

"Let's get out of here." I pressed the doorknob into her hand while I wound the Dictaphone's cord into a loop. "Now," I whispered.

She touched the doorknob to the hinge side of the door. Inhaling deeply, she mouthed, "Third-floor elevator."

The raw, red glow of the portal ignited like a beating heart.

Kylie and I stepped through the storage cage door and exited the elevator gates on the Jackrabbit Hotel's third floor.

The crimson glow faded behind us until it was simply the dark, empty carriage at our backs. The ceiling lights were off in the hallway, the bulbs long since broken or shorted out. When we'd been here before, dying sunlight had filtered in through the windows and cast hazy patterns on the rugs, but night had come now, and only weak light emerged from the few open guest rooms. I could barely make out a few pieces of candy that littered the hallway. The rippling form of a single camouflaged Thieving Crow roosting on a brass wall sconce.

A light was on in the last room on the left—Arnold's office.

Somewhere close, a person giggled. I spun, clutching my collar.

Kylie raised her blade, but I held out my hand.

"I don't think Andrzej and Hanna are threats. Arnold said himself that he took the wrong characters out of their movie."

"You haven't watched their movie," she whispered. "You don't know that for sure."

I jerked my chin toward the end of the hallway, where a person's shadow passed in front of the light source. Uncle Arnold was awake and moving around Room 341.

"I know for damn sure that *he* is."

It was too dark to read Kylie's facial expression, but her hand trembled as she handed me back the doorknob.

"Kylie," I whispered, low and urgent, turning to face her. I wanted to tell her that she didn't have to do this—to face Arnold again, re-subject herself to his spell—but the words didn't come.

Her head dipped in a nod when I didn't finish my thought. "It's all right."

A knot of fear clogged my throat. Facing Arnold's pacing shadow at the end of the hall, I suddenly doubted everything. Now I was glad *my* face was hidden.

I started, "Whatever happens . . ."

She shook her head sharply. "Like you said, it's not the time." Her voice faltered, but then she gave my shoulder a shove and urged softly, "You should hide."

I almost didn't. I almost called it off. I *wanted* to call it off. But Rafe and Miracle were downstairs, already enacting their parts in everything. We were all dependent on one another now. None of us could fail, or we all would.

Reeling, I started down the hallway. Saltwater taffy, wintergreen mints, foil-wrapped caramels littered the rug like a saccharine minefield. I stepped over the mints while also trying to avoid squeaky floorboards that would give away my presence. The Thieving Crow launched itself off the wall sconce and flew into a guest room midway down the hall where weak moonlight shone.

Glancing inside the room after the bird, I startled.

Two children sat perfectly, eerily still on the bed. They wore tan wool clothes and knee socks, and the girl was swinging her feet against the bed skirt. Rubber gas masks gave them the round eyes of insects.

Andrzej and Hanna.

I froze, pinned under their alien stares. Doubts flooded my mind. Maybe Kylie was right that we didn't know who the villain of their story was. . . .

When I didn't move, the boy did. He slid off the bed slowly, crossing to the doorway with steps almost as quiet as my own. My breath lodged in my throat. I backpedaled, barely remembering to watch out for the mints, until my shoulders pressed into the rear wall.

Andrzej said quietly, "The woman with the gun. Did she find you?"

He had to mean Miracle. I recalled that he had been the one to tell Uncle Arnold about her arrival. I gave a shaky nod, my body still primed for danger.

"I lured her into the hotel when that goat-man was in the basement."

What was he trying to tell me? That he had *helped* us?

Before I could ask for clarification, he pressed a small, sharp object into my palm and whispered, "Luck, luck, pretty teddy bear."

He eased the room's door closed until it clicked into place and I was staring at nothing more than knots in oak grain. I let out my breath in a sudden rush. My body was still tightly wound, prepared for a fight that didn't seem to be coming.

In my palm rested a key. A metal label said MASTER.

I glanced down the hall back at Kylie. Arms clamped across her chest, she shuddered in the same way she had during *Stitches 2*.

Ahead, Arnold's office door stood partway open; I waited until I heard him typing on one of the laptops, which meant his back would be to the door. Cautiously, I darted the rest of the way to the cracked door of Room 340 and peeked inside.

The Fear-Not Wife lay on her back atop the covers, her hair streaking the cotton pillow. Her dark dress left her body shapeless against the white bedcovers, like a void between universes. The deep gash across her throat gurgled wetly when her chest rose and fell in whatever semblance of breath a dead woman took.

Still asleep.

I slipped quickly inside, closed the door all but a sliver, and crouched in the dark.

The only sound that came from Arnold's room was steady typing, which meant he hadn't heard or seen me. It was hard to feel relief, however, when there was a sleeping monster behind me who might wake at any moment.

Working as silently and swiftly as I could, I plugged the Dictaphone's fraying cord into an outlet, then eased open the cover and pressed the button to start recording. The device let out a low swish as the disk spun. I cringed at the sound and checked the bed, but the Wife continued to wheeze her rasping, slumbered breath.

A moment later, Kylie's footsteps creaked down the hallway. Unlike me, she wasn't trying to hide her presence.

"Arnold." Her voice rang out. "You wanted to talk, right? Well, get the fuck out here. Let's talk."

Through the cracked door, I could only make out a sliver of the hallway. The tips of Kylie's shoes were all that was visible. Everything remained quiet, but then the hinges of Arnold's door groaned.

Plodding footsteps thumped in the hall. I braced myself for the old man's familiar voice, but instead I heard Kylie's sharp intake of breath.

"What did you do? How——?" The shock in her voice didn't sound like she was acting.

"What did *you* do?" Uncle Arnold barked back at her. I had to steady myself with a hand against the wall. It wasn't the same voice I knew, the watery timbre that painted fear in my heart.

It was a younger man's voice.

No, impossible.

I hadn't signed the draft of Arne Koning's sketch. I hadn't even finished it, leaving off some of the jaw's shading. There was no way the curse could have brought Arne Koning to life.

I struggled to peer through the cracked door. The place he stood was blocked from my vision. I was left with dry lips, anxious to know what—or *who*—Kylie was looking at.

Arnold warned Kylie, "If you've come here to kill me——"

There was something odd about his younger voice, something breathy and garbled. It sounded almost as distorted as the gas-masked Andrzej.

I tossed a glance at the bed again, praying their noise wouldn't wake the Wife.

"I haven't." Kylie had regained a measure of her composure. "And . . . and . . . don't compel me—not yet. Let me explain while I can still think for myself. Look, it's just me. I came on my own. I don't have any weapons. No earplugs. As a sign of good faith."

My pulse rushed deafeningly in my ears. I glanced down at the device, praying the Dictaphone was recording everything.

The hallway groaned beneath Arnold as he adjusted his stance.

"Go on, then. Say what you have to say." His old-fashioned speech patterns echoed within his new voice.

Kylie continued, "Haven doesn't know I'm here. She wants to stop you. And I'll be honest, you scare the living shit out of me, too. I don't know how you did *this*, but it only goes to prove what you're capable of. If you worked with the right person, you could do even more. I'm a curseworker. I can write you anything you want—"

"Stop," Arnold snapped. Kylie fell silent, though I could hear her unsteady breathing.

I let out a silent, frustrated hiss. He'd spoken in a regular voice, not the commanding whisper. At this point, all I had recorded were harmless words.

He continued, "You want to go against your sister? Work with me?"

"That's right." Kylie's voice faltered a little.

Arnold was quiet, probably taking his time to scheme over this new development. I resisted the urge to open the door wider to look at him. Was it Uncle Arnold—or Arne Koning? Were they *both* alive now? Finally, I heard him snort.

"Bullshit. Whatever you and Haven are plotting, it's painfully transparent. Why are you really here, doll?"

I braced myself, sliding a slow look over my shoulder at the slumbering Fear-Not Wife.

A pause followed during which I had no idea what was happening in the hallway. The tension in the air was thick enough that it had a smell, like waterlogged carpet.

Kylie growled, "How about to kill you, motherfucker?"

There was a rustle, and I imagined her pulling the Damascus knife from her rear waistband. Her shoes slapped as she ran toward him, an angry hiss in her throat, her steps fast—

"Stop what you're doing."

The whisper—*the* whisper.

I glanced at the Dictaphone in triumph, noting on the disk the numerical location of the phrase: 87-1. Once done, my attention immediately returned to Kylie.

At Arnold's command, her steps ended abruptly. I could only

imagine the hypnotic battalion marching through her mind, forcing the real Kylie a step back.

"Drop it."

Something clattered softly to the rug.

The floorboards creaked as Arnold approached her. He let slip a derisive snort. "You think I'm an idiot?"

"I don't," Kylie whispered, her words sluggish under his compulsion. "I'm sorry. It was my idea, not Haven's. She didn't think you'd fall for it, but I had to try."

"Your sister has more sense than you."

As the Dictaphone's disk spun steadily in the moonlight, I bit my lip. There was no way of knowing how long the disk would record, and Arnold could certainly bloviate.

Say it, I urged him wordlessly. Kylie had rushed him with a knife and admitted to wanting to murder him. Wasn't that enough reason to order her to kill herself?

"At least I was brave enough to try." Kylie's voice trembled. "You can compel my body, but you can't compel *me*. Not my soul. That will never be under your control."

She was challenging him. Trying to provoke him into saying the phrase we needed.

The Dictaphone disk stalled for a split second, and panic flooded me. I tapped it, and it skipped, then started spinning steadily again.

"You have no idea the things I can make you do." Arnold's footsteps eased closer to where Kylie stood. Through the cracked doorway, and in the light cast by Arnold's office, I could now make out the tips of his shoes, a few inches from her own. They weren't his usual worn-out leather loafers, but the expensive black-and-tan sneakers I'd drawn on Arne Koning's feet. "On second thought, *pick that knife back up.*"

I held my breath. My finger was poised over the button to stop the machine. The moment Arnold gave Kylie the command to kill herself, I needed to wake the Fear-Not Wife and rush to shock Kylie out of his hypnotism.

With my other hand, I readied the stun gun.

"Take that knife—" he whispered with relish.

This was it. My pulse thundered.

"—and go to those stairs, find your sister wherever she's cowering in this hotel, and plunge that knife into her belly. Don't stop stabbing until there's no more blood left inside her."

At his words, my finger slipped on the STOP button.

No.

My thoughts were a scramble. He hadn't said the right phrase. But it was too late to capture it now. As my mind raced, I jabbed the STOP button and frantically rewound to 87-1.

Out in the hall, Kylie seemed to vacillate. Arnold's command had been to go to the stairs to find me, but she knew I wasn't in the lower portion of the hotel. The contradictory command had her momentarily irresolute.

I took the opportunity to fling myself onto the bed and shake the Fear-Not Wife by her shoulders. "Wake up. Wake up!"

Liquid gurgled in her slashed throat. Her torn lips parted. Her glassy eyes snapped open.

"Oh, *fuck*," I muttered.

She lunged at me faster than I thought she could move.

I jerked the Dictaphone's plug out of the outlet and snatched up the machine a second before the Fear-Not Wife loomed over me, grayscale bloodshot eyes catching the moonlight, white hands outstretched, broken nails sharp as they reached for my neck.

CHAPTER THIRTY-SIX

—

THE CANDY HOUSE
© 1951 Sigil Pictures

INTERIOR — HOSPITAL CREMATION ROOM — NIGHT

The flames force Andrzej and Hanna back from
the kiln's open front. The nurse inside is
still now. Dead. TIGHT ON her bare feet,
already charred.

The siblings embrace, sobbing in relief and
exhaustion.

EXTERIOR — ROOFTOP — DAWN

As the sun rises, FRESH SMOKE comes from the
hospital cremation kiln's chimney.

—

HER DECAYED FINGERS brushed my shirt collar, tried to find purchase. I wrenched my body out of reach, crawling backward across the floor, dragging the Dictaphone with me.

Her body swayed as she teetered around to lurch again.

I scrambled to my feet, backing away until my spine pressed against the wall. My shoulder knocked into a painting, sending it crashing to the floor.

Out in the hall, Arnold snapped, "What's that? *Who's* there?"

My mind turned over, searching for ways out of this. I stepped over the frame's broken glass, moving to the far side of the bed where the pitchfork rested against the dresser. The Fear-Not Wife's dead eyes tracked my movements. She lumbered toward me, but her knee caught on the bed's edge. She bumped against the mattress a few times, robotically stuck.

"Go see what that noise in 340 is," Arnold commanded.

Kylie, a liability now as much as a victim. She was an extension of Arnold just as Tyler had been in Pharmacy Bar.

The door to our room swung open under Kylie's hand. The Fear-Not Wife's body gave a jerky turn toward the noise. When she saw Kylie, a hiss slid out of her throat.

"Kylie, stop!" There was no point in hiding my presence anymore. "Get away from here!"

Kylie's body gave an odd tremor—her real self behind the compelled one fully aware of what was happening, but unable to act.

I adjusted the Dictaphone's strap around my shoulder so I could pick up the heavy pitchfork. Climbing across the bed, I aimed my weapon at the Fear-Not Wife's back just as Kylie sprang at me, Damascus knife raised. The dead woman moved in time to avoid the pitchfork's full impact, though one tine pierced her torso between the ribs.

Kylie collided with the pitchfork handle, which knocked the wind out of her. She grabbed it with one hand, trying to shove it out of her way to get at me. I climbed off the bed on the opposite side of the handle.

The Fear-Not Wife yanked her body back toward me with a breathy growl, dragging the impaled pitchfork with her. With her bottom lip missing, her crooked teeth caught the moon's gleam as they gnashed in the air.

Kylie slashed the knife at me, but the Fear-Not Wife flailed, and the blade cut the dead woman's arm instead of mine.

I took advantage of their tangled limbs to shove the stun gun against Kylie's neck. Fifty thousand volts of electricity pulsed through her. Her eyes widened and rolled back. Her body jerked like a marionette. I immediately pulled the device back.

One second. Not enough to seriously hurt her—just to shock her out of Arnold's spell.

She fell to the floor, though she managed at the last second to catch herself on her forearms, which told me she hadn't taken too much of the jolt and wouldn't be incapacitated for long.

The Fear-Not Wife swiped at me, but with the pitchfork dragging behind her, her movements were as limited as livestock in a triangular collar. I skirted her until I could grab Kylie.

"Get up. Hurry!" I yelled, dragging her to her feet.

The Damascus knife had been lost somewhere during the fight, but I ignored that. Shakily, Kylie tried to stand. I gripped her by the torso, pushing her back out into the hall. I threw myself after her, then slammed Room 340's door closed behind me, holding the knob firmly.

The Fear-Not Wife's body thumped heavily against the other side of the door, her fingernails grating against the wood, trying to get out.

A male voice behind me said, "You shifty little bitch. *St*—"

I took one hand off the doorknob to jam the Dictaphone's plug into a wall outlet, then hit the PLAY button. The disk cranked to life at place 87.1. I made sure the device's speaker was aimed squarely in Arnold's direction so the brunt of the sound waves would only hit him.

"Stop what you're doing."

Arnold's voice crackled over the recording, halting the real-life whisper of the man behind me.

I turned to face Arnold.

Who was no longer Arnold.

Arne Koning looked like how I'd drawn him, down to the full head of dark locks and the tall physique. In fact, his appearance was *exactly* as I'd drawn him; a chunk of his jaw was missing where I hadn't completed the detail work around his mouth. The missing flesh showed his grinning skull beneath as well as the length of his tongue, all the way to the base of his throat.

Fury flashed in his narrowed eyes. His throat pulsed, but he didn't speak.

He can't compel me. He just hypnotized himself out of action.

The knob rattled under my hand. I strained to keep the door to Room 340 closed with all my strength.

"Let me." Kylie, exhausted but clear-eyed, took over at the door. "I can hold it."

I surrendered it to her and stepped back, breathing hard.

Facing Arne, I asked, "How did you do it?"

"I didn't do anything." His expression was sour with rage. "*You* made the drawing."

"I didn't sign my name!"

He pulled my crumpled illustration out of his vest pocket. He held it up to the moonlight, jabbing at the bottom right corner. "Didn't you? It's right there. Not in ink, true, but still there."

It took a second before understanding dawned on me. I'd signed my Thieving Crow illustration, not Arne Koning's—but I'd signed it *right on top of the other.*

My signature had bled through.

"I took this illustration off *him*," Arne said, sweeping his hand back toward Room 341. "Right after injecting him with a lethal dose of barbiturates. He changed his mind when I showed up, of course. Started blathering that there was room in the world for two of himself. Fat fucking moron."

Legs shaking, I leaned forward to peer through Room 341's doorway. At the edge of the bed, two stumpy, loafer-clad feet lay cold and stiff.

Jesus Christ. He really killed Uncle Arnold.

"Your jaw—"

He grimaced, the gaping hole in his cheek making the expression ghoulish. "You should have finished what you started, Haven."

Room 340's door rattled more fiercely in Kylie's hands. The Fear-Not

Wife managed to pull it open a few inches, showing a sliver of her snapping jaws. I grabbed the knob on top of Kylie's hands, straining along with her to keep it closed.

The right-hand corner of Arne's unfinished lips drew back when he realized that holding the door left us incapacitated. He picked up a hiking stick from a pile of the hotel's decorative detritus on the floor. Stalking toward us, he raised the stick, preparing to strike.

Clutching the knob with one hand, I used the other to fumble with the Dictaphone's button, trying frantically to rewind it back to 87.1 again to command him to stop—

The elevator dinged.

Caught off guard, Arne and I both briefly twisted toward the far end of the hall, but as the elevator doors rumbled open, he raised the hiking stick again and brought it down hard. I let go of the door, grabbing Kylie and pulling her away before it struck us.

The door to Room 340 jerked open.

The dead woman hurtled through the door, pitchfork still lodged in her torso. Arne Koning stumbled back, his face slack with surprise. He dropped the stick. For a second, his side was open, undefended.

I pulled the stun gun out of my pocket, flipped the ON switch, and rushed him.

It made contact through his vest and shirt. His body jiggled. His new blue eyes rolled back in his head. He gripped my arm, trying to stop me, but his legs buckled, and he fell. His body seized a few more times as he rolled into a fetal position.

I maintained contact for five seconds—enough to make sure he'd stay down.

Behind me, the Fear-Not Wife lunged at Kylie. Her undead hand closed around Kylie's left wrist. Kylie jerked backward, trying to twist free. She grabbed the fallen hiking stick and slammed it into the woman's decomposing head.

As soon as I was sure Arne was unconscious, I spun around. The stun gun wouldn't work on a dead woman, so I closed my hand on the Fear-Not Wife's shoulder, trying to pull her off Kylie. Beneath her dress's rough-spun fabric, something squished wetly and sloughed off her bony scapula. The smell of rotting meat permeated the hallway.

The elevator door opened, and Rafe stepped out.

He sprinted toward us as soon as he'd processed the scene. Candy crunched beneath his shoes, throwing up puffs of poisonous gas, but Rafe didn't seem affected.

The Fear-Not Wife's arm squished beneath my grip, her thin skin ready to pop like a water balloon. My hands slid down to her bony wrist, where I could get a better hold. I braced a foot against the wall and strained to tug her backward, away from Kylie.

Rafe slammed into the dead woman. One hand gripped the pitchfork's handle at her spine; the other curled around the base of her throat. He shoved her against the wall as her jaws snapped, trying to get a taste of him.

Kylie stumbled sideways to catch herself against the wall.

"You have to kill her with her own story," I reminded him breathlessly.

Rafe trapped one of her flailing wrists as she tried to claw his neck. "I'm clever, darling. I'll figure it out. Do what you need to do with Arnold."

"I . . . I used the stun gun on Kylie. She's too weak to come with me."

"I'll take care of her." He glanced back at my sister, and then his charcoal eyes switched to me, wavering with concern. "And you? You'll be all right with . . ." His gaze fell to Arne Koning's unconscious body. "I assume I know who *that* is."

I adjusted the Dictaphone strap around my shoulder, still struggling to catch my breath. I knelt and grabbed Arne's wrists. "I promised you I wasn't dying today."

Rafe grinned. "Good girl."

The Fear-Not Wife lunged at Rafe again, and he thrust her back against the wall hard enough to snap at least one of her bones.

"Go, then," he ordered. "Keep your promise."

It wasn't easy to drag Arne's body across the hall, especially since I was already near the point of exhaustion. Once I reached 341, I took out the brass doorknob. Thrusting it into the hinge side of the door, I whispered until the crimson light bloomed, and then dragged Arne's unconscious body through the portal, the reek of undead flesh falling away behind us, making room for something new.

Arne Koning groaned, stirring back to consciousness, as I hauled his body deeper into the basement storage cage. I dropped him unceremoniously amid the costumes, then stepped out over his splayed body, locking the wire door behind me.

I leaned my forehead against the cool metal of the door, letting out a tight breath. Arne Koning was now an insect I'd pinned beneath my needle, no longer able to flap in my ear or sting or draw blood.

Inside the cage, Arne rolled to his side, coughing.

I dragged over an old hotel chair and set the Dictaphone on it. After plugging the machine into the wall, I opened the lid to make sure the disk hadn't slipped.

Arne sat up slowly, wincing in pain, rubbing a hand over the back of his neck. His left side was turned toward me, hiding the unfinished section of his jaw, and from this direction he looked as human as his guideposts, LoneWolf or Balan Erner. Or me.

He faced me, and the missing cheek was visible once more. His exposed tongue pulsed in his throat, but I quickly replayed his command to himself not to compel me.

Pushing himself to his feet, he wove his fingers between the cage's bars, stumbling, still weak. "Haven Marbury. You *really* don't want to cross me."

My throat tightened from a muscle-memory fear of what he'd done to me before. I gave a cold smile. "I do, actually. I'm enjoying this more than you can imagine."

His fingers gripped the cage bars.. "You're going to kill me? You're going to give up the possibilities of what I can do for you?"

"No," I said offhand as I rewound the Dictaphone, playing back through the various phrases I'd recorded him saying. "*I'm not going to kill you.*"

We had planned to record his voice giving Kylie the command to kill herself, but, well, *plans*. Now I had a mishmash of random words I had to stitch together into some semblance of a command. I pulled out the Thieving Crow drawing I'd tucked into my bra along with one of the pens I was always finding squirreled away in my pockets, and started marking off the recording's timestamps.

Arne shook the wire cage. "Haven? *Haven!*"

I ignored him as I knelt over the Dictaphone, replaying his command again. "*Go to the stairs, find your sister wherever she's cowering in this hotel, and plunge that knife into her belly. Don't stop stabbing until there's no more blood left inside her.*"

I'd once recapped a horror movie called *Poster Child* that involved a ransom note made of cut-out words from magazines. When the words were rearranged, they revealed the missing boy's location.

I glanced over my shoulder at the staircase. I replayed the recording again and again, marking down the timestamps until I felt confident that I had what I needed in the right order.

I dragged over an antique speaker next to where I'd set up the Dictaphone. I plugged it in, then hooked it up to the Dictaphone's microphone port. The speaker started humming, feedback causing it to squeal.

Arne pressed his hands over his ears. "What the fuck do you think you're going to do with that?"

"Rewriting your world."

Arnold had been the one to explain to me that his power only worked if sound waves were targeted squarely on his victim—overheard whispers didn't compel anyone. I adjusted the speaker's controls to make sure the sound waves would project in his direction and loud enough that covering his ears wouldn't help. Arne reached through the bars, trying to swipe at me, but I just shot him a cold glare. I took a moment of greedy satisfaction to watch him kick and punch at the bars with the lithe young body I'd given him.

I might not be perfect, but, damn, I could draw.

I knelt over the Dictaphone and hit PLAY at the first timestamp. A burst of feedback screeched throughout the basement. The recording cracked over static.

"Go to the stairs . . ."

I stopped the recording, turned the dial forward to the next time-stamp, and hit PLAY again.

"Turn it off!" Arne threw his shoulder against the cage with enough force to make its hinges groan.

". . . don't stop . . ."

I paused the recording again and then dialed it forward to the final timestamp. The whole floor vibrated with the thunderous volume as Arne's own voice recited:

". . . until there's no more blood left inside . . ."

On the recording, Arne's voice was a whisper, but here, with the speaker at full blast and aimed directly at him, covering his ears hadn't made a difference. The rage in his eyes iced over until they were frosted, dull. A slow line of blood ran down his arm from where he'd punctured himself on a jagged wire.

He slowly took his hands off his ears.

I ripped the speaker plug out of the wall, breathing hard.

His right eye twitched. I knew what the compulsion felt like; knew the real Arne was still in there, seething. But his arms lowered in a strange, mechanical way. His jaw remained clenched.

My stomach pulled tight. *Go to the stairs . . . don't stop . . . until there's no more blood left inside.*

I'd done the best I could.

I turned the key in the lock, praying it worked.

The young-old man's expensive sneakers clomped on the floor as he stepped out of the cage. Slowly, he circled around to face the basement stairs.

"Go on, dollface," I whispered through my incisors.

He walked slowly, slowly, toward the wooden staircase. The carcasses of fallen birds around the stairs formed three- and four-foot piles; Arne Koning climbed over them on hands and knees, their blood staining his pristine shoes.

For a moment, I imagined I was back in Malice House, watching a horror movie on my father's battered old television set, taking recap notes with my usual shorthand notations. *TSTL: Too Stupid To Live. JSH: Just Shoot Him!* And *DLA: Don't Look Away.*

I didn't look away as Arne Koning crawled into the Vantablack of the birds' bodies. My heart rate shot up, my throat went dry, but I continued to watch until only the tips of his shoes remained in the overturned rig's spotlight.

A wet hiss turned into a squelch.

"No . . . no!" Arne's voice was a breathy scrape through his broken jaw.

A tentacle—if it could even be called a tentacle—appeared for a brief second. Bruise-black in color, a briny stench. Most chilling of all, it was made of dozens of human arms with outstretched fingers.

It dragged Arne into the darkness.

He screamed.

He screamed and screamed until his voice failed him.

I heard something like the clatter of human teeth. Then silence.

The smell of coastal waste drifted out from under the stairs. It mixed with the sugar-sweet smell of the caramels sticky under my shoes. I staggered several feet backward, sinking onto an old Jackrabbit Hotel sofa draped in in a white sheet.

A single Thieving Crow flapped up toward the sofa arm.

I leaned forward, elbows on knees and head in my hands, and let out a few racking breaths that were somewhere between sobs and laughter. I couldn't look at the bird. Couldn't face any of them, or the cursed candy, or think about the monsters still stalking the hallways upstairs. For this brief stretch, all I wanted was to sit. To breathe. To disappear into a timeless pocket if I could. To relish the fact that I would never hear those whispers again.

Weary, I dragged my hair out of my face and sat up.

I pushed myself to my feet on strung-out muscles.

The curse wouldn't allow me a moment of triumph, not yet.

There are others to end.

CHAPTER THIRTY-SEVEN

THE HUNDREDTH STAIR
© 1941 Sigil Pictures

INTERIOR — VICTORIAN BEACH HOUSE — DAY

Harrison has placed himself between the
menacing tentacle and his wife and daughter
on the sickbed. We hear wet gurgling as the
tentacle's humanlike fingers reach for him.

                    HARRISON
              (muttering resolutely)
          One hundred curses my folly has
          brought us. It healed you, my love,
          but it demands payment. Another body
          to add to its collection.

He steps toward the tentacle as a willing
sacrifice.

                    JANE
          Daddy, no!

THE JACKRABBIT HOTEL lobby was deserted. The dream smoke was gone, though its ozone smell lingered. Dead birds littered the floor alongside handfuls of crushed candy. I trudged past the Killarney Doorman's bullet-ridden carcass, which smelled equally of barnyard and stale cologne. I stopped in the center of the lobby, listening.

The hotel creaked around me, its bones still unsettled after all these years.

Limping from exhaustion, I made my way to the elevator and jabbed the brass call button. While I waited for it, I stepped back, letting my eyes sink closed.

When the bell dinged to signal its arrival, I opened my eyes, and froze. The frosted-glass walls of the carriage were splashed with blood. A collage of bloody handprints suggested a grisly story. On the other side of the opaque glass, an outline loomed of some creature whose malformed shape couldn't be called human—

—the metal gates opened.

I already had the stun gun in hand, but I didn't need it.

"Kylie?" Her name rushed up my throat as I flipped off the stun gun. "Kylie!"

What had appeared as one monstrous creature through the frosted glass was just my sister leaning on Rafe, who supported her. Her shirt-sleeves were stained with bloody muck, and a deep gash at the corner of her mouth oozed. Rafe's hair was plastered to one side, gleaming with slick blood. His hands were coated in putrid sludge up to the elbows.

Kylie fell forward to throw her arms around me. She felt bone-thin, yet sturdy where it mattered. An awful smell hit my nose. The glop covering them was the Fear-Not Wife's rotting flesh, I realized. It streaked Kylie's clothes and skin, but I clutched her harder until the familiar faint scent of her—floral shampoo, a touch of neroli oil—came through.

"Arne . . . ?" she asked, her breath catching.

"He's dead."

There must have been some hesitation in my voice, because she pulled back and fixed me with a close look.

"I mean, yes. He's dead. I'm sure. I used his own commands to make him feed himself to the thing under the basement stairs. There's no way anyone could have survived it."

Rafe asked, "You saw his body?"

"I couldn't without feeding *myself* to the stairs monster." I shook my head. "I heard his screams. Trust me, he's gone."

Dark approval shone in Rafe's eyes.

I indicated the blood-streaked elevator walls. "What happened to the Wife?"

"She's dead," Rafe said. "Well, dead*er*." From his shoulder, he removed a clod of a woman's scalp with long black hair attached. "We trapped her in the elevator, then used the pitchfork on her. It's from her own story."

"She was already a corpse," Kylie said. "So it took a *lot* of stabbing." She attempted to wipe some of the carnage off her hands. "Rafe eventually separated her head from her neck, and that did it. We left her body on the third floor."

I swept my gaze around the lobby, which was silent. Not a single caw from a Thieving Crow. "I suppose Miracle was successful with the birds. Where is she?"

Rafe wiped more gelatinous flesh from his hands onto his shirt. "I can hazard a guess."

He led the way across the lobby and into the Durango Ballroom. My muscles relaxed when I saw Miracle, alive and unharmed, seated opposite Doctor Vaughn Ellis, who was tied by cloth napkins to his buffet chair. His fingers extended slowly as though still trying to reach for his cup of cold tea.

Miracle pushed herself to her feet when she heard footsteps, one hand already on the Chicago Typewriter, until she saw it was us.

"Haven. Did you—"

I cut her off with a nod. "Arnold is gone."

"Killed with his own story?"

"Killed by his own command, so yes. He won't be bothering us anymore." I sank into a buffet chair, my legs spent, and pointed my chin toward the doctor. "Why did you leave him alive?"

"I haven't seen his movie. You have. You know better than me how to end him. We'll have to clear out the whole hotel eventually. There is still the doctor, the crows, the thing under the stairs, the children."

I sat straight again. "Andrzej and Hanna aren't monsters."

She didn't look amused. "They climbed out of a horror film."

"But they weren't the villains."

"Have you seen *The Candy House*? Have you seen what, exactly, is under those masks?"

I was silent. A decade of training in horror movies had taught me to beware of plot twists. I'd once recapped an Argentine film about an orphanage whose young wards were being abused—in the end, it was them doing the violence all along.

Miracle pulled a handful of wintergreen mints from her pocket and dropped them in Doctor Ellis's empty teacup. "I saved these so we can feed them to the children. With a big enough dose, they'll go easy, peacefully, in their sleep."

"*No.*" I surprised myself with my forcefulness. Taking a breath, I explained more evenly, "Andrzej was the one who unlocked the door so you could get into the hotel. He distracted Arnold in the basement. They've been helping us this whole time. I'm not going to kill them only because they aren't from this world."

Miracle looked dissatisfied. "You don't know—"

"Haven's right." Rafe's voice cut across the quiet banquet table.

Miracle snorted. "Of course you'd think so. Kylie? Tell me you don't agree with this insanity."

Kylie dragged a napkin over her chin, managing to wipe away most of the Fear-Not Wife's blood from her face. "They're kids. I don't know, maybe they're monsters, maybe they aren't, but I can't condone killing them because they *might* be evil." She dropped the filthy napkin on the table. "Those birds, though? I'll gladly slaughter those little traitors. The question is just how."

Miracle thought about this for a second. "You have their story?"

"On my laptop upstairs."

"We'll need to read it."

While Kylie went to get her laptop, Rafe pulled out the chair next to me and sat down. He rested his hand on mine. "It was right—saying we should spare those children." I could feel his pulse, slow and steady, almost in time with mine. He leaned in and lowered his voice out of Miracle's hearing. "We have to protect our own."

I stiffened, but before I could think of a response, Kylie had returned. She set the laptop on the buffet table and turned it toward Miracle.

Miracle tapped the keyboard as she scrolled through "The Thieving Crow."

She read aloud the line *"Its loyalty belonged to the tattooed girl with glittering shiny baubles dangling from her ears and pinned to affixed to her nose. To the powerful strong one. The leader."* Her head lifted. "Here is the problem. You marked out too much of the story. It left open too much room for interpretation. The birds were obedient to you because you made yourself their leader, but then one of them challenged you, and it broke the chain of command."

"That first bird who attacked you," I said. "The huge one. It's still in the basement. It didn't leave with the others."

Miracle closed the laptop and handed it to Kylie. "We have to get them back under your control. If you kill the one who challenged you, the others might fall back in line. Do you still have that knife?"

"It's in the room upstairs," I said, tactfully leaving out that Kylie had dropped it while trying to stab me with it.

Miracle continued, "Once Kylie has reestablished dominance over the flock, we'll turn on the basement boiler. She wrote herself into their story, so she's a part of it. She can order the crows to fly into the boiler one at a time."

It was a distasteful job, but Kylie executed it efficiently. Not a full hour had passed before we all stood in front of the rumbling boiler amid the acrid, earthy smell of burned feathers. They stank like singed human hair.

I turned away from the boiler and faced the wooden staircase. "And the thing under the stairs?"

Everyone was quiet as they also turned to face the stairs. None of us had seen *The Hundredth Stair*. As far as any of us knew, when Arnold had brought the creature out of the film, he hadn't also brought any objects that could destroy it.

"We could choke it with its own tentacle," Miracle suggested. "Joao and I did that with a demonic snake that had crawled out of an Indonesian folktale. We tricked it into eating its own tail."

I shook my head, still haunted by Arne's screams amid the noise of hundreds of human-sounding teeth. "None of us should go anywhere near that thing. Not until we've seen *The Hundredth Stair* and know what it's capable of."

Miracle held out her hands like I should say more, but I didn't have any ideas beyond what I'd already said.

"And the guy tied up upstairs? The Sandman Killer?" Kylie asked by way of reminding us.

Miracle pulled a silver scalpel from her back pocket and held it up to the spotlight that Arnold had turned on. "The doctor had this in his jacket pocket. It's from his world. He made it easy for us."

I took the scalpel from her. I'd been wrong to think of it as silver, I realized. It was in black and white.

Rafe scoffed. "Arnold was right about one thing. The Sandman Killer is a relic. He has no ill intent toward anyone anymore and hasn't for decades. He isn't a threat."

"He could be used for his abilities," Kylie pointed out. "Just like Arnold did."

Miracle threw her hands up, exasperated. "This shouldn't be a debate! He's killed several people. Relic or not, we don't let monsters live. You're an Acosta, Haven. You too, Kylie. If you don't end him, I will."

Rafe bent toward me and said gruffly, "He's one of us."

Turning to him, I murmured, "I can't let a serial killer go free."

"I'm not suggesting you do." He pressed his lips close to my ear, one hand cupped to keep his voice from being overheard as he suggested an alternative.

Kylie and Miracle watched our exchange with wary expressions. If I hadn't been holding the scalpel, I suspected Miracle might have run upstairs and done the job herself.

Rafe drew back, catching an errant curl and tucking it behind my ear. My stomach was churning, but I turned to face Miracle. "Maybe we can strike a bargain."

Her eyes shot accusatorily to Rafe. "You're listening to the wrong person if you think he's giving good advice."

Between my fingers, the scalpel almost had the reassuring weight of a paintbrush. I explained, "Joao is dead. You need a curseworker to fill his place. Let me ensure the Sandman Killer is incapacitated in a way that will guarantee he's no danger to anyone, and I'll help you in your work."

Miracle's attention darted between the scalpel and Rafe. The fact that she didn't immediately say no told me that she, too, had thought about how to fill Joao's shoes.

"They're my own kind," I said. "Let me decide what to do with them."

She shook her head slowly in a demonstration of her doubt, but then seemed to second-guess herself, and refolded her arms. "You can ensure he won't hurt anyone else?"

"I'm certain of it."

"And the thing under the stairs?"

"We'll shut up the hotel," I said crisply. "There are no roads or trails leading here. Arnold made sure the door locks are secure. Andrzej gave me the hotel's master key. We'll leave the Jackrabbit locked up, a tomb to the Sigil Pictures monsters. After we've watched *The Hundredth Stair* and prepared ourselves, we'll return."

Miracle studied me like she could dissect my innermost thoughts.

"Your friend can find us copies of the full Sigil Pictures catalog?"

"Rob is capable of getting his hands on almost anything."

She relented only after Rafe stepped in to broker final negotiations. Her first condition was for us to lock all the hotel exits and chain the doors. Second, I surrendered the scalpel for her to add to her backpack of otherworldly weaponry. Lastly, I vowed to help her with her endeavors, including coming back to someday end the Jackrabbit's remaining monsters for good.

Once we'd agreed, we went upstairs for one final walk-through of the hotel, stopping at its grand glass entrance.

"Good riddance," Kylie muttered.

I fished the Killarney Doorman's doorknob out of my pocket. "It's time to get the hell out of here."

CHAPTER THIRTY-EIGHT

———

```
End credits roll over footage of snowy alpine
mountains. There is no sign of the Lucerne
Institute of Sleep any longer. Nature's order
reigns once more.

          THE SANDMAN KILLER


     DIRECTED BY. . . . . . Max Faraday
     PRODUCED BY. . . . . . Richard Alton
     SCREENPLAY BY. . . . . Richard Alton
     MUSIC BY . . . . . . . Fran Cooper
     ART DIRECTION BY . . . Max Faraday
     FILM EDITOR. . . . . . Nigel Allen
```

———

RETURNING TO LA felt like tumbling back into a familiar dream. I'd never call the city home, but the creative energy that flowed through it was something I recognized even if I still felt one step removed from it. Its bright lights and scrabble for attention demanded too high a price—I'd rather leave the heady artistic ambition to those willing to carve out a piece of their souls for an audience: my father, Kylie, Rob. Like the moth that I was, I would take the vacant houses, the foggy islands, the shadows.

"I have to be at a meeting at five." Rob checked his watch, squinting to see the time in the dark theater, foot jiggling anxiously in his expensive leather loafers. "And traffic this time of day on the 101 is a nightmare. . . ."

"Relax. They'll be here soon." I didn't pack too much sympathy into my tone.

He stood up from a squeaking theater chair and paced the row's length. "Tyler thought I was being extravagant when I had this theater installed. He pushed for some generic home theater, converting a guest bedroom by sealing the windows and adding leather lounge chairs. Can you *imagine*? These theater seats came from the old Vaudevillian Theater in San Diego—"

"Rob," I groaned.

He folded his arms. "My point is, the theater's come in handy, hasn't it? And how about the transcripts?"

He pointed to the stack of yellowing pages in my lap. Salvaged original screenplays and transcripts from all known Sigil Pictures films—even a few *unknown*. It wasn't the same as having the films themselves, but it shed a lot of light on what Max Faraday and Richard Alton had created.

I set down the end credits page for *The Sandman Killer* that I'd been reading and dumped the whole stack of screenplays onto the chair next to me.

He shook his legs out, stiff from waiting. A heavy silence fell between us, and he grudgingly looked down at the floor.

"Look, Haven. You knew I was a shifty bastard from the start."

Rob had already apologized—in Rob's way, which included listing all the things he'd done for me—for going behind my back to try to get a documentary made about the curse. He'd admitted it was the reason he'd been so eager to help as I interviewed Nanette Fields and bribed my way into funeral homes, letting me do the legwork for him.

"Has your studio agreed to drop the project yet?" I asked.

He hedged as he adjusted his shirt cuffs. "Insight Entertainment paid a substantial fee to option the *Hollywooder* article. They want a return on their investment. It's just business."

I pinched the bridge of my nose. "Rob, you can't make that documentary!"

"If it was up to me, I would pull the plug!" he protested. "But Insight is a huge team of production executives, board members, senior staff. I tried to convince them it was a boondoggle, but what can I say? I guess I was *too* good a salesman when I first pitched the idea back in November. They parroted the points I'd made then back at me. Urban legends are hot right now, Haven."

Exasperated, I briefly considered Miracle's backpack full of monstrous weaponry. . . .

I glanced at the door, wondering what was taking the others so long. Then I held up my palms in truce. "Look, maybe we can strike a bargain. I have all the old Sigil Pictures props and costumes from *The Sandman Killer*. If I share those extremely valuable resources with Insight Entertainment, will they promise to keep the scope of the documentary limited to Sigil Pictures' history? Not poke around beyond what's specifically described in the article? That means no mentioning Nanette's murder, no Joao Acosta, no *me*."

Rob folded his arms as he slipped into producer mode. "Full access to *The Sandman Killer* props," he agreed. "*And* Max Faraday and Richard Alton's original audio visual equipment."

Was he seriously negotiating? After his secret nearly got me killed?

Of course, this was Rob.

"Whatever. Fine." I could get him the props and equipment without opening up the Jackrabbit Hotel property to anyone but me.

He nudged the stack of screenplays with his knee. "I'll pay you triple if you write up recaps of those."

I turned away, scoffing, before affectionately muttering, "You're such a weirdo."

The stairs outside the theater squeaked, and in another minute, Tyler and Kylie came in. Tyler was telling Kylie about a book he was reading, and how he was hoping to get a part in the adaptation once his burn marks healed and he could remove the bandages from his arm. Kylie wore denim overalls and a fluttery shirt that showed off her tattoos. A few days back in LA had done wonders for her. She'd checked out of the Jackrabbit Hotel in bruised disarray, streaked with the Fear-Not Wife's decomposing flesh, arms pecked by dozens of sharp beaks, but now, showered and rested and stuffed full from Tyler's kitchen, she'd returned to the twentysomething woman with a quick smile and spark in her eyes.

Her conversation with Tyler ended. She checked her phone. "They still aren't here? Do you think anything went wrong?"

As if on cue, the theater door leading to the driveway began to glow. Kylie and Tyler moved away from it, back toward the foyer with the popcorn machine.

The door opened. Rafe stepped through the portal into the theater, followed by Dahlia. She wore black wool trousers, a creamy blouse, and a clattering collection of necklaces. Behind her, I glimpsed the room they'd emerged from: a cramped shop whose shelves held baskets of crystals, vials of herbal remedies in brown jars, and an odd assortment of animal skulls. The smell of waxy soaps clung to their clothes. Even when they shut the door, the herbal scents of Dahlia's witchcraft shop idled in the air.

I nodded to the witch. "Thank you for coming."

She unwound her silk scarf breezily. "Portland is drowning in tourists this time of year. The shop is busy. Let's get on with it."

I gave a signal to Rob, who picked up the metal film case at the end of the aisle and patted it. "I'll set up the projector. Haven, maybe you can get our, ah, guest?"

I pushed myself to my feet, climbing the stairs to Rob's living room, where Miracle sat on the wraparound sofa, reading through a salvaged copy of a transcript of *The Hundredth Stair*, a duct-taped Doctor Vaughn Ellis next to her.

"Has he been any trouble?" I asked.

She shook her head. "He asks where Agnes is occasionally. Sometimes for tea. Otherwise, he's been out of it."

Even surrounded by midcentury movie memorabilia, the somnologist looked strikingly out of place. Cast in black and white as he was, it couldn't be more apparent that he didn't belong in this world.

"They're ready for him downstairs," I said.

Standing up, Miracle slipped his scalpel out of her shirt pocket and took the protective cap off the blade. She raised an eyebrow, looking at her reflection in the metal. "It's only us now," she said to me. "No Rafe, no friends. Are you sure you want to let him live? Compassion for monsters is a dangerous thing. You may think you can save them, but you can't."

"After today," I assured Miracle, "Doctor Vaughn Ellis won't be able to hurt a soul, whether he persists in some distant realm or not."

She didn't look convinced as she bent down to slice the duct tape around his wrists and ankles, freeing him, though he barely seemed to notice. She slid the protective cap on the scalpel and tucked it back into her pocket. "If you're going to be a part of this business, eventually you'll need to figure out which side you're on."

I rested my hands on my hips, refusing to let her intimidate me. "You told me once the monsters were on both sides of the curse."

She patted my shoulder, a smirk of approval on her lips. "You're finally getting it."

We guided the shambling Sandman Killer down the stairs into the theater. The projector was rolling, lighting up the screen with flickering images. Rob and Tyler stood in the rear of the theater on either side of the projector, watching the damaged frames play out through the wavering title card and opening images of the snowy Alps.

We watched the film in silence until we reached the early scene where Agnes stepped into the lobby.

Dahlia said, "Stop it here."

Rob paused the frame, and Dahlia beckoned us all forward. This time she used Rob, Tyler, Kylie, and Miracle to create the four corners of the doorway. Whispering, she cast the spell to open the rift.

A touch of Alpine chill, mixed with the smell of sterile equipment, came from the screen.

Rafe dragged over the stool from the popcorn.

"Time to go home, old man." Rafe hefted the somnologist onto his shoulder in a fireman's carry. The doctor was so frail that Rafe's extraordinary strength was hardly necessary. Rafe mounted the stool, carted the doctor up onto the institute's floor, and then hoisted himself in after.

My lips parted as I watched the screen eat up Rafe's warm color and leave him black and white. He turned around and extended a hand down toward me, light brown fingers pushing through the two-dimensional barrier once more.

I climbed onto the stool and into the movie. Passing through a cloud of tingling cold energy, I found myself standing once more inside the Lucerne Institute of Sleep.

The others in Rob's theater were gone. A frigid breeze came from the institute's entrance, where Agnes Fitzpatrick held the door open, frozen in place.

Rafe turned his head to take in the black-and-white decor around the lobby. He observed wryly, "I prefer it as a hotel."

"I'll pass on both." I squatted down to where Doctor Ellis slumped on the floor. "Help me get him up. Put him there, on that sofa."

We lifted the doctor to his feet and shuffled him to the closest white leather seat, facing Agnes at the door. His husk of a body sank shallowly into it.

I brushed off my hands. "Now he can forever dream about Agnes."

Rafe's hair ruffled in the breeze coming from the open door, but he wasn't shivering like I was. He took notice of my goose bumps and ran his hands along my arms. Surrounded by the grayscale setting of another time and place, I felt the sense of freedom that came with being hidden.

Rafe's hand moved to cup my jaw, his gaze falling to my lips.

I turned away. We couldn't see the others, but they could see us. "They're watching."

Rafe reluctantly abandoned the idea of the kiss, stuffing his hand into his jeans pocket instead. The absence of his hand's warmth left a void on my skin.

Whatever deal he'd made with Dahlia, I knew, would soon come to light.

A small rift in the floor opened, emitting blinding white light. Rafe swept his hand toward it, his velvety voice shrouding me. "After you, darling."

CHAPTER THIRTY-NINE

———

RABBIT HOLE
© 1949 Sigil Pictures

INTERIOR — THE PALEON SOCIETY'S UNDERGROUND
CHAMBER — NIGHT

>   MASTER OF CEREMONIES
> Those who interrupt our proceedings
> without an invitation are punished,
> Mariana. Do you wish to be punished,
> my butterfly?

>   MARIANA
> (breathing hard beneath her mask)
> Butterfly? No—I am a moth. Creatures
> of night know punishment and reward
> are merely different sides of the
> same dark wings.

———

NIGHT WAS FALLING over Los Angeles as sparks rose from the chrome firepit on Rob's deck. The wood crackled and hissed, damp from the light rain that had begun to descend. Our group gathered in a loose circle around the flames. Though Dahlia didn't seem bothered by the rain, Kylie and Rob and Tyler hunched against it, looking anxious to get back inside.

Rafe handed me the film reel. "The honors are yours, Haven."

I took the antique object, feeling for a few brief moments like a speech might be in order, and then I simply chucked the thing into the fire.

The film caught and smoldered. Frames of Alpine mountains melted away into oozy puddles of plastic.

"Doctor Vaughn Ellis won't be haunting any more dreams," I said.

The flames turned the reel's metal wheel black, and it wasn't long before any remnant of *The Sandman Killer*'s story was gone—from this world, at least.

The rain picked up, and Kylie peeked out from her jacket hood. "Yeah, bye, motherfucker. You won't be missed." She turned swiftly and headed back inside, followed by Rob and Tyler.

Dahlia stood tall and hoodless despite the rain streaking her face. She rested a light hand on Rafe's forearm. "Harbinger. It's time."

His eyes shifted to me. "Soon."

The witch went inside to the join the others, leaving Rafe and me alone in the misty rain. I ducked my head against the weather.

"What does she mean, it's time?"

He poked at the fire's smoldering embers with a marshmallow stick, not meeting my gaze. "I told you, the bargain was I'd return with her to Portland, to help her work."

I swallowed a lump that had sprouted in my throat. "A few days, right?"

He continued stirring the embers, not looking at me. "One year."

My mouth fell open. "A *year*?"

"I didn't have much choice. We needed her help." He finally met my gaze as rain caught in his long lashes.

I struggled to wrap my mind around the idea of Rafe in Portland under the Witch of Went's influence. Would I see him? Unlikely. The path I had planned took me in the opposite direction of the Pacific Northwest. And I doubted I would be welcomed by her anyway.

Rafe touched my chin, using his thumb to wipe away a raindrop on my bottom lip. "Another woman wants me."

I bit my lip, teeth grazing his thumb. Our gaze didn't break. He was joking. But *was* I jealous? Rafe and Dahlia were former lovers. Neither of them was known for loyalty, and both were known for ruthless lust. I was less bothered that he and Dahlia might sleep together, however, than I was by the hold she might develop on his soul. In the months since I'd known Rafe, he'd changed. Once, he'd been an often-cruel herald of chaos delighted to find a fresh new world as his playground; now I'd seen him put an end to monsters who threatened humanity.

With me, he'd become dangerously close to a hero. With her, what darkness would he slide back into?

"When will you leave?" I muttered.

"Now," he said. "Tonight."

His fingers still clasped my chin. It was clear that he didn't want to go; I didn't want him to leave. The rain picked up. We were both getting drenched. The damp soaked through my clothes to my skin.

I stepped back, out of his grasp—and he let me go.

Inside, the goodbyes were brief. Rafe had never been close to my friends, and Dahlia outright terrified them. As they took their places at the hall closet door, Rafe slipped the Killarney doorknob into my hand.

"You do the honors." His voice rumbled low, close. "Keep the doorknob. You never know."

A ripple of goose bumps rose on my skin where his breath touched it. I opened the portal for them back into Dahlia's witchcraft shop, and into the scent of burning sage they disappeared.

A quiet settled over Rob's living room.

Shortly, Tyler clapped. "Who wants a drink?"

Kylie turned to him in grateful desperation. "Oh god. Please."

They made their way to the kitchen, leaving me alone with Rob. I listened to Kylie's snort of laughter emerge from the kitchen as they made cocktails, and I smiled.

"I think they like each other better than either of us," Rob observed, unoffended.

I smiled my agreement, then paused. "Hey, I've been meaning to ask. The day we met, you said you had leverage on Kylie. I found out what it was—the short story she was working on, in the folder called Enigma. But I don't get why she'd call it that. Because of me, because I'm an enigma?"

His eyebrows drew up curiously. "No. No. Enigma is the name of her *publisher*."

It felt for a moment like time had paused, but it hadn't. The clock still ticked. "Her publisher?"

An impish gleam pricked up in Rob's eyes. "What, exactly, did she tell you?"

I turned in an unsteady arc toward the kitchen. Kylie and Tyler were only outlines through the doorway as glasses clinked together. Her laptop sat on the dining table. I lurched for it, opening it.

It was password protected.

"Kylie." My voice was hoarse.

My sister appeared in the doorway, her smile faltering to find me at her open laptop. I twisted the computer around so the keyboard faced her.

"Open the Enigma folder," I demanded, barely recognizing my own voice.

Kylie didn't make a move for a few seconds. As though sensing a coming storm, Tyler retreated into the kitchen, and I heard the sounds of cabinets closing. Rob remained behind me, however, watching in fascination.

"Why?" she asked.

"Let me see it. Rob knows all about whatever you're hiding, doesn't he? So don't try to lie this time, or he'll know."

Looking slightly pale as her gaze darted between me and Rob, she leaned over the laptop and typed a few keys.

"I don't know what you're worried about," she said in her bad-actress voice. "You read the story already."

"I get the feeling Haven didn't read *all* of it," Rob muttered. *The pot-stirrer.*

I grabbed her laptop, turned it toward me. She didn't try to stop me this time. I scrolled to the folder marked *Enigma* and clicked it open. My foot tapped against the floor, agitated.

There were several documents inside the folder.

WORK IN PROGRESS
BEFORE THE NIGHT COMES IN—DRAFT 1
BEFORE THE NIGHT COMES IN—DRAFT 2
FULL BTNCI OUTLINE
DOCUSIGN_NANCE_K_AUTHOR_AGMT_ENIGMA

There was "Work in Progress" as she'd said: the rewritten version of my life that I hadn't had the stomach to read more than a line of. But the other documents were a mystery.

"*Before the Night Comes In?* What is this?"

Kylie's hands twisted together like she was untangling invisible knots. She drew in a deep breath. "The latest manuscript I've been working on."

I clicked the "Draft 2" document and scanned through the first few pages. It looked like a short-story collection. I scrolled back to the table of contents and froze.

"Work in Progress" was the second story out of eight.

"*Eight* stories? You mean my story is just one part of this . . . whatever this is? What the hell are the other stories *about*, Kylie?"

She kept her lips closed, looking slightly ill.

She clearly wasn't going to volunteer answers, so I opened the author agreement next. I'd seen enough of my father's publishing contracts to know the key points to look for: Project description. Payment terms. Deliverable dates.

> *Clause 2.B. The Author [Kylie Nance, writing as Kylie Marbury] agrees to deliver to the Publisher [Enigma Publishing LLC] a completed manuscript entitled* Before the Night Comes In, *described as a series of interconnected dark-fantasy short stories set in a dystopian alternate 1950s populated by witches, demons, and monstrous creatures, and dealing with themes of obsolescence, impiety, and obstructed feminism.*

My breath stalled in my throat.

I leaned my weight onto my palms, still feeling robbed of oxygen. "This is describing *Bedtime Stories for Monsters*. This is our father's manuscript, not yours."

Kylie winced, looking toward the rain pounding the deck outside. "It's only roughly based on our father's manuscript. I never even had a chance to read the stories before you destroyed it; I only know what little you told me about them. I didn't plagiarize it."

"I don't care if you plagiarized it! It isn't about plagiarizing. Kylie, you wrote me into a fucking short-story collection! What am I to you, a character on a page? Not even worthy of my own book at that—*just one goddamn chapter?*"

She gulped in a breath like she was about to cry. "It isn't like that."

"It's *exactly* like that!"

"I don't think of you as less than human," she argued. "It was just my source of inspiration as a writer. That's what writers do, write from their own life—"

"It's *my* life. No, not even that. Apparently, my life isn't interesting enough to be a story on its own, so you had to change it. Change *me*."

She held her tongue, knowing better than to defend herself. I took a long breath that shook with anger. I saw only red, try as I might to fade myself back to normal.

"And did you even think about the curse?" I said in a barely controlled voice. "*Bedtime Stories for Monsters* activated the curse in the first place."

"Because it was a good manuscript," she mumbled, turning her eyes on the floor. "Obviously, the story had power. It deserved to be published."

I stared at her, speechless. Behind me, Rob slowly breathed in and out, nose wheezing. The troublemaker was enjoying this.

She dragged her fingers down the sides of her face and then held out her hands palms-forward, trying to calm the situation. "Look, our father never acknowledged me. I didn't get a thing from his life or his death. You know as well as anyone that there was no inheritance. We agreed that I wouldn't go public that I was his biological daughter, and I never did—I didn't find Patrick Kane, he found me. But our father *still owes me*. He's dead. He doesn't need the manuscript. I do. In case you forgot, we have nothing except what Rafe decides to dole out under whatever conditions he wants to set. No money. No home. And I refuse to be beholden to a monster."

"Was it for the money?" I challenged. "Or because you've always wanted to be published?"

Her lips parted, ready for a retort, but then she pressed them back together. More measuredly, she said, "I don't see what's wrong with taking advantage of both."

I dug my fingers into my temples, unable to believe what she was saying. The clock on Kylie's computer was counting the passing minutes. Time was moving too fast, dizzyingly fast.

I spun on Rob. "You knew about this?"

"I hacked into Kylie's email account while we were holding you two in the theater," he explained. "I found an email to her Enigma editor where she said she didn't want the deal announcement to go public until after she'd had a chance to tell you about it. I didn't know the exact significance of the project, but I knew she didn't want *you* to find out. That was leverage enough."

I needed to pace. My muscles were twitching, urging me to move.

"Kylie, how could you do this after all the times we told each other not to draw, not to write?"

"I was careful," she insisted. "I'm not an idiot. I know the dangers, and I know how the curse works. It takes both written word and artwork, right? So, if I write a story that is never illustrated—and check Clause 6.A. in the contract, I insisted that provision be included—then it isn't a threat. *Before the Night Comes In* is safe from the curse."

A strange energy ran over my skin. "You can't know that for sure."

"Can't I? How many books did our father go on to write and publish *after* he knew about the curse? Six? Seven? None of those ever triggered the curse, so we know it's completely possible for someone with Acosta blood to write books that are simply books. I was careful. I knew what I was doing."

Did she?

I could feel a part of her reaching out, seeking my absolution. "Our father made it work. I can, too. I refuse to go my whole life living in fear of the curse."

I faced the laptop again, one finger hovering over the keys, debating whether to open the *Before the Night Comes In* draft or if it was better not to know.

I whispered, "This is what you've been doing at night, isn't it? When I thought you were reading Dad's books?"

She swallowed roughly—it was enough of an answer.

Something hardened in my chest. "Kylie, you think you're in control of it, but you aren't. You don't realize this is the curse working through you. It's pulling the strings to make you write this."

The energy shifted in her face. All the guilt from her secret melted away, replaced by something sharper. It scared me, that look.

"No," she insisted. "I'm in control."

A blade of fear sharpened in my own mind. I didn't even realize how hard I was breathing until Rob touched my shoulder.

"Easy," he whispered, in a rare moment of sympathy. "She thought what she was doing was safe. It wasn't malicious."

I threw off his hand.

Outside, a rumble of tires on the wet pavement ended in a squeal. I heard a car door open and close in front of Rob's house.

Curling my fingers into my palm, I faced Kylie. "You have to decide what side of this thing you're going to be on."

Kylie's eyebrows rose at my scary-low whisper. She, too, glanced toward the front of the house. "Why, are you going to hunt me down if you decide I'm a monster because I wrote a *book?*"

There was an ugliness to her voice that didn't quite sound like her. I softened, blinking out of my anger. "I would never hurt you."

"I wish I could believe that, Haven, but I've seen what you can do. You didn't even say goodbye to your boyfriend, who you aren't going to see for a year. I'm not sure I made you human *enough.*"

Another car door slammed outside. Footsteps sounded on the front porch.

Rob took a few steps back, decamping behind the mannequin in a ball gown, watching from over her plastic shoulder.

My muscles were twitching now as the rain battered harder at the windows.

Keeping my focus on Kylie, I said, "I'd never hurt you. I'd never try to change you. From the day we met, I accepted you for who you were, scars and all. I never said anything about the forgeries. I kept you from the Witch of Went's dissection table. From the Robber Saints' story extractor, too. I promised you half of anything I get from the insurance company. I've treated you like a sister, and you've labeled me a monster."

Eyes flashing, she opened her mouth, but I kept going.

"So be it. Publish the damn book. See what happens. But you aren't going to have your sister at your side when it all comes crashing down just like it did for our father. He was weak. So are you if you can't even see what's happening here. And when Miracle and I start coming after the demons you create, you'd better have picked a side by then."

Someone knocked on the front door.

Face flushed, I took one long last look at Kylie's startled expression before twisting away.

Miracle was waiting for me on the other side of that door, stoic in a heavy raincoat. When the door opened, she stood peering into Rob's place for a moment, gauged the tension in the air, then went to wait by her Desert Wanderer van. Through the windshield, I saw her backpack along with boxes and duffel bags, each one filled with objects from story worlds that could help destroy demons that had escaped their pages. Joao Acosta's belongings were there, ready for a new hand to pick them up and finish his work at Miracle's side.

Miracle opened the passenger's-side door for me.

I started across the threshold.

"Haven, wait!" Kylie stood behind me, breathing hard. She looked exhausted, but there was a touch of softness in her eyes that hadn't been there during our fight. "Don't go. We can figure this out."

Did she even know me? And if so, why had she tried to change me?

Rob had said there was no malice behind her actions, and I believed that, but the curse didn't care where one's heart was. It could work just as easily through good intentions as evil ones.

Maybe I *was* a work in progress, but if anyone was going to pen a new life for me, it was going to be *me*.

I stepped the rest of the way through, shutting the door behind me, walking through the rain toward the unknown.

ACKNOWLEDGMENTS

No book happens by magic, though this one came close through the miraculous editing of Adam Wilson at Hyperion Avenue. You pushed the story to the right places, tightened when I rambled, and helped crack the mystery of these two sisters on either side of a family curse.

My agent, Barbara Poelle at Irene Goodman Literary Agency, offered all the support an author could ask for when writing about things that go bump in the night. Facing monsters is nothing compared to the terror of publication.

The entire team at Hyperion Avenue brought this story to life: Tonya Agurto, Jennifer Levesque, Olivia Zavitson, Amy King, Alex Serrano, Kaitie Leary, Sara Liebling, Guy Cunningham, Meredith Jones. Each of you own a piece of this book, and I hope you know how grateful I am for your involvement. Without your talents, this story would be a mere silent film without a soundtrack to give it a soul.

Shelley Walden gave the Los Angeles scenes a close look to make sure I was doing the city justice. The Bat Cavers cheered this series on with Wendi's cookies and wine. And a special thanks goes to the usual suspects: my parents, my husband, and my children, who love me despite my literary wanderings into the dark unknown.

And to my readers who followed me into those shadowy corners, thank you for trusting me with your curiosity. Here's to more wonderful nightmares.